THE UNMADE BED
Twentieth Century Erotica

THE UNMADE BED

Twentieth Century Erotica

Edited by Marti Hohmann

Credits:
"Harriet's New Charge" is an excerpt from *The English Governess* Copyright © 1990 by Masquerade Books; "The Murder of Juanita Appel" first appeared in *The Celibacy Club* Copyright © 1997 by Janice Eidus; "Alice," "Esmeralda," "Florence," and "Cunts" are excerpts from *White Stains* Copyright © 1998 by Masquerade Books; "Sex in the Pre-Apocalypse" and "Snakefruit" by Anne Tourney first appeared in *Paramour* vol. 3, no. 3 (Spring/Summer 1996) and vol. 3, no. 1 (Fall/Winter 1995); "1-900-FANTASY," "Antonia's Beast," and "Dial 'O' for Oysters" first appeared in *Bondage on a Budget: The Ultimate Guide to Low-Cost Lust* Copyright © 1997 by Alison Tyler; *Safe Word* Copyright© 1998 Molly Weatherfield.

ISBN 0-7394-0651-5

Manufactured in the United States of America
Published by Masquerade Books, Inc.
801 Second Avenue
New York, N.Y. 10017

THE UNMADE BED

UNDERGROUND INTERESTS

Amy Aldridge

Matt and Lucy had been seeing each other for about a month when Matt told Lucy about his fantasies. They had made love in every room in her flat, in every conceivable position. He loved her lithe body and her full breasts that seemed in danger of toppling her over.

They discovered that their bodies fit together very well, and if Lucy wore her very high heels, he could enter her if he were leaning slightly against a wall or something solid. They had set up candles around the living room, and had long ago lost all their clothing, except for a red garter belt and white stockings, which Lucy was wearing with high-heeled shoes.

Matt was leaning against the wall, his legs slightly apart, slim body shining with sweat, enormous cock erect and ready. Lucy steadied herself; her heels made balance difficult. She got astride him and felt him nudge her with the head of his cock. He adjusted for the angle and thrust inside her. He lifted one of her legs just under the knee to make entry easier, and by the time they had come together, Lucy had her legs around his hips, and he was supporting her. They collapsed onto her well-padded sofa and shared a glass of wine. It was then that Matt said, "If you didn't get so carried away, we could make love quite discreetly, anywhere."

Lucy looked appraisingly at him. "We *have* made love anywhere. I don't think there's a surface in this flat that hasn't been used for the purpose."

Matt said quietly, "I don't mean that. I mean outside. Somewhere where there are other people who don't know what we're doing."

"If you think I'm making love in the park in the middle of February, you can think again," she snorted. "Anyway, I've already done that—when I was about sixteen."

"No, I mean indoors. You know."

"No, I don't, and you're not explaining very well, either. Tell me. What is this idea?"

And so Matt told her. His fantasy involved making love to someone in such a discreet way that only he and she would know what they were doing.

Lucy thought about it for a while. "I can see it would be exciting. But how would we make sure no one knew? We could get arrested for outraging public decency or something."

Matt reassured her that he had it all worked out. "You know that huge greatcoat that I wear to festivals? The one you say was used as a tent by the Russian Army? I could wear that. You would wear your high heels and a skirt without any underwear. Come on, you could do that."

Lucy was reluctant to agree without a trial, and so the following evening found them dressed and discussing strategy and technique with all the seriousness of generals. "It's lucky our height is compatible," said Lucy. "It would be impossible otherwise."

"I don't think that's true," said Matt. "Love will always find a way," he winked.

"There are always people standing up in the underground, cuddling and kissing. We'll blend right in. Here I am leaning up against the glass in my big coat. You stand on either side of my legs." Lucy got into position. "Then I wrap my arms and my coat around you." And so they practiced and practiced and eventually brought a mirror from the bedroom to ensure that they weren't in danger of anyone guessing what they were doing.

They had decided to go out on Thursday night, onto a line of the underground they'd never traveled, where they were unlikely to meet anyone they knew. Matt spent the whole day with an erection, thinking about it, running it over in his mind. It intruded on his work, and it intruded on his lunch hour until he considered finding somewhere private to bring himself to climax.

Lucy felt increasingly nervous and excited. She had asked for two days off from work because she knew that she wouldn't be able to concentrate. She took a long bath in the morning, and then very carefully dressed and made herself up. She spent a couple of hours in the flat, her body buzzing with excitement. She decided not to wear any underwear at all, except for her stockings and garter belt. Her shoes would be uncomfortable without them, and anyway, they made her feel sexy. She put on her overcoat for added security—she didn't want to be attacked by sex-crazed men on the way to the station.

At six o'clock, Lucy left the flat and walked along to the local station, buying a ticket for their destination. She traveled by train to the station where they had agreed to meet, and she was so nervous she had to force herself to get off the train. Matt, meanwhile, had left work and taken a different train. He didn't sit down. His erection could outrage public decency quite well enough without showing it off to everyone, he thought.

Lucy was waiting for him under the clock, and they kissed. He said, "I wasn't sure you'd come; I knew you were nervous."

"I nearly didn't, but I knew how much you were looking forward to it. I couldn't let you down."

"Shall we catch our train?" he asked, with a smile.

The station was packed, and Lucy was wondering whether there would be enough room to do it without the cooperation of the whole carriage. Fortunately the line they had chosen was not popular: overground trains were faster, cheaper and more efficient, and so only those who were traveling a couple of stops took it.

Matt took Lucy's hand and guided her into the train. There were about twenty businessmen and women in the carriage, none of whom looked at them. Most of them were reading the evening paper. Matt leaned against the glass and whispered in her ear, "I think I could throw you on the floor and take you without anyone noticing!" Lucy settled against him;

she could feel his huge cock hard against her. When she undid his zipper, she realized that he wasn't wearing any underwear, either. He slid his feet away slightly and braced himself against the glass. Lucy hiked up her skirt and drew closer to him. She whispered: "I'm sorry, I don't think I can do it." Then she zipped him up again.

He pulled her close to him and whispered that it didn't matter; they got off the train at the next stop. It was an old-fashioned station in the suburbs, and they crossed an iron bridge to get over to the other platform to take a train back the other way. It had a tatty waiting room, with an early twentieth-century design, which someone had tried to modernize by adding larger windows. Matt took her hand and drew her into the waiting room, which was empty.

"What was wrong? Why did you stop?" Matt said.

"I didn't feel sexy in front of all those people going home from work," Lucy replied. "I felt sordid and dirty, but not in a sexy way at all."

Lucy walked over to Matt. "Now here, on the other hand—" She unzipped his trousers, took out his cock, which was rapidly regaining its hardness, and then turned away from him, looking out of the window. She lifted her skirt from behind, revealing the rounded frame of her dark pubic hair, with a glimpse of dark red beneath. Matt didn't need a second invitation to position his cock's head in readiness.

Lucy said, "Here comes a train," and as the glistening engine drew in on the opposite platform, Matt mounted her from behind, pushing in and sliding his hands under her top to cup her breasts. No one got off the train, and the doors closed and it drew away.

He withdrew, and asked Lucy to suck his cock; she obediently sat down on the bench and pulled him toward her. She tasted herself on his body, and licked the length of his penis, all round, like a child with an ice cream cone. Then she took it into her mouth. Matt stood impassively, looking out of the window, then quickly withdrew and zipped himself up. He said: "Watch out, there's someone coming along the platform." Then he exclaimed: "I don't believe it! It's Rob!"

"Who's Rob?" asked Lucy.

"My best friend from university. We used to live together and do everything together—even screw together."

"What do you mean? Were you lovers?"

"No, but we only had one double bedroom between us—we used to share the house with several other people. If I was seeing my woman at the same time as Rob was seeing his, we would all do it together in our room." Rob got closer, and Lucy saw a very attractive man in his late twenties, with short dark hair and the bluest of blue eyes. "He looks very nice," she said.

"You fancy him, you mean," Matt countered. When she protested, he added, "No, it's all right, everyone always fancies Rob. He has an allure, I don't know what it is." He left the waiting room, greeted Rob and gave him a hug, and then brought him back to meet Lucy.

After the introductions, Rob said, "What are you two doing in here?" Before Matt could say anything, Lucy said: "We were trying to find a public place to fuck." Both men looked shocked.

"Don't look at me like that, Matt," Lucy protested. "We were, after all. And I was just playing the trouser flute, if you know what I mean."

Rob said, "Well, don't let me stop you." He made to leave.

"Look," Lucy said. "Matt wants to do it with someone watching. I think he got into the habit when you were living together."

"He's told you about our escapades, has he?" Rob asked.

"Only a couple of minutes ago. But what I'm thinking is, why don't you come back to my place, and we can show off for you instead of all these boring old commuters?"

Rob looked at Matt. "Is that what you want?"

Matt looked embarrassed. "You must have been on your way somewhere. Aren't you going to be late or something?"

"No, I was just going to check out the comedy club tonight," Rob answered. "But I can do that any time." He slid his hand around Lucy's shoulders. "Lucy's proposition seems much more enticing."

They didn't talk much on the way back to the flat. Lucy went upstairs to open the door, and Rob caught a glimpse of her dark pubic hair. He said, "Your girlfriend is really beautiful, and she isn't wearing any underwear."

Matt didn't say anything, but led Rob upstairs. Rob turned to him. "If you're not happy with this, I'll go."

"No, it's fine, it'll be like old times."

They went into the bedroom, where Lucy lit some candles and positioned a chair for Rob. Matt went to undress, but Lucy said, "Leave your clothes on. It's much more sexy that way."

Matt knelt on the bed, and Lucy unzipped him, saying: "Where were we?"

She bent over to kiss the tip of his penis, sliding her hands around to hold and direct him. She started rhythmically guiding him back and forth as she tried to take as much of him into her mouth as she could.

She was more or less on all fours, and her skirt had ridden up. Rob could see her sex, and he longed to fuck her from behind. He was already fairly aroused, but the idea of slipping it into her from behind engorged his cock, and he shifted in his chair to accommodate his growing bulge.

Lucy sat back on her heels and said, "It seems mean not to let him join in, doesn't it?" Matt shrugged, saying, "Do you want to come over and help Lucy out?"

Rob quickly stripped. Lucy could hardly believe the thickness of his erect cock. While he watched, she went back to sucking Matt; then she felt her skirt being slipped up, and her hips grasped firmly. Rob didn't try to force his way into her immediately. He pushed only the tip of his penis against her, but she caught him unawares and pushed back on to him until he had penetrated her properly.

He had only thrust a couple of times before he withdrew, and picking up the trusty pot of Vaseline always kept by the bed, started to anoint her other place. Lucy stopped what she was doing and said, "No way, you've got to be kidding!" But Rob grasped her legs and pulled her back as Matt grabbed her wrists and pulled her forward. She said, "Oh, great, now what do I do?" Matt kissed her and said, "You be a good girl and lie still."

She sighed and said, "OK. But be careful with me."

He countered, "Remember, this was your idea."

Matt found the handcuffs and ties they had bought in a sex shop for a joke and discarded after one half-hearted try. Lucy said, "You don't need those. I will do whatever you want, you know I will." But Matt clipped her wrists to the bed, then tied her ankles to each corner. She was face down on the bed.

"It's my turn," Matt said. He swung his cock inside her, pushing hard. When he withdrew, he trailed his finger between her legs, entering there, but with more difficulty. Rob asked her to lift her hips and put one pillow beneath them—then a second, and then a third —until her bottom was well off the bed.

Rob entered her briefly and then withdrew. When she hadn't felt anyone's touch for a few minutes, she turned her head and said, "What's going on?" She felt exposed, on view. Then she felt every inch of her being probed, tested, explored. The trick wasn't to know whose fingers were here, or whose cock there; the trick was to lose herself in the feeling and the exploration, the sliding and the penetration. She felt them everywhere. She began to come, and Rob withdrew immediately.

"No! No! Come back! It isn't fair!" she cried, writhing and frustrated. They untied her and let her do whatever she wanted with them. She lay down and pulled Rob on top of her, guiding him home with her hands. She shouted, "Fuck me hard, let me feel you thrusting into me, come on, come on, do it, do it!" She felt his cock filling her to capacity. Matt watched for a moment, and then pulled Rob off of her and entered her himself. He pushed her legs up so that he went deeply, then came quickly.

Rob sat up, watching Matt, but Lucy came to him and pulled him to her, and he moved over her body and entered her once again. This time, the way eased with the lubrication left over from the lovemaking with Matt, they slid together very gently, and Lucy again started to make noise. She panted, "Oh yes, baby, there, that's wonderful, do it there, go on. I can feel you filling me, it's a wonderful feeling, come on, please." He pulled out of her, turned her over, and fucked her from behind until he said, "Can I come now?" The idea of his control so excited her that she came shouting, "Yes, yes, yes," and he came too. They fell apart and lay on the bed.

After twenty minutes, Lucy and Rob began to explore each other's bodies with their tongues. They slid around until each had his or her head supported on the other's thigh. His cock began to regain its erect size, and she was fascinated by it. She looked at it and ran her tongue over it and around it; she wanted to put it back inside her, so she did. He said, "That's not fair, I was enjoying that." But she wanted him to thrust as deeply as he could, to take her with authority. "Don't hold back for me this time," she said. "I want to feel you fucking me as hard as you want."

They were locked together for the third time before they realized Matt had left.

HARRIET'S NEW CHARGE

Anonymous

It was half an hour before Harriet descended to the library, where Richard had been awaiting her in all the throes of trepidation and uncertainty. On seeing her he became still more disturbed. She, quite at her ease, approached and tapped him lightly under the chin.

"Well," she said, "what have you been doing since I left?"

He blushed and tried to reply, but an excess of shyness strangled his voice. He was silent.

"Come, are you dumb?"

"No, miss..."

"Well?"

"I—I did nothing at all."

"Nothing at all! But that is unheard of. One must do something."

The last words were accompanied by a gaze of such penetration that he shivered, his eyes involuntarily falling to the region of his genitals for assurance that there were no traces of his indulgence. Harriet's shrewd gaze followed his.

"Come now," she said, with a faint note of mockery in her clear, pleasant voice, "tell me what you have been doing. Begin at the beginning."

She sat down, smoothing out her skirt, and taking his hands in hers she drew him close to her.

"I read—a little," he said. "But..."

"But what?'

"I couldn't read—very much. Then I—I looked out of the window."

"A praiseworthy occupation. And after that?"

He was deeply disturbed. The touch of the young woman's soft hands, the contact of her knees distracted him without his knowing why.

"After that," he mumbled, "I—I did nothing at all."

"Perfect," said Harriet. "You spend your time well. But you know all that is going to be changed from now on, don't you? We shall begin our studies tomorrow, and you will work hard. Where is your room?"

He led her upstairs. His room was only a few steps from her own. She cast a look of disapproval at the slight untidiness she saw there. "What is that jacket doing on the bed?" she asked, pointing. "Hang it up at once." He obeyed. As he opened his closet she saw his short nightgown hanging on the back of the door, and stepping forward she took it from its hook.

"You will not need this any longer," she announced. "From now on you will sleep without nightclothes."

"Yes, miss," he murmured.

"I shall come and see you here this evening, when you are in bed," she said. "You say your prayers at bedtime?"

"No, miss."

"That is disgraceful. We will say them together in future, in my room."

During the hours until dinner, Harriet and Richard talked together in the library. Thus she learned, almost without his being aware of it, not only of the events of her pupil's life but the immediate history of his family. From a few naive remarks she also learned of Mr. Lovel's addiction to pleasure and of the existence of his mistress.

The hour for dinner arrived. In her room the table was already set. Harriet seated herself with her back to the lamp, her face in shadow. Opposite her, the pale countenance of Richard was in the full light.

Bridget carried in the dishes and set them on the table with a sullen air, but she altered her manner at once on receiving a single glance from Harriet. The glance was so portentous that the old woman understood in that instant what her position in the household was henceforth to be, and she grasped at the same time the fact that she had everything to gain by making herself Harriet's subordinate. Her air at once became respectful, even obsequious.

The soup was served. Richard hungrily took a spoonful and was carrying it to his lips when Harriet leaned forward and stopped his hand. "What are you doing?"

"M-miss—I'm eating!" he stammered.

"And the grace before meals? You never say grace?"

"No, miss..."

"You will do so from now on. I shall say the words now, and you will remember them. Tomorrow you will be made to say them by yourself."

His head lowered, he listened carefully while she spoke the benediction. Only when she raised her own spoon did he venture to begin eating.

"You have often been in this room?" she said after a while.

"No, miss."

"You will be from now on. When your work is insufficiently done in the daytime, you will make up the arrears here. And when you are to be punished, it will be in this room."

A curious sensation of fear and fascination went through him as he heard these words and saw her beautiful gray eyes fixed on him, but which of these sentiments was uppermost he could not tell. Already he had felt his whole being profoundly disturbed by the personality of his governess, and now with this disturbance there was mixed a feeling of shuddering attraction towards her, a sense of fear at finding himself so absolutely subject to this young woman, and also something else, something indefinable but sweet, almost too sweet. The meal was finished in silence.

Later, when he gained his room, it was with a feeling of having drunk some heady draught that made his head swim deliciously. A peculiar lassitude invaded his whole body. As he undressed, the touch of his clothes slipping over his skin made him shiver, and as soon as he was between the cool sheets a feeling of profound languor made him relax his naked limbs with an exquisite sense of well-being. Instinctively, he turned his face towards his pillow and curled himself into a ball, as if feeling the need for warmth and physical intimacy. Then he closed his eyes, but wasn't able to fall asleep.

He had been in bed scarcely a quarter of an hour when, very softly, his door was half opened and then closed again. Between these two operations Harriet had slipped into the room without making a sound. She carried a small lamp whose feeble light was further subdued by a heavy shade. On tiptoe she approached the bed and bent over.

The boy was lying on his back now, dozing, his eyes half-closed, lost in a reverie of the one subject that engrossed him—the arrival of Harriet Marwood in the house, and the new life he was entering. But now, thanks to his afternoon indulgence, the sensuality of his temperament was no longer aroused by such consideration, and his little penis lay soft and inert between his thighs.

All at once he felt the sheet and coverlet lifted from him; for an instant he felt himself bared to the hips, and then, just as swiftly, the covers were replaced.

He had not time to utter a cry before he recognized his governess. He sat up in bed, shaken by a violent, indefinable fear. But Harriet's hand was laid gently on his head.

"Do not be afraid, Richard," she said softly. "I saw that you were not asleep, and I wished to make sure you were behaving yourself. You were, I see, and all is as it should be. Lie down now, and go to sleep."

He obeyed, stretching himself out, his hand crossed over his chest as if to contain the wild beating of his heart. It was then that he experienced his most intense emotion: Harriet leaned over his bed and kissed him, softly and lingeringly, on the mouth.

"When you have been a good boy during the day," she said, "I will come to you in the evening, like this, to kiss you goodnight."

He had a moment of daring. As the hand that had slipped beneath his chin was withdrawn, he raised his head suddenly and pressed his lips to it. Then, red as a peony, he turned his head to the wall at his bedside.

"Good night, Richard," she said.

And she disappeared.

At this moment Mr. Lovel was also in bed, lying beside his mistress in the rosy light of the bedroom in her flat, where he now spent the greater part of his evenings. He had just withdrawn from the warm embrace of her anal sheath, after spending in it with extraordinary satisfaction.

On this occasion Kate was wearing, for the caprice of her protector, the working dress of the high-class Parisian prostitute of the time—a short transparent chemise over a narrow, tightly laced corset with long black silk stockings tightly gartered at mid-thigh and a pair of leather kid boots with immoderately high heels. In this suggestive costume the whiteness and opulence of her superb body had appeared with such striking and voluptuous effect that she had to withstand two separate amorous assaults in succession before her protector's passions were momentarily sated and she was able to revert to the question of Richard's governess.

"Why," said Mr. Lovel, "I suppose you would call her a handsome woman, Kate, but it's a type that makes no impression on me. Miss Marwood is much too straitlaced, I find."

"That's just as well. But did she strike you as likely to break your boy of that habit of his?"

"I don't know. All I can say is that if anyone can do it, she is the one." He laughed. "She looks like a regular martinet, a holy terror. I don't envy the boy."

"Ah well, it's for his own good. He'll thank us all for it some day." And crooking a handsome leg in its tight black stocking, she coquettishly laid the soft kid of her boot in his lap, counting on it making its effect on his sensuality in due time. "Do you think it will take long?"

"I've no idea, Kate. That's a very handsome boot you have on, my dear. Raise it up, will you?"

"There you are," she said, raising her bare thigh. "You like my new boots then? I saw them in Dover Street yesterday and bought them with you in mind."

Mr. Lovel bit the toe of her boot softly, then pressed the soft kid of the upper against his cheek. "Ah, you're a dear girl, Kate. Do you know, I find I don't see half as much of you as I'd like. I've gotten into needing you at the oddest times, my dear—in the middle of the night, first thing in the morning, and so on. Yes, that's right, rub your other boot over my genitals." He kissed the smartly shod foot before him with slowly mounting emotion.

"My poor Arthur," said Kate. "I had no idea you wanted me so often. It seems that whenever you are here you are fucking my bum or my mouth, and I thought that was enough." She reached for his testicles with a warm hand and began kneading them delicately. "Oh, it's a terrible thing for a man to have an erection in his bed all by himself. It's such a waste."

"And with a mistress like you to remember and think of," he said, gripping her leather-shod foot, "one's almost obliged to masturbate as if one were a damned boy oneself. Listen, Kate, I'll tell you what. You must come and sleep at my house. Now that my poor wife has gone, there can be no complications. You'll come, won't you?"

"My darling Arthur," cried Kate, beside herself with joy, "it's what I have always longed for, didn't you know? Oh, many's the long night I've tossed and turned in this lonely bed too, with my arse itching to have your prick in it, my hands empty and craving to be holding your sweet balls, and my throat dry with wanting the taste of your seed. Yes, Arthur, let all that be over and done with, and let me share your bed and your pleasure every night as a man's mistress should."

He took her head between his hands and made the rare gesture of kissing her on the lips. "You shall come tomorrow," he said.

"Now who is the happiest woman in the world!" the good creature cried, jumping up. "For that, I must give you the finest frigging ever a man had! Come, sit down on the stool there now, and put your legs apart."

Arthur rose and sat on the low stool with his legs widely spread, while Kate, drawing up a high chair, sat down facing him. Raising her legs and laying her heels on either side of his testicles, she took his half-awakened member between the sides of her boots and began rolling and rubbing it skillfully against the velvety leather of the uppers. Arthur's eyes shone with pleasure as he followed the slow voluptuous movements of her feet.

"That's a grand way to be frigged when you're in the mood for boot, isn't it?" she said archly.

Arthur looked from her flushed face to his member, which was slowly swelling from the soft friction of the leather, and then to her own widespread thighs that, with her chemise now well tucked up, displayed the charming slit of her sex opening and shutting with the rotation of her hips as she kept masturbating him in this ingenious manner.

"Dear Kate," he said, "you can frig a man better with your feet than many a whore can do with her two hands, indeed you can."

"Ah, I'm only too glad I can, since you like it so well. But now you've got me so hot I must frig myself, too." She parted the lips of her vulva, and attacked her swollen clitoris with passionate fingers.

The sight completed the process of her lover's erection. As his member throbbed and pulsated between the churning, kneading feet, he kept his eyes fixed, now on it and now on his mistress' masturbation of herself, until he felt the pleasure of the crisis threading his loins imperiously and discharged his sperm freely into the air. Then, sinking back in happy exhaustion, he followed with critical appreciation the course which Kate was following in the achievement of her own orgasm.

† † †

The next morning at seven o'clock, Harriet, fully dressed, entered her pupil's room again. He was still drowned in slumber, and as on the previous evening she lifted the covers and with a swift glance examined the boy carefully. She at once noted the violent erection of his member, and smiled at this evidence of a temperament so consonant with her plans. Richard had not moved; to waken him she was obliged to shake him by the shoulder. He started up, rubbing his eyes.

"Well, Richard, what do you say?"

"Good—good morning, miss."

"Good morning. It is seven o'clock, the time when you will get up every morning from now on. Come into the bathroom."

He hesitated, all too aware of the distention of his genitals.

"Well, I am waiting," she said, her brows knitting in exasperation.

"But—but, miss, I'm not—I mean—I mean, my—"

"Your what? Come, up with you now at once." With a swift movement, she pulled the covers from his naked body. His hands went instinctively to cover his member. "Oh, so that is what is troubling you! Really, such false modesty is absurd. Get up at once! We are not going to wait for that morning tension to go down." And she turned away impatiently.

He rose in confusion, seized his dressing gown, and followed her into the bathroom.

"I have had Bridget draw your bath," said Harriet. "Get into it now."

He looked at her in embarrassment. "Yes, miss." But he remained motionless, standing before her uncertainly.

"Well, what are you waiting for?"

"I—miss, I shall have to undress."

"Of course. You do not make a habit of taking a bath in your dressing gown, I hope. Take it off."

He began untying the cord around his waist, hoping she would leave. Then he understood that she meant to be present when he took his bath. He slipped out of the gown and stood nude before her.

She sat down, examining him with her cool, intent glance. This was the first time she had seen him naked, and for all her air of outward calm she was deeply stirred by the beauty of this youthful body. Her eyes passed appreciatively from point to point, dwelling with connoisseurship now on the plump shoulders, now on the straight slender legs, now on the almost feminine swell of the hips. She fixed her gaze at last on the firm and nervous rondure of buttocks and thighs, and then centering inevitably on the puerile penis. By now soft and pendant, it had withdrawn coyly between his thighs where it formed, with the small tight testicles, a kind of dainty genital triumvirate in a state of modesty and repose. When he was in the water, she drew her chair beside the bathtub.

"I have been entrusted by your father," she said with a smile, "with the task of supervising your whole upbringing. That comprises more than school work, you know. So I shall be here every morning to see that you take your bath, whether you like it or not. Now hurry. Wash yourself thoroughly all over!"

Richard obeyed. He was reminded more and more of his little schoolmate's governess. How far would the resemblance go? And how downright and domineering this woman was! Suddenly disturbed by the thought that he might even now be keeping her waiting, he finished washing himself and was rising to leave the bath when she stopped him.

"What is this?" she said sharply. "Do you not wash your private parts?"

"No, miss—I mean, yes...I thought that—that—"

"You thought you would omit them this morning, I suppose! I told you to wash yourself all over. Kneel down and do so at once, if you please."

He scrambled to his knees in the bath and began soaping his penis with trembling hands. Harriet watched him closely, noting the accustomed gestures with which he was handling himself as he drew back the prepuce and ran his fingers around the head of the shaft itself.

She spoke suddenly. "You play with yourself a good deal, my boy, don't you?"

He gasped and went red as fire, his hands left their task abruptly. He tried to speak, but could not.

"You need not answer, Richard," she said. She fixed him with the piercing glance of her gray eyes. "I shall have more to say to you on this subject in a few minutes. For the moment, however, you will put your hands behind your head while I finish washing you myself." And rolling up her sleeves she lathered her hands and took hold of his member; in a moment her fingers were firmly palpating its head and neck, while her other hand, passing between his thighs from the rear, grasped his testicles and massaged them briskly.

As her hands plied their double task, the boy's penis, already accustomed to respond instantly to his own manipulations, gradually swelled and stiffened quite independently of his volition. He watched it rising with an indescribable feeling of shame, horror, and pleasure. Harriet, for her part, continued the ablution as if quite unconscious of what was happening. Even when she inserted a smooth finger in the boy's tight anus, the answering throb that elevated his penis to its full height drew no comment from her. Anyone looking at her would have thought she was even ignorant of the very meaning of tumescence. At last she ceased.

"Into the water with you now," she said calmly, "and rinse yourself well. And now get out and dry yourself at once."

The boy obeyed, awkward and embarrassed by the rigid member that was still standing out and swaying before him with an air of arrogance quite out of keeping with his own feelings of shame and confusion. When he finished, Harriet took the towel from him and sat back.

"Come here," she said, drawing him between her knees. "And do not hang your head like that. Yes, look at me. Now, are you listening?"

Her eyes were boring into his. He noted their warm brilliance, so much at variance with the coldness of her tone and the curl of her short upper lip.

"Yes, miss," he whispered.

She settled herself more comfortably in her chair.

"I am going to talk to you very seriously about this habit of yours, Richard. That is because I mean to impress on you the dangers you are running in giving way to it. In the first place, there is the danger to your personality. You are already, I see, quite weak and lacking in character, without this final indulgence of your senses to render you completely spineless. Lacking all willpower, a passive instrument of your own sensuality.

"In the second, there is the danger to your health. Do you know the physical results of constant self-abuse? I do not wish to frighten you, especially when it is not too late for you to turn over a new leaf, but the habit is extremely dangerous. Your present pallor alone is an indication of that.

"And finally there is the moral danger, the danger that this habit may master you to such an extent that you may never be able to find satisfaction in a normal and natural way. Think, Richard: one day you will wish to be married. How will you feel then, facing the woman who you wish to make your wife, if you are already so wedded to a shameful, childish, and weakening habit that you are unable to express your love as God and Nature intended you should?" The governess paused. She had been holding his hands, but now she released them and placed her own hands firmly on his naked hips, drawing him closer to her as she went on. "Those are all reasons for giving up this self-indulgence of yours, and I wish you to think of them constantly from now on. But there is one other reason that is perhaps better than any of those others, Richard, and one that may weigh with you more powerfully than they do." Here she paused again, and suddenly kneading the flesh of his hips with the harsh grip of her strong fingers, she gave him her warm, full-lipped smile. "And that is, Richard, that if I ever catch you playing with yourself I will thrash you to within an inch of your life."

With these words, which fell on him like the blow of a stick, she pushed him away gently and, as if to emphasize her threat, tapped his now subsiding member lightly with her fingers.

"And now, dress yourself, and come to breakfast."

As soon as breakfast was over, Harriet and her pupil repaired to the library, now the schoolroom. She pointed out to him where he was to sit, and sat down herself—not opposite but beside him, and in such a way that she could oversee his work at any moment. Thus the first lesson began.

Richard was nervous, awkward and embarrassed by the smallest difficulty. Not only had he lost the habit of study during his long period of idleness, but the presence of Miss Marwood at his side disturbed him strangely. Truly, the effect this young woman had on his imagination and senses was remarkable!

Sitting beside her, he felt the occasional touch of

her knee, her hand, her arm. Her bosom pressed his shoulder when she bent over him. At those moments he became giddy. Her cheek kept brushing his, stray locks of her hair tickled his temples, her breath intoxicated him. So great was his disturbance that sometimes his eyes filled with tears and he wished to break into sobs—and all for no reason. Or what could the reason be? Indeed, she was not threatening him now!

The lesson period lasted three hours, and work was resumed after luncheon without any incident to break the monotony of the day.

For a week matters continued thus. Richard, under the awe he felt for Harriet, was working hard and steadily, doing his best to deserve a word of satisfaction and encouragement—even a caress. Whenever she called him to her chair for him to recite a lesson or explain a problem, if his replies were correct she signified approbation with a few light affectionate taps on his loins, such as one might bestow on an infant.

He still wore the short Eton jacket and white trousers he had worn at school, and the touch of her hand, felt through the tight-fitting serge of the latter, had come to excite and disturb him immoderately. At such moments he had a mad impulse to throw himself into her arms, to crush his face against her breast, to huddle himself against her in absolute abandonment of his whole being to her will. It was then that the fever of his senses rose to a height. He felt the blood beating in his head and a sensation of wild and hopeless craving flooded his loins, while the turgescence of his member and the constriction of his clothing affected him with both the shame and the sheer physical pain of a confined and frustrated erection.

Every night she came to see him in bed. She smoothed his pillow and tucked him in as the tenderest of mothers might have done, then gave him a long kiss on the lips and withdrew, still calm, still apparently cold, leaving him prey to a thousand confused thoughts and in a kind of ecstasy. And then, alone and naked in his bed, he was left to the torments of his desire and temptation, lying on his back in the dark, his hands pressed tightly to his sides, desperately fighting the impulse to carry out the forbidden self-indulgence that he craved with every nerve in his body and every fiber of his brain. Had it been only the fear of punishment that restrained him, he would have succumbed long before this. But he was bound to this agonizing abstinence by a more imperious taboo, a sense that to give himself this sexual relief would be to commit an act of infidelity to the woman herself. It was often more than an hour before his flesh subsided sufficiently for him to fall asleep, worn out but almost happy in this victory over himself.

By the end of the week he had only one thought, one wish—to be tied always to this woman's apron strings. She was everything to him; he lived only for her. Let us admit it; he was in love with her. And, with the clairvoyance of love, he was aware also of the force and intensity of her own interest in him. Obscurely, he understood that he was a source of frustration for her as well, and this frightened him. He sensed the fact that she was waiting, waiting—but for what? And after a while, obsessed and tormented as he was by the sensuous ordeal he went through twenty times a day, the task of resisting the impulse to give way to his burning desire, he came to believe that it was that very weakness and resumed self-indulgence she was awaiting so she might put her threat of punishment into effect.

THINGS INTANGIBLE

Cara Bruce

"Are there different degrees of darkness?" Ryan asks me as he slides into bed.

"Not really," I say, moving closer to the warmth of his body. He wraps his arms around me and I run my fingers over his biceps. They are not too large, yet still well-defined.

"The fog is rolling in," he says, and I know he is looking out of the window above our bed. A cool breeze blows in, stirring the sheets, and I can hear the light titter of people walking on the sidewalk below. "What does fog look like?" I ask, turning my cheek so it rests upon the soft cotton of his T-shirt. He smells like laundry detergent, a sort of chemically fresh scent.

"Picture a blob," he says. "An intangible shape. If you put your hand through and drew it out again it would be wet."

"Go on," I tell him, moving my hand through the thin hair that has grown just a little bit over his eyes.

"It rolls slowly across the sky. Everything is light and it's like the heavens unrolled a thick carpet."

He picks up the soft blanket from the foot of my bed and draws it over us to make his point. He pulls it over our heads and we giggle.

I turn my face toward him and he brings his lips down to mine. They are soft and as soon as he kisses me I feel a stirring between my legs. His tongue darts into my mouth, running along my teeth.

"Fog smothers the entire city," he says as he rolls over on top of me. I like the pressure of his body and the soft touch of his hand as he places it lightly behind my neck. I can feel him hard against me, his cock pressing into my thigh. I know him. I know each of his body parts as if it were my own. The rise of his Adam's apple, the slope of his nose, the curve of his calf. His breath is hot. His lips, barely parted, start their journey. They begin in the hollow of my throat and travel straight down until they pause in the center of my breasts, leaving a tiny trail of moisture in their wake.

"Tell me," I say, as his mouth finds my nipple, "is fog warm or cold?"

He is sucking on my tit. His lips have formed a firm suction and his tongue moves in tiny circles.

"Fog," he says, his mouth hovering above me, "is like this." He lifts his mouth away and a burst of cold air rushes in to take its place. I feel my nipple double in size as it lurches upward searching for his warmth. I smile and he brings his lips down to mine. His callused hands are sliding down my thighs. They move to the insides, pulling me apart. His fingers stroke the tiny dip under my pelvic bone. He is teasing me. I want him to move over, to touch me. He brushes his fingers lightly above my patch of short hairs. I gasp.

"Fog touches everything," he says and I can hear the smile in his voice. His finger finds my clit and he gently rubs it, moving lightly back and forth. I raise my hips to encourage him to go faster. He does. He slides one finger inside of me. Immediately I tighten around it trying to feel every part. He draws it in and out but I want more of him.

"Tell me," I gasp, "can fog go inside of you?"

He shifts his weight until he is centered above me. He removes his fingers and uses them to guide his dick, which pokes stubbornly at my opening.

"Fog can go everywhere," he tells me, pushing himself in. "You can feel it in your bones."

He moves inside of me. He pushes deep and hard, again and again. I raise my hips to meet him as he thrusts. He starts moving faster, harder; I can feel him deep inside of me. I clutch his back and wrap my legs around his. He begins to groan and I can smell him beginning to perspire. He moves faster and the feeling travels through my stomach as he thrusts and I clench. Across the darkness of my eyes, I see a flash of light and my legs begin to shake. I gasp and come against him, my orgasm almost unbearably intense. He thrusts once more until his thighs tighten and he lies still.

He kisses my lips, my face, my neck, and I nestle my nose into his fine hair, breathing in the heady scent of sex and shampoo.

"Ryan," I whisper to him, "I'm so glad we moved to San Francisco." I lightly feel his eyelids to see if they are closed and I wonder how I ever lived without the pale gray light of fog.

SAME DIFFERENCE

Alex Cay

Decline bench press, his exercise: on his back, his head resting on the low end of the angled bench and his knees bent over the high end, his ankles under the padded support. He brought the bar down to his chest. It stopped halfway back up. The third set, seventh repetition, was one rep too many without someone to spot him. His face clenched his eyes squeezed shut his arms went aquake at the elbows. Nothing doing. Then, over his own grunting, a soft woman's voice: "Finish it, I'm here now, you can do it, come on. This is the one that counts."

The bar rose a little. A little more.

"Keep going, keep it up, don't stop now, don't stop. Come on, don't puss out on me, good, good. That's it, make it hurt, make it count, finish it, don't be a pussy, yes, yes, good." Gray couldn't hear her last words over his own cry and the clanging of the bar as it dropped back on the rack. His finish had not been his best effort, though he appreciated both her help and the encouraging white lies, ones he had told and had been told countless times. This woman knew her way around a gym.

Gray's eyes opened to a pair of turgid vastus medialis like giant water drops overhanging the rim of the kneecaps and solidified just before splashing him in the face. The woman had not yet backed off the bar. A Marine hair's length away from his head at ten and two o'clock, her stalactite legs emerged from either side of a lavender crotch with a negligible inseam, the kind of workout shorts that had high overlapping lateral slits for optimal freedom of movement. Her hands still held onto the bar, inside his, and they could have been a man's gloved workout hands except for the shaped, painted nails. Bright red. He could not see her upside-down face very well, but thought it promising. A blonde.

"Thanks." He took a moment to slow his breathing

and recover his heart rate before sitting up. Sometimes, when he stood or sat up too fast, his body retaliated with dizziness.

"Anytime." She stepped back. Her left hand stayed on the bar. "You know better than to push it alone."

Sitting up and turning toward his mystery spotter, Gray found that she fulfilled her upside-down promise, and then some: a knockout face, a killer physique: tall, pretty, and pumped. *Really* pumped. Veins strained the surface like an oak tree's roots. Her blonde hair sat in loose curls around her face, off her shoulders but touching at the base of the trapezius. She wore a black scoop-neck sportsbra, more scoop than bra. She didn't need the support, Gray noted, since her chest bulged like his.

"I've been out of my routine for a few days. I guess I was a little over-anxious."

"Do you compete?" she asked. *She must be trying to flatter me*, Gray thought. Anyone with as much bodybuilding experience as this woman displayed would have sized him up and instantly known that he did not.

"In my dreams. I want to, I figure maybe in a couple of years. You?"

"Started last November. Runner-up twice now in local amateur shows. Lost the first one because I was too ripped, too manly. One of the other girls told me, said the judges thought I was on the juice. Lost the second because I wasn't ripped enough. Guys are lucky—you don't have to put up with that crap. By the way I'm Tish, like 'tush' with an 'i,' short for Tisha."

"I'm Gray." Shaking her gloved hand felt like grabbing the handle for the upright row. "I don't think I've seen you in here before." When not working out, Gray worked at the gym as a trainer, and recognized nearly everybody. Every *body*, that is—Gray knew his fellow gym denizens by a glimpse of a calf, a triceps medial head, a set of lats with a particular knurling.

"This is my first time. I like it. A good mix of machines and freeweights, and plenty of both so you don't waste time waiting around. That's why I left the last place. It was packed all the time. Yuppies. I kept going there because Wendy, she's my old training partner, lived on that side of town. She's married and out to here now," Tish said, holding one hand several inches off her belly, "so here I am. Do you always pump solo?"

"Only when I have to. My partner moved back to Chicago this weekend. I need to find someone else to lift with." He liked her. He liked the way she talked, fast and brash, not unlike the way Dale, his recent ex-roommate and bodybuilding buddy, talked. Dale, though, was no Tisha. No sir.

But Tish had to leave just then—Gray was starting his workout, she had ended hers when, on her way to the locker room, she caught the flagging bar. They agreed to lift together the next day.

He was bent over at the fountain when he felt a firm pat on his right glute. "Are you ready for me?"

"Let's do it." Thus their workout, which would continue six days a week for nearly two years, began.

Gregory "Gray" Thomas Lacey had a Pater aesthetic: bodybuilding for bodybuilding's sake. He did not exercise for his health, neither sculpted himself out of vanity nor for the women. He did it for the sport: For the beauty of the sport, the beauty of manly competition. The integrity of his competition aesthetic combined with his respect for and faith in his body precluded steroids.

He had never been a handsome man, what with his flat, lipless face, but his long brown hair and his large athletic build made him at least not unattractive. He had hit his current height of 6'3" in the eighth grade, and at that age was one of the few boys taller than the girls. However much his size may have overwhelmed them, it at least lent him a masculinity the girls could recognize. He shaved daily throughout high school. In the tenth grade he accomplished that rarest of teenage Don Juanisms by dating a senior, a cheerleader and captain of the squad. While her friends partied in Lawrence at the frat houses, she picked him up, parked a block away from her house, sneaked him through the garage into the basement, opened out the old sofabed and showed him her moves.

Gray's other fame in high school came from wrestling. He had won the state heavyweight championship his sophomore, junior, and senior years. Most matches he won by forfeit, the opposing team having no heavy of its own. Gray, the one member of his squad who did not torture himself before every meet by running and swimming and starving and steaming himself to make weight, would rather have undergone the weekly masochistic regimen and wrestled, than not and not. He relished the sweaty, close-quarters physical contest on the mat, and victory's natural high. When he did wrestle, he won. Always. Except for the competition at the state tournaments, his opponents had been recruited to win the heavyweight matches, as Gray usually did, by forfeit. They were on the team because they were fat.

Gray told Tish a little of his history their first day as training partners. He told her he had wrestled in high school, and in college had powerlifted and played rugby. The yearbook facts. Then she told him his. Tisha Louise Kirk had had high aspirations as a gymnast, until she grew too tall; despite her pituitaries, she continued gymnastics for her first two years at Northwestern, long knowing that the Olympics were out of the question but continuing out of momentum, only to quit the summer before her junior year because if she couldn't be the best, why the fuck bother? Thus, already equipped with calluses and muscles and accustomed to the stares, she hit the weights. He took it all in that night at his now half-furnished apartment, over pasta primavera and a chilled plastic bottle of Evian; with *Classics for Romance*, *Sensual Strings*, *More Late Night Sax for Lovers*, and *Erotitudes: Classic Music with Subliminal Suggestions to Make Her Want You* in the discplayer; and under prints of Impressionist paintings and photos of his favorite self-sculpted Olympian masterpieces: Franco and Arnold during their legendary 1975 pose-down in South Africa, and Shawn Ray; and Corey Everson and Lennda Murray, the female deities, one light and the other dark, "like yin and yang" Gray pointed out, and not-recent, soft, glamour shots of Corey but shots from her harder-bodied competing days.

Today, over the usual black spandex shorts, he wore his oversized white lifting shirt from the powerlifting club at Kansas State, with enormously wide short sleeves, and cropped so that when he moved his belly sometimes winked. On the front of the shirt, a purple wildcat hit a three-quarters back double-biceps; on the back, purple letters shouted SHUT UP AND LIFT. Tish wore the same outfit as the day before, this time black on the bottom, white up top. Since both had worked chest and back the previous day, today they worked shoulders and arms. Pyramid up on the delts, superset biceps and triceps, and finish each exercise with a low-weight fourth set to rep out. Tish was more vocal than Gray remembered any previous partner being. The last few reps of a tough set stimulated the most and best of this kind of talk: "Come on now, come on Lacey, almost there, that's it, there you go, don't stop, all right, excellent, excellent, let's pump out one more, make it hurt, I've got you, yes, yes. Good job."

Tish didn't call him Gray. Mostly she called him Lacey. She also called him big guy, big man, and pussy, reserving this last for his most desperate lifting moments, when her words needed to push deep inside and pull him to his peak. When doing it, she leaned close, the shadow of her lips nibbling his ear: "Don't be a pussy. Don't stop now, you big pussy—finish it."

When not focused on his own body, or evaluating

one across the gym, Gray vetted hers. She worked heavy weights to bulk up her delts, lats, and rhomboids. With lower weight, higher reps, and slower movements, she strove to lengthen and tone her lower body. Which is not to deny that her legs nearly burst out of their skin, but relative to the proportions of her upper body and contrasted with other competitive female lifters, her lower body appeared, especially at the distance of the judge's table, elongated, sleek, as well as developed. All this effort toward a triangular rather than an hourglass figure (for himself he wanted the hourglass shape, a slender albeit rippling midsection and huge everything else). Each point of attachment between her pectorals and sternum stood out, her breasts less tits for copping than shoulderpad-like cushions kludged atop the muscles. They reminded him of parentheses, of lazy, fallen-over parentheses.

Outside the gym, Gray found himself, as Dale would say, eye-fucking her. And what a fuck it was.

"You have Frieda Kahlo eyes," he blurted.

"Is that supposed to be a compliment?"

"Yeah. They're big and brown. They're cool. She's a painter." Gray knew nothing about Frieda Kahlo beyond the caption facts; these he knew because he had memorized them, as he did those under the photos of whichever featured writers and artists he found on book jackets and in glossies at bookstores and newsstands. It was his way, his self-culturing program.

She swigged from her bottle. "Is that that All Sport Body Quencher stuff?" she asked.

"Yeah."

"You should drink Lite Carbo Pump, it's shitloads better for you," she said, holding up hers.

"Same difference."

"No, this has a lot more carbs, and more kinds of carbs. Sometimes I drink Cytomax, it's high on electrolytes, and almost as many carbs, but way more calories. Yours is a pussy drink."

"A what?"

"You drink it for the taste. It doesn't do flip for you. What's it got anyway, a little high-fructose corn syrup? It's for pussies. Don't be a pussy, Lacey. Do things all the way or don't do them at all."

Gray would not have guessed she talked that way outside the gym. Then again, they were still at the gym, if not inside, and in spirit their muscles, temporarily gorged with blood from the forced oxygen rush, were still pumping iron.

"You have quite a mouth," he said, grinning. Quite a mouth the other way, too—wide and suggestive—all the better to eat him with.

"Not ladylike enough for you? Not womanly?"

"Didn't say that."

"'Cause if that's the case, you can just suck my dick."

Gray's face flushed.

She pressed her advantage, standing up off the bike rack and holding both hands up to him, palms out, fingers spread. "Put your hands up, I want to show you something." She placed her palms against his, shifting hers until their bases were even. Gray had thought before that she had large hands for a woman, but he had no idea. Tish's fingertips extended a quarter inch beyond his own.

"If I were a guy, you know what that would mean?" Tish strutted a grin. Gray chuckled dumbly.

That night, after a dessert of a mixed fruit cup, Gray returned from the bathroom to find the futon cushion spread on the floor in the space Dale's coffee table trunk once owned, and Tish lying on the cushion on her side as if about to crunch her obliques. But for the tiny gold crucifix on its nearly invisible chain, she lay in her magnificence of buff. She had not dimmed the light—may have even switched on the lamp in the corner. They would not be two average bodies bumbling and hiding under sheets, a blanket, and poor lighting. They would be a fucking spectacle, a spectacle fucking, and would half-hear the audience of the walls roar their awe. Under the eyes, under the jealous-if-approving eyes, thought Gray, of the Olympians.

"It's pussy time," she said, decreeing her seduction. They did it until two in the morning, going through three condoms and three positions in a peculiar stamina competition. The sort of night Dale called a fuck-fest.

How she thrashed! And the talk she talked! Her tongue became her clit's articulation; her body her pussy's puppet.

Afterward they fell asleep, Tish in Gray's arms, their spooning, excrescent bodies two tectonic plates nestled along a fault line and forming a mountain ridge.

By the end of the month, Tish and her things had replaced Dale and his. She installed her several full-length mirrors, one for every room and two for the large living area, so that she could strike a pose whenever the pose struck her.

Tish and Gray built their life together from the outside in. Eating, training, and love-making formed the cornerstone activities of their affair, which rose monumentally above the flat desert plain of Kansas City's arid middle-class existence. The three parts of their modest library constituted the engineering manuals for the construction and maintenance of this pyramidal love: the no-fat high-protein cookbooks in the kitchen, and the bodybuilding and better-loving manuals on the shelves in Dale's old room. Books of the "fornicatory pleasures," Gray liked to say. The shelves, though, did not stretch as easily as their skin did to accommodate their gains, so the amassing couple soon had stacks mushrooming about the apartment.

Unawares, they loved according to the Weider principles by which they lifted, most notably the principles of intensity and variety. As in training they made gains by constant changes in the kind and technique of their exercises—one day, for instance, doing the flat bench press and incline flies at max weight, and fast low reps; and another day, the decline press and cable flies at low weight, and superslow on both the positive and negative motions—so too they achieved new levels of sexual pleasure by shocking the body with the unexpected position in combination with various strokes and gyrations. V-bar front pull-down, standing reverse-grip cable row, continuous movement hack squats, one-arm dumbbell overhead French press, side-by-side clasping, reciprocal sight of the posteriors, variant yawning position, the position of the Wife of Indra, cicada on a bough. Change the activity, change the angle, change the pace; change, change, change; new, new, new; yes, yes, oh oh oh yes.

Even the sounds of their loving and lifting concresced, the same grunts, gasps, heaves, screams, taunts, biddings, and brutish coos. Of this cross-fertilization, the most unusual strain had its roots in Tish's history with her prior lifting partner, and flowered in the gym during hack squats about six months into their partnership: "Come on now, do it for your Daddy, Lacey, do it to him, do it to him, what's so funny?—that's it, that's it."

"Do it for your Daddy?" Gray asked after completing the set. "Do it to him, do it to him? What's up with that?"

"Wendy," her old partner, Tish explained, "went to therapy twice a week—I always ragged her about it, I mean really, why can't people just deal?—because of severe self-esteem hang-ups on account of her father. Never good enough for him, never good enough for herself. So then once when she's about to puss out on the lat pull-down I leaned in and whispered, 'Do it for your Daddy, girl, do it for Daddy.' Wendy busts, right, loses her grip, the bar goes flying up, nearly takes my head off, and the plates crash down. Did more good for the girl in those fifteen seconds and for free than all that time and money flushed down the crapper at the therapist's."

In no time Wendy and Tish's joke became a part of Gray and Tish's liftspeak, and within twenty-four hours, their bedspeak as well. Tish invoking, Gray complying, both appeased: "Do it for your Daddy, Do it to Daddy, Do it to him, Fuck him, you pussy, Fuck your Daddy's cunt."

He called her pussy sometimes too, though absolutely not because she had a vagina. Not because she was a pussy, but because she called him one. A way of ribbing his pal. He also, though rarely and only long after she had established it as a part of her working vocabulary, called her cunt, which meant either bitch or pussy. Tish knew which. The first time he did it, one-upping her "don't be such a pussy" for his limp egg-beating technique by telling her not to "be such a cunt," it surprised her, but did not disarm her. Gray never could do that. "Are you prepared to put your dick where your mouth is?" she retorted, and he wound up balling her on the kitchen table. It was all he knew to do in such situations, though for the physicality of his loving he never knew the solution for what it was—surrender, placation, oblation. After, she dabbed off her sweat with whatever corner of clothing was available, and kicked back.

One postcoital Sunday morning Tish, who in her no-nonsense-get-down-to-sweating style flirted more after sex than before, told Gray that her last name, Kirk, meant *church*.

"Your body's one hell of a temple," he came back.

"I guess that makes you my personal lay priest," Tisha cracked. "I am," she continued, "an accomplished punnilinguist." (That she punned better than he did not bother him. Very little that Tish did bothered him. He was good-natured, proud of his woman—who wouldn't be?—and in love. Heart-fucked, Dale would have said.) Then she went down on him.

Gray loved oral sex from Tish especially. Beyond the language of musculature, fellatio and its kissing cousin was the only Latin he knew. Looking down at her he could check out himself, his own pecs and abs; and he could touch himself, and her, rub on her shoulders, grip her head, help her with the rhythm, finger through her hair, tug her hair and pull her off when he didn't want to come. He could see himself, and he could see her as she touched and teased him, as she licked nibbled and ate him up. And he could watch when the real banging began, her biceps and forearm flexors pumping him, her lips invaginating him, her head bobbing like a cylinder too eager to wait on its piston. Her mouth fucking him and him fucking it back while he looked down on the muscled mass on her knees before him, three perfect striated deltoid heads on each side framing her bouncing blondage: a total rush, the best head of his life.

He began painting her toenails weekly, and once, after some wheedling along the lines of don't be a pussy, he let her paint his. He didn't shower at the gym that day. Imagine two troglodytes painting each other's toenails cherry red, less troglodytes really than a pair of punchy, overgrown puppies.

Gray never talked about Tish with his parents. They knew he was dating someone, albeit casually. Someone he spent time with until he found *her*, you know, *the one*. They had no idea Tisha lived with him. Since leaving college Tish screened all calls through the answering machine; if either of them answered, it was Gray. Nor did his parents know that she also trained as a bodybuilder—the two college professors had had a hard enough time when Gray came out about his lifestyle. He talked on the phone more and spent more time with her family than his own. Gray's parents never met Tish, never spoke with her on the phone, never saw a photo of her. The doctors Gregory Sr. and Belinda Meredith Lacey—"Bee," he called her—never took Tisha Louise Kirk seriously.

They sometimes jerked one another off, sometimes jerked themselves off in front of the other.

It was while frenching his dick that she first slid a finger in his ass. He had already been in hers with his (not his finger, mind), and, as she later joked, what's good for goose is good for the gander. She had rimmed him with her tongue before—a first for him, and an unexpectedly thrilling sensation—and had wriggled a finger partially inside before. When she went a little further this time he squeezed in reflexive self-defense, and she paused. He relaxed, her mouth still worked on him up front, her finger still on hold in back. She continued. He tensed, she paused, he relaxed; and again, until she hit a nerve that felt tied fast to his balls, an unexpected erogenous lifeline, and when he came, God, did he come. They had been together three months; in another month she was doing him with a dildo while he was on top doing her.

Yes, he had already been there with her. She was his first that way. The idea had not previously appealed to him. Yet from their meeting he had loved her ass, its compactness very like his own, and ever since, the more his eyes and hands and mouth made that part of her the object of their admiration, the more they inched his imagination along. He was lying on top of her; his penis, pressed between the crevice of her asscheeks and his own abdomen, stirred, nuzzling her where it lay. She must have realized what he wanted. "Yes, pussy, yes." He dry-humped her; she writhed as if he were inside. The next time Gray found himself in the same position, again she must have known. From the topmost nightstand drawer, she pulled out and handed him their lubricant, then slid a pillow under her belly to lift her ass for an easier go. She knew what she was doing. "Go slowly now baby—that's right—how I've wanted you in my ass—yes, fuck me now, you pussy, fuck your Daddy up the ass."

That's "tush" with an "i," short for Tisha.

The competing body has to glisten and shine and ripple, so two days before their first competition together—his first ever, the Topeka Capital Contest—they shaved one another. Tish got carried away. Shaving his groin, Tish replaced razor with scissors and snipped away. She lathered him up, then picked up the razor again. With legs spread wide and a woman with a blade betwixt, Gray found his vulnerability titillating. The fresh air did a cool virginal jig there. He got hard. But he was too clever to screw her before shaving her, too. Not bothering to clean the lather residue, their following fuck was slippery like a water-park ride.

They did not celebrate Tish's first victory in Topeka because Gray lost, and this one thing, competition, she would never rub in his face. Gray had placed behind a nattily sculpted pipsqueak of a champion, and a runner-up both Gray and Tish judged asymmetrical.

"Measuring tape, I say," Tish consoled. "Let's have some standards. Methodically eliminate the puny and the asymmetrical, and then maybe we can get down to business. Damn wanker's arms."

They did not make love for an entire thirty-four hours.

II.

On May 24, 1995, two years after Gray had met her, everything with Tish went tits up.

She had decided to do an article for *Shape* magazine on women's bodybuilding. A photo essay, actually. No, we are not men, the article was to proclaim: we are women, strong women, with womanly curves, and womanly graces. The photographer, Miranda "Randy"

Randall, Tish had discovered through an announcement for a current show, pinned to the gym bulletin board. She tore the flier off the board in the afternoon and by nine Randy had agreed to do the shoot.

The woman made things happen.

The shoot took nine hours on a Tuesday. Tish posed in every stage of dress and undress. She wore a gown, a cocktail dress, a pair of jeans and a white tee, a miniskirt, a string bikini, a bedsheet, and nothing, covering herself with a hand, an arm, or turned leg, or such props as dumbbells, a frying pan and spatula, and even Randy's cat, Caleb.

The cat was Tish's idea. The idea of covering one pussy with another tickled her pink.

Gray participated in three shot scenarios. Dressed as a businessman in a standard dark navy suit, he took notes on his knees at Tish's feet, Tish in a power suit with skirt sitting crosslegged and unstockinged on her enormous desk's edge. Gray in a tuxedo danced behind her, his arms wrapped around to her front suggesting both paternal hug and grope; she in her exaggerated loincloth of a dress, its sides slit above her hips to her waist, one entire rock of buttock outcropping for these shots. In his last sequence, Gray, wearing only gym shorts, lay facedown on a bed, with teddy-clad Tish straddling his butt, making him appear birthday-unclad, while she pretended to massage his back.

Most of the shoot Gray watched from the makeup chair. Shelby, the make-up girl, sat nearby. He guessed her twenty-three, four years younger than himself. Her pageboy hairstyle and petiteness promised to preserve the girl in her while the woman matured. Because of their relative sizes, to work on Gray she had to drop the chair to its lowest setting. Shit, he could grab her around the waist with one hand and knock out some curls.

In the foreground, Tish released Caleb to the floor and plopped into the papasan chair where she waited between sequences. Randy was reloading her camera and adjusting the lighting. Not having bothered to cover herself, wearing only her bikini bottom, Tish cuddled coyly with a pillow in the round rattan chair and asked Gray, "Do you think *Playboy* will take me?"

She was, he realized, serious. "They'd be idiots not to." And they just might. Tish wasn't a bunny of nineteen, but she was Tish, and they just might.

Shelby's chair tilted as she stood, and Gray looked her way. As she approached, he turned his chair to face the mirror, in which, in the background, he could see Tish, now twice as far away, inspecting her nails. Shelby leaned over him to fetch the powder—she wore a fragrance he did not recognize, but liked—and bending between Gray and the mirror, began to prep him.

She had moved behind him and was doing his hair when he addressed her in the mirror. "Has anyone ever told you look like Donna Tartt?"—by which he meant, you are tiny with cropped dark hair. "She's a writer."

"I wish. She's so pretty. And she's a great writer. What a first novel. Didn't you love it?" She had stopped working. Her hands, the brush in her left, rested on Gray's shoulders.

"Yeah, she's great." He had not. He knew this author's caption facts from an article—had it been an interview?—in *Vanity Fair*. Having returned the magazine to the angled shelf and walking away he muttered off a set of synapse reps, to stress and grow his memory: *Donna Tartt, writer; Donna Tartt, writer; Donna Tartt, writer.*

Tish was in a silk camisole now, doing some shots before Gray joined her on the bed.

Shelby pointed her brush at the other woman. "You don't like her doing this, do you?"

His face went hot. Where had that come from? "Why wouldn't I? Look at her, she's amazing."

"She's a sight, all right," said this other, miniature woman.

† † †

Two days later Gray called the girl in the morning at the salon where she worked: "Shelby Nicholson, please." He asked to see her.

They met for lunch. He confessed that he had not read Donna Tartt's book, that the lie had been nagging him ever since. He wanted to buy her lunch to pay for his lie. He ate a salad, she had the chicken quesadilla appetizer and the taco soup. After his confession he said very little, and the tiny Shelby, obviously nervous, ran at the mouth enough for both of them. He chased each bite of his lunch with a swig of her life story: her mother's early death, her three older sisters, her father, and her last boyfriend, a cop, who had cheated on her with his butch supervising sergeant. She tried to get him to talk about Tish. He would not. She thanked him for the meal.

On Saturday, Shelby called him. She had heard through Randy the photographer that he had kicked Tish out. She said she called out of worry.

"I'm in love with you," he told her.

She hung up.

No mere makeup girl. This, this was an angel.

He dogged her. He had her scent and was all nose. He would not relent.

Dale, Gray knew, would not have considered the

girl a fuckable. But Dale let Bob Guiccione and *Baywatch* define his taste for him. He didn't know, didn't care, what a real woman was about. Shelby's realness twisted Gray in like a vortex.

The little cunt can't make you happy, he heard Tisha in the back of his head: *You'll snap her in two, you'll split her at the seam. You think she has muscles enough down there for you? She's not a woman, Gray, she's a mouse.*

Two weeks after he had told her on the phone that he loved her, Shelby agreed to a date, dinner, and a movie. "But I'm going to call you Gregory because I hate Gray, and don't you dare tell me you love me."

What don't I understand? Then tell me how it is, let's see if I can't grok it. Brother and sister? What the fuck does that mean? Brothers and sisters don't screw like berserk rabbits.

Finally, Gregory and Shelby kissed. In a matter of several agonizing days.

Are you afraid of what your tightass parents will think? Are you afraid you won't be able to handle me? Well, you're sure as shit right about that.

He would not sleep with her for months, not until all his body hair had grown back. He did not know how to explain why it was gone.

Don't be a pussy, Gray. Don't be such a damned fucking pussy.

When they finally did make love he was ever so

gentle. Her tiny body he could lift and place and move any way he liked. When he did lift and place and move her, he was ever so gentle.

They did not speak during. He discovered he preferred her whimpers of pleasure and her orgasmic gasps. If her lovemaking had a fault, it was that her blow jobs were not the feasting they could have been. Her small mouth tired easily, and she did not swallow. If her lovemaking had a fault. She even allowed him to make love to her ass, to slide himself between her baby-soft cheeks, she waiting patiently until he came into the small of her back.

Heaven.

With Shelby, Gregory did things right. They didn't move in together until after the wedding. He didn't propose until they had met each other's parents and he had secured her father's blessing. Yes, they slept together, though he arranged to feel sufficiently guilty about it.

Gregory moderated in other ways, too. He returned to All Sport Body Quencher. He no longer dreamed of being Mr. Universe, merely of owning his own gym. Instead of ending his quest for the ideal masculine form, he modified his vision. He now lifted for health, a little for vanity, and for Shelby. She liked her man strong. But not too much.

On their first wedding anniversary, Mr. and Mrs. Gregory Lacey opened a gym. Gregory ran the floor, Shelby ran the business. They managed quite well together.

Though Gray still masturbated, enjoying that most measly of orgasms, and on occasion—and as it shamed him tremendously he would never confess it, he would never even admit to Shelby that he masturbated at all—he did it with a lubed dildo up his ass, which he kept hidden from her, and fantasized Tish sucking him to kingdom come.

III.

Dale drove back to Kansas City to be the best man. Randy, the photographer who had brought them together, shot the event.

Tish was man enough to attend the ceremonies. Tisha Louise Kirk—who was man enough and big enough, more pumped than ever, sported her gold crucifix on its nearly invisible chain, and stood on exhibit in a barn-red strapless dress slit to the knees. And so it was that Tisha Louise Kirk—flaunting her unstockinged rockhard gastrocnemius and soleus muscles, forced by her high heels to flex, her dress revealing the smart rectangular fields of her adaman-

tine rectus abdominus through a sequin-bordered sheer cutout in the shape of a teardrop, a slender teardrop—Tish caught the bouquet.

BEEP!

M. Christian

As soon as he got home, he turned on his answering machine.

Beep! "Hello, slut. Have you been a good boy? Hmm? I bet you haven't, have you? I know you, slut. I know you've been bad. Yes, that's right—bad. You're a slut, after all; you can't help being anything else, can't help but be a slut. You crave sex, don't you? Yes, you do: you want it badly, want it *nasty*. Your body aches for it, your soul screams for it. That's what being a slut's all about, isn't it? Wanting it all the time, needing it so badly—"

Her voice was deep and purring, a moment before

a hard rain, a sexy rumbling that spoke of strong shoulders, a proud stance, firm eyes.

"But you're not just a slut, are you? No, you're not some run-of-the-mill slut. You're my slut. You're mine, do you hear me? You're my property, my boy, my plaything. You're mine from the tip of your nose to the tips of your toes. And your cock—especially your cock—is mine. You might carry it around with you, but your cock belongs to me. I let you carry it, and nothing more. You know you're supposed to keep your hands off it, not touch it without my permission, but I know you. I know you can't resist. I know you took your cock in your hands and stroked it. I know you stroked your cock and thought of me: my tits and ass and, especially, my cunt. I know you did it because you're a slut. But that doesn't mean I forgive you—because it was *my* cock you played with. My cock—and I hadn't given you permission, had I?"

The machine clicked as she hung up, then signaled the subsequent message.

Beep! "You were bad, and you know it. You stroked my cock and you came—you broke the rules. You know what happens when you break the rules. Even sluts, after all, have to obey. You have to be punished, slut. It's for your own good.

"So what'll it be? Hmm? Maybe I'll just spank you,

let you feel my firm hand on your tender ass. A few dozen smacks on your dimpled cheeks. Or maybe it'll be my cane you'll feel—the scalding pain of my birch rod. Too much? Well, who decides things, slut—*you*?"

Yes, it was powerful: there was no denying that. He was beyond hard, touching on *ache*. Almost unconsciously his hand dropped down and started to massage his cock. He didn't feel like muscles and tissue—he was so hard— velvet, silk wrapped in iron? Telling himself he wanted to feel how hard he was, he kicked off his shoes, hopped on one foot till he got his socks off, kicked off his shorts, and put one gently quaking hand around his cock. Yes, steel in satin. Yes, so strong, so painfully hard.

Beep! "Or maybe I'll use my clips—remember them? I thought you might: their exquisite bite on your chest, your nipples, under your cock, on your balls. Yes, maybe the clips. I do so enjoy watching your face screw up against their tightness, their pinching. I love hearing you whimper as they go on—and then hearing you cry when, after ten minutes or so, they come off. I particularly like putting them on your nipples. I love the way your brown nubs get fiery from their grip, crimson from delightful pain. And I love the way you love them. They might ache, and you might moan, and when the pain builds to a wonderful peak, cry out—but I know you, slut. I know every corner and crease of you. Ache, moan, and cry, but I know you do it out of joy—both because your pain readily becomes pleasure and because you know that it pleases *me*."

Spitting into his hand, he stroked himself—glorying in the coolness of the skin of his palm against the molten tissues of his cock. He felt his balls squeeze together: a glorious tightness. His mind was storming with images, a vibrant, fleshy and viscous torrent of pictures. Nothing stayed for more than a half-beat of his heart, but the lack of focus wasn't distracting—much as, in a rainstorm, the individual drops of rain are invisible, though the storm can be clearly seen. The storm in this case was tall, broad, with flaming eyes, a bountiful and strong body. She smacked a crop into her left hand with a well-practiced action.

Beep! "As you know, I have many toys. Many instruments with which to punish you—and please me. You've seen my playroom, you know what I have. Think of the dark wood cabinets, the leather bench, the sling, the stocks. Think of the bolts in the ceiling, the floors. Think of the many things I have at my disposal. So much to play with. Maybe I'll have you lie on my table, put your perky little ass in the air. You've seen that one special cabinet, haven't you? Oh, yes, you know about that one: the one with the heavy hooks to hold all those very heavy whips—my beautiful floggers. Maybe the red one, or the blue and silver. Ah, I know—what else for your sweet, slutty ass? What else but my special flogger? You know the one: my heavy whip, the black one. Oh, yes, that's what you need, what you deserve. Think of it, slut. Think of yourself on my hard leather table, naked, your cock squeezed between the tabletop and your smooth belly. Maybe the air in the room is just a bit chilly, so there's a sprinkle of goose bumps along your legs. You wait. Eagerly. You know it's coming, you know I'm standing next to you—and in my hand is my very special black whip."

He was there, the leather smooth and cool against his belly. His cock was too hard, gently quaking with frustrated desire. He could feel her standing next to him, feel her erotic scowl, her intensity. He wanted her, but he also wanted what was in her hand, on his ass.

Beep! "I'll make you wait, you know that. I'll make you wait till the waiting itself becomes more painful than any instrument I might use. Then, when you can't stand it any more, when the words 'Please, Mistress' finally slip from between your proud lips, then—and only then—will I raise the black whip and use it on you. Only then, slut, will I beat your pale ass. One stroke, two, three—but who's counting? Soon you won't be able to tell, won't care how many. You'll just be your ass, burning from my whip.

"I'll beat you. I'll pound your slutty ass till it's no longer anything like pain. You know that place, slut. You know it because I've brought you there—I've *taken* you there. You know the moment when the whip no longer is painful, when I'm no longer your Lady, your Dominant. You know that moment because you love it as much as I do, that special point when the pain stops and the pleasure starts—when I become your lover and not your Mistress."

Stroking his cock, his shirt and tie flapping against his chest, he wanted to be there more than anything else on earth. He would have given anything, done anything, to be there with her, on that table. He wanted her punishment, her whip, her strong arm pounding on his ass. He wanted her love.

Beep! "Maybe you'll come, slut, and maybe you won't. Maybe the pain will go so far beyond itself that your body will let it out in a wracking, beautiful come —a rose blooming among thorns. Maybe you'll be rewarded for your endurance, your suffering. Maybe, but maybe not—because, you see, that even though at that moment I will be your lover, and not your Mistress, I still own you. You will still be mine. Your pleasure makes me happy, but my pleasure is why you are here, what you breathe for.

"And I wish for pleasure, slut. I wish to punish you, because I want you as my toy, my plaything. That's what you're here for, right, slut? You're mine—every inch of you. Your tongue, ass, and fingers, and of course, your cock. You are mine, slut. Not that you mind—I know you live for how I will use you, what punishments I will inflict on you. We're a perfect match. But philosophy bores me, and what I want from you is service. Now!

"You know my cunt. You know it even better than I do. You've memorized every fold, every inch of it. You know how big my clit gets when you kiss it; you know the flavor of my juices when you lick them. You know the wet embrace of my cunt on your cock when I deem you to be used for such things. You know exactly what's going to happen when I step up to the table and tell you to roll over. Because you live for what will happen next."

He was there, on that table, rolling over onto his back, staring up at her with furnace-hot eyes, his steel cock bobbing against his tight stomach, straining upward at an impatient forty-five degrees.

"Kiss me, slut—on my special lips. Feel the smoothness of my labia, how closely I've shaved myself. I'll put a finger inside and paint your lips with my juice, offer you a tempting treat for what you will dine on soon enough. Then I'll part my lips, ever so gently, to show you the pink depths—your home, your temple.

"Lick me, slut—long and deeply. Taste the wine of my cunt, the special flavor of my pussy. Drink me and tease and cherish my clit. You know what I want from you. Make me come, slut, make me scream out my orgasm while my hands pull you closer, deeper.

His cock was pulsing, beating with the trip-hammer of his heart. He made animal noises; he burned to feel his cock in her cunt.

Beep! "What a pretty cock you have. It's long and strong—just like all of you. But it's mine, though. Right, slut? My cock. So I'll climb up on the table and lower myself, inch by inch, onto you, slowly filling my wet depths with your cock. Then, and only then, will I fuck you—up and down, back and forth. You'll want to come, of course, but I won't let you. You know the rules, slut; you know that only I can tell you when to come. And you can't come yet, not for a long time—not till my cunt juice paints your lap, your balls—not till I've come again and again from slamming my cunt up and down, up and down, on your quaking dick. Then, when you can't stand it, and the scream starts to tear its way out of you, I'll bend down and whisper, 'Now, slut,' into your ear. Only then, slut. Only then—"

Now!

An avalanche of pleasure, a torrential downpour of joy. He exploded and jetted across his living room, all over his couch. The quaking continued for what seemed like minutes. Then his body betrayed him, and he collapsed, hard, onto his small doorway rug, his legs quivering.

"You are mine, slut. You are a good, kind and noble slut—and you belong to me. Isn't that marvelous?" *Click!*

He lay on the couch, oblivious to the next message —his mother asking why he hadn't called in days— until all thoughts left his swimming head and he began to slip into a gentle nap.

Well, almost all thoughts. One surfaced before he sank down into a long dream filled with leather goddesses with gleaming skin and powerful desires—

Praise God for wrong numbers....

WHAT YOU FIND

Jameson Currier

He kisses you on the lips and says good-bye in a whisper. As you hear the door click behind him you are suddenly wide awake, aware of the morning stillness in his apartment. This is the first time he has left you alone in his place after eight months of dating, sleeping over occasionally at his apartment on the weekends, and you stretch you legs out in the bed, tensing the sleep out of your muscles. You feel the space where he slept last night next to you, still warm, you think, then run the palm of your hand over the flat empty space of the sheet and draw his pillow up to your face, breathing in the remaining scent of him. You think a moment about last night's sex, feeling yourself getting hard. You play with yourself for a moment, slipping your hand beneath your underwear, stroking yourself, then cupping your balls. You sigh loudly and get out of bed.

In the kitchen you make coffee, fiddle with yourself in your underwear some more, wanting to keep yourself semi-erect and edgy as long as you can. You sit at the table and eat a cranberry muffin he bought for you at the grocery store yesterday. You look at the digital clock on the VCR. It reads 9:17. You calculate he won't be back for another four hours—gone to his daughter's bat mitzvah in Connecticut. You don't know what amazes you more—the fact that he is forty-six years old and has a daughter old enough to be bat mitzvahed, or the fact that he is still married but filing for a divorce. You glance outside the window as you chew on your muffin, happy as you taste the burst of a cranberry in your mouth. You stare at the apartment building windows across the street, then watch a barge creep along the East River. He says he's gay, though he won't admit it to anyone except you and the tricks he meets at the Townhouse, his favorite bar on the east side. He's not told his soon-to-be-ex-wife the reason why their marriage is ending, not told his daughter why he no longer lives at home. He has no plans to come out on the job, no plans, either, for you, except to have sex with you when his schedule permits. He doesn't want a relationship, after all, you remind yourself—only someone to have a good time with. That's all you want out of this too, you tell yourself, but then you remind yourself you know that's not true. You've spent the last twenty years looking for a lover—and just when you found someone you want to fall in love with—just when you are ready—he tells you he wants to date other people and doesn't want to settle down.

The story of my life, you think with a big sigh. You get up from the table. You wash your coffee mug in the kitchen sink and place it in the dish rack. You wonder why he left you alone in his apartment—after months and months of insinuating that he was dating other men, that you weren't the *only* distraction in his life, that he knew you were the possessive and jealous type, did he think that you had changed after all that time? Or has he changed, you wonder? Is he ready for a relationship now? No, you remind yourself again. It's sex, not a relationship. You're just fuck buddies who go to the movies together.

At least it's good, you think. The sex. At least you find him sexy. At least he appreciates you appreciating him. At least it makes you feel good to make him feel good. Well, most of the time. You walk out of the kitchen and again are drawn to the view from his window. You watch a helicopter float over Roosevelt Island. Before he left you alone you had made up your mind you wouldn't snoop through his things—you knew enough about him already, and what you suspected of him you didn't need confirmed. You're thirty-nine years old. You're a mature gay man. You don't need to snoop through a married boyfriend's stuff. You don't need your jealousy piqued, your possessiveness inflamed. You already have enough problems with this pseudo-relationship—his age, his marriage, his money, his ego.

You suddenly smack yourself in the head with the palm of you hand, listening to the sound it makes. *Why, why, why are you here?* you ask yourself. Are you that desperate for attention? That needy for any kind of relationship? *Yes*, you answer. You're such a fool. And Kevin's dead. So are Jeff and Michael and a lot of the other boys you used to play with.

You turn on the television and check the weather on Channel 1—the box in the corner reads 49 degrees. You turn up the sound so you can hear it above the stereo and wait for the newscaster to read the forecast, running your finger across the head of your cock. The newscaster predicts that it may reach the high sixties today. You stand in front of the TV playing with yourself, looking out again at the view. You think about him sucking your cock, then think about sucking his cock, then imagine him on the couch, his legs apart and you feel yourself grow harder, frustrated. You fight off the urge to masturbate—he's coming back, you know, and he'll want to have sex—and so will you. You surf through the channels with the remote control, lingering for a moment on a wrestling program, admiring the body of one of the wrestlers—thick and muscled about the arms and shoulders. You wish for a moment he had a better body. Wished he were younger and better looking. You wish he was the wrestler. You're still hard and you squeeze your cock now, stroke it back and forth really good a few times, then click the TV off with the remote just when you're ready to want more. You switch on the stereo and begin stretching your neck, twist your waist back and forth and side to side until you feel loose, supple and awake.

You turn the stereo up louder and wander into the bedroom. You slip on his sneakers, hoping you'll stretch them out of shape. You laugh. Your feet are bigger than his. But he has the bigger waist. You look at yourself in the mirror over his dresser. You look better than you have in the last ten years. You've lost twenty-five pounds since you've started dating him—anxiety over trying to make it work for you, too, you know. But it has made you look younger, more attractive, you think. You certainly notice you get more looks now on the street. And you never walk out of a bar alone these days. You stare at your waist. Twenty-nine inches. You can even see the muscles in your stomach now. You couldn't when you were twenty-nine years old.

You turn on the treadmill, start walking at a slow pace. You turn up the speed, punch the reset button. Your erection drops off fast as the pace of your feet gets faster and faster. Even if he doesn't want you someone else will, you think. Even if this ends there will be someone else. He's not the only person you're seeing, you remind yourself. Your little joke on him. *As if he even cared*, you think. You walk and walk, noticing the furniture in his bedroom. You remember when they delivered the dresser. You suggested he get the mission-style headboard because it would work well with handcuffs. You were with him when he bid on the Hockney at Christie's.

You notice an unfamiliar envelope on the top of the dresser and it disturbs you. You don't know what it is. You think about stopping to snoop, but you don't. You keep walking, turning the speed up even faster.

He'll never lose the weight, you remind yourself. He eats too much junk—snacks and cookies throughout the day, every night potato chips, ice cream and a carafe of wine before going to bed. How does he do it? Consume so much food? You don't even have an appetite anymore. All you want is to feel good about something. All you ask from him is some kind of affection, which is the last thing he is willing to give.

You stop after thirty-one minutes and two-and-a-half miles. You are drenched in sweat; your cock is small, wet. You get off the treadmill and check the envelope on top of the dresser. It is the menu of the meal they are serving at his daughter's bat mitzvah. You look at the clock. Two hours and forty minutes left. He could get back early, though. You lie on the floor and look at the ceiling, then force yourself through one hundred crunches. You roll over and lie on your stomach, lift yourself up into a position for pushups. Your feet slide against his polished wooden floor. You inch your way down till the heels of your feet are against the bottom drawer of his nightstand. You do fifty push-ups and then rest. You make a note in your head to remind him to invest in a chin-up bar. He will never do it, you know. It would ruin the aesthetics of his apartment. You do fifty more push-ups, purposely banging your heels against his dresser drawer. That's where he keeps the dildos and lube. Where the condoms come from. Where he stashes the magazines he picks up at the bar.

You roll over and open the drawer and look inside. Oh hell, you think, you've started snooping. Just find it all out and get it over with. You've seen all the toys in this drawer before. Three sizes of dildos—thin, regular, and extra big with a double head. Nothing is new that you can tell except the recent issue of *Next* which is dated this weekend. That means he went to the bar this week.

You close the drawer and sit on the bed. You untie his sneakers and throw them on top of the treadmill. You open the top drawer of the nightstand. You've never seen him open this drawer. On top are his pay stubs. You read the year-to-date earnings column. You estimate he makes close to $400,000 a year. You are stunned. You had no idea he made *that* much. He did say once that he made more money than a doctor. Then you get angry. You pay for half of everything you do together—the movies, the theater tickets, the occasional restaurant, the trip last month to Washington, D.C. You barely make $25,000 a year. You try to shrug it off, but you can't. He once told you he would like you more if you made more money. Jerk, you think. Pig. All he's after is sex. All he wants is a good time. He's just using you. Using you for the sex.

You look through the rest of the drawer. There are scraps of paper with numbers and addresses written on them. You read each one. John at a Chelsea phone number, Peter on East Eightieth Street. There is another pile of business cards he must have gotten from tricks at the bar. You become perturbed because there are so many of them. You even find one of your old boyfriends in his pile. Small world, you try to console yourself, then laugh because you think they both deserve one another. They're both jerks, you tell yourself. Both nothing but pigs.

In the back of the drawer you notice a membership card to the baths. You look at the expiration date and are relieved that it expired one month before you started dating him. What a pig I've found, you tell yourself again. Why would you want to be in a relationship with a sex junkie?

You shake your head. That's not what you want. You wonder if he will ever want to settle down. He was up front when you confronted him with it after you had been dating each other for six weeks. He said he just got out of a fourteen-year marriage, why would he want to settle down with someone right away? You remind yourself that it was your choice to continue this. Then you remind yourself that since he cheated on his wife when he was married—of course he's going to cheat around on a *boyfriend.* Then you tell yourself that "cheat" is the wrong word. There's nothing going on between the two of you, after all. At least not in his direction. It's just sex. Just dating. You close the drawer. You don't want to know any more. You try not to get upset. Don't make him into someone he's not going to be, you tell yourself.

Pigs, you think. They're all pigs. Rich men, fat men, gay men. They're all jerks. Even yourself. When did you ever have a decent boyfriend? When were you ever a decent one yourself? You never told him about Peter, never mentioned the ad you placed in *HX* two months ago, never mentioned the string of blind dates you had, never mentioned whom you met on the phone lines. *But he provoked it*, you tell yourself. Didn't he *make* you look by reminding you of your every imperfection over and over? That you are far from the perfect boyfriend for him? That you weren't rich enough or young enough or cute enough or hot enough? And weren't you just hoping to find someone better than *him?*

You go into the kitchen and get a drink of water. You look at your watch. Ninety more minutes. You could read the book you brought, look through the notes of your novel that you think will never be finished. Suddenly you are aware that you will never have any money. You're a gay writer, you write gay stories, you write about gay life. You will never make the kind of money to be able to live in this kind of apartment. You look back at the view of the East River, at the wall of the apartments across the street. If you give him up you will never see this view again. But then you would never feel this lousy again, either.

When you first started dating him all you did was have sex. Sex in his new bed, sex in the kitchen, sex on the ottoman, sex on the floor. He was so cheap, he didn't even take you out for dinner. You wonder for a moment if you had his kind of money would you be dating someone like him? No, you think. You would be out of here quick. But you don't like him for just his money. And you want him for something more than just sex.

Then you remember how much you have in your wallet. Two dollars. You just paid the rent on your fifth-floor walk-up in Hell's Kitchen. You're broke. You don't even have enough to go out for a sandwich. Instead you walk into the bathroom and rinse your face. You open the medicine chest and count the number of new toothbrushes on the shelf. Four. None gone. None of the packages have been opened since you were last here. You know he keeps them for tricks. Just like he does the stack of disposable razors. You pull down a razor he has saved for you and lather your face with his shaving cream. You smile at yourself in the mirror. Fool, you think. You're such a clown. At least you can pretend to be happy. Maybe you should have been an actor after all and not a writer.

You shave and then brush your teeth. You look at yourself in the mirror, admire your waist and then flex your biceps. Treat me nice when I'm poor and I'll love you when I'm rich, you think.

You walk out of the bathroom and into his closet. You smell his shirts—freshly laundered and ironed cotton button-down. You touch his jackets, wave your fingers through the rack of ties, then thumb through them for the one he bought when you went together to Barney's. You play with yourself again and realize that you are already hard.

You try on one of his shirts. It fits nicely, but you don't even contemplate trying on his pants; there's a five-inch difference between your waists. You take the shirt off and look at yourself in the mirror on the back door of the closet. You strike a pose. You run your hand up and down your stomach. You cup your balls, twirling the ends of your pubic hair. You would never shave your balls, you think. You like it natural. You think about the times you've shaved his balls, the erection he gets as he's handled by you. You smile and then shake your head. Where is all this going? you wonder. Right into therapy?

You decide to explore some more. He once told you he kept cash hidden in the apartment, out of sight of his wife's lawyer. You wonder if you can find it. Suddenly, the prospect of this new game seizes you. You open his dresser drawers, looking beneath his underwear, between his T-shirts, inside his socks, through his shorts and under his slacks. You're obsessed with finding some money, any money, even if it's just a dollar bill or some coins he uses for laundry. You're not going to steal it, you just want to discover it, count it, touch it, know where it is because he makes such a big issue of how much he has and how little you have. Instead, you find a book of erotic stories under his jeans. You thumb through it. Nothing inside so you put it back. Maybe he's cash poor, you think, as you close the drawer. Maybe he's just a portfolio—all stocks and assets.

The bottom drawer surprises you, however, when you open it—there is a row of neatly stacked videos. You pick one up. It is *The Best of Joey Stefano*. You look at the photo of the guy on the cover. Dark hair, dark eyes, unshaven pouty looks. You've seen him on Robin Byrd's cable show a couple of times. Didn't he die? you think. Didn't he have a drug problem?

You put the video back in the drawer. You lift up another one. Same guy on the cover, full body shot, tattoo on his bicep. Joey Stefano in *Tattoo You.* You look at Joey. You look at yourself in the mirror. No contest, you think. He's younger. Hotter. Better arms. Better ass. You feel defeated. You put that video back and lift up one more. *Prince Charming*, with Joey Stefano's name on the cast list. As you turn it over an envelope falls to the ground. You pick it up and notice there is a phone number written on the front, with a 213 area code. California. You look inside the envelope, opening it carefully where it has been taped shut. It is full of small black hairs. Pubic hair, you think. An envelope full of pubic hair. It can't be *his*—his is gray. It must be Joey Stefano's pubic hair. *You have discovered an envelope full of Joey Stefano's pubic hair.*

What a pig you've found, you think. You had a big fight once over the porn. He wanted to watch it during sex. You wanted a little more attention from him. You sigh, aware that you will never be his ideal type—he's told you that, in fact. You've never insulted him, however, never told him that you think he could lose a little weight, go to the gym a little more, that the toupee really *is* noticeable. But then you're easier than he is. You're not so specific when it comes to men and body types and hair. All you want is someone to care—they don't have to look like a body builder or a wrestler or the bouncer you once saw in front of a club. OK, so you're jealous, you think. Deal with it. Get over it.

You go into the bathroom and flush Joey Stefano's pubic hair down the toilet. Then you open the medicine cabinet and find his nail scissors. You take off your underwear. You snip off some of your pubic hair. It is the same color as Joey's. You put it in the envelope and return it to the drawer with the videos. You kick the drawer closed with your foot, hoping you've made a dent in the wood.

You lie back on the bed again and stare at the ceiling, playing with your cock. How do you make things work, you wonder. You don't want to give up. You're not a quitter. Something is going on with this man if he trusts you enough to leave you behind in his apartment. You look at the photo of his daughter on his dresser. You could always blackmail him, you think. You could earn your fortune by threatening to expose him to his wife and his boss.

Grow up, you tell yourself. You would never do that. You're too gay yourself, too out, too proud to even think about doing something like that. What you want is to make something work, make this relationship work. But what if this is the wrong one, you wonder? What if you've picked the wrong guy again?

You squeeze your cock, rub your fist over the head.

You feel yourself getting hard. You close your eyes, feel the muscles of your chest tense. You think about the guy you saw in the sweater department at Bloomingdale's yesterday. Black hair, great arms. Better-looking than Joey Stefano, you laugh to yourself. You imagine him going down on you. The guy at Bloomingdale's. Not Joey. Joey's just a big bottom, after all, or so you've heard. You lift your legs up in the air, wet a finger in your mouth, and then begin to play with your asshole. You're hot, bothered, frustrated, and worked up. You pump your cock. Harder and harder. You push two fingers into your ass. Move them in and out as you work your fist up and down your cock. When you shoot you almost hit your nipple. You open your eyes and calm your breathing. You feel mean and nasty. You take some of your cum and rub it onto his comforter. You're such a pig, you think. Why are all gay men such pigs? You're no better than he is. You get up off the bed and go to the bathroom.

You piss and then step into the shower. You use his soap and shampoo. You find a clean towel and dry yourself off with it, just to make another one dirty for him to have to wash. You use his cologne and deodorant. You dry your hair with his hair dryer. You smell like him, you think, as you admire yourself in his mirror. He's all over you.

You look at the clock. He'll be back in about five minutes, you think. Your heart begins to beat faster and faster. You take a deep breath and hurriedly put on your jeans and sweatshirt, sitting on the couch and lacing up your boots. You get your jacket out of the closet. You take a last look at his river view.

Then you leave. You open the door and just walk out, listening to it slam behind you. He will never find your jealousy, anger, and obsession again, you decide. And he will not find you in his apartment when he returns.

KITTY

Roy Edroso

He was lonely. Worse, he was getting to be aware of his loneliness. For months he'd been busy enough that it only came to mind as he lay in bed waiting for sleep, which was bad enough but acceptable as the regular, contained nuisance of single life, like a diabetic's daily insulin shot. Now that the big electrical job was done, he was between assignments for awhile and had time to himself, and as he took the subway to museums or ate solitary meals in restaurants or lay on the sofa with his eyes half closed and a book open on his chest, loneliness more insistently made its presence known. When he emerged from a movie theater, he felt keenly the warmth of the chattering crowds moving on the sidewalk beside him, their voices recounting the story he'd just seen, but with names and events salted in that he didn't recognize. The further he walked the less of their animal warmth he felt; couples hurried ahead or fell back; fading ripples of their laughter dispersed down side streets. Then loneliness was there to meet him and see him home.

Home was no longer a comfort. He'd painted the walls, but they still felt blank and lifeless. He kept the TV on all night. He drank. The drink was a species of warmth. But loneliness waited; he would see it in the morning.

He dressed up in a good suit and chilled a bottle of champagne to watch the Oscars on TV. By Best Costume Design he had drunk the bottle and torn off his suit. At least now he didn't have to worry about Bette's fur as she climbed onto his lap. "I'm sorry you had to wait, sweetie," he told her, "Daddy wanted to feel special for Oscar Night." Bette purred and looked straight at him with a serious expression that softened when he scratched her under the chin. She stretched her neck at him and curled her toes.

Bette was a comfort. He'd had her for three years, and they loved each other. She was a pretty American shorthaired cat, black with white patches and paws, sleek and canny. She responded to his moods, not with the anxiety of dogs, but with the calm and beneficent curiosity of her species. He knew she was always sizing him up for petting or food, but he didn't mind feeding her and he loved to stroke or scratch her or play with her, to see her become limber with pleasure. And he was proud of her beauty, sensitive to her natural perfection, the reliable grace not only of her movements but even of her greed and willfulness. When he came back from a long weekend away and found that she had shit on the rug, he wasn't even mad, though he'd been fond of the rug. When she looked at him accusingly, then gave a short, scratchy meow and affected to ignore him, her butt high and tail swishing as she rubbed her face on the sofa, he laughed and scooped her up in his arms and nuzzled her. "My pretty, pretty girl," he whispered. She purred.

But even when loving and petting Bette he was not free from loneliness. She was a cat, after all. He needed human affection. But he didn't want to need it. People disappointed him, women especially. Over the years his disappointment had festered and putresced and its stink now permeated every corner of his soul. He had lost any facility for resisting or concealing it. So he avoided people, and petted his beautiful cat.

One night he lay in bed, drunk, with Bette stretched out and sleepy next to him. "If only you were a woman," he murmured. "You're my good girl. If only you were a woman." And as his last grains of consciousness gently sifted and mingled with those of sleep, he said, "I wish you understood."

He dreamt. In his dream he could not quite see what was happening, only sense it. Bette stood erect, and was much taller than she really was; indeed was almost as tall as he was. Her furry arms rested on his shoulders, and she was nuzzling him ferociously, her cool little nose butting his face, her thin lips streaking his cheeks with drool. He felt her belly brush his own with fine, slightly stiff hairs. Then suddenly her belly pressed his and it was no longer hairy at all, but fleshy, and it sank into his own skin and warmed it. His thighs tensed and felt her hind legs reach inward behind his shins and slowly sink in their claws.

Just on the verge of pain he opened his eyes.

He was only half awake. His mind still swam with the night. The room was dark, his head felt overly large and his face and mouth felt dry. His hand crept along the blanket and reached for Bette to stroke her. Her fur prickled his hand. It was very dry—scorched and gnarled like desert weeds. His fingers snaked in among the rough tendrils until they found a small daub of warmth and damp. His fingers eased in; the warmth flowed, clung to him like oil, and his fingertips drank it in.

He slowly rolled toward her. He felt her body rise under his hand. It was her haunch he felt—of that he was certain—but it seemed larger than usual. He could not feel the ridge of her shank, and again he felt no hair. The long, gentle slope of her haunch comforted him. Warmth radiated from her body and made him groggier, and at the edge of sleep a dab of cool like an angel's tear touched his throat with mercy and filled his soul with peace.

When he opened his eyes again, the sun had pushed through the chinks in the blinds. He saw a woman in his bed, her long back to him. She was partly obscured by covers and long, wavy black hair.

I must have gone out, he thought. *I must have gone out drunk and found a woman and brought her home.*

As if in response to his thought, the woman spun around with unimaginable speed and rose on one haunch. She fixed him with a stare, alert but not alarmed or unkind.

Her eyes were large, round, and dark-rimmed; it could have been makeup that rimmed them—the lines were dusty, like kohl—but he sensed it was not. All her other facial features were small. Her nose was small though fleshy, its tip round and full, with very small nostrils. Her ears were small—what he could see of them under that long, wild, black drape of hair—and they rode very high on her head. Her mouth was very small, too, though her lips looked full, perhaps from being gathered so closely together, almost puckered; they fit almost entirely under her nose.

Her chin was just a wide bump, and her neck rolled up to it without much definition, though this could have been caused by compression from the perfect erectness with which she bore her upper body. This was astonishing to him, for her lower body remained prone and relaxed on the bed, and he got the feeling that the one wiry arm that reached down to hold her torso aloft was not bearing much weight.

In contrast to her facial features, her body was broad, even full-hipped, yet there seemed to be no excess flesh to her—she was built wide, and well-built. Her shoulders were broad and straight; her breasts were full and also broad, crowding each other comfortably on her chest. (They had given one great heave when she had righted herself, then stood still, also erect, also alert). Her hips were wide and tapered gently to her thighs. Her legs were very powerful all the way down, yet the definition around her kneecaps was fine and almost delicate. She had large feet with long, perfectly white nails. Her hands were also large and long-nailed. *Her nails must be three inches long*, he thought. He wondered how she got her feet into shoes.

And then he realized that she had never worn shoes.

"Bette?" he said quietly.

She held his stare a moment, then let her torso fall to the bed, and rolled to face away from him. Her head moved back and forth in wide, looping, playful rolls, and she pushed her feet and hands straight out in front of her. He heard her nails scrape the wall under the window. Her shoulders hunched forward and her back pressed into his hands. He scratched her shoulders. From her shoulders to her ribs, waist, buttocks, thighs, calves, and feet, her body writhed with pleasure. Deep in her chest, she purred.

He was instantly hard.

Slowly he moved to her and pressed his body into hers. She seemed to like that; she undulated against him. Freed of its coating of hair, her flesh was moist and alive and seemed to thrill to his, push into his, spread and contract and catch his flesh in its own ebb and flow. Her buttocks actually closed around the top of his cock, squeezed and dragged along his shaft, and his mind went blank with desire. She pushed her head back, first into his face, almost suffocating him with her hair, then over and on top of his uppermost cheek. He heard more rapid scraping on the wall. She jerked her shoulders and moved her head forward and back, leaving streaks of spit on his cheek. Some of it seeped into his mouth, and he recognized a faint taste of cat food. But this didn't distract him from the steady contractions of Bette's body against his. He felt his balls tightening. Against the cool cheeks of her ass his cock throbbed. He felt as if he could come like this.

Suddenly Bette got up on all fours. He moved to enter her from behind, but she leapt from the bed and stood upright. Her posture was exquisite, like a dancer's. She walked beside the bed very slowly, with small steps, her butt rolling luxuriantly. As she walked she looked at him, then at the wall, then at him. Then she meowed. Her voice was deeper now, a human voice, but it came from her throat and was unmistakably the drawn-out, querulous yip of his cat. She darted into the other room, nails clacking.

He followed. She was standing in the kitchen by her food and water bowls, looking at him. She bent elegantly from the waist to the floor, her hair spreading over everything, and put her fingers around the rim of her food bowl, but her fingers were stiff and could not fully grasp the bowl. She moved her hands errantly, spastically, causing the bowls to skitter. She stood straight up, looked at him, yipped louder. Her face was slightly tense and her eyes glowed.

Keeping his eyes on her, he went to the cupboard and brought out a can—then, thinking better of it, got three cans. She quickly walked over and stood right next to him, staring in his eyes, breathing in his face. He was almost frightened, she was so close and focused, but he went about the familiar routine, ignoring her as he always did when she shadowed him in the kitchen. When he opened the cans she began to purr and when he started spooning food into the bowl she fell to all fours and dug her face into the bowl. He gently pushed her head aside to get all the food in, then stood back and watched as she took her breakfast.

She ate with pure animal pleasure, her arms and legs taut, her jaws thrusting. Her butt floated high up in the air. It was a beautiful, ripe, fulsome ass and it was his. She was his cat.

He stepped forward and gently placed his cock between her thighs. Bette quickly spun around and, with a short sneezing sound, brought one clenched, clawed hand up next to her face. She didn't look particularly angry, just wary, but the thought of those three-inch nails slashing with feline speed at his dick took the wind out of his sails. She went back to her bowl, and he went to his chair and, as he always had, waited for her to finish eating.

When she was done she walked upright toward him—he was apprehensive now—and suddenly swooped down her head and brushed her mouth against his knee. Her hair swept his cock and it tingled. She went to the couch, stood on it on all fours a moment, then collapsed and, with her legs hanging over the edge, fell promptly asleep.

For a while he watched her midsection gently rise and fall with each breath. Then he read *Newsweek.*

On and off throughout the day he read and watched TV. Bette got up from time to time and walked around upright with small, delicate steps. Her eyes glowed but her face was otherwise impassive. She looked wonderful naked, regal and unashamed, but now he was too intimidated to remain naked himself around her; he felt overmatched. He went into the bedroom to dress. As he pulled on his pants, Bette sneaked in on all fours and swiped at one dangling cuff. He yelled in terror and she flew out of the room. He wondered if eventually he would have to teach her to dress. His own clothes wouldn't fit her. He supposed he would have to start with robes and T-shirts.

That was planning too far ahead, he decided. He

went to his chair and sat; Bette plopped down in front of him, stretched out on her back, and swished her ass back and forth, her breasts lolling, her belly tightening. She was as graceful as ever, as beautiful as ever. And now she was also a woman, an incredibly sexy woman.

Who ate cat food, wanted her tummy rubbed, and threatened his dick with her claws.

She got up, looked him in the eye, and climbed into his lap. Though she appeared utterly comfortable and self-possessed folding her legs up and digging her head under his chin, he felt clumsy and got a mouthful of hair. He shifted just quickly enough to keep her from crushing his balls. She pressed hard enough on his chest to labor his breathing. She stopped wriggling and began to purr. He rested his arms on her back. Her body got very warm. It was like cradling a small lion.

She sleepily wiped her mouth on his face again. He kissed her cheek, then, gently, her lips. They felt warm and soft. He kissed her again. Her lips parted slightly and his tongue grazed hers. It felt a little rough, but not bad. He pressed his mouth to hers a little harder and her tongue arched in her mouth, becoming fuller and softer. Their lips were snug, though she did not seem to have the instinct to really reciprocate. He wanted to show her. His arms urged her toward him. Her jaws moved a little. *She'll do what I want*, he thought. *She's my kitty. She wants to please me.*

She shifted her weight and her knee pinched one of his testicles. The pain jolted him, and she flew from his lap and into the next room.

He gingerly massaged his balls, sighed, and took a shower.

The weather was getting warm but he kept all the windows closed. All he needed was for her to go wandering out onto the fire escape like that. He went shopping, came back, watched her napping, went out again. He walked up and down the street, trying to imagine her walking beside him in a nice dress, a floral print, and comfortable shoes. He looked forward to trimming her nails as soon as he thought it was safe.

When he came back again she meowed and ran to him. He stood very close to her and stroked her hair with both hands. Then he moved his hands down and rubbed her breasts. She stood there purring, hands at her sides, her head slightly raised, eyes half closed. Her breasts were warm and comfortable in his hands. He kept rubbing gently and soon felt her nipples rising against his palm. He reached one hand under her buttocks, and she immediately spun and trotted away.

He sighed and went out again.

When he came back he found a bunch of things

on the floor. There was a book, an empty milk carton he'd left out, and a bottle cap. He threw out the milk carton and as he was putting up the book, Bette came in and began kicking the bottle cap around. He picked up the bottle cap and put it in the trash and closed the lid. He went back to his chair and picked up *Newsweek*. Bette stood by the door of the kitchen, meowed, looked at him, then went into the kitchen, then meowed again. He ignored her. *For a miracle*, he thought, *she's getting to be a pain in the ass*.

He heard a ratlike scuttling in the kitchen. He went in and found her scraping the edge of the lid with her nails. She spotted him and ran out, her shoulder smacking his chest hard as she passed.

He walked off the pain, massaging his chest. Then he lay down on his bed, sullen and suddenly quite tired. Soon she came in and curled against his back. He sighed and went to sleep.

Deep in the night he was wakened by scuttling and meowing in the next room.

He snapped on the light and went to look. Bette seemed agitated. Her eyes were a bit wild and she was walking back and forth in the living room. She looked at him and yowled so loudly that he instinctively shushed her. She yowled again, but more quietly, and held his gaze.

"What's wrong, Bette?" he asked.

Yowl.

"What's wrong, poor honey?"

She walked in a small circle. Suddenly she flashed out a hand at the bookcase and swatted a few books to the ground. He ran to her and grabbed her from behind around the middle. She wriggled in his arms. It suddenly struck him that she could do some real damage to him, but she seemed not to have that in mind. She rubbed against him, first back and forth and, now for the first time, up and down. From her throat came a kind of low gurgling. She squirmed slowly but with great purpose. Even through his slacks he could feel her buttocks grabbing at him. She even smelled different. She smelled—he didn't know how else to put it—womanly.

He guided her into the bedroom and encouraged her onto the bed. She stayed on all fours and pointed her ass at him. Her bush looked moist; he even thought he saw a mist around it. Bette kneaded the bed with her hands and feet and turned her head back to look at him, eyes narrowed and fiery. Hair fell in her face.

He pulled off his clothes and climbed up to her and was guiding his cock toward her when she pushed her ass back and her cunt gulped and closed tight around the head. An unearthly cry came out of her, high and undulating, shrill and throaty at the same time. Her grip on him was tight, airtight. She shook like a broken lawnmower. The bed began to rattle.

He hooked his toes on the bedframe and pushed. She was so tight that driving in was almost like making a new hole. Bette's head reared back till it was almost upside down. Bubbles of sounds came out of her throat. He was all the way in and he didn't know whether he wanted to move. It felt like he belonged in there, like he was part of her. Then Bette started to rear and buck. She slid him almost all the way out, then she slammed him all the way back in. She did this again, then again, then caught his cock in the middle and began to vibrate, fucking maybe the middle inch or two of his dick incredibly rapidly. The head of his cock was numb—it felt as if it were floating in warm oil—but his shaft was getting the fuck of its life. He thought his cock might spray cum from the middle like a sprinkler. Suddenly her cunt seemed to yawn; instinctively he rammed back in all the way, and she gave another feline shriek and rose up on her toes and fingertips, her back arching to the ceiling. His knees jumped forward and his body fell back; but for the grip on his cock he would have flown off the bed. As it was she was practically holding him from above; his back arched toward the bed and his cock was jerked upward. Suddenly she roared like a lion and he exploded, his whole life shooting up and out of him. When she dropped him, his back hit the bed, his head hit the frame, his feet skidded forward, and he lay flat. The ceiling was full of light and stars. Air rushed in and out of his head.

Bette trotted into the next room and ate the rest of her food.

He fell asleep more or less like that, waking up a few hours later with Bette snuggled comfortably against his back. To his pleasurable surprise, she had loped one arm over him like a real girl. She smelled like a real girl too, like a real girl who'd been fucked: she smelled of sweat and the faint, vinegary finish of hard-worked pussy.

He slept, got up again in a few hours and took a shower. Bette followed him into the bathroom. What she had on her mouth was not quite a smile, properly speaking, but she certainly looked pleased, her eyes sleepy-bright and her face relaxed, unlined and radiant. She waited patiently outside the shower—he knew better than to pull her into the water with him, though he wanted to—and when he came out he was delighted to see her sitting rather humanly on the closed toilet seat (her knees were drawn up all the way to her chin, but still). "My good girl," he said happily, cradling her face in his hands. "My good Bette."

He went to the couch and she lolled merrily next to him on her back. He rubbed her tummy and her breasts, even squeezed them a little possessively; she purred. *Well, of course*, he thought. *She has a daddy who feeds her and rubs her tummy and takes her to the vet, and now he fucks her, too. How could a kitty be happier?*

He was happy, too. He went out and got a case of Fancy Feast and a giant bag of the best litter. He also got some mackerel fillets and a bottle of wine.

Bette was extra-happy and excited when he got home. He thought it might be the fish smell, but he eventually read in her repeated, happy mews that she had something to show him. Maybe she's caught a mouse, he thought.

She led him to the kitchen. At first he was confused. There were small gobs of leftover cat food all over the floor. *Why*, he wondered, *would she be proud of that*? But then she stood marching with dainty steps by the counter, and he noticed that the food bowl was on it. He looked at her with wonder and pride. She put her fingers around the rim of the bowl and clumsily tried to move it again; she still hadn't got the thumbs completely figured out. "No, no, honey," he purred. "It's okay. You did fine, my good good girl, so good—"

He embraced her, his heart full of love and pride. She accepted his embrace and even tried to reciprocate, her arms raised awkwardly like flippers to the level of his hips, her nails hooked to the seat of his pants. And when he kissed her she let his tongue in, and the awkwardness with which she kissed back only delighted him more.

That night he poached the fillets and set the table properly for the first time in many, many months.

As he did Bette prowled around the apartment in a newly free and easy manner. The lubricious, luxuriant roll of her walk, her buttcheeks thrusting a little to the side as she went, was not unlike that of a woman conscious of her effect on a man. And in truth he did enjoying watching her. As he cooked the meal she dashed into the kitchen, making expectant yips. He shooed her away; she dashed out, then poked her head in at the door and meowed again. He ran after her with the spatula in his hand, and she scooted into the living room and tried to push herself under the sofa. He smacked her lightly on the ass and laughed. Ten minutes later, they did it again, enjoying it every bit as much.

When dinner was ready he encouraged her onto a chair opposite his. She sniffed her fish, then carefully put her hands on either side of the plate and dipped her head to eat. When she had her first mouthful he asked her, "Is it good, honey? Good food?" She looked at him, held his gaze a few seconds as she chewed, then dipped her head again. He kept asking her, so she would look at him, and was thrilled each time she did.

He even poured her a little bowl of wine, but she wrinkled her nose at it, so he gave her milk instead.

After dinner he brought her to the couch and tried to find a comfortable upright position for them to be romantic in. She seemed to find this awkward, however, and finally stretched out on his lap, purring as he stroked her hair, back, and buttocks.

He eased her off, went to the bed, undressed, lay on top of the covers, and called her. He heard her splashing her litter around, then the steady clacking of her nails. She came in and leapt onto the bed and looked at him. He smiled at her. Bette spun around and nudged his hip with her butt. He just watched a moment, eyes twinkling.

"How about we try it another way?" he said, his voice low and a little slurred. "Come on, don't you want to please your daddy?"

He tried to pull her so that she sat on his cock, but she resisted, her hands and feet gripping the covers tightly. He gave her ass a slap; she gave a yip and her head spun around toward him, but she continued to push her butt at him.

Finally he got up and mounted her. As she began her frenzied shallow fucking, he grabbed hold of her buttocks and held them to slow her down. She gave a low, shaky, angry yowl and thrashed harder.

Suddenly he pinched her firmly at the base of her neck. The yowl sunk into her chest, like someone had suffocated it, and her thrashing became weak and spastic, as he had imagined it would.

He stroked slowly and with his free hand reached under and cupped and squeezed one of her breasts. Bette continued to gurgle and fight feebly against his nerve pinch. She rotated her head as best she could and gave him a shocked look. He released her breast, grabbed her shoulder and pushed her down onto her side. Her legs began to kick. The bottom one became enmeshed in the blanket, but the topmost one caught his shin a few times, hard. He felt it but didn't care. Blood filled his head and boiled in it. Keeping hold of her neck, with his free hand he grabbed her ankle and yanked it under his legs so that she was fully on her back. She struggled as best she could; her arms, tense but drained of power, flailed on the blanket like newly caught fish; her legs shuddered; her torso thrashed in its own rhythm, out of sync with his thrusts. He kept going. His mouth caught her nipple; he kissed it; he bit it. A thin sheet of scream came out of her. Her legs kicked out to her sides in an oddly inverted Australian crawl. Occasionally her knees came up and grazed his ribs painfully. He fucked her harder. He kissed her throat and suddenly he lost hold of her neck. She smashed her hands into his chest and he felt hot sharp pain, saw the ceiling, slammed to the floor. Bette's claws tapped rapidly across the floor and out of the room.

He ran to the bathroom, shut the door, and flipped on the light. He counted nine welts—not deep, but wide and filled with blood. He guessed she had hit him mostly with the meat of her hands, the nails pressing in only slightly. He shuddered when he thought what her nails would have done if she'd put her mind to it. He noticed that his ribs and shins hurt and saw the beginnings of bruises.

He carefully cleaned his wounds with hot water and hydrogen peroxide and went back to the bedroom. On the bed Bette lay looking at him mildly, with no air of menace. He didn't know if he trusted that, though. She was an alien breed, after all, so beyond morality and driven by ancient instincts. He was depressed at the distance between them.

Keeping his eye on her, he slid into the bed and

turned out the light. A few times she shifted and stretched, but other than that, it was as if she weren't there.

Bette stopped inviting him to mount her. He supposed that whatever heat she'd been going through had passed, but it had come and gone so quickly that he wasn't entirely sure. Maybe he had offended her, he thought; maybe he could persuade her back into relations. He despaired of appealing to her reason, but he thought extra efforts to please her might work.

He kept buying her the best food and litter. He petted her, spoke sweetly to her. He thought she must know that he still desired her. At night he nuzzled her shoulder and ran one hand over her breasts and belly while he masturbated with the other. She purred and stretched, but his sexual passion didn't seem to touch her, no matter how humiliatingly raw and evident he made it.

In fact, though she grew over weeks more adept at the mechanics of human behavior—dining at table, sitting upright, showing progress every day with her grasping ability—she remained in her instincts perfectly feline: aloof, self-interested, petulant. She'd take things off the tables and leave them in corners. When her pan was not perfectly clean, she'd shit on the tiles. When dinner wasn't ready fast enough to suit her, she would stand in front him and meow, her face as blandly demanding as a dissolute aristocrat's. He felt regret at what now seemed lost, and a dark, poisonous resentment.

He picked up a new wiring job and was frankly relieved to be out of the house for much of the day. At first Bette was confused. When he came home after his first twelve-hour day, she sat on the sofa, legs drawn up, hands beside each other on the cushion in front of her, and yipped continuously for half an hour. Silently he made her meal and left it on the table, then sat in the easy chair and watched TV—he'd caught a Chinese dinner at the construction site, and wasn't hungry.

At the end of his third working day Bette was strangely quiet. She sat and wandered about as she always had, but she made no sounds at all. She looked at him quite a lot, with a certain tension in her face that seemed significant to him, but he didn't see what the significance could be, or what good it would do to ask.

At the end of the night, as he undressed beside the bed, Bette came in, sat calmly in the center of the bed, and watched him.

"Whatcha looking at, honey?" he asked her with weary playfulness. "Huh? You want something from me? I wish I knew what it was." She continued to stare. He sighed. "I wish you understood," he said, then got into bed and started to pull up the sheet.

Bette caught the edge of the sheet with her claws and drew it back. Then she got up on all fours, turned, and presented her ass to him.

He was astonished. There was in her manner no agitation or sign of her previous sexual excitement. She moved her butt only slightly, as if to make her meaning plain.

But he didn't question it. He felt hope and desire and, after kissing her neck and back a short time, got hard. Her opening was not very moist or pliant. He turned, lay on his back, pushed his head under her butt, eased it down, and began to lick and suck. But though he was right on her clitoris and liked to think himself good at this sort of thing, he didn't detect much reaction. She did eventually lubricate a little and he got up and mounted her. He took his time, as he had wanted to before. She did nothing to stop him; in fact, she helped him with a steady, grinding movement. Although she seemed less than passionate, she was making an effort for him, he decided. *She wants to please me. Good kitty.*

This time went on longer than the others. Eventually her grinding became balky; he sensed that she was getting too dry to keep up much longer. He let himself go, coming less spectacularly than before but with relief and, he had to admit, a certain pleasure at having moved her to his will instead of the other way around.

He gently pulled out and crawled alongside her and kissed her cheek. "My good girl," he whispered. "I love you."

She ducked her head and rubbed her face on his chest. Again he felt spit—or rather he thought it was spit, until he realized that it was not her mouth that had touched him, but her eyes.

Bette sprang up, batted the light switch off, curled up on the far side of the bed, and was still.

When he came home from work the next evening, he felt immediately that something was wrong. The apartment was warmer than the air conditioning should have made it. He ran to the living room and found that the fire escape window that he had closed and locked was wide open.

He looked around for the things burglars would take. They were all there. Nothing had been disturbed.

But he didn't see Bette.

He walked around, called her name, then ran to the window and called her name more loudly. There was no sign of her on the fire escape or the streets below. *Well,* he thought, *someone must have collected her, taken her in, cops or someone from social services or a good neighbor: after all, a speechless nude woman crawling on the fire escape...*

Then he noticed black fur, chunks of it, lying on the metal slats of the fire escape landing. Strands of it stuck to the window lock, and a mist of hair particles floated in the gray light in front of him. On the window ledge itself was a cat's toenail, small and hooked.

Dazed, he went to his chair and thought. Could she really have gone back to being a cat? He supposed that was no more miraculous than her previous transformation. Had she been half-cat, half-woman, as she worked at the lock? Was she that way now, a monster? Should he look for her? What should he do? There must be something—

And then his heart sank as the reality he had been evading became inescapable. Whatever she was now, she had not accidentally gotten lost or been locked out. She had fled. She didn't want him any more.

Rain began to fall. He got up and closed the window, looked out at the people dashing across the street or into taxis. He thought of Bette the cat all wet and miserable, darting between awnings. His chest became numb and heavy.

He went to the bedroom to change out of his work

clothes. In the full-length mirror he studied his chest, the scars still visible, long and faint. Then he went to the kitchen and began to load the cat food and litter bags into boxes. Maybe the ASPCA could use them.

There was leftover salmon in the fridge. He supposed he should eat it before that, too, became fraught with memory. But he wasn't hungry at all.

He went to the window and stared out into the rain. Sadness flowed through him; how could it not? He had never been so close to a woman, never been so aware of her ways and her needs, or so in love, and now that she was gone, he was convinced he would never have another woman. And, he also thought, the sobs starting to crawl painfully out of him, he would never have another cat.

THE MURDER OF JUANITA APPEL

Janice Eidus

The Literary Exchange occupied two floors of a small, barely noticeable office building squeezed between a parking garage and a vacant lot on Amsterdam Avenue. I was there to attend the first meeting of Juanita Appel's writing class. A dozen of us—mostly males, like myself—were sitting around a large wooden table in a conference room that had seen better days. I felt self-conscious: fresh out of college, boyish and blond, still fighting an occasional outbreak of adolescent acne, the youngest person in the room.

It was a hot, rainy night. The air conditioner was

broken, and the ceiling was leaking. A puddle was forming on the floor. Juanita Appel, our teacher, was nowhere in sight.

From the conversations going on around me, I gathered that the workshop was divided roughly in half: those who were Juanita Appel's admirers, members of a fierce, but tiny, cult; and those, like me, who'd never even heard of her before they'd registered for the class. I had only Wednesday nights off from my job selling encyclopedias by phone, and Juanita's was the only class offered on Wednesdays. And since I intended to become a best-selling novelist as quickly as possible, I'd gone ahead and registered.

While we were sitting around waiting for Juanita to show up, I noticed that the guy on my left, who sported a pencil-thin gray mustache and a black patch over his right eye, had placed one of Juanita's novels on the table in front of him. The title was spelled out in fiery red letters: *Dancing Loving Dreaming of the Air Mountains Sea.* "Excuse me," I said, tapping him on the shoulder, trying to make my voice sound older and deeper, "I'm not familiar with Juanita's work. May I have a look?"

Sneering, he handed the book to me, letting me know how little he thought of anyone not familiar with Juanita's work.

Ignoring his sneer, I looked for her author photograph on the back cover, but there was none. Instead, there were blurbs from a bunch of obscure-sounding writers, all of whom had foreign names. "Juanita Appel is a brilliant Surrealist," Vladimir Goranoffski declared. "A magical realist with an erotic streak a mile wide," gushed Miguel "Pocho" Echeverria.

I didn't bother reading any more of the blurbs. I looked at her bio: "Juanita Appel was born in the banana country of Colombia, South America. She spent her childhood back and forth between that country and the Bronx, New York." It also gave her birthdate. I did some quick math; Juanita was forty—no spring chicken.

I was glancing over the list of the other books she'd written, when the mustached student deigned to look over at me with his left eye. "None of her books are even in print," he said, with a cold rage in his voice, as though I were to blame for what he clearly saw as a terrible injustice.

I didn't respond. I was too depressed at the thought that this out-of-print Surrealist writer was the person from whom I'd hoped to learn how to become a best-selling, megabuck-making novelist.

I read the first sentence of the novel, and grew even more depressed. I liked straightforward stuff. Not this female Latin/Bronx sexed-up pseudo-Kafka with her convoluted prose about rainbow-colored parrots hanging from trees while quoting Samuel Beckett and devouring pistachio nuts swollen like vulvas. I slammed the book shut. Writers like Juanita stayed poor and obscure. I decided that I would drop out after the first class session and demand a full refund. I handed the book back to the mustached student, who adjusted his eyepatch and sneered at me again.

Finally, Juanita Appel arrived, twenty minutes late. She hovered in the doorway for a moment, staring impassively at us. She was at least six feet tall. Her skin was bronze; her eyes pale blue; her lips a pink so pale they bordered on white. Her thick, wavy chestnut hair fell to her waist, and she wore a clinging black dress that came to her ankles.

Without apologizing for her lateness, she entered the classroom, taking long, graceful strides to avoid the puddles. Seating herself with regal posture at the head of the table, she looked up at the dripping ceiling. Her voice was soft but strong. "Go home, send me your stories during the week, and we'll discuss them next time. Any questions?" Her accent was a curious combination of elegant Spanish and tough Bronx.

There were no questions. Her fans seemed overjoyed just being in her presence, breathing the same air she breathed. The others seemed too bewildered to ask anything. I, too, couldn't speak. I could barely think. To my complete shock, I—who'd barely even noticed the girls in my classes during my four years of college—had fallen head over heels in love with Juanita Appel.

I lingered outside the building, waiting for her to come out. Discreetly, I followed her to the bus stop. Although I lived only a few blocks from The Literary Exchange, in an apartment on Columbus Avenue that my parents were helping me to pay for, I also followed her onto the downtown bus.

Taking a risk, I sat directly across from her. Maybe she would be pleased to see me. I would tell her I was on my way to meet a friend at a West Village café. I would invite her along. We'd sit together in a dark, smoky corner, sipping espresso. After a few minutes, I would excuse myself and pretend to telephone my friend, who would have met with an unexpected emergency and wouldn't be able to join us. Then I would be alone with Juanita Appel, the woman who had stolen my heart. But that didn't happen. She didn't even notice me.

She got off at the very last stop. Although it was growing dark, the rain had stopped, and the West Village streets were crowded. With a racing heart, I followed behind her. She stopped at a greengrocer. The sight of her choosing among the bin of swollen, hot pink grapefruits made me weak with desire. She paid for two grapefruits and then continued on, swinging the greengrocer's plastic bag as she walked.

Near the corner of Sixth Avenue, she pulled a metal key ring from her pocket and opened the door of a nondescript building across the street from a shop that sold kinky sexual devices, and next door to a tiny restaurant known for its varieties of bagel sandwiches. Without turning around, she disappeared inside. I stood outside her building for hours in the darkness, craning my neck, trying to figure out which window was hers, and wondering how I would survive until the next Wednesday.

The following week, the class was smaller. Only her fans had returned. While waiting for her, they argued about "subtext" and "intentionality" in her work. The mustached fellow, whose patch was over his left eye this time, argued the loudest. I didn't join in their conversation. Instead, I sat there wondering what Juanita would do if she knew that all week long, between my telemarketing stints, I had wandered back and forth in front of her building. I'd also wandered in and out of the kinky sex shop across the street until the proprietor became suspicious and I felt obligated to buy a black leather mask. And I'd sat in the bagel place next door to her building, composing a short story for her class on a legal-sized yellow pad, hoping she'd come through the door. I had eaten bagels with jam, with butter, cheddar cheese, roast beef, and sturgeon slices until I'd wanted to throw up. But I hadn't seen Juanita once, not even from afar.

At last, again twenty minutes late, Juanita came through the door of the conference room. This time she was wearing a short, strapless red dress that showed off her full, round breasts, her narrow waist, shapely calves, and strong ankles. It was raining again, and as she stepped over the puddles, I caught a glimpse of bronzed inner thigh.

She sat down, appearing unfazed by the reduced size of the class. With no preliminaries, she began to discuss our stories. She read sections of them aloud, and it soon became apparent to me that all the other students were trying to mimic her style. "I'm sure that you meant well," she would say listlessly to each student, "but this just wasn't written from the heart." Eager to please her, the student would nod vehemently, "You're right, Juanita, not from the heart! Next time, definitely, from the heart!"

Juanita would sigh, moving on to the next story, continuing to speak softly, occasionally licking her pale lips. Sometimes her Colombian accent dominated; sometimes her Bronx. She seemed utterly bored.

At the end of the class, she said, "OK, send me more of your stuff for next time."

I felt stricken and ashamed. I was the only student whose work hadn't been discussed. I rose along with the others, keeping my head down.

As I was walking out the door, I heard her speak my name. "Please," she said, wearily, "remain after class a moment."

When all the other students had gone, I stood before her.

"Listen," she said, remaining seated at the table, and looking up at the ceiling, "I don't think this is the right class for you. Maybe you could transfer to Margot Madd's class. Or Bill Smith's. Did you know they both teach here?" She looked at me hopefully.

I nodded. I knew they both taught there, although neither on Wednesdays. Originally, Margot Madd and Bill Smith had been the writers I'd most wanted to study with; after all, they were both famous, and they both wrote about real life. I'd read Margot's novel, *At Play*, about a rich girl whose parents neglect her, and who develops a cocaine habit, and I'd found it both sexy and moving. Bill Smith had written lots of novels, and they were all deep and brutal, about men who drank a lot and got into fistfights. But I no longer wanted to study with either of them. I wanted only Juanita. "No," I answered weakly, "I can't."

Juanita picked up the loose pages of "One Night at a Bar in Philly," my story. "It's really not my kind of thing," she said. "I can't be of help to you."

I dropped to my knees in front of her.

Her pale blue eyes widened.

"I love you," I said pleadingly, looking up at her. A lock of my hair fell into my eyes. I was sweating.

"Hey, is this some kind of sick joke or what?" she demanded angrily, in her Bronx accent.

I shook my head. "I love you," I repeated stubbornly, pushing my hair from my eyes so that I could look directly up into her dark, exotic face. "I must make love to you tonight or I'll die!"

"Whoa, calm down." Her voice became maternal and kind. She rose from her chair and stood. She looked down at me from her great height. "How old are you?"

"Twenty-two," I mumbled, realizing for the first time that I was just a child in her eyes. I felt humiliated.

"Why, you're just a boy, just a child," she said, echoing my thought.

Tears filled my eyes.

"Get up, *pobrecito,*" she said softly in her Colombian accent.

I got up from the floor, the knees of my blue jeans wet from the puddle in which I'd been kneeling. I stood before her. To my astonishment, she pushed me down onto the top of the wooden table. I began to tremble. She lay on top of me. Her red dress rustled as it slid up her thighs. "Ay, *Dios mio*, such a young and pretty boy!" she cried, sounding very Spanish and very hot-blooded.

From that moment on, Juanita and I had a sex life that knew no bounds, no inhibitions. We were insatiable. I loved to lick and bite and stroke her body's every nook and cranny, and she did the same to me. But despite my taste for her flesh, I just couldn't develop a taste for her writing. At first I didn't let on. I was so grateful, so amazed, that she loved me. I couldn't believe my luck as she fell into my arms night after night, her muscular, lithe body resting beside mine.

After a few weeks, however, I grew bold. Despite our age differences, despite the fact that I was her student,

I became increasingly forward in my objections to her work. "I'm just a simple guy," I would tell her, after we'd made love in the creaky loft bed in her tiny, dark studio apartment overlooking a back alley, "like most people. But simple doesn't mean dumb, if you know what I mean."

"No, my little darling," she would answer, lying back and playing with her nipple in the way she knew never failed to arouse me. "I don't know what you mean."

"I mean, I don't go for all these arty inventions of yours. You've lived a fascinating life, Juanita. Write about real life. Your *real* life."

"What is 'real life,' my darling?" She played teasingly with her other nipple.

I turned away, growing impatient with her teasing, with her pink, hard nipples. I knew all about her real life, because she'd confided in me late at night, after we made love. I knew about the exotic locales in which she'd lived, and about her divorced, ill-suited parents—her Colombian, macho millionaire father; her Bronx Jewish socialist mother—the hard times, and the many star-crossed love affairs. If only she would write it straight, I thought, without fancy language, pretentious parents, and sexy pistachio nuts, people would love it, and she'd be able to sell her books for big bucks and appear on talk shows like Margot Madd, and win prestigious awards like Bill Smith. "What I mean is," I tried not to let my impatience show, "you should write about the night that you lost your virginity to the bearded peasant who worked on your father's plantation, and about how your father disowned you when he discovered the two of you beneath his banana tree. And about how you accompanied your mother on political demonstrations when you were so small that your little arms ached as you held onto the picket signs she made you carry, and how you marched alongside her with tears in your eyes, wishing she would love you, her only daughter, as much as she loved the masses, the downtrodden of the earth. Really, Juanita, it's highly marketable stuff."

To please me, she bought Margot Madd's novel. "I'm studying *At Play* for you, *querido*," she announced, covering my face with kisses.

One night, however, when she was out, I peeked at the notes she'd scrawled in the book's margin. "This one's a bimbo," she had written. *Una loca!*"

I had another idea. "Call Bill Smith," I told her. "Ask him to come out with us for a drink. And listen to what he has to say about writing. He's a great man. OK?"

"OK," she nodded, without enthusiasm.

Bill Smith suggested a bar on Eighth Avenue. It smelled of cheap wine, urine, and cabbage soup. "Great place, isn't it?" he greeted us expansively, stroking his bushy, crumb-laden beard. "A bar for real people, not quiche eaters."

Juanita was the only woman in the place. She was wearing a black catsuit and high heels. The men who lined the bar couldn't take their eyes off her.

We sat at a table in the back. Bill Smith quickly got drunk and began reminiscing about the alcoholic binges and fistfights of his youth.

Juanita studied her fingernails. Stifling a yawn, she stirred the ice in her Cuba Libre. Finally, she looked up at him. "I must ask you one thing, Mr. Smith. Don't you ever get bored, just telling it like it is?"

He, like all the other men at the bar, kept staring at her full breasts. "Call me Bill, Juanita," he said thickly. "Nope. How else can you tell it?"

"Oh," she said, throwing back her shoulders proudly, so that her breasts appeared even larger and fuller, "you can tell it as it *should* be. Or as it *could* be. Or as it *would* be if one thing—one particle of dust, one atom, one alpha ray—just one tiny thing in the universe suddenly shifted."

Bill Smith rolled his eyes. I tried to show him, by

rolling mine, too, that even though I was her lover, I shared his sympathies.

"Or," Juanita went on determinedly, ignoring our rolling eyes, "one can show it as one fears it, dreads it; one can expose the dark side of *what is*...."

"Damn," Bill Smith said, opening his wallet. "I left the house without any cash. Would you mind?"

"Yeah, right, I'll just bet you did," Juanita said, scowling and suddenly sounding very Bronx. Nonetheless, she paid.

Bill Smith pinched her butt on the way out of the bar.

She gave him an icy stare and walked haughtily ahead of us to the bus stop.

"I like a girl with spunk," he whispered admiringly to me. "And big bazooms."

"You alienated Bill Smith," I said angrily to her when we got back to my airy, high-ceilinged, one-bedroom apartment, where we'd been spending more and more time. I'd grown tired of her tiny, dark excuse of a home.

"I'm sorry, my darling, but he's such a bobo..." Still, she seemed genuinely upset to have displeased me. She walked over to my desk. "OK, I'll do it!" she cried passionately. "I'll write my memoirs —the real thing! Not merely a thinly disguised novel, like your idols Margot Madd and Bill Smith. And," her features grew strangely grim, "you shall be the executor of them when I die."

I went to her and held her tightly. "Don't talk of death," I said. "Talk of rebirth, talk of huge sales and megabucks...."

After that, Juanita sat at my desk every day, every night, writing her memoirs. She frowned and sweated, cursing in both Spanish and English as she labored. I stopped making love to her. After a month, I asked her to read me what she'd written. "My father, the rich, cruel banana baron, was an alcoholic," she began.

"Go on, that's terrific," I said.

She read me the next sentence. "He was also a monkey."

My heart sank. Juanita had written, instead of the first chapter of her memoirs, a Surrealistic tale about a family that was half-human, half-monkey.

I was enraged. She was deliberately tormenting me. She had led me on and mocked me. I no longer loved her. In fact, I hated everything about her: her large, bulbous breasts, her Amazonian height, her Spanish-Bronx accent. I raised my hand to strike her.

She drew back, looking pale and fearful. "Please," she cried, placing her hand over her left breast, "my heart!"

My hand remained in the air, ready to strike. "There's nothing wrong with your heart," I said, in a mean and surly tone that matched my mood, "other than that you're cold-hearted, not to give me the one thing—the only thing—I ask of you!"

She lowered her eyes. Tears ran down her cheeks. "I tried to write my memoirs, I really did," she said, "but it just wasn't any damn fun, *muchacho*. And," her sobs grew louder, "I've hidden something from you, my darling. I didn't want to alarm you, but my heart...it really is weak." Eyes still downcast, she proceeded to tell me of the rheumatic fever she'd had as a child, and of the doctors who continually warned her that too much excitement in any form would kill her.

I couldn't say a word, I was too amazed by Juanita's revelations. I allowed my hand to fall by my side.

"You didn't mean what you said before, did you?" she asked, raising her bloodshot eyes to meet mine, "about my being cold-hearted? You weren't really going to hit me, were you?"

I waited a long moment. She seemed a stranger to me, a Surrealist writer with large breasts, a tear-stained, red face, and an inadequate heart. "I love you more than ever, Juanita," I spoke slowly. "You are even more precious to me now that I know about your heart. I will never, never hurt you. Come here." I was acutely conscious, at that moment, of my long eyelashes, my fine, blond hair, my cheeks as red as a girl's, my very strong, very young heart beating loudly against my very strong, very young chest. I rubbed my hands against her nipples until she moaned. I lifted her blouse and stuck my hands down the front of her tight black stirrup pants and inside her pink nylon panties.

In the months following, I made love to her constantly. Our lovemaking grew wilder, more intense. Her orgasms were tidal waves, earthquakes, tornadoes of passion. I rarely came myself, but that only inflamed me more. I was perpetually erect, an animal in heat, a howling beast, never satisfied. Juanita and I didn't eat, didn't sleep. All we did was make love. Until the night her heart gave out. She died in my arms, in the midst of an orgasm so violent the paintings on my walls shook.

Gently, I eased her off my body. I checked her pulse just to be sure. I shut her eyelids tight, and planted a farewell kiss on those pale, full lips. I had every reason to feel proud of myself, and I did. Here I was, only twenty-two, and I had just committed the perfect murder.

† † †

At Juanita's funeral, her skinny, gray-haired mother eyed me suspiciously, but I let my hair fall into my eyes. That way, she couldn't really see me, and by the time I pushed the hair away, she was walking out the door of the funeral parlor, her back erect, no longer conscious of me at all.

Shortly after the funeral, I began writing Juanita's memoirs. It was easy work. I remembered everything she'd told me. I finished the memoirs in six months, ending them at the point where Juanita reads my story, "One Night at a Bar in Philly," and tells me that I'm destined to become one of the world's greatest writers, and declares her love for me on the spot. I conveniently "discovered" her memoirs in a trunk hidden beneath her bed, and a publisher bought them for a decent sum of money. But they sold poorly and went out of print almost overnight.

A year later, a famous literary critic at Yale published a book about Juanita—*Bronx Surrealist*—which won a Pulitzer. All of Juanita's novels were reprinted with brightly colored drawings of parrots and women's breasts on the covers. Juanita's work had entered the canon. Suddenly, everyone was teaching her, from the deconstructionists to the feminists, the elitists to the populists.

Juanita's books were selling like hotcakes. Her mother, the executor of her daughter's fiction, grew rich and started a progressive magazine with her money called *The Old Left Writes!*

All Juanita had made me executor of was the book she'd never written, the book I'd written for her, the book which was viewed as her one weak effort and not reprinted. "Not up to snuff," Bill Smith had written in his review in the *Times*. "Appel's memoirs are too down to earth, too real for her. Unlike those of us who write best of what we know—drinking and fighting, for instance—Juanita's true calling was to write about the exotic universes of her imagination."

So these days I lie in bed, sweating, staring at the ceiling, unable to sleep, trying to understand what happened. And what I think is this: Juanita had been aware of my murderous intentions all along. Juanita had been in control every step of the way. After all, she's the one who told me about her weak heart and the doctors' warnings. And then I think that I don't even exist at all, that Juanita had simply conjured me up—so very young, hungry, pretty, and greedy—to help her achieve her wild and glorious climax, the ending she'd undoubtedly yearned for. But most of all, as I lie here, night after night, never sleeping, I fear that soon I shall be forced to create my own climax, my own ending. Because I see now that a life without Juanita is really no life at all.

THE CUT

T. Ellis

Michael was a young man with sweet buns of steel, a strut in his walk, and a chest you could make look better only by rubbing it down with coconut oil. And he knew it. He had blond curls around a pouting cherub's face and an attitude like the worst infant you ever potty trained. He was a model.

At the moment he was working for Gino, the genial, portly, white-haired and leather-vested mogul of the Rome-based Viva empire of designer goods. Gino, a gentle spirit, liked a nice firm piece of ass, but he also liked a soul above the hole, and Michael seemed to have one, somewhere deep in his sulky blue, watery eyes. But such trouble the boy caused whenever he came in for a session. And then there was the business with Cosmo.

Cosmo was across town—a bastard, a street thief—as Gino put it—and they'd been rivals since the two had come out of the gutters thirty years ago. Cosmo was also white-haired, also wore leather vests, but there the identification ended. Where Gino was round and jovial, Cosmo was a rail, a swaying cornstalk, a veritable tower of loose-limbed, ravenous energy. He would walk, swaying, down the night streets of Rome, stalking the new youth, new styles, new dirt in the air. His eyes roved a boy's body like ants, heading right for the honey pot. He too had seen Michael, in cafés, in the clubs, on the floor, shaking his little money-maker, and he'd seen, more importantly, Gino paddling on his arm, waving him to his table, and airily inviting him to the silvery champagne buckets that were always sweating there. Cosmo saw the look in Gino's eye and he smelt a ripe fruit.

Michael found himself invited to another photoshoot on the day of Gino's upcoming Viva fall catalogue show. It was a last-minute assignment and he didn't know the client but it paid thousands and he was going. That's what he told Gino, anyway, on the phone; he didn't even have the decency to come into the office and tell him himself, the punk. "You *punk*," Gino screamed into the phone. "You don't even have the decency?!"

"Hey, I'm a free agent," Michael drawled; he sounded barely awake. "I'm an artist and I need my unpredictability."

"Do you ever walk anywhere without wiggling your behind, Michael? Your unpredictability—" Gino growled.

"I don't care about you and your tantrums. I gotta go where the money leads, right? That's what a professional is, isn't it?"

Gino hung up on him and smoked three cigarettes, one after the other. Then he called Cosmo.

"What do you want for him?" he said. He didn't need to introduce himself, didn't need to say who he was talking about, didn't need to ask anybody where Michael could have been hired at such short notice. Cosmo didn't miss a beat.

"Seven thousand," he said.

"For what?" Gino scowled, looking at the wet tip of his filter.

"For every hour he works for you on that day and not for me," Cosmo rolled liquorice around his tongue.

"An hour?" Gino screamed, "On top of what I pay the little whore anyway? You want seven K an hour?"

"Hey, you're the one in love," Cosmo says. "I think the boy is trash."

"I don't love anybody," Gino says.

"Yeah, tell your momma," Cosmo says, hanging up.

Gino wrote a check and sent it to Cosmo via a leather-clad messenger, and the thin man smiled beatifically while faxing Michael's new instructions to him: to turn out for the rival assignment at the halls of Viva's palace, where the draughty marble corridors would display the new fall line for the cameras. Meanwhile, Gino sat at his desk, drafting a new project, an invitation to send out for a special guest.

Monday arrived and the aforementioned Viva spectacular was almost under way. Models slouched against bare white walls; clothes, the heat of the stitching still not quite off them, hung on long stands of tubular metal. The air was crackled with Gino's tension and the walkie-talkies of the security he'd hired at the last minute, nobody knew why. Michael, whose mind was always on higher matters, only realized on the morning of the assignment that the new address on his invite was in fact Viva Palais, the home of his former mentor, sugar daddy, and guiding spirit.

"Alright!" he mutted to himself as he walked into the marble halls. "I get to do both gigs!" And then a dim realization trickled into the fog behind his perfect, wrinkle-free brow and he wondered, as he saw the column of security advisers in black leather advance toward him, who the other client could have been who would want to hire him to have photos taken at the same time as the Viva show.

"Michael!" Gino said. He was behind him and Michael jumped, despite his usual torpor.

"You scared me," he mumbled. "What's with the leather riot police, huh?"

"Your new employer has his eccentricities," Gino said.

"You know him?" Michael said.

"Kinda," Gino said, "Come this way."

The riot police grabbed Michael's arms and dragged him after the waddling, leather-waistcoated, white-haired gentleman up the stairs.

At the top of the stairs was a rotunda, a small stand of raised marble in the middle of a plain of black and white squares. All around the rotunda were chairs—the usual assembly of reporters, assembled fashion critics, buyers, and other Eurotrash were gathered on the folding metal, smoking long, slim cigarettes and saying mean things to whoever would listen. Camera flashguns were popping already and no clothes were to be seen. Above the rotunda was a curtain, presently raised, that could fall to conceal it, and at a small distance, an enclosure where the clothes were and where Gino, followed by his riot police in black regalia, took Michael. As he struggled pointlessly to free his arms, Michael found a small boxer's protective plate jammed into his mouth to block his speech and a dozen hands disrobing him and putting new clothes on him. Before he could blink he found himself hustled to the white rotunda, hands still grasped by black-suited police and his face pointing the wrong way. He was carried, ass-first, his feet off the ground, toward the platform, where a single cane-backed mahogany chair stood, facing the audience.

"Ladies and gentleman, *cognocenti,*" Gino began, his plump arms waving above his leather waistcoat armholes, the stubble on his chin a little wetter than usual, perhaps with sweat. "We are proud to present to you today, a little something different. As a prelude to the fall collection, a new concept in designer outfits—The Changing Mood!"

With that he waved his hand at the chair, where, bound by the wrists with handcuffs, Michael had found himself, ass raised toward the audience. He was sweating. As the police handcuffed him, he felt the quiet smiles and growing titters of the crowd; they rose to a gasp and then a slow murmur of perhaps erotic interest as Gino made his announcement and the police moved away, baring Michael's ass to the whole of the gathered audience. It was no secret that a preponderance of the men in the audience were gay, and the women were not averse to a nice firm ass on a man either, even if it were just for the looking at.

"Gentlemen, the canes!" Gino said, and Michael twisted to try and look at him. He could barely see anyone and the blush on his face made him feel as if he could see even less. "Do not concern yourself about my colleague and model Michael, ladies and gentleman. This clothing is so precise in its stitching, the science of it so revolutionary," Gino explained, "that for his own protection Michael has begged me to handcuff him so that he cannot make a mistake and interfere with the smooth running of this exhibition."

Michael choked on the boxer's plate crammed in his mouth. You couldn't see it but he couldn't spit it out.

"You're a trooper, aren't you, kid?" Gino's hand rested on Michael's rear. He was standing feet barely apart, smiling at the audience. "A champion!" Gino smacked Michael's ass, not a vicious slap, just a proprietorial paddle, a slap to show everybody who owned whom.

"The canes," Gino said, and two canes were brought in on yellow pillows of velvet by policemen in black. He took the longer one. They were crooked-handled at one end and had notches up and down their whippy lengths. Michael couldn't see them from his position but he heard the whistling cut of the first one chopping air as Gino showed it off before the audience. He wriggled his ass, trying to pull free of the handcuffs, but he was held tight.

"Now, gentlemen, ladies, the heart of the new Viva Changing Mood concept is the ability to have an outfit serve, as it were, any function. To change, if you will, to suit your whim. To help me demonstrate, I want to ask an old friend, an old dear friend, to help me up here. Ladies and gentlemen, a big round of applause for your friend and mine, Mr. Cosmo Lianno!" The thin man arose out of the crowd and joined Gino on the platform, flanking Michael's upraised and slightly swaying ass. Taking the other cane off of the yellow pillows and swishing it through the air, he muttered in Michael's ear, "It won't be long now, baby."

"When you are out," Gino addressed the audience as if telling a children's story, "do you want to go home if your plans change? Do you want to have to go shopping? Do you want to have to feel uncomfortable or inappropriately dressed if you go somewhere where your outfit doesn't fit? No, you do not. And what do you want to do about it? Don't you want to have a choice when you dress your loved one? Not a choice just for yourself but also for him, for those you love? Don't you want him to have a chance to please you, no matter where you go? Well, now you can."

He turned to Michael. Through the lights were shining on his upturned bottom, Michael could feel Gino's glare as he turned and put one hand on the back of Michael's neck. It was a terribly intimate gesture and Michael pulled against the cuffs till he thought his wrists would bleed.

"My friend is wearing the morning outfit, with the white pants, white shirt, white face—a virginal look," Gino was laughing. "But what if you want, around lunchtime, a slightly hotter look, for a cocktail party, perhaps? My friend," Gino addressed Cosmo and Cosmo bowed. He rose from his bow and with his entire and considerable strength, bent the length of the cane in his right hand and brought it back, swinging like an arrow and whistling through the air, at Michael's exposed arse. It cut like a whip into his buttocks just below where his underwear would end at the top of his thighs. Michael lurched, bound and gagged, on the chair back and gave a muffled cry. One seam of the morning trousers gave and he felt the air brush against his bottom.

"I will do the other, my friend," Gino said, and he swung the white cane into Michael's ass from the other side, hitting again at the spot just below the buttock, where the briefs would be. Another cut. Then Gino and Cosmo both tore at his legs. They each reached a hand into his buttocks and for a moment he didn't know what they would do to him, but they merely ripped away the fabric that covered his legs. The seams gave and the legs came off the slacks, unveiling another pair below, in evening blue.

"That's how your lover should look to you, ladies and gentlemen," Gino said. "If you strike him he should change right away. From virginal to raunchy. How you say? A little something blue?"

They rained blows on him with the canes till the white jacket came away as well, and they bared his feet to the audience too, which seemed a frightful humiliation. He was facing away from them all, his sore ass still swaying, streaked with black and blue. Michael fought back the tears.

"But after blue what happens, ladies and gentlemen?" Gino was saying. "What comes after blue, do you know? What do you want after the blue? Something simple, no?"

He tapped his cane, just the very tip of it, between the cheeks of Michael's bottom. He could feel the tip of the cane coming through the suit fabric.

"My friend," Gino said to Cosmo, and the tall man swung again with his seemingly impossibly long arms. The cane swiveled through the air and its melancholy whistle cut down. Michael screamed—this time the cut reached all the way to the flesh. Gino applied his cane, and one blow, then another, and then another, fell upon Michael's ass, as if a concerto of bowing were being played upon his rear. As the blows fell and the jacket sleeve fell off, followed by a pants leg, then another pants leg, Michael felt the air meeting the sweat that had tracked its way down his ass, and the hot trickle from the lights that flushed his back. When they were done, he was naked. He was placed on all fours, his ass facing the audience, his cheeks bared and parted. The flashbulbs popped for a little while, but then they stopped. Even the industry veterans realized they were in the presence of something more than fashion. There was silence as Gino finally stopped beating the boy and ripped off the last piece of cloth. Michael was naked and weeping in the chair, crouched, hoping to fend off future blows. His ass was still swaying temptingly, pale and beautiful, in the air.

"Ladies and gentlemen, tell me now, what do you

want of your love? How else would you want your love to change, after you got this outfit on them? I can only think of one thing, but it's not for the open air." Gino snapped his fingers and the curtains round them fell and hid both Gino and Cosmo and the boy from the assembled audience. Gino reached to the bent-over boy's mouth and pulled the boxer's plate roughly out of his teeth. His face was pushed up over the cane back and Gino pulled up his chin and held it. "Do you understand love, Michael?" Gino asked.

"I understand it," Michael slurred, his eyes puffy with tears.

"I don't think so," Gino said. "You have to show me. He should show you too, Cosmo?"

"I'm always happy to see something old but good," Cosmo said, unzipping his trousers. Michael heard the zipper descend but was in no condition to respond to it. He saw Gino unbutton his own fly, exposing a graying, curled, ashen, but definitely hardening cock. Gino's cock was stiffening and brown, had a birthmark on its fat left side, and had a little drop of pre-come already winking in its eye. "Show me, Michael," Gino was saying, hoarsely. "I don't believe you."

Michael looked up at him through puffy eyes, already tearing up again, and was about to answer when Cosmo's prick between his cheeks made him stiffen up and whimper. With tears coming down his face, he opened his mouth to say something to Gino and then just shook his head and hung it. Gino lifted up his head by the hair and Michael looked into his eyes, grunting from the force of Cosmo's thrusts. Looking deeply into Gino's eyes, he took the whole of his cock down his throat. There was restlessness in the chairs behind the curtain while the two designers took their pleasure, but they felt that they could wait. After all, there were some things that could not be rushed for money, *coutoure*, or even love.

NURSE, NURSE

T. Ellis

Suzanne worked at the hospital where the nurse's uniforms were short in the skirt rather, for her taste, but where her best friend Marie looked quite good filling hers. They had come up through nursing school together and found their first posting together, two years at the Geriatric Ward in Waterman's Town Center Hospital. She settled in quickly to the new routine, the ward with its cold blue tiles and coughing men, the endless beeps and groans of the hospital at night and the sharing of a small rented apartment with Marie, but she felt something must be missing. She had a sudden shock one morning as, taking her tea as she came back from her night shift, Marie dashed across their small kitchen, late to leave for her own shift. She was naked, and her small, perfect, white breasts were still wet from the shower she'd just finished. She was running a towel through her wet blond curls and shaking water from her fanny like some strange parody of an erotic dancer, only she was just trying to dry as quickly as possible and said, seeming not to notice the blush that rushed to Suzanne's face, "Can I borrow a uniform, Sue? I'm dead if I don't get out in two secs!"

Sue nodded twice, in confusion, and lowered her eyes into her tea. Marie dashed off, her white bum retreating and the slight peek of blond tufts between her cheeks disappearing with her. Sue realized with horror she could not help watching avidly till Marie disappeared into her room. She had honestly never thought about her friend in any way resembling that, she assured herself, even though she did enjoy shopping with her and helping her pick out the tightest outfits, skimpiest thongs, and smallest bathing tops. "Must run, you're an angel," Marie said, dashing in the kitchen, barely zipping up Sue's rather smaller-chested uniform over her own bouncing, braless breasts and giving Suzanne a peck on the cheek. Suzanne found herself reaching up to touch the place she had kissed in wonder as the slammed echo of Marie leaving the flat slowly died.

This would certainly not do, she thought to herself, walking into the hospital that night to start her own new shift. She had spent the day in restless wandering about the apartment and tossing, unable to sleep, upon her bed. The vision of Marie, her blond curls between her legs, those white droplet-covered breasts, even her face as she dried her body off, haunted her and would not let her sleep in peace. She found herself reaching between her legs and feeling the moisture gather and an explosion rock her body at the thought of sinking down into Marie's wetness, just sinking down and burying her face in there.

She walked into the geriatric ward. The usual men were shuffling from the bathroom to bed. She went to her desk and found that her rotation had changed. The sister would be off for the night, a case of flu.

"Hello!" Soft familiar hands covered her face from behind, blinding her.

"Marie!" she whispered, not daring to say the name out loud.

"Got it in one!" Marie giggled. She was still wearing the outfit that was too small for her. The skirt, which on Suzanne was simply too short, on Marie was a miniskirt of sorts, and the tightness of her top made her look voluptuous. She had left the front zipper a little undone, Suzanne suspected, to enhance the effect.

"Guess who's been drafted to pull a double shift?" Marie pulled a face, half-heartedly, over her natural smile. "And guess who's found us a nice little money-maker?" Suzanne looked at her. Marie pulled her deep into the nook where the sister's desk was hidden, taking care that no one in the dark ward's empty corridors could hear.

"There's no one here tonight," Marie said, almost into her ear.

"Mmm," Suzanne said. She couldn't look in her friend's eyes. It was embarrassing having her this close. *Stop it*, she thought to herself. *Stop it right now.*

"We've got a real winner in Private Room 7," Marie said.

"Mr. Walker?" Suzanne said, "He's harmless. A nice old man."

"That nice old man offered me five hundred dollars to strip," Marie said.

"What?" Suzanne was stunned.

"I got him to make it five hundred for the two of us," Marie said, smiling wickedly and looking straight into Suzanne's eyes.

"I couldn't," Suzanne said. "You're crazy!"

"Not even for me?" Marie said, and she looked straight at her. *She knows*, Suzanne thought, and her cheeks filled with color.

"Not even for your roommate who always needs help with the rent?" Marie said, and Suzanne found herself breathing shakily.

"Do you really have to?" Suzanne said.

"I need the money," Marie said, and she picked that moment to stroke Suzanne's hair, pushing it back off of her flushed face. She pressed up against her, whispering, "It'll be fun, won't it?" Suzanne swallowed, closed her eyes so Marie couldn't see her thoughts, and nodded.

Mr. Walker's room, with the gold-plated number on its door, was shadowed; it was lit by only a single lamp, which was near the old man's bed, where he lay, lightly snoring. After glancing quickly each way down the corridor to make sure no one was coming, Marie crept into the room first, then waved for Suzanne to follow her, *They could all die up and down the ward for the next half hour*, Suzanne thought, *for as much as the two of them were concerned*, but she couldn't find it in herself to feel guilty. Marie looked adorable bending over the old man's bed and Walker stirred, his snore coming to an abrupt halt in mid singsong as he glimpsed Marie's slightly unzipped chest over his face. He smiled as she leaned in to tell him, "If you've got the money, Mr. Walker, I believe you'll have your show this evening."

He counted the notes on the rolling carts that they used for bringin meals to the bedside: Ten crisp fifty-dollar bills, dusky green on the tabletop. Marie went to pick them up. The old man's hand moved surprisingly quickly and a slap echoed in the room. Marie rubbed her hand. "Not before the curtain falls," the old man's dry voice boomed, just this short of laughing. "I want to see the warm-up act begin." He looked at Suzanne. She realized, with a start, that she'd have to undress in front of both of them to get things rolling.

"You didn't say I'd have to do this cold," Suzanne said, her back to Walker. Marie sidled up to her to get her going.

"Keep him friendly," Marie whispered, "we could get more out of him." She looked back and smiled. Walker's wallet was under his pillow again, but it wasn't empty. He sat up in his bed, his yellow hands on the sheet top, gazing placidly at Suzanne's uniformed bottom, which she bared slowly, pulling her dress up over her head without unzipping it. *Why bother with the chest when there's so little there?* she thought to herself. *Maybe he won't bother.* She stood, with her back still to him, in her garter belt and stockings and small frilly panites.(The day of thinking about Marie had affected her choice of underwear — not that she'd thought anyone would ever see it.)

"Come here, child," she heard the old man say. Stomach churning, she turned and faced the two of them, blushing more when she saw Marie looking at her bared body. The old man beckoned to her, with a slow hooking gesture, to approach the bed. Looking at Marie, not him, she found herself obeying; she stood not two feet from Marie, just beside the bed and within the man's reach, should he have wanted to touch her. He pointed at her panties and she blushed. Marie smiled. "Nothing I've not seen before," she murmured.

"You haven't," Suzanne found herself saying, blushing deeply.

"Then I'm sure it's time I did," Marie said. Suzanne was stunned to see a fierce fire in her eyes when she looked up, with difficulty, to meet them. She pushed down the elasticized trim of her panties and felt the air hitting her bare bottom and realized she was wet between her legs. After she had awkwardly slipped off her panties, she rose shamefacedly to stand before them in only her stockings and bra, wishing she could cover herself with her hands.

The old man's eyes bored into her brown, now-hot curls. "Help your friend," he said to Suzanne, and she found herself, blushing once more, reaching out to Marie.

When, bare once more, Marie stood in the middle of the room and shook her hips as if trying to dry off, Suzanne couldn't help wondering at the beauty and grace of her, at the desire that burned within her to kiss that girl she thought she knew so well between those beautiful, stone-white breasts and to fall in front of her. She gasped as she felt the old man's hand on her bare buttocks, and she got even more confused when she heard Marie say, when she assumed the position the old man asked for, "No touching, unless you want to pay more."

Negotiation ensued, and the old man's hand stayed on her rear for what seemed days till Marie and he struck a bargain. She felt his hand, like a small leathery paddle, suddenly lift, and she realized with a start that she should have been listening, because the negotiation had apparently involved her. The touching Marie had mentioned, she realized, was not by the old man and was not of her. As she saw the old man's wallet come out from behind the white pillow again, and ten more crisp notes counted out on the table and disappear into Marie's discarded uniform, she heard words extended in the air but could not hear them. She heard her name but she could not attend to it. Then Marie placed herself on the wooden table over the old man's bed, her legs spread wide. Marie pointed for her to come before her and she found herself, wearing only her bra and stockings, clambering up over the old man's blankets, leaning, with her bare bottom spread almost in front of his face, into Marie's gloriously parted thighs. "Kiss me, darling," Marie said, with a slight hint of triumphant mischief. "It's for a good cause." Suzanne sank into the heady scent of Marie's blond curls with a grateful and open mouth.

"Not yet," Marie gasped, when, after she came once, then twice into Suzanne's mouth, Suzanne tried to rise. "There's more," Marie smiled, and Suzanne found herself lying spread-eagled on her back, her legs wide before the dry old man. Sweet Marie clambered over her and started to kiss her between the legs until slowly, then not so slowly, she found her hips bucking up to meet Marie's, as her pussy, which had felt so much was missing, sweetly, sweetly began to writhe.

IT'S NOT HIS FACE

Bonny Finberg

You walk into the Death Row Bar and Lounge wanting a drink and some conversation. It doesn't have to be too profound: just a little off and ephemeral. There are no empty stools so you stand next to the forty-something guy with the greasy blond hair and killer, blue-as-ice eyes. You're not looking for a pick-up so you open the newspaper. A quick look at his profile reveals a long-healed broken nose. His face is sad and brutal, occasionally lit by a hero's boyish grin. You exchange a few words with his friend, two stools down. You go back to your crossword puzzle.

"What was the clue for 'Toledo'?" His voice is soft, tentative.

Words about words, sense organizing chaos. A reference point. Or maybe a time and space malfunction. Now you talk about Spain and he talks about Spain. He's lit a lantern and you walk the beam. As you approach you feel like the only member of a secret order, the follower of an oblique philosophy, fending off the plague at gloomy altars. Who could fall in love with such a brittle hurt?

You're almost shoulder-to-shoulder with this icon, a strange man in a bar drinking too many beers. You've been raised to think he's dangerous, but now you're old enough to take the risk, make your own judgment calls. He knows the bartenders, the flushed-faced regulars. He's from the Bronx. He shows you an old family photograph that his sister had framed for his birthday, which is today. They're all wearing winter coats with mouton collars, his mother in the center with stockings and sensible pumps, in front of a brick building with an iron banister. He points himself out, the little blond boy of four squinting into the white sunlight. Then he shows you eleven brothers and sisters, all with names like his: Patrick. He tells you about his father, a traveling salesman, who drank and had a bad temper, who couldn't be in the picture because he was taking the picture. He doesn't know he's telling you all this.

You're telling him about the Hindus in Bhaktapur and the Sufis in Istanbul. He's telling you about the fortune teller in Barcelona who lived in a house with too many cats, who frightened him, whom he ran away from, out of fear, when they met in the airport. He looks like a fireman who would never run from anything, but he's vulnerable, and he doesn't know he's telling you all this.

He's read *The Gnostic Gospels*.

"I always see both sides. Duality," you say. "I'm drawn to pantheism. It recognizes the multitude of attributes of the one God, the ultimate unity of the many. I like graven images. The more the better. We're sensual beings, born illiterate. Images appeal to our most basic aesthetic, our first aesthetic pleasure—the sight of our mother's face. It's evolved into Disney."

"*De*volved. I was raised in the Catholic Church," he says. "It's all about aesthetics anyway."

"Absolutely."

Together you walk the fifteen blocks back to your apartment in the rain without an umbrella. He tells you he played football in high school. Maybe that explains the nose. Though you sense a hidden violence—could have been a drunken brawl.

He ends up on your couch, playing your guitar with the broken G-string, singing Beatles songs, forgetting some of the words and you help him, both of you singing "Let It Be." Your voices don't mesh and the air is weak. His presence is suddenly flat, irritating. He wants to hear Bruce Springsteen, the early stuff. He knows all the words. You don't know these early songs, you came to Springsteen late. You may never want to hear Bruce Springsteen again.

He asks if you have any Dylan; suddenly he's the true poet, petting the cat, but maybe you want him to leave. You put on some later Dylan, one of the many overlooked ones, telling him how fine Dylan is, how he gets better the older he gets.

He asks, "Is it all right if I close my eyes for a few minutes?" He stretches his legs without waiting for a reply and leans his head back against the big pillows you bought in Nepal.

"No problem," you say.

It's a good time to take care of the neglected stuff in the sink.

There's a man sleeping on the couch and you're washing dishes. He's made himself at home. Snoring.

Dylan's over and you decide to play something that only appeals to you. Something eccentric and obscure. Maybe he'll hate it.

You're standing over him, hoping he hasn't passed out for the night. He stirs, opening his eyes. The rain has set his hair into a waxy mass, clinging to his face. You smile politely, wondering what he'd look like after a shower and if he weren't three sheets to the wind.

"How about a hug?" he asks, extending his arms, smiling that trust-me smile again.

What the hell.

His tongue fills your mouth like a giant hard-on. He tightens it into a big wet muscle with a pointed tip. This is bad for kissing but maybe he's trying to tell you it's good for something else, or maybe it's just your imagination.

And suddenly that Cole Porter song pops into your head, *It's the wrong time and the wrong place....* You rewrite the words: *It's not his smell, but it's an acceptable smell; it's not his tongue, and I don't like this tongue, and it's not right with me.*

"Maybe we shouldn't start what we can't finish," you say, not sure if you're being explicit enough.

He's doing to your breasts something boys used to do when you were thirteen: lifting your sweater, tugging clumsily at the back of your bra.

What the hell. You undo it yourself. He's opening your jeans, trying to slide them over your hips, which have always been an asset except when you are lying down and need to get off your pants quickly. You do it yourself.

You're completely naked and he's not. He unfolds you back over the length of couch. His head is between your thighs and he's happily discovered you shave there, unaware it's someone else's preference. You look down along your stretched-out body and see he's smiling. You've decided there's little in this for you unless you take a completely exploitive position. It's not a very arousing idea at the moment, so you think about the tongue and the long wiry body of someone who always makes you feel taut and vibrant. The phone rings. The answering machine clicks on but you've turned down the volume to avoid complications. There's a silent pause before the machine clicks again to rewind the tape.

After you come, you're sure you want him to leave.

"Let's go to sleep," he says.

He's already in bed. You're turning off lights and doing bathroom things, wondering if he's forgotten where he is or if he treats all women like wives. You crawl in next to him; he's even taken the outside half of the bed, leaving you up against the wall. You lie there with a merciless tickle in your throat, resigned to a sleepless night, weighing the pros and cons between whether he falls asleep or stays awake. He opens his arm to pull you close and your face is on his chest, nose close to his armpit. There's a spicy smell and it's a familiar gesture but it's like a movie remake that's been miscast. You turn over because you really want to fall asleep now, lying on your stomach. He says your name and orders, in a proprietary tone, "Lie this way," pulling you in with his arm. *This movie is taking a turn for the worse*, you think, you've come this far, you might as well see it to the end. He puts your hand on his cock, which is not so hard as to make all this seem worth it, or as hard as it might be, considering you're two attractive strangers lying together naked in a clean, comfortable bed. Something starts happening and you remember the unopened box of condoms in the dresser from last summer that you never got the chance to use because you don't really like sex with strangers.

"I have condoms," you say, distracted by the degree to which your pleasure is eclipsed by guilt.

The phone rings, the muted answering machine silently recording. The silence is brief, then you hear the mechanical clickings and clackings of the machine rewinding the tape. The lump of flesh in your hand is responding poorly. He takes the back of your head and lifts it. You're not sure where he intends to direct it and you don't feel like doing him any favors.

The phone rings again. This time it goes on longer. Something is building on the other end of the line. You sit up suddenly.

"I can't do this, Patrick."

You look over at him and he's got the squinting, blinking look of someone waking up as he's being tossed overboard in the sunny glare of his last day on Earth.

"You'd better go."

"Okay, I just need about an hour to get myself together and then I'll leave."

"No, you have to go now. There's something I have to attend to."

"I understand," he says, now sitting up as well, the two of you side by side, naked. He strokes your head; then he's standing, tucking in his pockets, zipping his pants in a flash. "Will he come here now?"

"No, I'll go there."

He asks two more times if he'll come here, as if he isn't sure and doesn't want to be mistaken.

"You're a weirdo, but a good weirdo," he says. "I like you," he adds, addressing you by your name again. "I hope this man is worthy of you."

You don't know.

A few rushed minutes. He hugs you a second time at the door. You return his embrace.

He exits, diminishing between the elevator doors.

You close the door and pick up the phone.

LAST CALL

Jamie Joy Gatto

"I have loved strangers, and after them I will go." (Jer. 2:25)

I never would have worn my bathing suit to a bar, especially at night, especially to that bar where I know everyone, unless I was in "a mood," as my husband calls it. But I put on the suit, and only the suit, with no change of clothing, to go to a pool party where rumor had it my ex would be with his new wife. Actually, not just *my* ex, but also the ex of my husband. The new wife would be there, too: Baptist to the bone. I couldn't resist.

The suit was a fabulous, fine jersey knit, a flirty one-piece 1940s glamour-girl number. It was sleek and black, with an oh-so-low halter neck and a peekaboo skirt that fell just over my ripe, smooth ass. Classic, dangerous, perfect. I simply couldn't resist.

Even though the pool party was a bust due to a typical temperamental New Orleans downpour, that last lingering stare at my husband's crotch, and that one haunting whisper, "You look hot," as we passed *him* in the hall, was all I needed to accelerate "the mood" and take my suit elsewhere. Oh, Paul and I were not going home yet, and furthermore, we were walking. I practically skipped to St. Joe's bar, shiny sling-back pumps clacking on the pavement, leaving Mr. Ex to his abysmal Baptist bride.

The bar glowed dimly with the promise of a perfect martini in a V-shaped glass, crystalline chilled and tasting of baby tears, wet with olives and a whisper of vermouth. The bartender made my mouth water. I knew him by name and little else, and I was thirsty.

Figuring that my bare feet couldn't stand in Bette Davis pumps forever, I angled and vied for the only available seat at the bar. Paul kissed me as he slipped away to say his hellos and probably grab a game of pool in back. The moist crowd pressed around me as I slid onto a leather-covered stool.

Crosses dangled and danced overhead in the breeze of antique ceiling fans, some handmade, some seemingly from churches, others jeweled and sparkling in the glow of a Victorian gothic chandelier. St. Joseph stood vigil over the oak altar crowded with whiskey, wine, and imported beer, his aureole outshone by a row of fat Christmas bulbs while Ren, the barkeep, took my order, "Dirty, up, and dripping wet."

"How salty do you want it?" he asked.

"Filthy," I said smiling, believing fully in transubstantiation.

I wiggled on the sweaty stool to keep my rump from sticking to it, then lifted the glass with two hands, savoring each heady sip. A multitude of possibilities surrounded me. The long, smooth neck of a leggy woman invited me, her head tossed back in laughter. The wink of an older man glistened with seedy desire. The biceps of a college boy rumpled boastfully as he lifted a pool cue, pocketing the bright red three-ball.

Faces hummed, laughter tinkled, something shimmered inside me just below the surface, at first a pale weakening, then a rush. My seat dampened, not only from sweat. I bit my lip and tasted the curve of my lacquered nail. My pinkie barely parted my mouth, touched the wet inner surface with tiny traces along my lips.

In my head, armies of men lined up for miles, filled me with cocks of every size. Come flowed out of me like milk. Rows of round luscious milkmaids followed, licking the cream from inside me, their breasts full, brushing my thighs, stuffing pink nipples into my mouth.

I swirled the tiny sword stacked with olives in my drink. My eyes searched the room for Paul, but he was not in sight. Ren bustled about serving drinks. There was no one else I knew well enough to talk to, much less share the goddess that stirred within. From behind me, a familiar pair of broad palms brushed my hair aside, squeezed my shoulders.

"There you are, Paul," I said.

"I love it when you do that," he said, "I had to come see the look on your face."

"Do what? What look?"

"You were biting your finger."

"I'm not biting my finger."

"You were, and I love it," he said, "It means you're in a mood." He pointed to a small group at a table drinking beer, "I'm with some school friends in back, if you want to come meet them."

I really wasn't in the mood to remember names, smile and nod, be polite. Not tonight. Play the straight-wife role in my Betty Grable bathing suit? What was he thinking?

"No, I think I'll keep my chair," I said, eyeing Ren.

"Well, behave," he winked.

"Never," I said smiling, looking up at the painting. "My Painting," as I had named it, hung in an elaborate gold frame high above the service area. Painted in Roman-style text across the top of it were the Latin words, "Porten Se Bien," which meant, loosely translated, "Behave Well."

It was done by the same interior designer who had hand-sponged the walls a rich hue of *terre verte*, having had the sense and taste to leave the ceiling untouched, blotched and burned, aged in a shell-shocked patina that no faux finish artist could ever hope to reproduce.

In the painting, a robed, bearded sage floated in a blue sky dotted with clouds, along with a great human eye, a large pair of smiling lips, and a single human ear. All seemed to watch over, perhaps even protect, the earthly scene below. On mortal ground, a man whose back was to my gaze stood nude. Before him a nude woman, arms opened, offered herself to him. On his left, a nude man leaned over, buttocks raised in invitation. Their vulnerable naked flesh was surrounded by thorny blooming cacti, a paradox of potential pain and fleeting beauty. Below the figures, three open roses blossomed under cracked human skulls.

Life is short; why should anyone have to choose? *Pick both*, I urged the faceless man. *Go for it. Take the risk before your perfect flesh turns to dry dust. Besides*, I laughed to myself, *they probably both like to watch*.

That's when I noticed her. She didn't seem like much at first, just a college girl, especially because she had been seated. When she stood she was at least as tall as Paul, even wearing flats, her caramel legs resplendent against her brown shorts. I could not see her face because of the way she stood, talking to Paul, her with that honeyed ponytail cascading down her back, barely brushing the smooth curve of her spine.

When she angled to the left, I caught the warmth of her high cheekbones, her smooth skin. She laughed, shook her head. I glimpsed a taste of her full lips, white teeth contrasted with golden skin. I could not see her eyes, but nearly got up from my seat to do so. When I realized I was staring, I ordered another drink from Ren. "Do you know her?" I pointed casually, pulled my stool closer to the bar.

"Who, Alana?" he said, "Sure. She comes in all the time. She works at PJ's. Why?"

"Just wondering," I smiled, tried not to look at her. I waited a beat, took a sip of my martini, looked over at the table. Paul and Alana were sitting alone, their chairs pulled close, as if they were whispering to one another. She tugged on her long pony-tail, twisting it around her hand. Finally, I could see her eyes; I could not discern their color, but she looked at him as if she meant what she was saying. Paul put his hand on her shoulder; she nodded. He got up from the table and walked toward me. I chewed on an olive, pretended not to see him as he approached.

"Having fun?" I asked.

"Yes, as a matter of fact," he said, "but there is someone who would very much like to talk to you."

"Who?" I asked, taking a huge slug of vodka.

"My classmate, Alana. You met her before, don't you remember?"

"I met *her* before?" I said, taking another gulp, nearly choking on an olive. "When?"

"New Year's Eve, don't you remember? At the Columns."

"New Year's Eve at the Columns. After I drank how many bottles of champagne?"

"Oh, I see," he laughed, "You really don't remember her."

"Was it before or after I danced on the table with Duncan?"

"I think after. But don't tell her you can't remember her. She recalls you *well*."

"Me?" I said. I gulped my drink, finishing it.

He pushed my hair aside and leaned into my ear. "She wants to talk to you," he whispered, "about sex."

I spun around in my seat. "What about sex?"

"Ask her," he said. "She likes you."

"She likes me?"

"Yes," he said, "go talk to her."

I tugged at my bathing suit straps. "OK," I said, standing up in time to see her go into the ladies' room. As I sat alone at the table, I turned to look for Paul, but he was already chatting with Ren. I watched the door of the ladies' room, wished I could go in and fix my hair. I found my compact, then began to touch up my lipstick.

"Your lips are beautiful," Alana said.

I nearly jumped.

"So red next to your pale skin." There was a hint of something foreign peppering her voice. It was a gentle voice, husky but soothing. She sat in the chair exactly next to me, then turned to face me. She was close, right there.

"Thank you," I said, sounding strange to myself, "where are you from?" I said, "You have a lovely accent."

"Brazil," she said. "My family is from Brazil." She smelled warm like coffee, and at last I could see that her eyes were a pale jade green. She leaned closer. "I remember the first time I saw you," she said, "at the Columns. You were dressed in that beautiful gown, those gloves. I remember your smile," she said, "and your beautiful lips."

I couldn't speak; and if I could have, what on earth could I have said?

"Your husband tells me you are like me," she said. "That you love other women, too. I have been infatuated with other women before, but I have never shown it. I want you to show me how it's done, to teach me," she said, "I think it would be beautiful. What do you think?"

I tried to think of something to say, but couldn't, so I nodded.

She touched my knee lightly, with her fingertips. I could smell her breath, so human, so sweet. "Imagine," she said, "how it will look, you and me. Your ivory skin, and mine, so dark."

She searched my eyes. "You will teach me how to please you," she said. "You will teach me how to love a woman." I opened my mouth to speak, but she said, "Don't answer, not yet. There is something I must ask you first. Do you find me beautiful?"

"Oh, yes," I whispered. I touched her hand.

She looked relieved. "There is something else. I—" she looked deeply into her glass, turned it slowly. "I would really like it if my boyfriend could be there, too. You do not have to touch him if you do not like him, or even let him touch you. He will only watch. You see, I told him that I would do it for him," she said. "But what he does not know is that I am doing it to please myself, and to please you, if you will let me."

For the life of me, I could not speak. All I could do was stare.

She said, "Do not answer me now," and placed a business card in my hand. I held it up as if to read it, but my eyes would not focus. I could only see her. "Please call me in two weeks," she said, "after my final exams. If you want to show me, I will learn. I will please you." She leaned into me, whispered in my ear, "Two weeks."

I sat in my seat holding the business card until I could read what it said, "Alana Zocchio, assistant manager, PJ's Coffee." I tucked it in my purse.

"Last call," Ren said.

ADVENTURE

Michael Hemmingson

Phone Call

I got the phone call while I was watching television. *Babylon 5*. I think I could've been watching too much television.

"Hello," I said.

"Hello," a woman's voice said. "Who is this?"

I was surprised and amused. "Who are you?" I asked.

"Andrea," she said.

"Do I know you?"

"I don't think so," she said. "I found your phone number. I was curious. I was angry. I called. I'm sorry."

Angry? "I don't understand."

"I live in San Diego," she said. "My husband's name is Barry Redman. Do you know him?"

"No," I said.

"I found your phone number on the back of a matchbook," she told me. "It was from a bar. I pulled it out of the jacket pocket of my husband's gray suit, which he was wearing two nights ago. He was out late. He came home drunk."

"Is this some kind of weird joke?" I said. "Did Lisa put you up to this?"

"Lisa?"

"My wife."

"I don't know a Lisa."

"I don't know a Barry Redman."

"Where is your wife now?"

"Is this a joke?"

"I'm sorry," she said, and hung up.

I thought about it. I went back to the television.

Lisa

Lisa called later that night. She'd had a few drinks. She likes to drink, and so do I. It's the one thing we immediately had in common when we met seven years ago. She was down in San Diego, on business for the company she worked for. She'd been in San Diego for five days. This was her last night. "I can't wait to get back home," she said.

"I got the strangest telephone call today," I said.

"What?"

"It was—" I said. "I don't know," I said. "It was nothing."

"I'm beat," Lisa said.

The next afternoon, I drove to the airport and picked her up. We kissed and didn't talk. We went home. From the corner of my eye, I kept looking at her to see if she were different.

Home, I made us two vodka tonics and we sat in front of the television. The television wasn't on.

"Do you know someone named Barry Redman?" I asked.

Lisa was about to take a drink. She stopped. "What?" she said.

"Barry Redman," I said.

"Why do you ask?"

"I got a funny phone call yesterday," I said. "A woman called. She was in San Diego. Said she found our number on a matchbook from a bar. Her husband's name is—"

"Yes," Lisa said, "I know him."

"A business associate?" I asked.

"No," she said.

"A friend?" I asked.

"I don't know him that well, really," she said.

The Truth

We didn't make love when we went to bed. She didn't seem to be in the mood, and I wasn't either. We were a little drunk and sleeping naked.

"So who is Barry Redman?" I asked.

She didn't answer. She lay there, her back turned to me.

"Lisa?" I said.

"What?" she said. She sat up, looking at me. She pulled the sheets across her breasts. "What the fuck do you *want*?" she said. "What do you want me to say?"

"I don't know," I said.

"What the *fuck* do you want me to say?" She was crying now. "You want the truth? OK. I'll tell you the truth. Barry Redman is someone I met at a bar in San Diego. A—a man."

"Oh," I said. I got up, went to the bathroom. I didn't have to pee. I looked at myself in the mirror. I put on my robe and went back to the bedroom. Lisa was naked on the bed, looking at the ceiling.

"Why did you give him our number?" I asked.

"I don't know," she said. "I don't know what I was thinking. Like I could *really* take a call here. I must've meant to give him my pager number and, I don't know. *I was drunk*. I was really drunk."

"Did you fuck him?" I asked.

She still looked at the ceiling.

I approached the bed. "Lisa," I said, "did you fuck him?"

She sat up. "No," she said. "I wanted to. But I didn't."

"Oh," I said.

"I sucked his cock," she said, looking at me.

I went to the kitchen.

I made some drinks.

I fell asleep in front of the television.

Hash Browns and Eggs

I woke up to the smell of food. Lisa was making breakfast in the kitchen. She wore a T-shirt and shorts.

"Do you want hash browns with your eggs?" she asked.

"You sucked his cock?" I asked.

"Yes," she said.

"Why?"

"Why?" she said. "Don't ask dumb questions," she said.

"Did he come in your mouth?" I said.

"Yes," she said.

"Just like that?"

"People come."

"You didn't make him wear a condom?" I asked.

"I don't like the taste of latex," she said.

"That's dangerous," I said.

"He seemed pretty safe," she said.

I sat down. "What did I do?" I said.

"You didn't do anything," Lisa said. She didn't look at me. "Our marriage has dulled. You know that. There's no—excitement. I'm a bad person, I know. We have a good marriage."

"Have there been others?" I asked.

"Yes."

"How many?"

"I won't answer that," she said.

"*How many?*"

"I guess I should pack some stuff," she said.

Second Phone Call

The phone rang while I was watching television. It was the news: Wolf Blitzer on CNN.

"Hello," the woman's voice said. "I called the other day. From San Diego."

"Andrea Redman?"

"Yes," she said. "I need to talk to you."

"Your husband met my wife at a bar," I said.

"I know," she said. "He told me. He said they didn't sleep together."

"No," I said. "Lisa only gave him a blow job."

"What?"

"You know what a blow job is?"

"I *know* what it is," she said. "I don't believe it."

"That's what my wife told me," I said. "She's gone now."

"With Barry?"

"They hardly know each other," I said. "I doubt they have anything romantic going on," I said.

Silence. "I shouldn't be surprised," Andrea Redman said. "He's done this before. I'd hoped it had stopped."

"Ask him what it was like," I said.

"What?"

"What it was like," I said, "getting his dick blown by my wife."

She hung up.

Lisa's Call

Lisa called me from a hotel room. "What should we do?" she said.

"What will you do?" I said.

"I'm not sure what to do," she said. "Do you want a divorce?"

"I'm not sure."

"I love you," she said, "no matter what."

"I want to know how many?"

"Is it important?"

"Yes," I said.

"Six," she said, "I think. But they didn't mean anything."

I hung up.

Los Angeles

Andrea Redman called in the afternoon. "I thought you might call," I said.

"I'm in L.A.," she said.

"Why are you in L.A.?"

"It's only a two-hour drive," she said. "I was hoping —I was hoping maybe you'd meet me."

"OK," I said.

She arrived forty minutes later. I was watching for her. She drove a small station wagon. She was tall and slim, with short blonde hair and a thin face, too gaunt. Maybe it was the glasses she wore. She rang the doorbell and I answered.

"Andrea Redman, I presume."

"Hello."

"Did you find my house OK?"

"I got lost once, but I'm here."

Coffee

I offered her some coffee. She said that'd be nice. I got us both a cup and we sat in the living room. The television was on, sound off. We sat there quietly sipping coffee.

"Well," I said.

"Well," she said. "I don't know what to say. I was rehearsing all kinds of things in my head on the way down here. My mind is blank now."

"Relax."

"I *am* relaxed. I just can't think. I don't know why I'm here. I got into my car and started to drive. I thought you had some answers. I don't know what the questions are. I woke up this morning and my husband was gone. I don't know where he is." She added, "I wasn't surprised."

"I don't think he's in L.A," I said.

"No," she said.

"But you are," I said.

"Yes," she said.

I looked out the window. "Listen," I said. "It's starting to get dark out. You want to go to a bar, or something?"

"Sure," Andrea Redman said. "Or something."

Tequila Tonics

We took her car. We went to a little bar I like, one Lisa and I used to go to. We'd been here last week. Andrea and I sat at the counter. "What would you like?" I asked.

"It doesn't matter," she said. "Whatever you're having," she said.

I ordered two tequila tonics.

"Strong," she said, sipping.

I drank mine fast and ordered another.

"I'm not much of a drinker," she said. "Barry likes to drink."

"Lisa likes to drink," I said. "I do too."

"I should take up drinking more," she said.

"Wouldn't hurt," I said.

We sat there.

"Do we have anything to talk about?" I said.

"I don't know," she said. "I feel uncomfortable."

"I'm sorry," I said.

"It's not you," she said, taking her glasses off and putting them back on. "It's this bar. I never feel comfortable in dark bars," she said.

Beer

We left the bar and picked up a six-pack of beer from the liquor store. I told her where to drive, near Santa Monica. I told her where to park.

"It's peaceful here," I said, opening two beers.

"I like the sound of the waves," Andrea Redman said. "We don't live near the beach. I always wanted to live by the beach," she said, drinking beer. "This is good beer. I usually don't drink beer. If I drink at all, it's wine. Not a lot of wine, a glass, two at the most," she said.

"When I drink wine," I said, "my eyes itch like crazy the next morning."

"I keep trying to picture them together," she said. "But I can't. I don't know what your wife looks like."

"I have a photo," I said, taking out my wallet.

"I do, too." She opened her purse. "Barry."

We exchanged photos.

"I still can't see them together," she said, giving my wallet back. "Can you?"

"I don't know."

"He swore they didn't make love."

"He just got his cock sucked."

"If he wanted that, why didn't he ask me?" She drank her beer. "I give him that when he wants it." She drank her beer and looked at me. "Would you like me to show you? Would you like me to suck you?"

"Yes," I said.

"OK," she said, "take it out."

I unzipped my pants.

Andrea finished her beer. She looked at me holding it. She bent down. I barely felt her mouth graze me. She came back up, adjusting her glasses.

"I can't," she said.

"It's OK," I said.

Motel Room

We got a motel room near the beach. There was a bar connected to the motel so we went there. She was getting drunk. "I want to get really drunk," she said, and I had no problem with that. There were mostly men in the bar. I ordered us two drinks and we sat in a booth. "I think I can go through with it this time," Andrea said, kissing me on the mouth.

A man with a thick mustache joined us in our booth. He was heavy-set and smiling. "Hello," he said. "I'm Rick."

"Hello," Andrea said.

"Can I join you?" he said.

"No," I said.

"There's this joke I wanted to tell you both," he said.

"A joke?" Andrea asked.

"Yeah," Rick said, "but now I can't remember it. I think I drank too much."

"Haven't we all," Andrea said, and giggled.

"You're cute," Rick said. "I mean, gorgeous. The both of you. All hugs and kisses. Like you're on some adventure. I envy you."

"Thanks," I said, "but we'd like to be left alone. We were having a private conversation."

"Yeah," Rick said. Something changed in him. "What's so private about it, huh? Tell me. What's so goddamned *private* about it?"

"Would you please leave," I said.

"What're you gonna to do about it?" he said.

Andrea laughed.

Rick looked down. "I'm sorry. I'm just drunk. I haven't been with a woman in over a year. When I see a pretty woman—" He got up and left.

"That was strange," Andrea said.

Surprise Visit

Back in the motel room, we started to kiss and undress. There was a knock on the door. Andrea went to get it, stumbling, wearing only her skirt and bra.

"Ignore it," I said.

"Maybe it's room service," she said.

"Motels don't have that," I said.

I don't know what she was thinking. She opened the door, half-naked, and said, "Surprise!" She was laughing, until a hand shoved her back. She collapsed on the floor, her glasses falling off her face.

Before I could move, Rick was in the room. He shut the door. He was holding a black revolver.

"Hello again," he said.

"Oh boy," I said.

"I had to do this," he said. "This is what's gonna happen. I'm robbing you, because I've been out of work longer than I want to remember and I need money. Then I'm gonna fuck your lady friend because I haven't been with a woman for a while."

Andrea just stared at him.

"Don't make this difficult," Rick said. "This can be fun if you'd like," he said.

I rushed Rick. He wasn't expecting it. I slapped the gun out of his hand and hit him a few times in the face. He went down. It was all a silly, drunken moment and probably would've been funny under different circumstances.

"Are you crazy?" Andrea said. "He could've *shot* us!"

"No." I picked up the gun. "It's fake."

"How can you tell?"

"You look at a revolver, you can see bullets in the chamber. This is a fake chamber. The whole thing is fake."

"Oh," Andrea said, picking up her glasses.

Coffee and Pancakes

We sat in a diner that was nearby, eating pancakes, drinking coffee, getting sober. We'd left Rick in the motel room bed; he seemed to be sleeping well.

"I guess I should go home now," Andrea said.

"Can you drive?"

"Yes. I need to go home. I've had enough excitement to last me the year, my life. Barry is probably wondering. Maybe he's even worried. I've never stayed away from home before."

"What will you tell him?"

"I don't have to tell him anything."

"Are you staying with him?"

"Yes," she said. "He's my husband."

6 A.M.

Andrea drove me home. I wanted to kiss her good-bye. We smiled at each other, and that was enough. It was 6 A.M. Lisa's car was there. She was in the bedroom, packing. We looked at each other. I went to the kitchen and made myself a vodka tonic. Lisa followed, looked at me.

"I just came by to get more of my stuff," she said. "I have to look for an apartment today."

"Don't," I said. "Don't."

Lisa came to me then, putting her head against my chest, and I held her.

"Lisa," I said, and felt her hand at my crotch.

CONFESSION

Paul Hill

This is not a confession. I have nothing to confess. Sin is only the breaking of an enforceable law, and so confession is merely a legal term.

I am forty-five years old, a professor of history at a small college in upstate New York. I live alone, have few material needs. I do, from time to time, strike up acquaintanceships with young, female graduate students —but never those I might have occasion to teach or mentor. I am all propriety. I am a proper gentlemen, too old to be copulating in the backseats of cars, or dorm rooms, or sofas, or against the walls in deserted bus stations. I am a gentleman and a scholar. Often, during academic breaks, I'll spend some money and invite my most recent acquaintance to a weekend in the city. We'll take in shows, eat at restaurants. I always reserve a room with two beds, take nothing for granted.

I am not unattractive, I think—thickening a bit with age, but I have a quick mind and listen well. I have enough money and, at the risk of sounding immodest, am not unknown in my particular field. More often than not, the young lady, my guest, finds her way to my bed, which is why I've taken her away in the first place. I may seem aloof, distant, removed, and I have no close friends, but I enjoy pleasuring women. I am a patient man and it pleases me to please them. It is my fascination to know them to such an intimate extent, without really knowing them at all. Once back at school, my demeanor, my schedule usually distance us. We remain friends, but they go on and I stay—we drift apart, I suppose. Some few mistake curiosity for passion, but I explain that we cannot be that "free" on campus—it's a stupid bird that defecates in its own nest.

Tall, with long blond hair, and in her early twenties, Sarah was no different from the others I had invited away for a weekend. She was a poet, or at least, a graduate student in the English Department. She was really quite lovely, and I had struck up a friendship in the usual way—asking about her studies, her goals, lightly belittling myself for my age, and then more pointedly, the misfortune of the distance between our ages. She made the appropriate objections sweetly, saying that she couldn't stomach the immaturity, arrogance, and bombast of the male students her own age in the department. We took to meeting a couple of evenings a week for coffee or walks around campus. She read me some of her poetry. When I suggested we spend a weekend in the city to take in a show, she seemed excited by the idea.

We arrived at the hotel in Manhattan on Friday evening. I had made reservations for dinner and had tickets to a show. I was surprised that Sarah did nothing to hide her sense of wonder at Manhattan, the hotel itself, the suite. She had apparently been in the city only once before, and then for an afternoon between bus connections.

As I say, we checked in, took the luggage to the room, and I, as I usually do, went down to the bar—both for a couple of drinks and to give the young lady some privacy in case she wanted to bathe or change. I am a patient man, and I could feel a certain sexual tension in Sarah that could only heighten by my paying no attention to it whatsoever.

I stayed in the bar for an hour, watching the people

there. I had only two drinks, as usual. I thought about Sarah's protestations, her feeling that my leaving was unnecessary, that she could ready herself for dinner without putting me out of the suite. I am the perfect gentlemen, I think. I remember telling her I would be away an hour.

I went back up to the room. I remember wondering, as I put the card in the lock, what state I would find her in. Aloofness is sometimes a strong aphrodisiac. I was about to call out as I entered, to let her know I was there. As I turned the corner of the partition that gives the room a small foyer, the first thing I saw was Sarah lying on the bed closest to the window. She was still wearing the black tank top she had worn in the car on the way down. Her eyes were closed and I thought she might be napping. As I came around the corner, I stopped. Sarah was naked from the waist down. Her bottom was resting on the foot of the bed, her legs were spread, knees bent, feet resting on the foot. Kneeling between her legs was a bellhop. His head was bobbing and I noticed his neck and shoulder muscles were taut. Time stopped.

Looking back at the moment, I don't know how I felt—cheated in some way, perhaps, although I understood that these weekends meant little or nothing to any of the parties involved. Certainly the bobbing black head, the tongue parting her labia and flicking her clitoris, the tickling of her abundant blond pubic hair, and the taste of her sex, the smell of which, I could now sense, filled the room, were all delights I had anticipated for myself. I can't say how long I stood there or how I felt. Jealous, perhaps—but it sounds a strong, strange word.

Sarah was the first to notice me. She turned her head, opened her eyes, and said two words: "Christ, David." The young man seemed to stiffen, turned his head, and made to get up. I saw that he was also naked from the waist down and that his erection was quickly fading in my presence. I had interrupted foreplay—minutes later they would have coupled there on the edge of the bed.

Sarah's legs were closing. The bellhop made a motion as if to rise from his knees. I then noticed his name tag: "Carlos."

"Stay where you are, boy," I said.

Carlos stammered, "Excuse me, sir...I didn't know... I'm leaving now."

I replied, scooping his trousers from the floor, "You're not leaving unless you want to return to your post in that condition." The threat of having to return to his post without any trousers stopped his movements. Sarah had turned her head to the window as if none of this had anything to do with her. I continued, "Keep licking her, boy, she seems to like it. Continue—if you don't want to lose your job." He probably had a family he was helping to support, so he spread Sarah's legs with his hands and recommenced licking her pubis—if with less enthusiasm.

I walked around his legs to the window. Sarah's eyes were tightly closed, as if with that gesture she could be somewhere else. I unzipped my fly and took out my penis. I knelt on the bed, stroking myself fully erect, and put my penis to her lips. Sarah ignored me until I cradled her skull with my other hand and pushed harder against her lips.

She opened her mouth and took in my cock, moving her tongue and making light sucking sounds. I looked up and found Carlos watching me with scared eyes. I motioned with my head for him to continue working on her.

Sarah's mouth, tongue, and lips started to move faster on me, almost as if she had the idea that once I climaxed, this uncomfortable tableau would be finished. I eased myself deeper into her mouth, down her throat, but somewhere in an obscure place in my mind, I had already decided that this would not end with my orgasm.

When I was on the verge of coming, I pulled away

from her. Because her eyes were still closed tightly, her lips and tongue continued to reach for my cock, and make sucking sounds for a split second after I removed myself.

Unimpressed by Carlos' lackluster performance on Sarah's cunt, I stood, addressing him: "Hey, boy. You don't seem to want to play with her anymore. Do you want to fuck her now?" His cock had shriveled and appeared to retreat farther as I asked him why he now seemed not as interested in fucking Sarah. I still had his trousers in my hand. I told him that he'd better start to perform if he expected his clothing back. I ordered him to sit on the other bed and lie back.

"But sir—" he protested.

"Do what I tell you," I ordered. "Shut up now, you're playing with your job." I stepped into the open bathroom and threw a small complimentary bottle of hand lotion to him.

"Get ready," I growled.

During this short interlude, Sarah kept silent, closed her long legs, and faced the window in a fetal position. I understood little of what I was doing, mostly driven by a need for completion, for closure—certainly, if they had planned a fuck, even a quick fuck in my absence, then that is what should take place.

Carlos' efforts at arousing himself were sabotaged by

his fear—and I could see now that he feared me. I went to Sarah, turned her on her back from the foot of the bed, and made her stand up by pulling on her shoulder. She was limp, without will, content to keep her eyes closed and be directed. I stood her in front of Carlos, facing him, and put her arms up and pulled off her tank top. I lifted her, now naked, onto the boy's hips. She fell forward on her hands and knees above his flaccid cock. "Penetrate her," I said to him, sitting her up to force her hips down on him. With the contact of cunt on cock, his penis became a little stiffer, but it was still insufficient to enter her. "Use your hands, boy," I directed. Carlos spread her with his fingers and then used his hand to introduce his stiffening cock. I pushed her hips down on him.

Sarah may have murmured something. It may have been, "no," but I wasn't paying attention. I was directing Carlos. Once he was safely lodged inside of her, I pushed her forward on top of him. "Take her," I said, meaning for him to trap her arms with his.

I can say now that up until that moment, I had little idea what I would do next. Had I thought I would force them to fuck until Carlos had climaxed? Had I thought that I wanted to watch the young Hispanic come inside of her tight, blond cunt? I don't know. I stood there, above them.

I hesitate to write what happened next. No one will ever read this, of course, but still—writing it is perhaps admitting it to myself. It was something I had never done, never felt the urge really to do. That is not to say that I'd ever been fellated with another man watching, nor that I'd ever been in a position to force a young woman's hips down on another man's cock, and watch as that man accommodated his entrance with his fingers. Somehow that moment late Friday afternoon seemed out of time and space and I did not seem myself. This is not excuse as much as an honest wonder at my own actions.

After I had pushed Sarah flat on Carlos' chest and saw that his penis, at least for the moment, was wedged safely inside her, I noticed her anus—a pink, clean puckering of flesh. Sarah, as I have said, was lanky, without excess—thin, maybe. Her breasts were small, her hips slim, and astride Carlos' hips in this position the cheeks of her bottom separated. I felt my penis stiffening and scooped the hand cream from the bed where Carlos had left it. After applying some to my cock and stroking myself once or twice, I wiped my hand on the spread and put the head of my member to Sarah's anus.

I imagine her eyes opened, although I couldn't see her face. At this point even Carlos had his eyes shut tightly. She stiffened and she made as if to sit up, but I grabbed her shoulders, both pushing her back onto Carlos and pulling myself into her.

I have deflowered two or three young girls, students whom some might have found plain-looking. I am a patient man and penetrating these virginal women was a slow, pleasant process. However, I had never sodomized anyone and was a little surprised at the difficulty I had in penetrating Sarah's ass. She was very tight, even with the lotion, and it was not a slow sliding but took a number of short powerful thrusts to get myself firmly inside. I only stopped when I could feel my lower stomach against her cheeks. Her ass was too tight, too new for sensation. It had to hurt, and it was to her credit, I suppose, that she didn't cry out, although I really don't know what I was expecting. With every thrust of my cock, however, there was some articulation, a sudden gasp, a short, explosive sigh of protest. I assaulted her anus again, in one hard thrust this time, and was rewarded with her short, sweet, whispering groan.

I don't know how many times I rammed myself into her that way, but I realized after a while that I was only sliding my now-very-swollen penis into her only to hear that little shocked groan. I would withdraw my cock to its head and then ram my hips to her ass, only because I wanted to hear that breathy "uh." Perhaps I liked what I imagined to be the sound of punishment; perhaps I also wanted to break that sound barrier, move Sarah to a still-more-desperate noise.

As I said, eventually I realized the motivation behind my thrusting at her, and also realized that, although Sarah's anus had widened and was easier to penetrate, she was still too tight for me to get much sensation. I was no closer to climax. Carlos had became aware, obviously, of my activities and must have been mad with terror, trapped as he was beneath our two bodies. I abruptly stopped ramming my cock up Sarah and stepped back. Carlos' penis had shriveled, literally falling out of her cunt, and looking very much like a small animal trying to hide. He protested weakly as I brushed aside his cock with mine and entered her. Sarah was a little dry, but with what was left of the hand cream, I quickly penetrated her and moved cleanly inside. This was a more familiar orifice and it was, I think, only a short time before I came, my semen pumping from me for what seemed like a long time.

No sooner had I finished and withdrawn than did Carlos push her off of him and scurry out from under her body. His penis was almost comical now, little and jiggling as he stood, crouched and trembling. I threw him his trousers and almost laughed as he stumbled, trying to dress and run at the same time. I doubted he'd be able to finish his shift, whatever it was. I had nothing to say to him.

I turned and entered the bathroom, where I cleaned my penis on one of the large white towels the establishment provides. I briefly adjusted my clothing, washed my hands, and splashed cold water on my face. Turning from the mirror, I could see that Sarah had moved again into a near-fetal position. I tossed the towel, the same one I used to clean myself, onto her hips from the bathroom doorway.

I have been here in the bar, writing this account, for the past three hours—first on scraps of paper I had in my agenda, and then on hotel stationery the bartender procured for me. I've had four or five drinks and been undisturbed, although the bar traffic has busied and slowed in waves. I confess that I do not know what to do now. I must go back to the room. Will Sarah be there? If she is gone, will I ever find out why she invited Carlos? Where is Carlos now? What is he doing at this moment? If Sarah is still in the room, will she be lying in the position I left her in? What will she have to say to me, or I to her? She has changed, no dobut. Will I propose marriage? Will I strike her if she does not speak?

I confess I know nothing about myself, or what I

may do next. I have two fears: the fear that what happened to me this afternoon, three hours ago, happened; and the fear that nothing like it will ever happen to me again.

SIGMUND'S CIGAR

Dasien Korangar

Dr. Velda Krebbing had dismissed her last client fifteen minutes before either Jeff or Caitlin had arrived. Jeff Tucker's file lay open on her desktop and she was making a pretense of rereading her notes. Jeff was a convicted sexual offender and it was her offer of treatment, as part of her studies in deviant sexuality, that was keeping him out of jail. His most recent arrest would have been for simple assault, had he managed to stay dressed. Evidently he'd been on his third-floor balcony, naked and gigantically erect, throwing water balloons at the adolescent ballet students lining up under his building for the Nutcracker tryouts. Several news photographers there doing stories on the annual cattle call had captured the attack on camera and Jeff's picture had run on every wire service.

According to the police report, Jeff, though seated, had remained visibly erect throughout the entire arrest procedure. Off the record, one cop told her that they had tested his resolve by cuffing him to the chair, removing his pants, and leaving the room to watch him through the one-way mirror in the interrogation room. Her cop told her that he'd maintained his posture straight into the second shift, till they got sick of looking at him. No doubt, the cop said, there was plenty of holding going on in the holding cell that night.

Tucker leaned up against the corner and jiggled the change in his pocket. He wasn't sure how he felt about the photographs of overripe fruit that decorated Dr. Krebbing's waiting-room walls; it seemed as if the institutional aroma of buffed hallways and ecofriendly citrus-based disinfectant was being riven by the heavy scent of lurid, overabundant nectar. He walked over to the large picture of a half cantaloupe wrapped in plastic film. It looked like the kind of neglected take-out lunch he'd seen so often in office refrigerators—the dye from the maraschino cherry had leeched into the loose, runny scoop of cottage cheese and the gas and heat from the decaying melon had bloated the plastic wrapping. He followed his nose to the next photograph in the series, a bowl of mortifying peaches and coagulating cream. He leaned in to get a closer look at the yellow jacket wasp mounting the swollen hump of sliced peach and noticed minute crystals of sugar rimming its thorax.

"Excuse me," Jeff said. He looked down and noticed he'd been looming over a pretty young woman seated underneath the photograph. She lowered her magazine and said to his belt buckle. "They're weird, aren't they?"

Jeff looked down her dress, saying, "They're voluptuous; it's almost as if I can smell them." She crossed her legs, forcing Jeff back a bit and picked up the copy of the *Kinsey Journal* she'd been reading from off the chair next to her, smiling kittenishly. Jeff realized that she was the source of the fructuous odor and plunked himself down into the chair.

While she was telling him that she had arrived early for her appointment just so she could skip out of work, Jeff watched Caitlin's dress part over her thigh. Velda was curious to explore Tucker's erotic triggers. She wondered if it were the ballooning itself, or the foreknowledge that he would be apprehended that had brought about his priapsis. She was interested in creating some clinical trials that would help explain his motivation.

As a graduate student, she had studied under Dr. Kurt Friend, who had pioneered a clinical method of registering sexual arousal with his phallometric device. In the early days of the study, subjects would be brought into his small Atlanta clinic under police escort. The test subjects, usually young men culled by the young Velda from the city's jails, would be strapped, pantless, into a chair. Next, a glass tube would be placed over their penises. The device measured degrees of sexual arousal by detecting the amount of air displaced from the tube by their growing erections. Under the careful supervision of Dr. Friend, Velda would then engage in a series of progressively more perverse sexual activities, in order to calculate the subjects' level of sexual deviance.

For example, in order to determine if a test subject had latent homosexual tendencies, Velda would tie her hair back and hide it under the collar of a loose-fitting suit jacket. To approximate the typical gay liaison, the experiment was performed in a simulation of a public lavatory. First, Velda would stand in front of the urinal, with her back to the subject, and pretend to relieve herself. She would then pantomime the arrival of another man in the restroom by looking over to the urinal beside her. (Dr. Friend was unavailable to participate in these studies due to his advanced age.) She indicated her sexual availability to the imaginary other man by pretending to stroke her own (imaginary) penis and whispering "frontsies or backsies?" If the subject displayed no arousal, they would conclude the test and move on to the girls' school gymnasium trial.

If, however, enough air was displaced in the phallometer, Velda would pretend to accept the stranger's sexual advance by rubbing her behind with her hands in a circular motion. Then she unbuckled her pants and dropped them, along with her underpants (she wore men's briefs in order to maintain strict clinical objectivity). Gripping the flush mechanism of the urinal with both hands, Velda would say something like, "Bugger me, you big hairy brute," while wiggling her bottom in a masculine fashion. To simulate authentic homosexual penis-to-anus contact, Velda would use a phallic analog she kept concealed in her breast pocket. Lowering her voice to a heavy grunt, to suggest a larger man, she'd say, "Look what I got for you, sweetcheeks," and then gasp, "forgive me, Lord." She would then thrust and rethrust the phallic analog into her rectum forcefully while maintaining a dialogue of guttural "hmphf hmphf"s and squeaky "mercy, mercy"s If the subject ejaculated during this clinical trial, his semen was analyzed for homosexual tendencies by mixing it with another homosexual subject's semen and observing whether the sperm mingled or retreated to the side of the petri dish.

Velda's student days were behind her now and she had become director of the Friend Institute before she moved on to private practice. Though she was in her early fifties, she still had the same lithe figure of her youth. She swam regularly at the university pool and had, in fact, been for a quick twenty laps just after lunch. Since she had been in a rush for her next appointment, she'd stuffed her pantyhose and bra into her purse after her shower, thinking she'd find some time later to put them back on. Tucker's file had reminded her of the "good old days" and, despite herself, she found her fingers straying up her skirt and in between her legs. As she made quick little circles over her stiffening clit, her nipples, brushing against her blouse, swelled in concordance. Despite the fact that arousal clouded her concentration during therapy sessions, she found a certain degree of friskiness helped her empathize with her subjects. She opened her desk drawer and pulled out another diagnostic tool that Dr. Friend had made especially for her. Sigmund's Cigar, they'd playfully named it, and Velda used it to match her sexual stimulation to her clients' so that she could gain further insight into their particular pathologies.

Constructed in the pre-battery days, Sigmund's Cigar was attached by a pair of insulated wires to a transformer in her desk file drawer. When she used it at work, Velda was effectively leashed to the desk. It was a crude tool, but it was effective and had tremendous sentimental value. Turning its dial to a medium setting, she hiked her skirt up to mid-thigh and moved forward so her tailbone was resting on the edge of her chair. Then she used the Cigar to part her labial lips and rested the length of it over her clitoris. She slipped off her shoes and rubbed the soles of her feet on the carpet. As her toes curled, she slid the device up inside her. She turned it down to a low hum and sat as far back on her chair as it would allow her, then uncapped her pen and buzzed her receptionist. "Send in Mr. Tucker, please," she said.

Jeff noticed the boxes of Kleenex first, then the open box of surgical gloves centered at the front of her desk, where an executive pen and pencil set would typically be displayed. He sat down at one of the two chairs across from her desk and rose again to shake her hand. She sat back down awkwardly and appeared flushed. She was wearing a simple white blouse and her hair was twisted into a neat dancer's chignon. As she introduced herself, she swiveled in her chair and he found it hard to meet her gaze, since she was squinting with one eye while the whites showed all around the other's pupil.

"You understand why you're here, Mr. Tucker?"

"The judge said if I went to all of your sessions for a year, I would get parole and not have to do any time."

"Good, and I'm sure you realize that I'll be communicating with your parole officer after each of our meetings and reporting on your progress." The doctor paused and seemed to cross her eyes for a moment. She continued: "We're going to begin our session today with some preliminary testing. I'm going to show you a series of pictures and I'd like you to tell me what's happening in them. OK?"

Jeff said the two orangutans in the first picture looked like they were trying to remember something but they didn't know what. He said that the naked boy on the little potty chair looked like an orangutan. The boy and the girl holding hands and running through a field looked as if they were on a picnic. When he explained that the two pro wrestlers were actually friends and were faking it in the ring, she gasped. So he told her that the next one with two men kissing was probably just a couple of European guys. When he looked up, her eyes were rolled back and he asked her if she were all right. She told him, after biting her lip, that he should just pay attention to the pictures.

He said that the photo of the hanged man was a picture of an executed murderer. That the mule in the barn was probably just a pet. That the naked man and woman loved each other. When he said that the girls in leotards were on a high school gymnastics team, she flipped to a different set of photos and asked him to explain them. First came a woman in a old-style bikini who he said looked familiar—maybe she was a friend of his mother's. Then she flashed him a picture of a woman wearing a gas mask, thigh-high leather boots, and nothing else. All he said was, "Wow."

"What about her?" she asked, with clenched teeth. He looked at the photo of a young woman being spanked by an old man in a lab coat. He said she looked like she'd been a bad girl. "How bad?" she asked. "Does she need to be punished?" Jeff said he figured she'd been very naughty and deserved a spanking, at least.

Velda looked like she might be suppressing either

a giggle or a belch; along with pivoting her chair left and right, she rocked her chair back and forth. Jeff could see the upturned soles of her bare feet sticking out from under the desk. An aroma of flowery shampoo, chlorine, blood, and nectar filled the room. He didn't even need to look at the next picture to know it would be of her. The photograph was in color and it depicted Dr. Krebbing in an open lab smock teasing a nipple with one hand and covering her vagina with the other. She smiled at him and purred a little. "How about her?" she asked.

"I still thinks she looks naughty."

"Mr. Tucker, I think we can rule out latent homosexuality and pedophilia, as well as necrophilia. What I'm most concerned about are your sadistic tendencies." She paused, closing her eyes for several seconds. "I have one more battery of tests for you before you leave. I need to measure your level of arousal to a specific set of sexual criteria. OK?"

Jeff nodded.

"In order for you to do this you must relax. I want you to lean back in you chair and close your eyes. OK? Relaxed? Now I'm going to ask you to lower your pants and shorts. We'll have to keep a close eye on your phallic response to this situation." This wasn't a problem for Jeff, who rarely required much of a prompt to expose himself. "Good, Jeff. Now lastly, please hold your arms behind the chair, just like you did at the police station."

"You're not going to cuff me, are you?"

"No, not unless it becomes necessary." As Jeff slid his pants down, Velda pulled her skirt up. She was moments away from an orgasm and therefore in an ideal state to empathize with her client's arousal. She unbuttoned her shirt, climbed up onto the desk top, and told Jeff to open his eyes.

Jeff confirmed his suspicion that she was indeed the woman being spanked in the photograph. The bottom she had presented to him there on her hands and knees on the desk had grown a bit broader since the photo was taken, but the more the better, he figured. She was naked except for the skirt pulled up around her waist and a pair of wires leading from between her legs to her desk drawer. The insides of her thighs glistened.

"All right Jeff, whatever I do, don't touch yourself, got it? In order for this test to be objective, I need to observe your penile response without manual stimulation." Velda began to wag her bottom back and forth, all the while massaging her clitoris. Jeff found himself swaying back and forth, like a bird hypnotized by a cobra. "Jeff, describe what you see."

"I see a very naughty girl."

"What's she doing?"

"Begging for a spanking."

"Like this?" she said, and began slapping herself. She watched Jeff's penis swell till it reached his sternum. "Come help me, Jeff." Jeff stood behind her and slapped her. "No, Jeff, harder, louder, we have to see just what kind of a sadist you are." As he spanked her, she began to howl and the slaps echoed off the walls. "Yes, Jeff! Spank me!" she said.

Jeff was a bit shocked; he hadn't expected her to be such an exuberant clinician. "What about your other patient?"

Velda, whose bottom was as red as her face, was breathing in tiny gasps. Between shudders, she whispered, "Yes, of course, you're right. Hold on just a second." She punched the button on the intercom and yelled, "Caitlin, get the hell in here right now!"

MARYANN

Marc Levy

Martin saw the ad in a magazine, plucked from one of several tin boxes chained, "handcuffed," he had said to himself, to a traffic light on Seventh Avenue. He was in the habit of reading them, and kept a stack of fresh one-dollar bills in a desk drawer.

Insert your response in an envelope. Do not seal it. Put the box number you are responding to on the front of the envelope. Put a stamp on the envelope. Now place the envelope and two dollars into a second envelope. Seal the second envelope. Address it to City Singles, P. O. Box 4041 Ansonia Station, New York, NY 10025. Make sure

> you have placed sufficient postage on the second envelope. For multiple responses, repeat the above.

Martin was forty-four years old and straight but he read them all. Women Seeking Men, Men Seeking Men, Women Seeking Women, Couples, Anything Goes. Afterward, he would return to the straight section. On a good day he would think to himself, *Well, you never know.* On bad days he was less positive about himself. He scanned.

> SWF, 40s, attractive, well-traveled, successful, outgoing, literate, enjoys Bach to Bon Jovi, museums, art, theater, culture, seeks honest, caring, successful man for committed relationship. Note, photo, phone.

Too much for me to handle, he thought, and continued to finger down the line. The uncommon epithets, those with wit or clever wordplays sometimes made him laugh. Most often it was the odd or eccentric that attracted him. His favorite was, "Yeah, I know the drill. I am woman, I am strong. Lonely SJF, 46, seeks nice guy to fill a bowl of chicken soup for. Be sane and interesting. Got a job? Great! Let's meet!"

He thought of writing her, but the ad had disappeared the following month. Martin felt he had missed the opportunity of a lifetime.

"So far so bad," he said to the lead-painted walls. In five months he had moved six times since returning from a year's travel in Asia and Europe. Depressed and fragmented in the cramped and stuffy $300-a-month YMCA room, he realized it was the same as in '92, when he had traveled in Central America for several months. It had taken him a year to readjust. How was it that he could leave and travel, occasionally find himself in good company for extended periods of time, and then come back and *crash and burn?* Where had he heard the phrase? From a chopper pilot. After the war.

> Good news, Aquarius. Your moon is in transit with Mercury. This is a good time to invest in stocks and bonds. Or buy that new 4x4 Rover you've been eyeing. Your special powers of imagination are now working for you, Aquarius. This is a great time to communicate your innovative ideas to those special persons around you.

Martin settled back onto the dismal foam bed and laughed through the haze of his anxiety. "Who you kidding, man?" he said to the four plaster walls and brown wooden floor. The words echoed off the rusted footlocker two feet from his head. Outside, in the firetrap hallway, someone shouted street directions into the pay phone.

"Left, bitch. Two blocks south, then hang a damn

right. You got that? Bitch! 'Ho! You got it?" It was Larry the Crackhead speaking with his girlfriend.

The phone slammed down hard. A moment later coins dropped into the machine; a deep voice spoke softly, perhaps to a wife. There were fifteen transient men on the floor. After six weeks Martin had grown used to the human parade.

He turned the page and continued down the list of Women Seeking Men, reading just the first line of each ad.

"Let me be the chocolate icing on your thick fudge cake!"

"SWF vegan sex goddess seeks thick hunk of dark meat."

"SWCFNS seeks Clint Eastwood look-alike with Richard Nixon values for LTR."

He smirked. They were hilarious, flowed like poems, and took his mind off himself.

"The chocolate icing on your thick fudge cake," he mouthed, and tasted the wordplay.

Outside, Martin recognized the shuffling step of Jeremy the ex-Marine, intent on his evening toilette. Sixty pounds overweight, a chain smoker, the USMC bulldog tattoo still visible on his bloated arm, Jeremy collected welfare and visited his parole officer twice weekly.

Once Martin heard Jeremy talking to himself in front of the cracked mirrors over the communal sinks.

"Gonna make a good-looking corpse," he repeated over and over. He had fought in Korea. He drank.

Martin wanted to speak to him, another vet. Jeremy kept to himself.

Fucking Marines, Martin thought. *The Cav saved your ass beaucoup times*.

"Sexy senior seeks gentleman for the company of his pleasure."

"People say I have a lot to give but I give too much of myself."

Martin read on. Women were in search of white knights, candlelit dinners, and all life has to offer: ballet, sailing, opera, cats, mensch, hot times. He ran his finger once more over the black-and-white column of babble.

"...the company of his pleasure. You will not be disappointed."

He put the paper down, closed his eyes, recalled past encounters. Judy had written back immediately, she would be glad to meet him, once out of prison.

"The police pulled me over because of a broken tail light. When they opened the hood they found ten kilos. But it wasn't mine. Honest. Anyway, I'll be getting out soon and would really like to meet you, Martin. You sound *so* interesting." He'd thrown the scented letter and soft-porn photo into the garbage. Bonnie promised high heels and negligees, but when they spoke by phone she rattled off a list of unquaint conditions, including $200 each time they had sex.

"Well, no thanks," Martin had said.

"That's your choice," she had countered.

"Have a pleasant day," he rejoined, then hung up.

Ann from Canada sent a computer-generated letter, the dot matrix crotch shot poised above the following:

> I *really* want to meet you, Martin Berry, 1482 River Street, Tarrytown, New Jersey 10591 USA. But first I'd like you to see my very personal video, only $19.95 plus $4.95 for shipping and handling.

He had called the postal inspectors in both countries.

Once, three weeks before leaving the country for Central America, he wrote to a woman advertising in a literary magazine. "While the mouse is away the cat will play. Forties SWF has nine months alone while husband is on sabbatical. Seeking good lover." Martin expressed his desire to make love slowly; foreplay was most important. He had a fondness for standing in front of full-length mirrors and undressing women while he stood behind.

> I'll raise your skirt up and enter you, your breasts cupped in my hands. Would you like that? I'll kiss you everywhere. Where do you liked to be kissed? Afterward, when we're spent, I'll kiss you to sleep.

He sent off the note and forgot about it.

Her reply came ten days after the plane tickets for Guatemala arrived.

> Dear Martin,
>
> Of the forty-one responses I received, yours was the only one that was straightforward and to the point. I too enjoy lovemaking standing up, but seated as well, and standing face-to-face, and in the bath. Martin, I would love to see you. Please call me soon to arrange our first meeting.

He wondered what to do. Stay, and lose the chance to travel? She seemed sincere. He wrote her the truth and departed a week later.

Martin carefully circled the oblong box. Sexy senior. She can't be that old, he reassured himself.

Maryann called a week later. Her voice reminded him of cake sales and hand-knitted sweaters. They made small talk, chatted about the weather, music, their likes and dislikes, her garden, his travels.

"And what kind of work do you do, dear? To go to all those places?"

"Well, I get a pension from the Veteran's Administration."

"A government pension? Goodness! Were you wounded badly?"

"Yes," he lied.

"But you can, well, you know..."

"Make love?" Martin said to the older woman.

"Not that I..."

"Yes," he said, "I can do that."

There was a momentary pause.

"You're certainly welcome to drop by," she said flawlessly.

"I'd like to," said Martin, as calmly as possible.

"Three o'clock on the twentieth?" she asked. "You can take a cab from the train station in Crestwood. I'll pay for it, dear."

"Sure," he said. "I'll see you then." He gently hung up the phone. *Well, what have I got to lose?* he thought. *She can't be* that *old*.

Martin worked out extra hard for a week. Stretching and calisthenics. His body was trim. He weighed 155 pounds. Afterward, he would look at the war photo of himself taped to the wall. He could see no difference between then and now. It was a good shot, taken on patrol somewhere off Tay Ninh. He stood bent slightly forward, head tilted up, straining under the weight of his helmet and pack. The M-16 hung sideways, a stiff metal flag draped across his chest over three bandoleers of ammo, his aid bag, the .45, his canteens of water, the fragmentation grenades. He hadn't smiled, but looked directly into the camera, the angular features shock set and weary.

"Say cheese," Larry Roy the point man said. But he hadn't, and they were ambushed soon after. And Bill Williams had died. When Martin looked at the photo he cried.

Pools of sweat glistened on the wooden floor. Even the window had fogged up. He stepped out to shower, his face flushed, sweat streaming off his body from exercise in the cubicle room.

"What you up to, man?" Larry whined.

Martin looked directly at the pitiful human being; the endorphins generated from exercise always burnt a pleasant hole through his private agony.

"Fucking," he said, dead serious.

The communal shower was empty. The cold water felt good on his head and body.

"You're a sick motherfucker, man," the young addict shouted. "Sick, sick, sick."

The shrill words echoed and drowned in the chipped-tiled chamber. Martin grinned. The words rolled playfully off his tongue.

"The chocolate icing on your thick fudge cake."

He stepped out of the shower, toweled down, brushed his teeth. *Why was he doing this?* he wondered, though he secretly knew. Depressed and anxious, Martin saw himself incapable of all but the simplest of emotional encounters. Besides, since the war it had always been this way, only now the government gave him money for post-traumatic stress disorder. He recalled the exam through the fractured mirror.

"All I know is that I went back to Viet Nam last year and something snapped."

The psychiatrist had nodded curtly, raised his eyebrows with muted concern. Martin had burst into tears, then cried for the rest of the hour.

Well, he thought, thinking of his impending date, *at least it's a start*. As far as he could tell, she lived a few towns over, had money, and they were both discreetly horny.

He took the train from Grand Central, got off at Crestwood, walked down to the stationery store, bought a scratch-off lottery ticket, won three dollars, and hailed a cab.

"Thirty-two Lincoln Lane," he told the driver," his voice uplifted. "Where you from, man?"

"Haiti," the cabby said. The whites of his eyes flashed in the rear-view mirror, the afternoon sun absorbed into his dark brown skin.

"Haiti," Martin echoed. "You come over here before or after Papa Doc?"

"I left in the time of Baby Doc, my friend. It was hard. Very bad. I am here now many years. I have a house, a wife, children; the taxi, she's mine. For me that is enough. And you? Are you from Crestwood? I haven't seen you before."

"Tarrytown," Martin said. "Just visiting a friend."

"She's nice, Tarrytown, yes?"

"Can't complain. And Crestwood?"

"Oh, Crestwood, she's very nice. What number did you say?"

Martin looked out the window at the manicured lawns, the unfenced yards, the well-kept Tudor and neocolonial homes; felt the wealthy sway of the road.

"Thirty-two," he said.

"Yes, my friend. Twenty-eight, thirty, thirty-two she is." The driver glided to the curb of a large house with a red painted door.

"Here," Martin said, handing him a bill and stepping out before the man could give him change.

"Have a good afternoon," he said, and snapped the door smartly shut.

"Yes, a good afternoon," the driver said. He eyed the three-dollar tip, then sped off.

Maryann looked remarkably like the mother of a friend from college, which, he calculated, would make her roughly sixty-four. She was old. They sat at her living room table.

"Not too long," Martin said, in answer to how long the trip had taken. He noted her bronze-tinted hair, over-rouged cheeks, liver-spotted hands, the deep wrinkled lines of her face. Yet beneath the blue silk blouse, she had intriguing breasts. She was not very pretty, he thought, but at least...

Martin had not slept with a woman in nearly two years. He imagined how he would unbutton her, take the delicate cups of her breasts into his hands and mouth. He would close his eyes, suckle long and hard, recall other women, unfasten his pants, penetrate her as he had not done in so long. He suddenly recalled the Columbian prostitute in Amsterdam, where he first "crashed and burned" on the way home from his travels in Southeast Asia. They spoke in simple Spanish. About the price, what he wanted, and what he didn't: SIDA. He spoke to her easily, without shame. "I want sex first. Afterward, will you let me hold you? Will you hold me? That's all I want." She undressed, set her clothes on the back of a wooden chair, filled a plastic bowl with warm water; placed a yellow towel nearby. After a powerful orgasm, she let him fall asleep in her arms. His head spun less for hours.

Maryann said, "Let me show you around." She gestured to the rest of her home.

"The bedroom?" Martin said, surprising himself.

"Why, I hadn't really thought of that, dear, but, oh, why not?" she feigned. She offered her hand; he led her upstairs to the second floor of the spacious house.

"It's the second door on the left, dear."

They undressed quickly.

"What's wrong?" Maryann said, looking from his limpness to her parted legs. "Honestly, dear. Don't you like me?"

Martin looked at her splayed naked on the double bed. She was spindle-legged, her belly a cummerbund of fat; it was one thing to sit in the company of this older woman, quite another to have sex with her. Still, she had well-proportioned, near–Venus de Milo breasts. And it had been so fucking long.

Maryann rose, touched him, drew him near. For several minutes he lay with her, not moving. She stroked the back of his neck. *How did she know? That's all I want for now, old woman. Just keep doing that. I'll pay you. How much? Thirty guilders? OK, we'll do it, for God's sake. I'll probably explode. Let me hold you. Hold me. Hold me. That's all I want.*

She grew restless, trailed her fingertips up and down the length of his cock.

"Oh, dear," Maryann said, fondling his splendid erection. "Martin, please."

Martin paused to collect his thoughts, to dilute the anguish of his reply. She really *is* old, he thought, and looked at the white-and-gray spangled stubble brooding between her legs. In college the girls called him Mr. Hips, in awe of his churning loins. It was something he'd learned on R&R.

"Can you help me out a little?" he had asked the pretty young prostitute at the Five Star Hotel in Yokohama, Japan. "I've just come out of combat. I'm not sure I can, you know, do it."

She smiled, unzipped the black cocktail dress, removed the long-haired wig, counted his 30,000 yen, rapidly circled her hips clockwise, then counter-clockwise; and ground his virginity to a pulp.

"Me good fuck, G.I.," she yawned. He took a photo of her while she slept. The college girls went wild whenever he duplicated her technical sex.

Martin looked at Maryann. *Not in a million years, baby. Not in a million fucking years.* Still, her breasts were beautiful. *Oh, Christ.* He lay down next to her. It had been too long.

"Please, Martin, dear. Goodness, look how big you are. Don't you want to make love to me?"

"Like this?" Martin said. With startling ease he entered her, closed his eyes, performed.

They awoke two hours later. He thought of the time it would take to return to Tarrytown. Cab. Train. Walk up the hill. Go to the Chinese take-out next to the VFW hall. He would give them money.

"Buddhist Delight," he would say. They would give him food.

"Goodness, it's late," Maryann said. "Are you hungry, dear? I can fix you something to eat." She began to dress.

"Not yet," Martin said. He pulled her down beside him, nestled his head between her breasts, suckled ravenously, then softly kissed the perfect nipples, the aromatic cleavage.

"Oh, Martin, dear, it's ten o'clock. I have to work tomorrow. And I have to take my pills, you know. Can we make it another time? Shall we?" She slipped forty dollars on the night table. The sight of it made him uneasy.

"I'll call a cab," Martin said, letting her go. In the lamplight he imagined she was good-looking in her youth.

"You'll call me next week, dear?"

"Yes," Martin said. He put on his coat. Maryann hugged him before he walked out the door.

"Goodness, wherever did you learn to do it like that?" He felt her frailness push up against him. Was she reliving her youth? She was old enough to be—he would not admit it. He had fucked her and fallen asleep in her arms.

"The cab's here," he said. Eyes closed, he kissed her on the cheek.

"Get home safe, dear. Have a safe trip."

"Four dollah," the Chinese girl said, handing him the order.

"Chopstick?" he said. She always forgot.

"Soy sauce?"

"Just one, please." She tossed in three, plus a thimble of hot-and-spicy mustard and two of the sticky goo duck sauce. It was their nightly ritual.

"Good night," Martin said.

"Goo night, mistah," she always replied.

He went immediately to his room, wolfed the food down, slurped water from a cold water faucet in the bathroom, brushed his teeth, lay down on the foam bed, clicked the overhead light switch off, and drifted to uneasy sleep.

THE BIRTHDAY PARTY

Marilyn Jaye Lewis

I opened my eyes in the middle of the night and at first I thought I was dreaming.

Danny was there, standing next to the bed, shaking me gently.

"Get up, Louanne, I have a surprise for you," he was saying.

"What's going on, Danny? What time is it?"

"It doesn't matter what time it is. I have a surprise for you."

That's when I realized we weren't alone. There was someone else in the dark there with us.

"Who's here, Danny? What's going on?"

"Relax. It's that guy from the bar, remember?"

I remembered all right, but I wasn't sure he'd been serious.

"You've got to be kidding, Danny."

"Don't tell me you've changed your mind. He's totally into it, Louanne, and he doesn't even want the money."

"I'm more than happy to do it for free, honey. For a pretty girl like you."

I couldn't believe it when I heard his voice coming at me in the darkness. It was really happening. The only thing keeping me from my dream lover was my own nervousness.

"Don't be scared, Louanne," the voice continued. "I know exactly what you want. Danny told me all the details, right down to keeping the lights off."

I pulled the blankets around myself protectively and listened to my heart pound.

"Danny," I said quietly, barely able to get the words out, "I don't know."

"I'll be right here," he assured me. "It'll be perfect, the best birthday gift you could want."

"All right," I heard myself saying. "All right."

"Do you have the outfit? Can you find it in the dark?"

"I think I can."

"Do you want us to leave you alone while you get dressed?"

"No, Danny. Stay here. I'm afraid I'll change my mind."

The room grew incredibly quiet as I got out of bed and felt through the closet and dresser drawers in the dark. All I could hear was the two of them breathing.

I felt a little awkward dressing like that, like I was overdoing it; a black velvet gown and high heels, and my best pearls, all in the pitch blackness. I knew full well what was coming. I wasn't sure I could go through with it. I felt too vulnerable, yet kind of excited at the same time.

"I'm ready, Danny," I said at last, "but swear to me you'll keep the lights off."

"I swear, Louanne. I'll keep the lights off."

I sat down in the chair by the window and raised the blinds so that the dim moonlight could filter in. I smoothed down my full skirt and waited. It seemed like an eternity that I sat there with my heart pounding.

"Hey, birthday girl," he finally said. "You look pretty in the moonlight."

He was planted firmly in front of me. I was afraid to look up at his face for fear that I might see him too clearly and decide not to go through with it.

"Thank you," I said softly.

He knelt down in front of me then and carefully removed my high heels.

"These are awfully pretty," he said. "Probably expensive, huh?"

"A little," I replied, still unable to find the full power of my voice.

His hands were warm as they slipped under my long skirt and felt for the tops of my stockings. His fingers brushing against the exposed area of my thighs aroused me, and I couldn't help but part my legs. The crinoline lining of my dress rustled against him as he lowered first one of my stockings and then the other, sliding them off completely.

He reached around me and put my hands behind my back, tightly tying them with one of my stockings. As he knelt before me, his face even with mine, I could feel his breath and had to admit that he appealed to me. I couldn't help but look at him, at his shadowy presence in the darkness. He leaned over, pulled me close, and kissed my mouth, pushing his tongue in; his hands pulled down the front of my strapless gown and exposed my breasts.

He kissed me for a long time, his tongue filling my mouth while his hands squeezed my breasts and tugged at my nipples. He was almost too rough; he was making me moan.

Suddenly he collected himself.

He stood and made me scoot off the chair. "Get on your knees," he said.

Danny abruptly lit a cigarette and the match light seemed blinding.

"Danny!" I cried, startled.

"Sorry," he said urgently. "I'm sorry, keep going, Louanne."

The sudden burst of flame in the dark had unsettled me. It had lasted just long enough for me to catch a good look at myself, on my knees, my most expensive dress tugged down to expose my breasts, my hands tied behind me. Thankfully the darkness returned before I'd had a chance to see the guy looking down at me. That might have made me change my mind altogether.

Instead we kept going.

The man unzipped his jeans and his erection sprang out full and hard. He grabbed my hair and guided my face to his cock. It felt warm.

"Go on," he said. "Kiss it all over."

I did as I was told, almost overcome with lust. I pretended I didn't have a choice, that this good-looking stranger from the bar was overpowering me, forcing me to kiss the length of his erect cock.

"That's good, that's right," he said. "Lick it. I want to feel your tongue. Go all the way down to my balls.

Oh, birthday girl, that's good. Now come back up and circle the head."

I couldn't believe he was playing his part so perfectly. As he held tight to my hair he said, "take it now, suck my dick"; then he drove his shaft in and out of my mouth feverishly. I tried to keep my balance in front of him, but I was unsteady on my knees, my hands too securely tied behind my back. Once or twice it seemed the only thing keeping me upright was his grip on my hair. My jaw was starting to ache and the spit was collecting in my mouth. He was pumping into me hard, not giving me a chance to swallow.

Finally he helped me up and led me over to the bed, where Danny was sitting, quietly smoking in the dark. The man tossed me face down on the mattress, but he wasn't too rough. Right away his hands were under my skirt, tugging my panties down. I was so wet that when my panties came down I felt unusually exposed. When they were off completely, he wedged some pillows under me to raise my ass in the air. He shoved my dress up until I could feel the rough hem against my bare shoulders. He spread my thighs as wide as they would go.

"Oh, God," I moaned softly when I felt his mouth on me.

"Birthday girl, you are so wet. You must be having a really good time."

His hands spread my swollen lips completely open and his tongue darted all over my engorged clit. He licked me thoroughly, even burrowing his tongue deep into my soaking hole.

Danny put out his cigarette. He knelt in front of me on the bed and undid his jeans. He took his erection out and slid it into my mouth; the position hurt my neck a little bit.

I sucked him eagerly, though, while the other guy kept licking my dripping pussy; while he pressed his face flush against my mound and jammed his tongue down into my hole, his strong hands keeping my thighs spread wide. I could tell it had been a while since he'd shaved, but the friction felt good on my engorged lips and when he started to groan I squirmed against his face.

"Louanne," Danny was saying as he worked his dick in and out of my mouth, "you look so pretty like this, so hot. Spread out and wiggling your little ass, you look like you want to get fucked, you know that? You want to get fucked, Louanne? You want a hard dick in your hot little hole?"

I was moaning crazily while I sucked Danny's cock, but my hands were still tied behind me and I had no choice, I had to go at the pace they chose.

"He looks to me like he might be ready," Danny

continued. "You want to get fucked now, Louanne? You want to get fucked really hard?"

Danny lifted my head then. "What do you say, birthday girl?"

"Yes," I said. "I do. I want to get fucked really hard, Danny."

Then I heard the guy get off the bed. I assumed he was getting undressed. In an instant he was back, his thighs were slipping under my thighs to steady himself, and he grasped my ankles tight, forcing my legs farther apart. Then he pushed his dick into my hole. He was substantially endowed. The full length of his cock going into my vagina made me cry out. He pumped into me hard and deep, and all I could do was lay there—with my ass propped up on the pillows for him, my ankles pinned to the bed—and take the full measure of his force all the way in.

Danny was back at my mouth, going at me in a brisk rhythm. I knew he was ready to come.

"Jesus," he was chanting, clutching my hair. "Jesus, Louanne."

I was whimpering and carrying on from the force of that cock thrusting into me from behind. Danny jerked against my face hard and started to come down my throat.

When Danny had finished, he scooted aside, lit

another cigarette, and watched me get nailed in the moonlight. I really started to sputter and cry then. The harder and deeper the guy fucked me, the better it felt.

"Oh, God," I was crying, as he pounded away at me until my spread legs ached and I thought he would never come.

When he finally did, I felt embarrassed. Everyone was coming down to earth again quickly and I realized I didn't even know the guy's name.

"That was really fun," he said while he started to put on his clothes. But when he moved to untie my hands, Danny intervened.

"Don't," Danny said. "Leave them tied just a little longer."

"Why?" I wanted to know. "What's going on?"

"It's well after midnight," Danny explained. "We're deep into the birthday zone."

"Danny, no," I protested, knowing him too well.

"Come on, be a good girl."

"Danny, no, I mean it."

Danny ignored my half-hearted pleas and told the guy to sit back down on the bed.

"She's already got on her prettiest party dress," Danny told him. "It's a shame not to give her her birthday spanking, too."

The guy seemed more than delighted to oblige Danny. He shifted me over his knee and raised my skirt while I struggled lamely to squirm away. "Come on," he said, slapping my naked ass. "You're a big girl. You can take it, Louanne. The pain won't last too long."

"That's what you think," Danny laughed as he leaned against the headboard and relaxed in the dark. "Wait'll you hear how old she is."

THAT ALICE NEEL SMILE

Tsaurah Litzky

She remembered going to an art gallery one time and seeing a portrait that the painter Alice Neel had done of herself nude at the age of fifty. Alice Neel was overweight. Her skin was stark white like library paste, with none of the rose and gold tones that accompany desire. Her breasts hung down like bags. Her pudenda sagged; her pubic hair was gray and sparse. The artist was standing in what looked like a living room, gazing directly out of the canvas. Her lipstick was bright red. She was holding a cigarette and smiling, joyous in her aging body, happy to be alive.

Regarding herself in the full-length mirror on her bathroom door, Babette tried to duplicate that Alice Neel smile but the face that looked back at her was bitter. She had not noticed before how pronounced the furrows on her forehead were and the lines that had formed from the edge of her nostrils to the corners of her mouth made her already-too-prominent nose look larger. In the months before they had split up, her husband had started to call her "banana nose." In retaliation she had called him "limp dick" because he would no longer have sex with her. Contrary to what she had hoped, this did not wound him; instead, he just laughed in her face.

She studied her breasts; they were definitely traveling south. Her nipples were large and had once been chocolate-colored but had paled to pink. She couldn't tell if her pudenda sagged because her pubic thatch was still black and thick. In his kinder moments, her husband used to call it her garden. She still masturbated to the vision of his big, gnarly, pink dick plunging in and out of her, stirring the earth inside of her. The memory was making her wet right now. She put her finger inside herself, then put it in her mouth and tasted it. Her juice was bitter and sticky but she sucked it down, wet her finger with saliva, and stuck it between her legs. She lubed her asshole with her spit, then turned to look at her ass.

She pulled her asscheeks apart to show her anus, still a tight little flower in spite of all the times her husband had buggered her there. At least her ass did not show the ravages of age; it was high, full, fleshy, and firm. The thought made Babette smile. She didn't look bad at all, she decided. She looked kind of pretty in a vintage Simone Signoret way. There was a caper or two left in her; she still remembered all the moves. She thought about seducing the only male student in her "How to Write Romantic Poetry" class. He had a sweet face, but with her luck she would probably get caught and lose her job. She made a conscious decision to be optimistic—you never know what destiny will bring your way. She decided to allow herself a generous glass of scotch, toasting destiny with each sip. Once happily tipsy, she climbed under the covers, picked up the book she was reading, *The Queen and the Beggar Boy*, and read herself to sleep.

She woke up feeling zesty even though it was a gray, cloudy day. She got out of bed and went to the toilet for her morning pee but when she flushed, a jet of pissy water shot out of the pipe that connected the john to the wall. This had happened before, and it meant that the drycap screwbob needed a new washer and the wingbat dingslip had to be tightened. She called her landlord, but his secretary said that he was in Switzer-land taking the radish cure and would not be back until he had lost sixty pounds and that she, the secretary, was not allowed to authorize any repairs. When Babette got off the phone she realized she could probably fix it herself, but she would have to buy a wrench plus the new washer and money was, as always, tight.

When she went to bed that night, she prayed for a plumber angel to descend from the heavens while she was sleeping and fix the toilet by waving his wings over it. However, when she used the toilet the next morning the leak had worsened so much that water covered the whole bathroom floor. As she mopped it up with her worn-to-shreds old sponge mop she thought: *So much for the power of prayer.*

She would have to try to repair the stinky thing herself; she could not afford a plumber. It was gray and overcast outside and she decided to dress up a bit, wear her new leopardskin minidress to cheer herself. Who knows? In the five blocks between her building and the hardware store, some lost French jazz musician driving by in a Mercedes might stop to ask her directions and admire her dress so much that he would invite her for a drink.

When she got to Barney's Cut-Rate Hardware Store,

Barney, who had been selling her nails, Lysol, gizmos, and spider traps for fifteen years, was nowhere to be seen. Maybe he was in the back of the store stocking the shelves or wanking himself. He was a bald sixty-year-old bachelor who looked as if he did a lot of wanking.

"Barney," she called out. There was a noise from the back of the shop and a slim figure half Barney's bulk came down the center aisle.

"Can I help you?" he asked. He took a step back, looked her up and down, and then ever-so-faintly licked his lips.

"Well," he said.

"Where's Barney? What's going on?" Babette replied, feeling disconcerted by his frankly appreciative stare.

"He's getting false teeth," he told her. "I'm his nephew, Kerry, down from Alaska."

He was quite cunning, this Kerry, with jet-black hair, eyes blue as hope, and a body that was thin and edgy, standing straight as a blade. "Hi," she said, noticing he had large, toughened workman's hands with big thumbs.

"How can I help you?" he asked again, but this time his voice was soft, almost tender.

"I need a washer for a drycap screwbob and a wrench to tighten a wingbat dingslip," she said.

"Anything to oblige a lady," he answered. Bowing slightly from the waist, he motioned for Babette to precede him up the aisle. She felt his eyes on her back and wondered if he was rubbing his crotch, but she couldn't summon the nerve to turn and find out. Feeling very conscious of her big, bouncy ass moving under her short dress, she suddenly felt a gentle patting, a few taps on the left side of her bum; suddenly her whole asscheek was seized in his big, hot hand. She was surprised; she didn't know what to do. As soon as she had seen those hands she had known she wanted them on her ass, but so soon? She had read in *Elle* that it was always better to play hard to get, but she really wasn't the *Elle* type—she was happy when she got the attention of any interesting, attractive guy. All the same, she wasn't sure she wanted to succumb to Kerry then and there, in aisle two, between the nuts and bolts section and the assorted screws. She swirled around to face him.

"Look," she said in a cool, dignified voice she didn't know she possessed, "aren't you being kind of—"

He supplied her with the word. "Fresh? I couldn't help myself. Besides, where I'm from, when a man sees what he wants he claims his territory."

This sounded so ludicrous that she was hardly sure she had heard him correctly, but then he stepped back and flashed her a 24-karat smile and she realized he was, if astonishingly naive, at least sincere. She felt her cunt grow moist and had to force her eyes away from the big lump between his legs, a lump that looked as if it were about to split the seam of his jeans. Suddenly he said something even more surprising. "I'm sorry if I shocked you. Do you want to go out, maybe for a drink and to a movie?"

She thought perhaps that she had stumbled into the promised land but she was quickly called back to the real world because right then some big guy in army fatigues and a hard hat came walking down the aisle towards them.

"I need some cement mix," he called out.

"Be right there," Kerry said. He quickly got her the drycap screwbob and wrench and they went back to the front of the store. Once at the register, she took her wallet from her purse and fished out a fiver to pay him. He waved the bill away. "Don't offend me," he said. When she handed her card to him, he grabbed her hand and kissed it. The guy in the fatigues and hard hat rolled his eyes. "Very cute, you two," he said. "But how about my cement mix?"

When she got home she put the washer Kerry had given her on the drycap screwbob; using the wrench he had supplied, she tightened the wingbat dingslip.

She flushed and nary a drop leaked from anywhere. She wondered if Kerry was as efficient at everything he did; then she allowed herself to hope he would call her soon. She got out her romantic poetry class homework poems to review but found she couldn't focus. She kept pausing, listening for the phone. She started to think about what she wanted to do with Kerry. Everything seemed beyond the pale. She wanted to tie his wrists with her Wonder Bra and spank him with her tits. She wanted him to take her doggy-style in the park during the day when someone might see them. She hadn't even known him for a full day and already she was totally obsessed; this was dangerous. She decided to go out, take a walk, go up to the library, maybe pick up a book.

At the library, she perused the self-help section but nothing interested her very much so she wandered into biography. She was about to take Joan Collins' autobiography, *Forever 22*, off the shelf, but a tiny, wizened woman who looked like Bart Simpson darted in front of her and grabbed it first. Then she saw a book called *Originals: American Woman Artists*. She took it over to a reading table and turned to a chapter on Alice Neel. Apparently, Alice Neel hadn't had an easy time of it: she had had a series of mental breakdowns in her teens, then had married a jealous overbearing husband who, when they split, had won custody of their kids. Then she had taken a string of exotic, unrewarding lovers.

Alice Neel and I are kindred spirits, Babette thought, reading on. One guy, a cokehead sailor, suspecting she was carrying on with someone else, burned her drawings and paintings, more than three thousand in all. Somehow Alice Neel picked up the pieces, moved to Harlem, and started over again. Eventually she had two sons by two different men, both of whom wanted to marry her, but she refused. Finally, when she was in her sixties, she had a big show at the Whitney and got the recognition she deserved. On the last page of the chapter appeared a painting of Alice Neel as an old woman. She was naked, with red lipstick on, smiling and smoking a cigarette. Next to the picture was a quote: "I only wanted to paint. Who knows why anyone wants anything? Whatever you want, whatever you're doing, be true to yourself, and always move forward."

Babette thought about her own jealous, overbearing husband, all those times she had come home unexpectedly to find him going through her appointment book. He had said he had a stomachache and was looking for the number of their family doctor, but she knew she was his stomachache and he was looking for appointments he imagined she had with other men.

She was surprised to find it was already dark out when she left the library. *It must be after 6:00*, she thought, which meant that Barney's Cut-Rate would be closed. She quickened her pace, thinking maybe Kerry had called and there would be a message on her answering machine. She was right. The little red light was blinking merrily on and off. Her breath caught in her throat as she pressed the playback button. She wondered what he would say, wanted to hear him pronounce her name. However, her husband's voice came floating out of the machine instead. "I've been thinking about you a lot," he said. "I can't stop thinking about you. I miss you; I've been selfish, a fool. Can we meet and talk, maybe tonight, tomorrow, very soon? Please call me." She used to love his voice: he had lived his first ten years in Dublin and had the faintest hint of a brogue. When it got rough between them his voice lost its appeal: he would yell and use his voice to bludgeon her.

"Get off your fat, lazy ass," he'd shout. "The kitchen's a mess."

"If it bothers you, clean it up," she'd retort and, going to her workroom, put her earplugs in and turn on the computer. At night his mood would turn again;

coming fresh from his shower, he'd jump damp and fragrant with cologne into their bed. He'd pull the covers up over them and bend his head to lick her toes; then he'd kiss her feet, her ankles, all the way up her legs to the tender fissure between. Since he'd left he'd always been in her head. She realized with a little shock that she hadn't thought of him at all since she saw Kerry coming down the aisle towards her in the hardware store. Now he was back in her head again. The phone rang again, startling her out of her memories. She answered it.

"Hello," a deep voice said. It took her a minute to realize it was Kerry.

"Er, hello," she said,

"How are you?" His voice was merry, a smiling voice. "Did the wrench work all right?"

"Yes, thanks, it worked fine."

"I was wondering," he said, "are you free for dinner tonight? Barney told me about this Italian place on Willoughby Street. What do you say, will you go out with me?"

"Yes," she said. "OK."

"That's great," he boomed into the phone. Giving him directions to her place, she told him to come at 8:00. "I can't wait to see you again," he said, then hung up.

She decided to wear her short, black, leather miniskirt and her pink V-neck sweater, with black tights and black cowboy boots. She went into the shower and stayed there a long time. A vision of her husband's face, the way it looked after they had sex, flushed and rosy like the face of a boy, kept flashing across her mind, but she struggled to push it out.

She was ready by 7:45. Her sweater was bright mauve, the color of her vulva; that was why she had chosen it. She hadn't been out to dinner with a man in a very long while. She checked herself in the mirror. Not bad. She practiced smiling, trying to smile a wide-open, all-across-the-face smile while not crinkling up her eyes. He knocked at her door at 8:00 precisely. She put the smile on her face and opened the door. He was wearing a gray suit with a plaid flannel shirt and a red tie, and his dark hair was slicked down with pomade. He looked like a cross between Rudolph Valentino and James Dean. His huge hand, holding out to her a single, perfect red rose, trembled slightly. She realized he was nervous.

"Thank you," she said, taking the rose. "Come in, sit down, you look great. Do you want a drink?" she said in one breath. She was nervous, too. He looked around. He must have approved of her Salvation Army decor because he said, "I like it here," and sat down in the big white wicker rocker her husband always sat in.

"I only have vodka. Is that OK?"

He nodded and smiled. "That's what I drink," he said. While she put the rose in a Poland Spring water bottle and poured their drinks, she could feel his eyes on her. As if he could read her mind he said, "I love watching you move." She had never known a man who expressed his admiration so directly. Maybe they were all like that in Alaska—or maybe he was one in a million. Or maybe she had finally flipped out and this was one long hallucination brought on by her masturbation marathons.

"Are you a dream?" she asked him as she set their drinks on the table and took the straightbacked chair beside him.

"You're the dream," he said, raising his glass. "To Barney's Cut-Rate," he said.

They clinked glasses and drank. He took her hand, brought it to his lips, kissed her palm, and traced her lifeline with his tongue. She could always tell as soon as a man kissed her if the fucking would be all right, and his kiss was so all right it pulled her off her chair and into his lap. He was gentle at first, then became more insistent, his mouth pressing her mouth open, breathing into her, their mouths forming a congruent "O." She felt her other mouth moisten and open, and he seemed to know this had happened, which made her feel sexier than she had felt in a long time.

"Give me your tongue," he whispered. When she ventured it, probing past his lips, he sucked her tongue in like it was sweet candy. Then he put his big hand down the V of her sweater and cupped her tit. With his thumb and index finger he found her nipple and gently pulled. How did he know this was the way to make her heart sing? His touch on her breast filled her with sudden passion. She started to fumble with the snap above his zipper.

"No, let me," he said, and he picked her up by her elbows and sat her back on the chair. He stood up, unzipped his fly, let his trousers fall to the floor. There he was, uncut, pointing due north: the pride of Alaska.

"Are you ready for me now?" he said. She loved it that he had asked her and she nodded her head yes.

"Let me look at you," he said. He knelt before her, pulled off her boots, her tights. He parted her thighs with his big, hot hands and gazed inside of her. She wanted him so much that she started to grab him and pull him into her but then she remembered something.

"Condom?" she asked.

"Yes," he replied, and he leaned down and took a package out of the pocket of his pants. She took it from him, ripped it open, and shook out the condom. Putting it in her mouth, she slid it on using a trick she had learned from a book she had mail-ordered, *The New Love Without Fear*.

"I love it that you can do that," he said, pulling her out of the chair and right up onto him.

She was so wet inside she felt like a river. She put her arms around his back and they moved together gracefully. It was so easy she started to laugh; they were swimming together, and a few short strokes was all it took to get them home. After it was over, he leaned back in the chair and hugged her to his chest. He was stroking her hair with great tenderness when she heard footsteps in the hall and then three sharp, loud knocks on her door.

"Who's that?" Kerry asked.

She said nothing, struck dumb, knowing exactly who it was.

"Hello! Are you in there? Your lights are on. I can see under the door," her husband said.

Afraid of what he might say next, she called out, "I'm busy now, go away."

"All right, but call me," he shouted through the door. His steps faded away down the hall. Kerry's prick had grown quite small; it slipped out of her, falling disappointed between his thick, round balls.

"What was that?" Kerry asked, his brow furrowed, his voice worried. She thought about saying, "Just a neighbor." She thought about sprouting wings and flying up through the roof into the night sky. She fished around for a believable lie and all the while a little voice inside mocked her, whispering: *Bye-bye Kerry, bye-bye Kerry*. She didn't want to lie to this man. She remembered Alice Neel saying, *Be true to yourself*, so she told him. She told Kerry that the man outside the door was her husband; she told him about their happiness, their alienation, their fights, their final separation.

Kerry listened, looking down. They were seated across from each other now, the red rose in the Poland Spring bottle standing between them like a referee. Finally he raised his face, looked her in the eye.

"But why no divorce yet?" he asked.

She was silent then, trying to get the answer right. After a few minutes she said, "I guess I wasn't ready to let go."

"But now?" he asked.

Alice Neel's words came into her head. *Always go forward*.

"I want to," Babette said. "I want you."

He kept looking at her. "I don't know," he said, shaking his head.

"Please believe me," Babette said, hating the begging tone in her voice. He didn't answer; she felt as if he were going far away. She was about to get down on her knees before him, but then he leaned over and kissed her.

"OK," he said. "We'll see."

ALICE

Anaïs Nin

I used to meet her at dances during the winter. She was a wonderful dancer and a little beauty. Needless to say, holding her in my arms in dancing made me wish to know her better. It was not long before little pressures of hands and arms were asking and answering unspoken questions. Without a word said, she let me know that some day she would consent to more.

Later, in the spring, we used to go walking together in the hills on pleasant afternoons. We would drive out into the country, hide the car somewhere on a quiet road, and wander off into the fresh green woods. We were fond of a most secluded little glade which we found one day, where we often rested sure of being undisturbed. But Alice, though generous with kisses and dear little caresses, entirely withheld herself otherwise, and I was entirely too fond of her, and too interested in discovering under what circumstances she would give herself, to press the matter beyond showing her clearly what I wanted. She quite understood, all the time, and I knew it was only a question of time until she would be brought to the point of giving me all that I asked.

Her surrender came under the unusual circumstances which I am about to describe. One lovely, warm afternoon in May we found our way to our little glade, but were very much surprised to find two other young lovers there before us. Totally engaged in each other, they did not hear us, and we stealthily withdrew a little distance and sat down in a little pocket among the bushes to see what would happen. Alice, I could easily see, was very much excited and interested.

The girl was lying on her back in the shade of a tree. The man lay beside her, and their lips were together. We could hear the indistinct murmur of their voices. Hunched up as we two were in our little hiding-place, quite close together, I did not find it hard, nor think it wrong, to put my lips to Alice's.

Alice clearly thought my conduct fitting, for she returned my kiss, with interest. The interest was paid in a tiny flutter of her tongue-tip against my lips. Our kiss lasted quite a time.

When we looked again, the scene had changed somewhat. Alice gasped a little, and well she might. The lover was lying on one side, propped up on an elbow, and his free hand was disturbing the formerly smooth folds of his sweetheart's skirt. Perhaps to keep her attention from what his hand was doing—at any rate, to keep her attention divided—he was kissing her quite ardently. But his hand was under her skirt and had pulled it up so that we could see two shapely legs in pale blue stockings. Two small feet in pale blue slippers (very unsuitable for walking in the hills) were calmly crossed. The lover was caressing the pale blue stockings.

"Peter," whispered Alice, remonstrating. For as she crouched, somewhat curled up, one very attractive leg, as far as the knee, lay outside of the shelter of her skirt, and my hand rested on the dark green silk that covered it. But her attention must have been distracted, for after that one remonstrance she leaned forward, her eyes intent on what she might see, while my hand enjoyed the delightful touch of green silk stretched over a beautifully modeled leg.

I turned from admiring the contours of the dark green leg to see what was happening to the pale blue ones. My hand, not being needed to see with, stayed where it was most comfortable. The blue legs had become most interesting. The skirt had been moved still more—the length of the blue stockings was now measurable. Not far above the knee they ended, and considerable was to be seen of two plump, white thighs, with the hand of the lover tenderly touching and stroking them. The pale blue slippers now lay side by side, and the girl's two arms, while her legs were being so lovingly caressed, were tight about the neck of her lover, holding his face to hers for kisses.

"Peter!" warned Alice again, in a tense whisper. For somehow, when I turned my eyes from the pretty green leg, my hand, left to its own resources without the guiding eye, had wandered somewhat; in fact, had strayed beyond the green stocking and was thrilling to the touch of soft, warm flesh. Alice stirred a bit, as if impatient, but it was satisfying to note that, in so doing, she thrust her legs still further from under her skirt. On looking to see what change her new attitude had effected, I was overjoyed to see that right close at hand there was a most enticing bit of plump, white thigh for me to appreciate. Close at hand, indeed; my hand made haste to embrace its opportunity, in fact to grasp at the unseen, as it felt its unhindered way to discover yet undiscovered pleasures to the touch.

"Pete, look—" whispered Alice again. And we looked. Not fifteen feet away the other pair, unsuspecting still, pursued their own amusement. The girl had moved—her skirt was drawn clear above her waist; her legs were all exposed, and her hips as well. Quite evidently the young lady had worn no panties or drawers! The young lover was sitting up, fussing with his clothing, his eyes enjoying a vision of loveliness. Those two pretty legs were slightly parted now, and such a dear little nest of hair was seen.

"Oh, Pete!" Alice gasped this time. For as the man's clothing was released, his sweetheart's hand reached out and took hold of something. The lover stretched out an instant, wriggled, and one bare manly leg came out of his trousers—bare, that is, except for shoe and sock and red garter. This bare leg was then placed across another bare leg, the man's between the woman's two, the woman's between the man's and, satisfied with this arrangement, the lover lay upon his sweetheart, his arms about her, hers about him. They moved delicately, as if rubbing on each other.

I had found Alice's hand and by placing it in a certain position I showed her that I, too, had something which might be held, should her hand care to hold it. Soon, indeed, she was holding it, and by playing with it as if absent-mindedly she caused me no little pleasure. But she could not remove her eyes from the scene before us.

We could hear soft cooing and murmurs. Alice and I ceased to regard the others for a time. She came somehow closer into my arms, lay quite heavily there, in fact, and in so placing herself managed to arrange her clothing so that both her legs lay bare. To my real surprise, Alice too was guiltless of wearing drawers or panties. Much reassured, I let my hands move freely over the delicious surfaces of her thighs and hips. Our lips were fast together, and now I learned how Alice could kiss when really interested. When my hand in its wanderings encountered certain soft curls, her lips and her tongue assailed me with a quite impetuous ardor.

But curiosity drew my eyes again to the other lovers. "Look, Alice!" I whispered to her, and as we looked our hands became very busy and our eyes drank in a most lascivious sight. Side by side now, the girl and her man were sitting, all outer clothing removed from their waists down, and the girl had further so opened her blouse that the dainty breasts hung out. With one arm each embraced the other, and their lips were crushed together. With their free hands they were playing with the most delicious playthings that the hands of man and of woman can touch. The man's hand was moving between his sweetheart's parted legs, the girl's hand held something hard and stiff, which she manipulated gently.

"Oo-oo-oh!" gasped Alice, and fell to kissing me wildly. Needless to say, I kissed wildly back. Her hand held something hard and stiff, and her treatment of it was as skillful as it was delicious. My hand was between her lovely legs, and the manner in which she received its ministrations showed that I had not forgotten how to play upon that organ which, if properly touched, causes a woman's body to re-echo with most delicious harmony.

Alice had at last abandoned her reserve, her withholding of herself. The discovery that she had worn no drawers gave me reason to suspect that this day she had intended from the start to give herself to me before our return. But as a matter of fact, I had no knowledge based on proof of any kind that she ever had worn drawers, when with me or at any time. As a rule, women wore drawers, or panties, or leg-covering of that general character—women in Alice's status in society, at any rate. This I knew from having seen them, from having removed them, in fact, on other and different occasions. It was not, therefore, an altogether unnatural assumption on my part that, under ordinary circumstances, Alice wore them also, and that she did not wear them this day because she had intended to be more than ordinarily gracious and complacent to me.

However, this is all a digression—Alice wore no drawers, and her very lovely naked thighs lay exposed to my hands and eyes. But her intentions towards me were shown even more clearly now by her conduct. Somehow, at some time, Alice had had experience. She had learned how to be charmingly wanton without being shameless. Her kisses were delights of art and skill, her movements were delicate and yet effective, her grip on what her fair hand held was possessive without being painful, and her handling of it, without being obtrusive, was obviously intended ultimately to bring it between her legs.

"Pete, darling, look there!" Alice whispered between her kisses. Our lovers were at last in earnest, the man lying between the girl's legs, which were embracing and holding him while he moved with vigorous thrusts of his hips. "Peter!" cooed Alice, and "Alice!" I cooed back—and somehow her weight was upon me, her legs spread far apart, and she took me into herself.

In the course of time we sat up again and looked

about. The other pair were sitting up, smiling at us. We were discovered! In our excitement we had moved so that our former shelter no longer concealed us. Either she was accustomed to intimate acts of love with others—which I really do not believe—or else she saw at once that we must make the best of the situation and, perhaps, improve it. At any rate, she laughed quite gaily and stood up, shaking her skirt down to where it belonged. I stood up, too, but not so easily, as my trousers needed attention.

The other man called out, "What luck?" "Fine," I said, "a bull's–eye!" Alice laughed again. "Same here," he answered, stepping nearer, "my name's Bill." "Mine's Pete." And we shook hands. "Gladys," said Bill, "here's Pete and Alice—come and get acquainted." So, all introduced, we sat down, Bill and Gladys on either side of me, and Alice on the other side of Bill. We talked a bit, about anything but the events of the past hour. After a time conversation waned. Bill was whispering to Alice, so I began to whisper to Gladys. What I said was of no importance to the other two, but it made Gladys laugh, with her eyes shining. Furthermore, she put out her hand to see if what I had told her was true. Finding that it was, she seemed satisfied and lay back, smiling enticingly. Somehow I found that I was embracing her naked legs. Bill did not seem to care—he was doing the same to Alice!

It was most interesting, to play this way with another man's sweetheart while the other man played with mine. There lay Alice, who had just given me a delicious half-hour, doing the same for Bill, and believe me, I knew that Bill was lucky! And here lay Gladys, giving herself to my caresses as she had given herself to Bill not long before—and believe me, I soon knew that both Bill and I were lucky, twice!

Gladys was not so voluptuously formed as Alice, but she knew her part and made every little movement have just the meaning that it should. Her little breasts were just as satisfactory to my hands and lips as Alice's fuller ones, and she responded just as delightfully to the skillful touch of my fingers. She was all woman, and ended by giving me a most glorious moment as I scored another bull's-eye. Unless all familiar signs failed, Gladys received as much pleasure from my success as I did. Bill scored his second center shot almost at the same time. Both girls were flushed and radiant.

"Bill's bigger," confided Alice in a whisper as she nestled up against me, "but he hasn't your finesse, Peter darling. But it was wonderful to get that twice—oo-oo-oh!" Gladys was whispering to Bill, and I heard his heavier voice whisper back, "I'm glad you liked it, honey"—so I guessed that Gladys told him she had been pleased.

Bill produced some liquid refreshment. I don't drink much, but it was awfully good whiskey, and the little glass went around among the four of us several times. The girls got just a little drunk, and I began to get interested. There is something about taking a girl who is just a little bit intoxicated that is most fascinating. Even the ardent ones become just a bit more so, and the movements of a girl on the way to becoming drunk are most wanton.

It wasn't so very long before all of us, stimulated a bit, were huddled in a most intimate group. The girls lay all over us two men and kissed us with wet lips. We fondled them and kissed them, on the lips and on the nipples of their breasts, which they had left bare. The whiskey and these caresses soon had their effect. "Pete, what's that?" Alice exclaimed, and made her eyes round with mocking amazement. For there it was again, as large as ever! "Gladys, see what I found, see what I found!" Alice called, as she unfastened my trousers and held her discovery in her hand. Without a word, Gladys unbuttoned Bill and took out what she found. No doubt about it, Bill's was bigger. But the girls were each satisfied—I know we all four laughed at the picture: two very pretty girls, somewhat flushed with whiskey, their breasts bare, each sitting beside a recumbent man holding in her hand something she never could claim as her own except a man gave it to her. We all took another drink.

Alice was getting very gay, and her kisses more and more amorous. She handled me lovingly, and called me, or that part of me which her hand held, all sorts of amusing names. But I was surprised when, with a sudden change of position, she put her head down and began to kiss it. Gladys immediately did the same to Bill. We two men lay there awhile, too contented to speak, and watched our sweethearts kiss and suck us. Alice knew how to use her mouth! I have often wondered, and have never found out, where and how she learned it.

Neither man nor woman could stand that for long. Gladys curled around and got her leg over Bill, and Alice imitated. I soon felt her, after a bit of rubbing, slide down upon me, hot and moist. The girls rode us so, and rubbed upon us as we bounced them with our knees and hips. They laughed and exclaimed and crooned and cooed, each holding the other's hand as they jounced about side by side on their willing mounts, and they must have given each other some signal, for both sat erect at almost the same moment with that look of wondering delight that lovers love to see on their sweetheart's faces, and then collapsed together, gasping, as Bill and I rang up our third bull's-eyes!

It was now getting late. We all promised to meet again, and went our separate ways. On the road home, lying with her head against my shoulder as I drove, Alice made the most extraordinary remark I ever heard from her lips—"Pete, I'm fucked to a frazzle!" Perhaps she was, then, but after a couple of cocktails and dinner at her house (friend-husband being away) she invited me to her room, and there, on her own bed, and all naked this time, both of us, at her own request, I—well, the lady used the word first—fucked her again!

And as she lay there, stretched out so beautifully and happily naked, when I kissed her good-night and good-bye, she murmured tenderly, "Four times in one day, each time a wonder, but, Peter darling, the last was the best!" And as I recall her naked body in my arms, with every fiber leaping with passionate desire, I still think it was the best.

ESMERALDA

Anaïs Nin

The woman placed the lamp on an old table, descended into the stairway, and closed the trap after her. As her footsteps creaked down the miserable stairs, Phoebus hastened to push the floor bolt in place. The old woman heard the sound, and laughed to herself, saying, "It's many a lesson Master Phoebus will teach her before sunrise."

And now the officer was alone with the fair prize he had persuaded to come to this secluded garret with him. Well she knew, virgin though she was, the object of his desire. And now, as she found herself alone with him, in spite of her love for the handsome soldier, she was blushing, trembling and confused, as he came from the fastening of the trap and seated himself on a great old chest beside her. Next to the chest, the foot close against it, was a dingy old bed.

For some moments he held her dainty hand in silence. Her cheeks were flushed; her long drooping lashes shaded her eyes. The officer, to whose face she hesitated to raise her glance, was radiant. A luxurious warmth was already stealing through his eyes, which were beginning to grow misty. At last, with a trembling voice, she said, "Oh, my lord Phoebus. Do not despise me. I feel that I am doing very wrong."

"Despise you, my pretty child," he replied, "and why?"

"For coming here with you."

"On that point, my beauty, we are not agreed. I should not despise you, but hate you."

"Hate me!" she cried, in startled eagerness, "what have I done?"

"For requiring so much urging," he replied.

"Alas," said she, "that is because I am breaking a sacred vow. But what does that matter? Why should I need father or mother now?"

So saying, she fixed her large dark eyes upon the captain; she was silent for a moment, then a tear fell from her eyes, a sigh from her lips, and she said, "I love you."

There was such an odor of chastity, such a charm of virtue about the young girl that Phoebus had not felt entirely at his ease with her. But this speech emboldened him.

"You love me," he said rapturously, and he threw his arm around her waist. He had only waited for such an opportunity.

"Phoebus," she said, gently removing his eager hands from her girdle, "I love your name; I love your sword. Draw your sword, Phoebus and let me see it."

He unsheathed his rapier with a smile. She studied the handle, the blade, examined the letters on the hilt with adorable curiosity, and kissed the sword, as she said, "You are a brave man's sword. I love my captain."

Phoebus took advantage of the situation to imprint on her lovely bent neck a kiss which made her start up red as a cherry.

"Phoebus," she resumed presently, "walk about a little, so that I may have a good look at you, and hear your spurs jingle. How handsome you are!"

He rose and gratified her; he walked about a little, gazing at the fair face and form of the beautiful creature; then he came and sat again beside her. Passion was now beginning to work in him.

"How hot and stuffy this old garret is," he said, "you

are lighter clad than I and do not notice, but I am suffocating. This May night is like early summer."

And, without comment from the girl, he arose and took off the heavy collar, belt, sword and outer garments which the custom of those times prescribed for an officer, and the heavy boots with the jingling spurs, leaving but his knee-length trousers and his long stockings to cover his limbs, while above his waist but a thin undergarment covered his body. Esmeralda started involuntarily as she saw his action, but again relapsed into thoughtfulness. Then he came and sat beside her again, this time very closely. The warmth of her body quickly penetrated the thin garment which he wore, and still further intoxicated him.

Words of love rose to his lips, to which the happy girl listened with increasing delight. Wrapped in her own thoughts, she dreamed for some moments to the sound of his voice. With his arm around her waist, unhindered now, he pressed her and again told her of his love.

"Oh, how happy you will be, how happy you will be tonight!" he murmured at last, and gently undid her sash. This rude action startled her from her reverie for a moment, and then she again became pensive and silent. Made bold by her gentleness, he again lovingly pressed his arm around her waist, and then silently removed her girdle. She was still dreaming, and with ardent gaze and trembling hand he began to unfasten her bodice. Hardly was this delightful task half performed when the soft garment began to fall away from the bright neckerchief which it had held in place. The blissful lover, quick to seize the opportunity, drew the pin which held the folds of the handkerchief together, raised her slightly from the wall against which she was leaning, and snatched it off. Her lovely shoulders, rosy and polished, shone above the top of her loosened bodice. She started like a frightened fawn as she realized that his eager eyes were feasting on her nakedness, even so little, but almost as quickly she became dreamy again and let him have his way.

And the captain quickly applied his active fingers to the remaining laces of her bodice; in a moment the task was finished; it was entirely open, and through the filmy gauze of her chemisette he saw the lovely hillocks of her beautiful bosom. With a cry of joy, he slipped the bodice off first one arm, then the other, and madly tossed it away, while to the rapturous lover whose white arms seemed worthy of Venus herself.

Gasping for breath, he devoted his attention to her skirts; eagerly he loosened them. Then he knelt before her and removed her slippers. Boldly now placing his hands under her garments up to her knees he unfastened her stockings; he pulled them both off. She started involuntarily when his hands touched her limbs, but again became passive, though with an ever-increasing flush on her cheeks.

Then he murmured to her to remain quiet; he rose quickly to his feet, and with mad eagerness tore off his remaining garments. In a trice he was naked, and as studly and white as Apollo himself, a splendid specimen of manly vigor.

Now he stood boldly before her. He cried out, "Esmeralda, be mine," and extended his hands. The dreaming girl was roused from her reverie by the sound of his voice; she opened her eyes wide, saw the ugly red bandage of his lusty manhood before her, and for an instant she hesitated and turned her head away, the last resistance of virgin modesty in the first presence of lusty manhood (not uncommon at such a moment). Then he spoke, with tones tenderly passionate; nature overcame that momentary hesitation; the inborn desire of the flesh asserted itself; she gazed into his eyes an instant, her own brimming with moisture; his hands were still stretched to her; and she rose to grasp them. As she did so, her two loosened skirts fell to the floor, and the gauze of her chemisette, reaching only halfway to her knees, was all that covered the trembling beauty. He took her hands, and she stepped out of those perfidious garments. For a brief instant he gazed into her sweet face; he saw in it the answer to his own glowing passion; with hands shaking with excitement he undid the fastening of that last garment; it fell open at the neck; one last instant he stopped, before the final unveiling of those lovely beauties; then he pushed the straps off her shoulders; the garment was soft as silk and dropped unhindered to the floor.

His whole body trembled as he looked upon her naked flesh. Her hands and feet were most dainty; her arms and legs exquisitely turned; the rosy freshness of her skin heavenly. With all these, she possessed fullness of breast more voluptuous than classic, and hips of almost Eastern heaviness. Withal, there was a suppleness and vigor in her appearance that told the practiced eye of Phoebus that here was the richest prize that he had yet been permitted to gather to his arms.

With an effort he restrained himself from seizing her, as she stood there with eyes half closed, but he laid his hands upon those polished shoulders, thrilling even at that touch of her fair skin, and exclaimed in a voice broken by passion, "Esmeralda, tell me again that you love me."

And she, gasping with emotion, cried out, "Oh, come, do with me what you will; I am yours. Take me, take everything. What is my mother to me now? You are my mother, for I love you, Phoebus, my adored captain, it is I; look at me, it is that little girl who comes in search of you. My soul, my life, my body, are yours. I am all yours, my captain. I will be your mistress, your pleasure, when you will; always yours. Take me, Phoebus, this is all yours."

As she said this in a voice choked with passion she hung her soft arms around the officer's neck; she gazed into his face imploringly, her beautiful eyes swimming with tears, and an indescribable smile on her lips. The enraptured captain, though careful not to allow his body to touch her, pressed his lips to those beautiful shoulders. The young girl, her eyes fixed on the ceiling, her head thrown back, trembled beneath his eager caress. Finally he joined his burning lips to her own, and each drank in from the other a long draft of love. With moisture now falling over her eyelids, they kissed long and deeply, till at last, in a little closer embrace he allowed her snowy hillocks to be pressed for the first time, though careful not to let his hips reach hers, nor his lustily throbbing tool to scarcely approach her snow-white form. But that pressure of her luscious breasts was a charming introduction, for her, to the beautiful story which she read that night, the first tortured beginning of that sweet delight of the flesh, the first step in that delicious contact of strength and beauty which ends in the dizzy climax of the supreme inner kiss of Venus triumphant.

And when her breasts joined the thrill of their pleasure to the sweet sensation she was drinking in at her lips, the new delights were too much for the young girl, and she leaned heavily against her lover. He understood and led her to the old couch, whose dingy furnishings were now to be the bridal bed of Esmeralda, whose glorious beauty would lend to that old couch the charm of the King's own.

She lay down upon it, and moved toward the back; she knew he would soon be beside her. He stood, partly turned away, for a short time, gently caressing his inflexible rod of steel, burning to possess the treasure house of the lovely maiden. Then he came to the bedside, and looked down upon her. With parched lips, distended nostrils, and swimming eyes he gazed for a brief moment upon the round, full titties, the richly developed thighs, the amply cushioned hips, and, in the midst of this rich whiteness, the mossy nest of dark hair which surrounded the place where were soon to be gratified their now mutual desires.

Her languor gave place to ardor. She opened her

eyes, turned slightly toward him, caught his lustful gaze fixed upon her treasure house; for just one last instant, as she looked upon his rod for the last time before it ravished her virginity, a slight feeling of dread came over her, then desire again conquered, she was willing, nay, anxious, now to know what were the sensations which this crimson instrument of torture could impart, and she stretched out her shining arms toward him, smiling.

Instantly he placed himself beside her, quickly placed one arm beneath her neck and shoulders, clasped the other around her warm body, and drew her full length against him. And she, too, threw her lovely arms around him, pressed her supple form close to his body, and then, each thrilled too greatly for words by that exquisite contact of the flesh, they lay a long time in silence, immovable, only the heaving of their breasts as they were pressed together, and the constant throbbing of his tool extended between his belly and her fair, white form being an exception to that loving rigidity.

Then, after what seemed an age of pleasure, and when the inexperienced girl had been thrilled through and through by this embrace, he moved down just a little, placed one leg over hers, and allowed the heat of his tool to nestle in the mossy fringe a little above that spot where their supreme love was soon to be consummated. It was too much for her equanimity; at that near approach of the male engine she cried out, and pressed her hot lips close against him. Firmly she held her body to that steel. Then he, teasingly, moved back a little, but now she pressed close to him as he did so, unwilling to lose any of that contact. Then they played many times thus; now the hairy, muscular leg of the man would embrace the white fairness of the girl's limbs, and, when he drew away, she would embrace him in turn. But each was careful not to separate far enough to take for very long that fiery spur from the mossy nest where its rod head was buried, only a couple of inches above the amorous lips, beyond which lay paradise, and directly under that mossy covering, already drinking in, through the skin, the magnetism of that lusty steel, was her exquisitely sensitive clitoris, fully distended, and throbbing with mad anticipation. The girl was now sighing and moaning with delight, and Phoebus was charmed immeasurably by the delightful beauty and her steady and rapid advances toward the beginning of the real act, which was now at hand.

For the heat of her hips, covered with perspiration, the sexual odor which her whole body began to give out, the steady pressure of her firm, round breasts against him, the moisture which filled her eyes and now and again overflowed on her cheeks, told him that the time for taking full possession of the beauty had come.

Gently he turned her on her back, still holding her against him, though relaxing the pressure upon her love spot as his weight came upon her, and moving his rod backward, so that when he had her entirely upon her back his rod was poised between the snowy luxuriance of her thighs. Quietly they lay again from some time, until she became accustomed to the weight of a man upon her, and realized the fact that the very pressure, upon the breasts of a girl who is not regularly thus treated, is productive of a pleasant sensation.

Then at length, when he thought she was prepared for the great lesson, he gently raised himself slightly and with his right hand sought the love spot and moved carefully away any hair which might have covered the treasure. Then he placed his lusty tool toward the entrance. With his right hand he pressed it down a little, till it was just at the gateway; then he moved forward just a little more. It touched the moist lips, another slight movement, another; a smothered cry from the girl, and his head was inside.

The utmost care was necessary to keep from spending; she had almost overpowered him already by her intense magnetism; so he remained motionless a short time; both hands were now underneath her shoulders. Absolutely still they lay, though he could distinctly feel the mad beating of her heart. So they remained quiet, till he felt he was fully in control of himself, for he knew what she, in her innocence, did not understand, that a severe trial must come to both before their passion could be realized. Her sacrifice of pain must be made before her fruits of pleasure could be gathered.

So now, being more calm, he gently began to push the tool into that virgin sheath. She could not remain quiet then, but gasped and moaned with every fresh movement. The distention of her sheath by that steel caused a continual augmentation of her sensations of delight, until he had advanced about half the length of that rod when she suddenly drew back, involuntarily. He had reached her maidenhead. Now, for the first time, he had to reassure her, telling her that there would have to be a little pain before their pleasure could be consummated, but only for this once, and ever after that nothing but joy would attend the operation. With such words he calmed her as best he could, then clasped her soft shoulders, and made his first charge, a rather strong one, at the barrier. It held firm, but the girl cried out in pain. He knew it was useless to talk to her any more, for the deed had to be done, regardless of the pain, before they could complete their divine union. Again he drew back slightly, and pushed against the membrane. It still held, and poor Esmeralda cried aloud. Another backing, another push of the tool, and another failure, but now the poor creature was frightened. "Oh, Phoebus, spare me," she moaned, "spare me. Oh, I'll do anything for you, but let me go. Oh, please let me go. Oh, oh, oh." He knew he could not, for it would have to be done sometime if he released her, and she would be too frightened afterward undergo the ordeal. So he waited a little, and pleaded with her, cheered her as best he could, and tried to calm her fears, though he was not entirely successful.

But when she was somewhat quiet, he again, without speaking, braced himself for a fourth trial; his hot hands clasped her shoulders again, his feet were against the chest, he drew his horn back half an inch from the bar, and charged it again. Again no result, except a scream of pain from the panting girl; though her fair arms clung around him, she bitterly lamented her fate now. But he, in silence, drew back again; a fifth ram, and only cries and sobs. Oh, how he pitied the poor lamb to whom he was forced to be so cruel! Tears stood in his own eyes, as he raised his head and looked into her dear face, drawn with pain, the lovely eyes dim with crying, and he sank down and poured his own tears upon her neck. But nature roused him again. Again he drew back his thus-far baffled tool; over half an inch away he stopped; gave another push; but oh, unhappy girl, only your sad cries were the result. "Oh, my darling Phoebus. I can't stand it. I can't stand it. I can't. I can't. Please, please, let me go. Oh, Phoebus; please; help me; Please! Please!! *Please!!!*"

But he did not answer; he felt that the poor girl's agony must be ended, at any price; he could not endure those pitiful cries; there was but one way, and that was the right way, cruel though it might be. He put his hands quickly under her shoulders harder than ever, he drew back over an inch from the barrier, he braced his sturdy legs hard against the chest, the unhappy girl sobbed aloud as he did so; but he was adamant; and this time his rod was adamant too, for he gave a massive thrust, its hard head struck the bar vigorously, and it broke and the impetus of his stroke caused him to pass a good inch beyond it, at which the poor creature screamed aloud again and again. Had one outside listened, he would have thought the unhappy lass was being severely punished, instead of being prepared for the consummation of the greatest happiness that could come to her. Her pain, however, was most real, and for a long time after the conquering of her last resistance to her violation, she lay there and sobbed and her dear body quivered with emotion.

But all things have an end, and eventually she became calm. He encouraged her all he could, and gradually nature began to instill passion into her veins again. He moved slightly in that clasping sheath, and the healing oil with which he had anointed his tool before possessing her had done its work, and the motion gave her only pleasure. The instant she realized that, her passion increased rapidly, and soon he felt emboldened to push on toward the goal. As he advanced further into her treasure house, the pressure upon her mount of Venus became heavier; the exquisitely sensitive organ which lay beneath that mossy hillock was forcibly diminished in size, and every added pressure upon it added to her sensations of delight.

Now both were eager for the climax. The ever-increasing heat of the beauty, only temporarily subdued, caused in Phoebus an irresistible desire to try the powers of the fine white body he embraced and to bestow upon the lovely virgin the first burning stream of passion from man's loins, while as for Esmeralda, now that the pain was over, she was not only sexually anxious, but mentally curious, to know the manner in which that rod would operate to end forever her state of maidenhood.

He took a firm hold beneath her soft shoulders; this time it was to give her the divinest of pleasure; she knew it, and wrapped her lovely arms tightly about him, one around his neck, the other just below his shoulders. An observer would have noted the ecstatic look on her face as Phoebus stiffened his arms, pressed his legs against the old chest, and pushed his rod of steel half an inch within that sheath. Then, for the first time, those maiden lips which guarded her supreme sanctuary felt the touch of a man; from head to foot the virgin trembled at that first kiss; she cried out with joy. For an instant, fearful of too sudden a result, he drew back slightly; then, when each had recovered from the first shock, he again placed the head against the sanctuary. And now, from the conjunction of those parts, a thrill of delightful sensation began to flow back and forth between them. Rising from her virgin lips, as they were pressed by that hot head, she could feel that thrill of exquisite pleasure rush up through her spine to her brain, most beautiful visions passing before her eyes; than plainly she could feel it descend again to her treasure house and flow in an electric current into his iron spur, and then she could feel him quiver slightly as it mounted to his brain and filled him with the glorious bliss it had her. Again and again it flowed back and forth from one to the other, and with each return to her body it was more intense, more delightful than before. More tightly she wrapped her arms about him; she pressed her fine legs close against him; higher rose her pleasure; still more tightly she clung to him; quicker and quicker came her hot breath. He exerted every effort of will to prevent throwing the rush of his passion into her, as she panted and quivered and clasped him, and suddenly, as he expected, her arms and legs relaxed, the rigidity of her form was gone in an instant, and she lay perfectly quiet. He raised his head; her eyes were half closed; her cheeks were crimson with passion; she was giving up the first tribute of her fountain of love; it was her virgin oil, this time, which never can flow but once, that was pouring from her cup to anoint the conquering instrument of the lucky Phoebus. Very quickly he felt its effect on the head of his tool; with difficulty he restrained himself; his breath came quicker; his hips began to twitch in spite of himself, so eager were the driving muscles to ram the beauty. Now his head was bathed in the steady flow, and every instant it sent a deeper burning thrill through his nerves. He could not last much longer, but now the girl was fast recovering her strength. He raised his head once more; she opened her eyes wide, they were brimming over again, but this time with the intoxication of her present and anticipated happiness. She wrapped her glorious arms around him once more; she again pressed her ivory legs close against his. Her virgin tribute to her lover had been paid, and now she was eager to give up that virginity.

With a mad cry he tightened his arms; he stiffened his legs against the chest; he pushed the ravisher against the thrice-willing victim firmly.

The sight of those two white bodies in that divine embrace was indescribable.

With every nerve and muscle tense, they strained their eager forms together.

There was one last supreme instant of silence, immobility, exalted anticipation.

Then a mighty throb shook the whole length of that vigorous tool, nestling in her virgin lips.

She realized the climax was close at hand.

They gasped, once, for breath.

A second throb, stronger than the first, the seed was near the goal.

The secret of life came to her.

For with the third magnificent convulsion, the first stroke of that passion seed was thrown upon her treasure house.

Her purity was gone forever. But the divine glories of heaven itself were hers.

She screamed aloud, as she felt that first destroying and revivifying blast of passion's substance, the happiest cry a man can hear, that of the despoiled virgin who is happy.

He had cried out, too; a sound strange to her; a girl hears it only once; it is the rejoicing in the delighted ravishment of a virgin eager to learn all that life has in store for her.

A second massive stroke dashed its hot fluid all over the deflowered place, and she again cried in ecstasy, but this time her cry was that of knowledge gained, and desire consummated.

Then as his lusty strokes continued, pouring their hot cream upon her, she began to struggle with pleasure under its lashings. She cried aloud again and again:

"Oh, Phoebus, please let me go. Let me go. Let me go. You are killing me, Phoebus. Oh Phoebus, I love you, I love you, I love you so. Oh, Phoebus, please let me go. Please."

The lover had heard such words before, though surely never from as charming a creature as this. He began to bend his back slightly and move his horn forward and back. The motion was maddening to the already agonized girl. She cried out in supreme passion as he thus tortured her. He rammed a little harder; and again, sweet music to his ears, she moaned out:

"Oh, Phoebus, my love, let me go. Please! Please! Oh, my love, my Phoebus, what are you doing, what are you doing to me? Don't kill me! Don't kill me. Oh, don't—don't—please, oh, please—don't!!!"

She swooned away, as his attack ceased. Her defilement was complete.

Slowly they returned to earthly consciousness; gradually the fierce heat of their passion cooled. But for some time the fair bride of love clung closely to the man who had violated her chastity; then after many a whispered word of love was exchanged, and her happy sighs, he gently disengaged her fair arms, and carefully withdrew.

And as she lay there her bosom was still heaving with the rush of her feelings. The beautiful round globes which had seemed so lusciously large when the flimsy chemisette fell from them were well pressed down from the attack they had experienced. Her eyes were still staring; her disheveled hair lay round her shoulders; her fair, round arms lay quiet at her sides. In that short space of time, long as it has taken to tell it, she had been transformed. But her thoughts, when thoughts returned, were not of regret. The world had revealed itself to her in a new light, and she, though physically fatigued for the moment, was supremely happy. The modest, trembling, confused virgin, who had entered that garret so short a time before, had been touched by the magic wand of man's strength, and now she lay there holding in her treasure house, so ruthlessly violated, the invigorating seed of her lover's loins. Her maiden purity was gone, but she realized from that one blissful experience the wealth of her own charms, and knew what they meant to a lover, and was not aggrieved at the discovery.

After a time she rose from the bed for a few moments, and then, when she was ready, came in her sweet nakedness back to it, and lay down again. Well she knew that their night of love had only begun; that soon again her gallant lover would seek her fair body for their mutual delight.

When Phoebus approached the bed, she turned first her shining dark eyes, then her lovely white body freely toward him, with very different feelings from those with which she had met him the first time. His strength had returned, for he was in full lusty health and vigor, and he gazed with sensual eye upon the loveliness of the girl he had so madly violated. And the appeal of those shining eyes, those warm lips, those lovely titties, those ivory legs, those sweet white arms, those ample hips, and that dark nest of love in the midst of that white voluptuousness, could not be resisted. He quickly lay down beside her, and they closely embraced again. Again and again he kissed her hot lips. This time it was a novice, but an ardent young beauty that he clasped in his arms; she had tasted the luscious fruit, foolishly called forbidden, and was soon eager to repeat the feast. Nature urged her on; the hot breath and lustful kisses of her lover roused her desire to draw from him gain a tribute of his strength to her beauty. His animation was heightened by the increasing warmth of the happy girl, who now lay panting on his greatest, half on top of him, offering herself again to be loved. Again his organ pressed against her fair body. She felt its hot head against her. Her animated curiosity, now no longer restrained by modesty, made her bold enough to slip her dainty hand down and grasp the lusty instrument which had violated her virginity. She wrapped her soft fingers around it and squeezed it gently; she ran her hot hand down to his hairy storehouse and grasped it in her warm clasp. Several times she pressed the hairy nuts in her unaccustomed hand; you must pardon her, fair reader, for she had never seen a man all for herself before, and her interest in his make-up was perfectly natural. She pressed, as I have said, the hairy balls in her dainty fingers, the hot head of his throbbing rod lying along her soft, white arms as she did so. And with every pressure of the bag, drawn up tightly as it was, a thrill went through him from head to foot. She noted this, and laughed at his uneasiness. He was soon trembling with passion, and mad to mount her. Convulsively his hips began to work the tool up and down against her lovely arm, as he held her against him.

She knew what that movement meant now, and she would not have that treasure seed spilled, except just as nature intended it. She instantly let go his bag, took her hand away, clasped both arms around his neck, and crowded her luscious hips against his tool. Clinging together, she turned on her back. She cried with joy as the pressure came on her mons veneris. Once more his hand sought the love spot; with breathless eagerness she remained in absolute silence while he pressed his head for the second time against her outer lips; eagerly they welcomed the steel spur now, not a stranger nor a ravisher this time, but a loving friend in the fair one's distress.

With delicious cries of happiness she received it as it entered her hot sheath, and advanced toward her sanctuary, unhindered now by any barrier; nothing but delight was hers and his. Closely her arms enwrapped his body; tightly did she press her to him in the bliss of her second surrender. She was not merely receptive now, she was eager to assist.

And her lover, overjoyed with the ardor of the young beauty, desired this time to bring the passionate bliss to a still higher plane than before, gratifying his lust with the most extravagant sensations which her richly developed hips and hot temperament could be made to afford.

He advanced upon the fair girl and soon his head nestled in her cup again. He pressed his raging head upon those lips; thrills of delight again and again flowed between them, just as before; from her flushed face to the tips of her dainty feet she was happy, and in the center of all sensations, between her fine legs, seemed to rest all the blessings of paradise.

And now he told her that their passion this time must rise to greater heights than at first; and with her assistance, they would climb to the most dizzy summits of ecstasy. The young girl, already brimming with passion, listened to his words with thoughts which cannot be described. She had learned all there was to know; she did not realize that she had for her lover a man of great experience in the art of love. If there were greater delights than she had experienced the first time, she did not think she could endure them.

But she determined to try and, as she found out, her powers kept her with him to the last.

He slipped his hands now under her hips, her plump buttocks pressed heavily upon them. And now he began gently to stroke her. She put both hands around his neck. He pressed her hips tightly with his strong hands, and, at his direction, she curved her back somewhat, helping to raise her hips to meet the arms. For quite a little time they did this, she thrilling with joy at every stroke. Then, as the ramming continued (it was not very happy, of course), he told her how to join in it. And now, assisted by his hands, as he stroked, she lifted her hips to meet him, and soon they were rocking in blissful union. The delightful girl was quivering already with passion, but her good sense told her to be as calm as she could and enjoy it as long as nature would possibly allow. So, for many strokes, they rose and fell together, though the passion of both was steadily rising. Finally she began to cry out with the sensation; he was fearful of her passion oil flowing, and they rested.

Quiet they lay, till each was more calm, when he whispered to her; the observer would have seen, as Phoebus whispered, that he spread his legs somewhat, though still keeping them firmly against the chest, then he would have seen her raise her lovely legs and cross them over his, her shapely calves resting on the back of his hairy limbs, and her dainty feet together. And when he felt that sweet, smooth flesh pressing upon him a rush of passion dashed over him, and he drove his angry rod tightly into the cup of the beautiful creature. Thrilled instantly by the magic pressure, she trembled in his grasp; she clung to him an instant more tightly, and then, with moans of delicious pleasure, she opened the rich fountains of her treasure house and madly poured her oil upon that straining head. Prepared for this, she did not relax so much this time as at first, but much of her strength remained. Abundantly she poured out her glorious oil, and quickly her full animation was at their mutual service.

Each knew that now the dizzy heights were to be reached.

Well nigh crazed already by the passions each had roused in the other, they pressed their panting bodies together with immense eagerness.

More tightly, if possible, he wrapped his arms around her steaming haunches.

Nervously she slipped her arms down around the middle of his back, pulling him upward upon her with all her strength.

Tighter she pressed her exquisite calves and polished legs against his straining muscles.

And when that embrace was tightest, he began to drive his rod against her cup.

It was the beginning of the mad rush to heavenly joys.

She curved her supple back, and came up with every stroke; they rocked up and down for about a score of strokes until he knew that now it must be.

He told her what to do.

Instantly she reversed her ardent motions.

She stayed up, after she had rocked up with him, till he drew back.

Then, as he drove her, she came down against him.

At the very first thrust, she screamed aloud.

When he drew back, she moved up; his rod came within an inch of the outer gateway.

When he thrust, and she drove down to meet him, his cock ran nearly the whole length of that sheath, and pressed against her sacred lips.

How could any girl endure such an attack!!!

Again he drew back; again she rose, again he came nearly to the outer lips; again he drove; again her scream delicious agony resounded through the room.

It was taking every conceivable effort of willpower for him to hold off so long.

For the fourth time, he pulled back; close to the outer opening he came; once more he rammed, and she came to join him; once more his head ran the torrid length of that oily sheath and crammed hard against the cup.

She cried out harder than ever; she was sobbing, too, but with consuming passion.

Five times; back he came; forward he went; down she came, he pressed it heavily against the tender womb lips; her cries were maddening.

Suddenly from her crazed womb poured forth a second spending.

But it did not weaken her.

But when he drew back the sixth time, clear to the door, with a cry of intense agony, and rammed it in, she did not come down to meet him.

She was rigid with madness.

His head tasted her spending, and instantly sent the message to his brain, and all over his whole nervous system.

She was a beautiful demon of crazed womanhood; her whole soul was centered in her maddening sensations of passion.

Seven times he drew back; she held strong, curving her back.

He rammed it down the whole length of her oily cavity, with one lusty movement, and plunged its red head into that oil for the second time.

He understood her.

She reached down still farther; she grasped his haunches; she strained her calves harder against him.

He wrapped her hips in a mighty grip; she held her lovely back in a rich curve.

She exerted every muscle of her glorious arms and legs to pull him up harder against her thighs.

And, in that supreme embrace, they reached the heights of paradise.

Without a preliminary throb, but with a mighty rush of scalding sperm, in the very first stroke of that maddening climax, the mighty realization of their desires was inaugurated.

With a wild cry, their very souls rushed into mutual ecstasy.

They were one; they knew nothing but love: mad, mad, mad, passionate love.

Of their two bodies they were now scarcely conscious, for their whole existence centered in that sheath, where the culmination of earthly desires was being enacted.

They knew no other sensations save those that emanated from that passion center.

He could only give short rams now, so slightly were they clasped.

But the sensations were not intermittent.

They were continuous.

Usually, the delight in sexual union runs in waves, coincident with the thrusts of the ejaculations.

But such were their bodies, and their souls, that from the time that first immense spurt of seed was thrown upon that already exquisitely tortured cup, the sensation of supreme pleasure, superb intensity of passion, exalted delight of possession, mad delight of realization, the crazed delirium of the union of two such ardent souls, never ceased, till long after the mighty rush of passion from the lusty loins of Phoebus into the glorious body of Esmeralda had ended its magnificent flow!

And now we must leave the lovely Esmeralda and the handsome Phoebus to pass the remainder of the night. We have not time to relate, how, after this supreme encounter of passion, they lay long in each other's arms, enjoying innocent conversation. Both were wearied by that mighty convulsion of their mutual passion, and Phoebus knew, too, that the way to win a repetition of favors is not to urge them too frequently. But before they finally disposed themselves to sleep, their desires reasserted themselves and they again went to heaven together. Then the now tired, but not satiated, girl fell asleep, and he soon joined her.

But when the next morning's sun aroused them both at once, each looked with delight upon the nudity of the other, and it was not long till interest turned to desire. Her eyes sparkled as she saw his tool raise its head proudly, as he gazed upon her naked charms, and, after taking a good look at her vanquisher by daylight, she was nothing loathe to be gathered in her lover's arms, and have that ugly monster concealed from the light within the eagerly encircling sheath of her fair form.

When that charming act was accomplished, they arose and began to pick up their scattered garments, which the haste of the night before had left where they might fall. And it took so long to find everything and playfully to begin to dress that his tool became erect again. And she in her chemisette and one flimsy skirt, murmured not when he playfully threw her back on the bed, just as she was, opened the chemise and let her glorious bubbies out, to press his still naked bosom, threw her thin skirt up to her waist, and buried his amorous rod once more in her delighted cavity; and there, in that unconventional manner, they clung together, until nature had had her own sweet way again with loving Phoebus and lovely Esmeralda.

And how many times this blissful tale was repeated during the long friendship of those two, I must leave you to guess.

FLORENCE

Anaïs Nin

Nineteen, dainty, but not slender, with rosy cheeks, and the brightest shining eyes, vivacious, jolly; she was, in short, wholly attractive; a girl whom the best of men might love, and, on the other hand, one whose round form less than a saint might long to fondle. For two years she had been employed in the office of M——& C, away downtown in New York City; and for a long time had the junior partner, Mr. Thompson, admired her beauty and grace, not to say, in summer, the exquisite, white roundness of her pretty arms and that glimpse of her charming neck. But he was sensible, and simply admired her, and took pains to conceal it; and so time passed.

But in September, 1919, a new office boy came to the firm. He was a bright young fellow, a well-knit boy, good-looking and brimful of health. His youthful vigor seemed to cast a glow over the entire office, which, of course, Miss Florence noted as did all the rest. But none but she felt it as deeply. There was something about the boy that made her thrill gently whenever he was near her, and when his hand touched hers, accidentally or otherwise, she seemed to feel a distinct electric shock. Horace did not attempt to conceal his liking for her, though to what extent he hoped to advance in her favors only he could have told. A month passed; they seemed to be more attracted to each other daily. And by the first of December, the girl used to find some excuse to be the last one in the office (the rest left at about half past four), and she and Horace used to visit with much pleasure. Their attraction for each other could not be stationary, of course, and ere long she used to let the sturdy youth take her in his arms and hug her closely, and then kiss her repeatedly, which gave her more pleasure than she would have admitted. Perhaps she thought he was only a child, but in this she was much mistaken.

Now he became bolder, so that there was no mistaking his desires, and she would often make up her mind to break off with him altogether, and then when night came, she would find herself in his embraces once more, saying to herself, after that pleasure, that tomorrow would be different. And so one day came, when, after they were left alone, he coaxed her to go to another room with him, where he said he had a bottle of cider. She thought of nothing wrong and went with him, and found herself in the place she had never been before, a bedroom used by the night floorwalker, after his duties at midnight were over. She was a little frightened at first, but the young man really did have a bottle of cider, and they drank some. Of course there was nothing wrong about this fact, but there must have been a little of something else in it. At any rate it made her head a little giddy, and still thinking nothing improper, she lay down upon the floorwalker's bed.

Now, whether the boy had had this in mind, or simply that the sight of the lovely girl lying there stimulated his desires, I do not now. I know, however, that he quickly came to the bedside, and, while she seemed not to be aware of what was taking place, he gently raised her skirts, until her round, plump calves, with their soft black stockings, were exposed; and after an instance of excited admiration he quickly got on the bed, and ran his hand up under her clothes. Before she could prevent him, he pressed and tickled her between her thighs in a way that made her cry out with excitement. Try as she would then, she could not get his hand away, for as soon as her strength would be roused to repulse him, he would again tickle and press her, and all her power would be lost through that delightful sensation on that unaccustomed spot. And with each attack her powers of resistance grew less, till finally within five minutes after she had fallen upon the bed, she lay there with his hand still under her clothing, absolutely helpless, trembling all over with nervous excitement, and between her legs there was an indescribable sensation, which she had never felt before.

And now, when she fell back helpless, and lay still, he knew that she was his. She did not even turn her head when he leaped off the bed and tore off his pants, exposing his lusty rod, stiff as a red-hot poker. She hardly moved a hand when he boldly climbed on the bed again, raised both her skirts to her waist, and in feverish haste unfastened her drawers. She only cried out, but did not stir when he pulled those drawers down and off, exposing the matchless whiteness of her polished legs, so round and charming, and between them that dainty dove's nest. The sight of her virgin whiteness inspired the boy to no pity; he quickly planted himself between those ivory columns. He bunted his head against her sanctuary for a few times, then, seizing it with his eager hand, he found the spot, inserted its end into the sheath, and there, before she was hardly conscious of his crime, she found herself impaled upon the tool of that devilish ruffian, she who would have been a prize of the gods themselves.

Her maidenhood gone, she offered not the slightest resistance to his onslaught, and scarcely had he penetrated to the citadel of love when she spent all over him, in the exuberance of her nature. He felt it, and gloating over his prize, prepared to do the act quickly. Even yet someone might have saved her from this shame, but, alas, succor came too late. For it was not until he had given her several rams of his lusty tool, that there was the sound of a key being put in the lock of the outer door; he heard, but nothing would stop him; stiffly he stroked her; now his rod tightened; there was a great throb of the lecherous muscle. Then the door opened; a man rushed into the room, took in the situation at a glance, ran to the bed, grabbed the vile youth by the hips, and pulled him away.

But the poor girl's ruin was accomplished, for while Mr. Thompson was hurrying across the long room, the youth had squirted a charge of seed upon her pure lips, and now, as the angry employer jerked him away, his sperm still spurted in jets from his stiff rod. But quickly, with blows and curses, did the infuriated Thompson throw the fellow out of the room, with warning never to let him see his face again.

And now the poor ruined girl was left alone with the man who had admired her so long, and whom she, too, had secretly admired. Instinctively she had lowered her skirts, but she was too much excited to attempt to flee; she remained motionless. Mr. Thompson then came to the bedside, sat down by her, and tried to calm her by not appearing to think of what happened. But, honorable though her friend was, the vision of those exquisite legs and the deep flush of excitement still covered her pretty cheeks, troubling him greatly. Let us tell the whole truth and say that, try as he would, the recollection of that sight forced itself so often upon his mind that soon he had an erection as great as Horace's, who had actually reached that haven of desire, though only for an instant.

He stretched himself on the bed; he had locked and bolted the door, before he came back; he lay at a distance from her; she did not object to his lying there; in fact, it seemed to him that her moist eyes were becoming alluring. Nature had, in truth, been roused in her. And finally he could no longer keep down his rising feelings, and began to talk of what he had seen. And at last, to be certain that anything had come from that scoundrel's rod to pollute the lovely girl, he openly asked her that question. She read his thoughts, and blushed still deeper when she replied, "Yes, Mr. Thompson, only one stroke; but that was enough; I felt it, and I am not a virgin any longer."

In a flash he clasped her close in his strong arms.

"Oh, dearest Florence, you know I would never have done this act to you; your purity would have always been safe with me. But now, if it is gone, and you surely know if his seed did touch you, if it has, then come and lie in my arms, and we will love to the very heights of heaven."

And what could the delighted girl say, but to murmur, "Yes," blushing ever deeper.

With a cry of pleasure, he sprang off the bed and kissed her pretty eyes shut, warning her not to open them until he should tell her she might. Then he quickly tore off his every garment; and his fine, white body and muscular back, arms, and legs were a glorious sight. She was blissful as she heard the rustling of his clothing; she knew real happiness was rapidly approaching.

Then he came to the bed, tool lustily standing; she

kept her eyes closed as he wished. "Don't be frightened, sweetheart," he said and gently began to remove her shoes; quickly they were off, and her stockings soon followed. Then he gently raised her up; she understood and herself unfastened her collar; then her waist was an easy matter. Now he raised her to her feet; taking care that her hands should not feel his naked flesh; her two skirts came down easily around her shapely form; then her girdle; and then her rather long chemise. The beauty's eyes were still closed; she felt no fear though she knew she was nearly naked.

He could not refrain from a cry of delight as he paused a moment and gazed at her beautifully turned legs, her supple, not to say voluptuous hips, where lay heaven itself. Next, with trembling hands, he raised her flimsy shift; he uncovered her snow-white belly with its deep navel, then he came to the luscious barrier of her breasts, where he had to make a considerable effort to raise the garment over them without pressing his hands against her glorious hillocks, with their already-erect nipples.

"Now raise your arms, darling," says he.

She does so, up he slips the garment over their beautiful white roundness, and the wonderful girl is naked.

He takes her by the hand, and tells her to lie down

on the bed, whispering to her to lie back a little way upon it, which she quickly does. The room seems to be aglow with passionate desire.

He stands for an instant more and gazes at the exquisite, bare, white form lying there, already so delighted, and soon to be fairly crazed with delirious passion.

Then he bids her open her eyes; she does so.

She sees for the first time his well-knit, white form, with gloriously stiff standing yard; she almost faints for an instant, with the rush of many thoughts, then passion overcomes all else, she stretches both lovely arms toward him; he instantly climbs upon the bed; she half rises to meet his embrace, they wrap their arms about each other passionately and sink down together, moaning out their delight as they press their glowing forms tightly against each other, while those luscious hillocks, which had never before felt man's touch, thrill with the sensation.

No mortal can describe such sensations. So all we can say is that they lay there a long time, simply drinking in the sweet delight of each other's flesh. Locked in that embrace, they mutually sighed and moaned out their extremes of pleasure.

And so gradually, but steadily, did their longing increase for further joys, and so mutually did they act, that they hardly noticed the degrees by which they slowly turned, till he was stretched upon the exquisite form of the happy creature as she lay flat on her back. His body matched hers perfectly. Cheek pressed against cheek, shoulders matched shoulders, breasts pressed breasts, and true it was, though strange, that the fully erect nipples on her luscious hillocks kissed exactly the little nipples on his bosom, and seemed to create, by that very contact, a gentle current of pleasure through each other. Belly matched belly as they lay; his legs extended exactly on top of her lovely round columns, until his firm built feet gently clasped her dainty, white ones between them. And, best of all, his rod stood gloriously stiff, straight upward between their bellies, and his big balls hung just below the beginning of that hairy nest in which were her already burning lips, showing just how they would lie when the lovers were united in true love.

For a long, delightful time they lay in that position, neither speaking. The divine kiss of her perfumed flesh was for some time satisfaction.

But after a time, that very divinity of sex inspired him to the consummation of the matchless act; his passion, like hers, was now imperiously demanding full satisfaction of every sense, which the coupling of their matchless bodies together should soon produce in both.

So, at length, he gently pressed his feet between

those dainty ones of hers; her round, white calves bade each other good-bye; her knees gave each other their last token; and, finally, her round, full thighs kissed each other's velvet fullness and separated; those lovely charms were not to be united again till the very heights of heaven had been attained by their lovely mistress, in the mossy nest which their parting now left exposed to the welcome thrust of that throbbing rod, which had so long knocked for admission to its sacred portals.

Still neither spoke, when the outpost of the citadel was now unprotected. Both sighed in mutual delight; once more cheek pressed cheek, shoulder pressed shoulder, breasts kissed breasts; she was now oh-so-eager to give. Then his careful hand sought, found, guided. This was, of course, not new to her, but, oh, how much sweeter at even this approach. And as his rod surely, but slowly and carefully, entered her moist sheath, it seemed to her as if magnetism thrilled from it already. Gradually he advanced until he nestled its head against her womb.

Instantly a current of electricity was established; the delighted girl felt it, and quivered in pleasure; he felt it too, and was as joyed as she. Entirely still then they lay, drinking in, without motion, each other's internal delights, as previously they had feasted on the pleasures of flesh alone.

And soon the alternating stream of magnetism, so much desired and so seldom felt, began to flow between them. Suddenly he felt of warmth flowing into his cock; it filled it, and then he clearly felt it run in his spine to his brain. There for a brief period it burned and fire flashed before his eyes; he could see nothing else. Then swiftly down it went again to his tool, and he distinctly felt it running into her womb. Then she, in turn, thrilled as she felt her whole womb quiver with a current of delight; then it rushed up to her brain; her brain reeled with the shock and she was in lurid delight while it lasted. Then, finally, down it hurried again, and crowded into his horn.

This continued again and again and each time it seemed more entrancing. In absolute stillness they lay, while this steadily increasing current of magnetism flowed back and forth.

Four delicious times it passed from her to him; four times, each intensified, it ran from the point of his rod, clasped by her inner lips into her womb.

Now she felt this was the last she could possibly endure, as for the fifth time she poured its magnetic strength into his cock. And he felt it that fifth time; while it rushed as before to his head, it left in his balls a stinging sensation that almost overcame him at once. Vivid lights flashed before his eyes; his brain seemed on fire; intoxicating perfume rose from her body now profusely sweating with passion.

Now a final rush of that flame seared his spine; his horn seemed fairly to shoot out a flame as the fiery glow poured into her womb, she felt it coming, and thought she would surely faint, but, oh, a thousand joys, she was spared that misfortune; she felt every thrill of it. The fire rushed up her spine; now lightning flashed before her eyes in turn.

The fire that had been left in his balls, from that great rush of magnetism, caused them to press hard against his root; the burning sensation extended now to his cock itself, and it began gradually to swell. He convulsively pressed her white shoulders a little harder, though his lips did not move. Then, for the last time, the blaze started down her spine; it reached her womb, and she noted that a slow, but gradual expansion of his rod began; her womb seemed to be consumed with fierce flames. Then suddenly, nature offered a moment's respite, for she spent vigorously.

For a very short period this was a relief, then the stream of passion's electricity began once more to scorch her sanctuary. The perfume of the hottest animal the world knows, a vigorously passionate girl about to be fornicated, filled the nostrils of both, and urged them on.

A cry from the trembling lover; he clasped his hands on her shoulders; his cock suddenly quivered, wriggling, as it were, from side to side without his hips moving.

The mighty head swelled in the clasps of her torrid lips.

A great throb shook the tool from root to head; she cried out; he reassured her, but without moving a muscle.

Then another throb; with it, a little more swelling.

The swelling head, enwrapped by her womb lips, opened that holy of holies ever so little.

Then the third throb, big as the other two combined, was the climax.

She screamed aloud when a blistering, stinging, mighty charge of seed was squirted through that small opening into the very center of her quivering womb itself.

Another massive stroke quickly followed, then another; all throwing their load of passion upon the trembling interior of that lovely creature's sacredest place.

And with every hot charge thrown into that sanctuary, the tortured girl screamed again and again, until the strokes came faster, and she simply lay there, half fainting, and gasped and moaned and shuddered in her passionate ecstasy, while he kept pouring from his lusty loins his glorious charges of passion's offering.

There the panting beauty lay under him, gasping and moaning and sighing and moaning again, and sometimes crying out, as the caress of joy thrilled her beyond restraint, until her lovely next had received to the fullest extent his tribute of manly strength to her sweet, fresh, young beauty.

And there they lay, for a long time, slowly returning to earth, as handsome and ardent a couple as a bed ever brought together.

We must leave to imagination the recital of the second blissful contact of that evening, where the amorous young beauty was thoroughly stroked, and also taught the mysteries of undulation.

To say that that day was their only day of love would be far from the truth.

CUNTS

Anaïs Nin

Pretty young women have nice tickly little cunts between their legs for ardent young men to put stiff pricks into. Let any young man see a young woman's pretty, hairy cunt, and watch how his prick will come up standing! If a girl will sit with her legs apart, and then pull her dresses up, uncovering the lovely soft white thighs and the delicious little hairy place between them, any young man's prick will come out and get hard and stiff, and eager to come close and touch the soft young cunt.

Think of all the pretty cunts between young women's legs as they walk about the streets, or lie asleep at night, and of all the manly pricks covered up in trousers. What joy when one of the cunts and one of the pricks come together! In dancing, bodies held close together, prick and cunt near to each other. It is not strange that young women and young men learn to desire each other and want to go from dancing to lie together somewhere—even if they do not say so!

What a pleasure to meet at a dance in the country some girl who knows the delights of fucking, who will go gladly from the hot, noisy room, where her desires have been aroused by the closeness of your body to hers, to some quiet, cool, dark corner of the woods and there lie down and open her receptive cunt to the thrusts of your eager prick! It is a joy to find such a girl, press your body to hers in the rhythm of a delightful waltz, feel her arms tighten, and know that as you touch her legs in the dance her cunt is beginning to twitch and tingle. Hold her close and let her feel the pushing and throbbing of your prick as it begins to get stiff from feeling the warmth of her body through the clothing. Then take her outside and kiss her until she opens her mouth and clings to you in the delirious kiss that means surrender. After that, put your arms about her, and walk up the road to the pitch-black grove. She will know why you are going there, and will stop you on the way for more and more ardent kisses, holding you close and rubbing her body against yours. In the darkness of the grove she will let you feel her young breasts, firm under your caressing hand, and will press against you with her legs. She will stand with her back against a tree, and let you lean against her and kiss her more, and as you raise her dresses she will part her legs, so that your fingers will find her hot young cunt, moist and open. How she will tremble and thrill as your fingers play with that lovely, hairy organ! She may put her hand on you, and find your prick, all hard and stiff and throbbing, and take it out and put it between her legs, and even make you fuck her that way, leaning against a tree!

Or she may sink to the soft ground, drawing you down to her, and lie there with her legs far apart, her cunt ready and open, and take you with sucking kisses, gasping and shaking with desire, her whole body enjoying the delicious fucking you will give her. And through the darkness you will hear the soft sounds of other happy couples, not far off, all aroused by the dance, enjoying their fucking-play in the soft night.

But even in the cities there are cunts that like to be fucked. If you know a full-blooded young woman, a young married woman who is keen, or a young widow who has not had a man for some time, take her out to a good dinner and after a few drinks drive her in your automobile to some quiet street in the suburbs and stop at some secluded spot away from the lights. Take her in your arms and kiss her, and she will be glad. If she is just drunk enough, or careless enough, and you are skillful, she will become so aroused with desire that she will let you take her to the backseat of your automobile and there give her the good fucking she longs for. Let your trousers down, sit there with your legs stretched out, and put her soft little hand on something big and hard. She will gasp and pull up her skirts and put herself astride of you, and let her quivering cunt come down for a delicious, satisfying fucking on your stiff prick.

Best is a discreet young widow or divorced woman, who has learned the delights of fucking and must indulge herself every few weeks. By waiting a month or so between times, she becomes so eager to feel a manly prick thrusting between her legs that she will not hesitate at all to let a suitable man know, by unmistakable signs, that she longs for a good fucking. Her cunt wants to be tickled and pushed and crowded by a nice thick prick, and if you are the man who meets with her favor at the time she will give you the opportunity to take her and fuck her to the delighted satisfaction of both of you.

One summer I met a young divorced woman, who

soon showed that she liked me. I used to call at her apartment for tea. We often kissed, and she kissed warmly, but I withheld myself, curious, to see what she would do. I knew that she desired me, and she knew that I desired her. One afternoon, after we had had our tea and a few highballs, and a few more than usually ardent kisses, she excused herself and left the room. After a few minutes she called to me. I found her in the half-opened door of her bedroom, clad only in a most delicious diaphanous pink nightdress, through which her beautiful body glowed blushing. No need for words; I carried her to the bed and there, naked in each other's arms, we enjoyed hours of the most delightful fucking, until both of us were quite exhausted.

There are so many pretty little cunts that ought to be fucked every now and then, and there are so few of them that get as much delicious fucking as they should have. Young women mistakenly keep their cunts secreted and never use them, unless perhaps they finger them themselves, or let other women finger them or rub them sometimes. Such innocent diversions are better than nothing, of course, but to enjoy all the pleasure their cunts can give them, young women ought to let themselves be fucked. Of course, there is danger in promiscuous fucking—the danger of horrible diseases and the danger of nameless children. But if a woman is discreet, careful to associate with clean young men, and see that proper precautions are taken, she can get a good, satisfying fucking now and then with no danger at all.

A woman can easily show a young man what she wants without being too bold, and if he is any sort of a fellow at all he will be more than glad to give it to her. Think, ladies, of the thrill of knowing that "it" is going to happen to you! You will be scared at first, when he comes to you, but if he is a decent fellow he will soon love you, and kiss you, and hold you close and play with you, so that in a very short time you will be kissing him back, and clinging to him, and wanting him to love you more. And you will not mind, then, when he puts his hands on your legs. How good it will feel to have his hands touching your bare legs, coming closer and closer to your maiden cunt! Let him finger you for a while and fondle you there, and you will want him so much that you will be glad and excited to see his long, hard prick come out. Then lie back and surrender yourself to him; open your waist so that he may play with your breasts; pull up your dress, put your legs apart, let him come in between them and put his prick in your cunt—then close your eyes and feel the dear lad with your whole body, your first man, as he fucks you. As you lie there, with your body held tight in his arms, you will think, "At last I am being fucked! I am a woman now, and a man is fucking me! His hard prick is actually in my cunt, and this delicious sensation which I feel as he pushes and thrusts is from his big, loving prick fucking my cunt."

Girls, after you have once been fucked by a nice, lovely boy with a big, thick prick, you will enjoy living, and nothing in the world will give you more satisfaction than letting your cunt be used now and then—but not too often—for a sweet-delicious fucking.

WHEN HE FOUND ME

Kevin Sampsell

We are in the sparkling white surroundings of the men's bathroom at the Dallas airport. I've never seen a place so bright and clean; even his shoes seem to sparkle and gleam.

I follow him in there. He turns around when the door closes and gets this look on his face, as if he is thinking the place is too clean for what we are about to do. He scans a slow 360 and then looks at me sideways, craning his neck to look at my ass.

"You want to go into town first? Go on a date?"

I walk over to the sink and splash my face with water, all the while trying to figure out what my answer should be. I rub the bubble gum-scented soap into my right eye by accident. I look down at my shoes; they are falling apart.

"Yeah, we can do that, I guess." I say. "I've got my credit cards. My schedule is messed up, but I still have to be back in five hours."

He has his car parked in a garage at the airport. It costs him $200 for parking. *Do this often?* I wonder.

We drive into Dallas and I am startled at how big and metropolitan it is. I'd always thought it would be ugly and full of cowboy hats. We go to a part of town where there are a lot of drug dealers and nice-looking women pretending to talk on the payphones. I try not to think about Rhonda or John.

"First you say 'Hey, baby,'" he explains. "If he acts like he's paying attention, you say, 'You workin'? That's about it. Let him lean in the window so he can take a good look. Tell him you aren't a cop, but don't say anything about money because *he* might be a cop. Let *him* tell you how much his dick is worth."

I tell him this isn't my scene, but he says it doesn't matter. He likes to break in new ass—and he likes to suck cock as he does it. He's usually bored with just one guy.

"Where's your wife?" he asks, spotting the ring on my finger.

"She lives in Hermiston, Oregon."

"You got kids with her?" he asks.

"One."

"You think he might be gay?"

"He's only ten," I say.

"Does he look at porno yet? Any hard-core stuff?"

"Never found any in his room before," I tell him. "That surprises me. When I was his age, I think I was into really big tits. Raquel Welch and Dolly Parton. The whole mother's milk fantasy, I suppose."

"You should try boy nipples more often; they're not as flabby," he informs me.

"My wife is flat-chested," I say. "Sometimes I pretend she's a boy. I bought her a fake mustache once."

"Do you tell her you pick up men?"

"I've told her about things in the past. She even slept with someone I did once; we talked about his tattoos. She wanted me to get a tattoo down there, just like him."

The next morning I wake up and realize I've missed my flight by several hours. I get up and look for a telephone to call the airport. A handsome young black man is putting on a coat and opening the door. He gives me an uneven, nervous grin and slips out of the apartment.

"You don't even know my name," a voice says.

I look over and see the man I met on the airplane standing in the bathroom doorway.

"My name is—" I start to say, confused by waking up in a stranger's apartment. "I mean, what's your name?"

"You can call me Jeff," he says, smirking.

"I've missed my plane," I tell him, looking for my shoes.

"It's OK. I took a look at your ticket this morning, then I called and postponed for you. I thought you'd want to rest after last night. In fact, you should probably just stay in bed."

He walks over to me, letting his towel fall away from him, his washed cock coming at my lips like a cigar. I take it in my hands and kiss it politely, glancing around the room for something to drink, or wash my mouth out with.

"I just shaved it," he says. "Smell the winto-green?"

I do, almost gagging as the strong scent of his shaving cream slips down my throat. He must sense this because he lets his dick slide out of my mouth. "There's some water and an extra toothbrush all ready for you," he says, waving toward the bathroom.

As I brush my teeth, Jeff yells something from the bedroom. I have the water running loudly, but I think he says: "You fucked my boyfriend last night."

† † †

"Something smells queer in here," one of the three men at the bar says when we sit down behind them. They circle their barstools to face us. "You're not cruising while we're in here, you got that?" His black cowboy hat says CLYDE on the front, the letters arched around an eagle.

The bartender walks over and says something to the men. They huff a little bit and then return to their drinking. They're all wearing leather and denim in different combinations.

I want to move to another table but Jeff grabs my hand. He seems only slightly concerned about the men, but warns me: "Those guys are nasty. Don't do anything stupid, unless you're into pain." A Dwight Yoakum song plays on the CD jukebox. Jeff sings along to the chorus and then leans over to me. "The small guy there, with them—" he starts to say, but is stopped quickly by unwanted eye contact from the bar.

"Why don't you talk so we can hear you," Clyde suggests. The other two keep their mouths closed tight, as if they're not allowed to speak. Their mouths only open when they sip their beer, and Clyde addresses them in an almost-fatherly tone. I notice that he is the only one in the bar who keeps his cowboy hat on. His butt slides off the stool, his boots clicking the floor loudly, and he stumbles as he steps toward our table. He seems drunk.

"OK," he says loudly, as if he's going to make an announcement to the whole bar. His hands go up, palms out. "I got to apologize to you boys," he says. "This is a public bar and you can do what you want to. I've been here long enough anyhow. It's time to get my men back home." The other two get up and pull on their jackets. The man motions to the bartender, and says, "Get Jiffy and his friend here a beer on my tab." The bartender winks and the men leave the bar.

"Have you lived in Texas all your life?" I ask Jeff.

"No," he answers. "I grew up in Baton Rouge, Louisiana."

I take a slow drink from the thin, watery beer. "When I was a kid, my favorite football team was the New Orleans Saints, so I always wanted to live there."

"Louisiana's no place for kids. For strung-out grown-ups maybe, and criminals, but not for little boys," he says.

"What did you do while growing up there?"

Jeff scoots closer to me and I feel his hand hover over my leg, near my crotch. Despite myself, I have an erection.

"My friend Truman and I would play a game. I think we were nine or ten. I'd wear his sister's clothes and hide somewhere in his house. When he found me, I'd act scared and weak. He had a pocketknife." Jeff's hand presses against my hard-on as he speaks in a steady whisper. His breath fills my nostrils. For some reason, I try not to breathe. The neon window lights around his head pulse like a sick halo.

"I'd have to lie on my back when he found me. I didn't wear any underwear and if I did, he'd pretend-hit me until I slid them off. Toward the end of the game he'd let me have the knife, and I would rub the dull side along his dick as if I were whittling a stick. I'd suck on the head and whittle the rest. The first time I did that he got scared and pissed on my chin. I thought it felt pretty good. After that, he'd always piss on me after he came. He'd wash the sperm off me that way."

I jump as the bartender sweeps our beer bottles away and replaces them with full ones. He looks at Jeff and smiles knowingly, as if he knows the story being told. I look at Jeff and see his strange smile but also something on his cheek, like tears, or maybe just sweat.

Jeff and I spend the rest of the day shopping and sightseeing. He wants to buy a pair of women's panties and a bra. "You can give these to your wife when you're home," he says, and I feel some relief knowing he realizes I have to go soon. "What size does she wear?"

At 8:00 P.M., we begin eating dinner back at his apartment. I tell him I have reservations for a flight home at a quarter after midnight.

"I wish I was married," Jeff says. "To a man. I get pissed sometimes because you have to be in a straight marriage to have a family and kids. Sure, there are rich fags and closeted dykes with children, but there aren't too many of us who are middle-class and out of the closet."

We are drinking wine. On the couch are several small bags from the day's shopping. Toys and books for my son, John. A pair of panties and bra for my wife, Rhonda, courtesy of Jeff's Visa card. A gift box of assorted cheese and crackers for myself.

"Do you spank your son?" Jeff asks me.

"I did once. He was four. I didn't want to, but I was under a lot of pressure. He was playing underneath our neighbor's police car after I'd told him twice that week not to. What's odd is that I never saw the guy drive it at all, just noticed it in front of his house every morning. He worked the night shift. I never even knew what he looked like until he died last year and his picture was in the newspaper. But I spanked my son for him."

Jeff shifts in his chair, sensing I'm drifting off the subject.

"Did you feel love for your son as you were spanking him? Or anger?" he asks.

"Both, I guess."

"Have you ever hit your wife?" he asks.

I think for a moment, wondering how the word "hit" is being defined in this question. Invisible blows last the longest, sometimes. "No. But she hit me once. Drew blood." My finger touches my nostrils lightly. My face feels unreal.

"I want you to be your wife," he says, standing up. He grabs one of the bags from the couch. He looks at the clock and his eyes say, *There is just enough time for this last charade.*

He is biting my nipple through the cloth as he pulls the straps down off my shoulders. "I think this looks sexy," he says. He is completely naked, and I am wearing the bra and panties he bought for my wife. One of his fingers is pushing into my ass, through the black lace of the panties. It feels good, better than it would have without them.

"Move like your wife would move. Make her sounds," Jeff whispers in my ear. "I want to know what it's like." My son's toys and books have been taken out of their bags and scattered around near us.

Part of me shuts down. I don't want to play this

game. I feel as if I'm being mocked in some way. Despite this, I become more aggressive. My hand wraps around his warm cock, and I want to feel it inside of me. Two of his fingers are starting to stretch me out, pushing more of the soft fabric in my anus. I feel him getting bigger and wider in my hand. He takes his hand from my ass and pushes me to my knees, then stands in front of me and tells me to squeeze my tits. He grabs his dick and rubs it against my cheek; when he pulls it sideways and slaps me with it, my cheek stings. He guides his cock into my mouth; it presses down on my tongue. I have to breathe through my nose; I try to suck it like a straw but almost gag. I start to masturbate but he stops me.

"You need to save it, " he says.

His hips pull back and his dick slides out from between my teeth. I gasp for air, struggling to mouth the words I desperately want to say to him. "I want you inside me. I want you to fuck me. I want—"

I am interrupted. His cock sprays me with cum. Some of it flies into my eyes, my face, and down my neck and chest. He aims a last shot into my open mouth, then grabs my head and softly nuzzles it against his chest and belly. We stick together awkwardly.

"I know what you want," he says softly. "It might change you forever. Maybe you'll come back to me.

Maybe you'll bring your son here next time. Maybe we could be a family. Maybe you'll still fuck women and I'll still fuck street boys."

The clock says 10:25 P.M. My body still twitching with a pulsing erection, I try to keep him hard with my hand.

"If I'm the first to fuck you, will you fall in love with me like a schoolgirl? Will you sneak away on weekends to come see me? Will we be romantic?"

I look at his face and drift into his eyes. He is beautiful—an angel, someone I've ever seen before. I lust for who he might be.

"Do you understand what I'm about to give you—" he asks.

SUNDAY IN THE PLAYPEN II WITH ROGER

Lawrence Schimel

It was 11:00 A.M. Sunday morning when I called Roger up and begged him to take me to a porn palace. "What do you think of the peeps?" I asked him when he picked up.

"Lisa, is that you? You woke me up at this godforsaken hour of the morning to ask me about Easter candy? You know I'm a Jew, we don't go in for that stuff."

"Not Easter peeps, you ninny. Peep shows. Girlie booths. I want to go to one before they clean up Times Square, and I need you to come with me." There was a long pause on the other side of the line. I was afraid for a moment that Roger had fallen asleep again; he never wakes up until 1:00 or 2:00 P.M., when half the day is already over. "I'll pay for everything," I added.

"Why should I want to go to a girlie show? Why do you want to go to a girlie show? And why do you want to go with me?"

"Well I *do* like girls, you know. Besides, I want to go with you because I can't go alone. They don't let unaccompanied females in to the kinds of places I want to go to." I laughed at the wording they used.

Roger laughed too, and then asked, totally seriously, "Why won't they let women in by themselves?"

I sighed. "For someone who sleeps with as many men as you do, dear, you're remarkably naive about sex."

"I may be a slut, but I'm a very traditional fuck-and-suck kind of boy—totally vanilla. So tell me, why don't they let girls in?"

"Unaccompanied women are usually hookers poaching on the territory of the place's girls. A john's not going to shell out money for a woman behind the glass if there's a chick who'll blow him in a video booth for twenty bucks."

"Fascinating," Roger said dryly.

"You need to expand your horizons, dear. That's why you need to come with me. Think of it as an education in heterosexual culture. For both of us."

"Maybe I'll hang up and pretend this was all a nightmare."

"Meet me at my place by 1:30 and I'll buy you lunch as well. If you're late, you buy your own food."

"I don't think I should eat before we're going to see what we're going to see," Roger said. I could imagine him wrinkling his nose and I smiled. I was glad he was planning on coming with me, even if he was still playing hard to get.

"I'll take you to Pietra Santa," I said.

"I'll see you at 1:29," he said, and hung up.

Roger, true to form, was far more cheerful after I'd paid the bill for lunch.

"So tell me," he asked, as we walked down Eighth Avenue toward Forty-second Street, "why do you want to go to a peep show? On a Sunday afternoon, of all times?"

"Isn't it just perfectly blasphemous?" I said. "That's why. It's always been so taboo—I want to see what it's like. You've never been even a little bit curious?"

"Not in the slightest." He made an exaggerated expression of mock-innocence.

"And why me?"

"Saves time. If you're with me, I won't have to call you later and tell you how it went."

Roger laughed. "Do you know which one we're going to?"

"I figured we'd just find one that looked especially sleazy and try it."

"How about this one?" Roger asked. We were right outside one such porn emporium—the Playpen. Eighth Avenue seemed to have more of these video palaces/girlie showplaces than I'd imagined—one or two on every block here in the mid-forties.

"Live Nude Girls," a voice cried over a loudspeaker, as if the announcer knew we were lingering out on the threshold. "Real Live Nude Girls!"

"I was thinking we should do something on Forty-second Street," I said, "for the sake of tradition." At the same time, I was afraid Roger might change his mind by the time we'd walked the extra few blocks down there. Maybe he'd have digested lunch by then and balk when it came time to go in. "But since we're here," I said, "let's give it a try."

My stomach tensed as we went in. I'd always wondered what it was like inside one of these places, if they were really as degrading to women as everyone claimed.

I felt as if every man's attention were suddenly on me the moment I stepped through the doors. There was a hungry anticipation in their looks, and I was glad I had Roger with me.

"I don't feel comfortable," Roger said. He was staring at all the merchandise, as if he were afraid he were about to be attacked; there were racks and racks of straight videos and inflatable dolls and such. "I think all the guys can tell I'm a fag," he whispered to me.

"Nonsense," I said.

"Live Nude Girls," the woman's voice on the loudspeaker said again. "You there in the jeans and white T-shirt. Don't be shy, come have a look. Real live nude girls!"

Roger looked over both shoulders, trying to see if anyone else in there was wearing jeans and a white T-shirt.

"Bring your girlfriend with you."

"How'd she do that?" Roger whispered, his voice cracking.

I smiled, pointing to the peep booths. One of the girls was peering over the top, with a microphone in her hands. She waved when she saw us looking at her.

"Shall we?" I said.

"If we must."

We approached the bank of doors and the girl disappeared from her perch—to prepare to give a show for us, I guessed. "That one," I said, pointing to one of the doors. Roger was squeamish about touching the doorknob, and I knew he was imagining what most of the hands that touched it had been touching before touching it.

There was a small closet on the other side, with a solid window on the inner wall.

"We need to buy tokens," I said, indicating the window. "You're holding all my money. Go get us some."

"I'll be back in a moment. Wait here."

Where did he think I was going to go? I wondered.

A guy was staring from the aisle into the cubicle at me. I felt dirty under his gaze, but I stared back at him until the door shut. Is this how the girls on the other side of the glass felt? I quickly latched the door and felt better immediately. I turned toward the window, imagining the girl on the other side, waiting for us. She was beautiful. Did she know which booth we were in? Was anyone else in one of the other booths? Was she performing right now for one of them? I was jealous at the thought, even knowing she must show off her body all day long to anyone who paid the tokens to lift the partition.

I tried to imagine what her body would look like naked, based on the brief glimpse of her I'd gotten when she was staring at us from above the peep show.

I was wet with anticipation, so I shoved a hand down the front of my shorts. The door was locked, and I didn't have the money to open the window. I was alone with my raunchiest fantasies, safe in this little closet in a porn palace.

It felt weird being here with Roger. I needed him, or I couldn't be here; but at the same time, I was embarrassed to be sexual around him. He was my best confidant and listened to all of my wildest exploits, but that was sex at a remove—after the fact.

And while I was feeling horny as hell here, Roger, I imagined, was feeling totally nonsexual. He was nervous and edgy, maybe even uncomfortable; I hoped he was curious despite what he claimed. I was glad he was sticking this out with me.

The door jiggled. "Shave and a haircut," Roger said from the other side. I pulled my hand out of my pants. My fingers were sticky. I licked them, tasting myself, then wiped them on my shorts. I let him in and locked the door again.

Roger wrinkled his nose. "This is all so weird," he said, handing me the tokens. "Being here, I mean. It'd be one thing to be here to get off, if that was your thing, but we're not here to do that, just to look. It's all so tawdry."

I could get off here—simply from being here more than anything we could do or see. I stood in front of the window. "Don't be a wuss," I said, making him stand beside me as I dropped the coin into the slot.

The partition began to lift. There were two girls on the other side, an African-American woman who was completely naked and the girl who'd called to us, who wore a T-shirt but no underwear. They both turned immediately toward the opening window, but the one who'd seen us first from above staked her claim.

"It's so great that you brought your girlfriend," she said to Roger, sticking her head through the opening. She had small, pert breasts, all but visible beneath the tight fabric. "It's $2 a peek, $5 a touch, $10 for a leg spread."

He doesn't want to touch you, I thought. *I do. Pay attention to me.* The intensity of my feelings surprised me.

"Give me a five," I told Roger.

Grinning, he tried to slap my hand. "Just kidding," he said, digging in one of his pockets.

I pressed my legs together nervously as he handed me the money, pressing on my clit as I did so. She stuck her hand through the window for the money and I gave it to her. She stepped away from the partition and lifted her shirt, exposing her small breasts. I had to lean forward to reach them.

Suddenly, I didn't feel sexual any more. The idea of the peep show, the anticipation of it, had aroused me more than the actuality.

It wasn't that I didn't find her attractive. But suddenly

I was gripped—literally—with the realization that she was a person, and not a fantasy. She had a name, a family, all that cultural baggage I hadn't wanted to deal with.

"My name is Lisa," I said, squeezing her breast gently.

She smiled at me, as I held her breast, and for a moment I felt we had a genuine connection, beyond the money that had passed hands. Then the window began to close and I jerked my hand back, as if I'd been caught doing something I knew I shouldn't have and felt guilty about. I wasn't sure whether I felt guilty for being here, or for having broken the shield of anonymity.

"Put more tokens in," she said, bending down to peer under the partition at us.

The window stopped moving and shut with a click of finality.

"Should I?" Roger asked.

I shook my head. "The tokens are also good in the video booths, right? Maybe we can find one with the Bobbitt *Uncut* video—just for curiosity's sake."

Roger headed down the steps. I hesitated, looked over my shoulder, hoping to see the girl from the peep show peering over the top of the booth, summoning clients to her again—or looking for me.

She never appeared, and after a moment I followed Roger down the stairs.

WORTH MORE THAN A THOUSAND WORDS

Lawrence Schimel

I have never been good at keeping a diary. It presupposes an audience—supposedly one's self, but I have never been comfortable with the idea. I am afraid someone will find it, and read it, and I will have bared my soul to a stranger—or worse, someone I'm close to. I am afraid because I have done this to others. Friends of mine. My sister. I have always been a voyeur.

Reading someone's diary is the thrill of the forbidden. The knot of worry in the stomach, the fear of being discovered. When I was younger, I read porn that way. I didn't need to. My grandfather kept stacks of porn magazines on top of the toilet in the bathroom of his apartment; I could have read them at leisure, in that small locked room, poring over the pictures. But I would go to a bookstore and sneak porn magazines from the rack, hiding them inside a copy of something innocuous like *Sports Illustrated.* I would walk back to the middle of the store and stand in an empty section to flip through the pictorials. I hardly even looked at the pictures, glancing down for a second and taking a mental photograph, my heart racing as I quickly glanced back up to make sure no one was coming down the aisle where I stood, to make sure no one ever saw what I was doing. As soon as someone came near, or even if I thought they would, I closed the magazine and moved from Gardening to Humor, to wherever there wasn't anyone else.

My heart pounds the same way when I read someone's diary, even if there's no chance of my being discovered—they're away for the weekend and I have the only key to the apartment. It is forbidden, and I feel there is someone watching me as I reach for the slim, clothbound book that's hidden beneath the bed. I flip through the pages, scanning for any mention of myself, or anything else that catches my eye. I look for moments where the handwriting changes, clues to highly emotional scenes. I'm like a vampire, thirsting not for blood, but vicarious emotion. Thirsting furtively, at night, when no one else is around, lest I be discovered.

I am always careful to replace the diary exactly as I found it. If it were my own, I would notice if it had been moved, even if anything around it had been moved. I guess that's why I've never been able to keep a diary before. I'm too paranoid. Afraid of exposing myself. I've broken the trust of too many friends who left me alone in their rooms while they went to class or work, while they went on vacation for a week, trusting me to water their plants. Trusting me not to read their diaries.

So I know someone else will read this. I can't help being aware of you. I feel as if I'm writing for you, not for myself. But I have something I want to write down, need to write down, so I don't lose it. So I don't forget. I know you're reading over my shoulder, so I'm going to fill in the background for you. After all, who knows what will happen? Fifteen, twenty years from now, the stranger who finds this book again, buried in an attic at the bottom of a box of books, might be myself. And my heart will begin pounding as I realize it is a diary, and I will open it and read all the details I'd long since forgotten.

† † †

There are some who consider thirteen an unlucky number. Not *I*. But I've got reason; I have a lover thirteen years older than myself.

Not unlucky, but still witchy. She's definitely a witchy woman. Enchanting seductress. It's almost impossible not to be drawn in by her. When we go out together, I watch it happen to the men around her. And I was drawn in, as well, although it's harder for me to know what happened, trapped in her glamour.

I've wondered sometimes if it was a potion she made, something she wore. She's an aromatherapist, always using subtle essences of plants to influence mood. Lavender. Ginger. Scents I've never been able to identify. Her home is suffused with a rich aroma of comfort and warmth, an amnesiac to anxiety.

Yet each time a man is ensnared by her spell she is taken by surprise. It is perhaps that very aspect that is so appealing: she does not wield her sexuality like a weapon or tool, but is so familiar with it, so intimate, that it sits upon her as an integral part of her being, as simply as the features of her face. If you saw her, you would understand what I meant. If you saw her, you would be drawn in by her, too.

While she may not understand the effect she has, she is aware of it. We met at a poetry reading in Boston and exchanged business cards. Later that week, a story showed up in my mail, a piece entitled "Desire." It was our first flirtation. I know not to assume that a first-person narrator is the author, but I could not help noticing similarities, how men seemed drawn to the protagonist like moths to a porchlight on a summer's evening. The writing was infused with the same sensuality that surrounds her presence. Though the story wasn't full of explicit sex, it played a strong role, tantalizingly alluded to or glimpsed. And the writing itself was lush, like a flurry of caresses moving up one's thigh and across one's belly and chest.

A writer myself, I appreciated the sumptuousness of her prose. I was also very turned on by it. Words have always held strong sway over me. Perhaps she'd sensed this, and thus chosen to make her first move in print, subtly, yet relentlessly, working on my weakness.

Perhaps because she understood the power words held over me, I was able to persuade her to let me read an erotic fantasy she had written for another lover of hers. Showering after the first night we spent together, I'd found her aromatherapy jars in the medicine cabinet. Later, I asked her if she ever used them in lovemaking. She said she had, and also mentioned a fantasy sequence she had written. The moment she realized what she had confessed she said, "I can't believe I just told you that."

I begged her to let me read it.

I was curious. I wondered who he was, what he looked like, why she had chosen to write something for him. I wondered what the sequence would reveal about her, her desires, her fantasies.

The idea of reading something meant for someone else thrilled me. In college, I would lie atop the window seat for hours, warmth on my stomach from the radiator underneath as I stared across the courtyard. I could never see much—the buildings were too far apart—but what I saw was never really the issue. It was the looking. Often I would spend an entire night staring at the yellow squares of light across the way, waiting for the brief shadows to cross their frame, unaware of how much time was passing, lost in the act of watching.

Reading a fantasy for someone else held the same appeal. Already I could feel myself begin to grow hard with anticipation.

She relented. I'm still not sure why. She'd never shown it to anyone but the man it was written for. But for some reason I convinced her to let me read it. Maybe because she had realized how powerful words were to me, and wanted to help me change, to grow.

I remember almost everything I read. It's as if I had a photographic memory, which I don't, since I only remember words. But eventually I will forget, or not be able to remember exactly. I'm sure that already I must have changed things, remembering what I would have found more erotic rather than what she actually wrote.

He was an actor in horror films. Naturally, he lived in L.A., across the country from her. Most of their relationship therefore took place in words, on the page or the phone. Once, it took place like this:

For Paul

I woke up this morning with the most luscious fantasy in my mind. Here, let me share it with you. Then we can both enjoy it.

We are in a luxury hotel; it is night. You sit on the bed in a white silk robe, gazing through the window at the panorama below: a city bejeweled with light. A muffled whisper of traffic filters through to your ears, almost as soothing as the surf.

Your back is to me. I can see from your reflection in the window that your eyes are closed in quiet contemplation, listening to the city sounds below. I ease onto the bed and move toward you, circle your chest with my arms from behind, rest my head against yours. Your hand lifts to caress mine; you smile, sigh, eyes still closed. A gentle squeeze, and I pull my arms away, letting my hands glide beneath the collar of your robe and slide the silk away like milk pouring from your skin. I knead your shoulders for a moment and am pleased to find you already so relaxed. My fingers wind through your hair, soft, like a spider sorting threads for her web. Your moan is barely audible until it evolves into another sigh. I am so happy to please you.

Knowing how much you enjoy it, I let my fingertips sneak down to your neck and feather your back with caresses. They play at your shoulder blades, tease your spine, explore your sides as you wriggle against them. I switch to a calmer touch, flat hands soothing nerve endings, then tickle you once more, enough to bring delight, no more.

You turn to kiss me. Once, softly, then again. Our mouths open, and we feel the warm moistness of each other's desire. I hear a tiny sound of surprise from you and you move away, smiling. "What's that scent?" you ask, leaning forward to sniff and kiss again.

"Can you guess?" I ask.

"Let me smell that again." You turn yourself fully around to embrace me and kiss me deeply. "A flower," I think.

"Yes, a flower. A special flower."

Another kiss. Another sniff. "Not roses. Not lilacs; not so sweet."

Another kiss. "Ah! Lavender."

"Yes!" I smile. "Do you like it?"

"Love it. Did you put it on your entire body?"

"Nothing so dull as that, sweetie."

You are intrigued, guessing that there is more. I know the notion of impending discoveries excites you. I can feel your erection against my thigh as you guide me down onto my back. Your hands are delightfully warm; I feel heat through the wine-colored silk of my robe as they find my breasts. You whisper my name as your mouth reaches my neck. You kiss, and then you lick.

"Lemon. That one's easy!"

I turn to bare more of my scented neck to you. My fingers find your hair again as you clasp your hungry mouth to my neck. My turn to sigh now. A wave of passion crests inside me and I press you away and onto your back so I can devour you with hot, wet kisses on your neck and face. The fingers of one hand are still entwined in your hair. The other dances across your chest, down your stomach, finds you hard and holds as your hips push against me, a promise of delights to come.

Both hands move now to your face, learning the features with my fingers as a blind woman might. I close my eyes to enhance the sensation, resculpting the lines of your face. Your hands grab my wrists. You press them to your lips.

"Peppermint," you say. "Peppermint wrists."

"You're very good at this," I answer, kissing your hands. My tongue presses along the inside of your palm, spreads your fingers as it dances between them.

"Have you done this before?"

"Never," you declare, tugging at me until I rest on top of you. You suck at my wrists like a child with a candy cane until the scent is gone. "But I hope to again." Straddling you in this way, I notice how very wet I am by the way you nearly slide into me without effort. But not yet, no.

I move forward, kiss the top of your head, rub my body along yours until my breasts are at your lips. Your lips part automatically and my right nipple stiffens in response to your tongue. You taste the left nipple before making your guess. They are both the same, but you are not sure you've got this one right. "Does it smell like gin? It tastes like gin." Determined to make your guess conclusive, you taste once more, moving between my nipples, licking, sucking, thrilling me.

When I can find my voice, I tell you, "Yes. It's juniper berry. What they make gin from." You release my breast long enough to grin and say, "Ah, educational as well as nutritional," then return to sucking. Your right hand nudges between our bodies and finds me wet and wanting. One finger slips inside me and I press against it, moaning softly. Two on the next gentle thrust. Oh, I could almost come right now! But no—there are still discoveries to make.

Playfully, I push away, sitting up and pulling you with me. Our skin is flushed with passion, our breath quick, eyes sparkling. "I just want to make it last," I explain. "Savor it."

"Savor it," you repeat, "I get it." You pass back through the familiar lavender garden, the lemon of my neck, and I lean back to let you revisit the juniper of my nipples. You brace me at the waist as I lean back farther, resting on my hands as your tongue circles my navel. It's ticklish, and I giggle and squirm as you make up your mind what it is.

"Spicy. Hot."

"Like you," I say through my giggles.

You taste again, then declare triumphantly; "Cinnamon!"

"Go to the head of the class!"

With a raised eyebrow and a boyish grin you say, "I thought you'd never ask," and move lower still, to the final scented spot. This is the challenge, since you have to get past my own musk to find the herbal aroma.

The moment I feel your tongue probe the soft, moist folds between my legs I no longer care about herbs or slowness or anything except that you don't ever stop! How wonderful you are with your mouth; your tongue is tentative, yet firm. You move your head away, trying to guess the aroma, I imagine, but I gently push you right back, moving my legs out from beneath me and letting you settle in. The heat and wetness release the herbal scent into the air around us. The earthy scent envelops us as your tongue carries me to a pleasant plateau, then coaxes me over the edge into the warm rolling ocean of orgasm.

As I begin to float back to the coherent world, I find my voice and say, "Paul, I want you inside me." I feel your weight and then I feel you push into me, a delicious feeling with the area so highly sensitized and flushed. My legs encircle your waist as your hips grind against me. With one hand I grasp your hair, baring your neck, smothering my moans there. I arch to let you reach farther into me and orgasm again overtakes me. You move slowly, helping to prolong the delight. When I have settled back to earth once more, you let your passion take control, pounding against me with increasing lust.

"I'm so close," you whisper, your voice hoarse with pleasure.

I quickly turn you over so that I can be on top of you, sitting up. "Lay back and enjoy this," I tell you, as I regain the rhythm we had a moment ago. You manage to smile broadly through your sighs, encouraging me with a word or two until eloquence deserts you altogether and your back arches and you buck and grunt and grasp my hips and hold me against you until you are spent. Keeping you inside of me, I bend forward to hold you and let you hold me as we catch our breath.

After a moment of quiet, you ask, "Are you going to tell me what the final aroma was?"

"Won't you guess?"

"Something earthy, like the woods. Like you."

"It's patchouli," I say. "From India."

"It's magical," you reply.

"You're magical, my dear."

We fall asleep there, in each other's arms, the moist fairies between us and the aromatic fairies watching over us.

With Love,

Laura

Writing it down, I found myself aroused again. Often, I paused and put down my pen, rereading the passage I had just written as I took off my shirt and ran my hands across my chest and back, along the line of hair that runs down my chest. With my left hand, I undid my jeans and stroked myself through my underwear. Slipping my hand underneath the brim, I avoided my cock, teasing myself, running my hand along the inside of my thigh and letting the backs of my fingers tickle my balls. As I write this now, I hold my balls in my hand, gently squeezing and rolling them, pressing deeply against the muscle underneath, the root of my cock, so hard. Enough of writing for now—

† † †

The afternoon I first read that piece stays firm in my mind. We woke at two in the afternoon. The house was quiet. Outside, the neighbors could be heard in the yard, as could the trills of birds in the dogwood which bloomed outside her bedroom. It felt like a lazy Sunday afternoon in spring as we reveled in the indolence of rising so late. Laura had called in sick earlier that morning, at dawn, when we decided finally to go to sleep.

The night had been spent in a revelry of physical sensation. I'd had no idea what to expect when she'd offered to put me up for the night after a poetry reading in New York. I'd figured it was likely I'd wind up on a couch in her living room. Instead she'd given me a massage, by candlelight, on her bed, since my back was sore from lying on floor cushions at the reading. I had injured my wrist, which was in a splint, and thus could only lean on one arm during the entire performance, cradling my injured hand in my lap.

She rubbed scented oils into the muscles, a soothing sensation I had never before experienced. The combination of smells from the oils and candles, the lighting, the lingering sensation of her fingers along my back—it seemed natural as we were lying next to each other, to reach out and pet her stomach over the satin of her chemise. Though my hand was in a splint, my fingers were still free and danced across the fabric, thrilling the skin beneath with the light friction. Later, our clothes off, we rubbed our bodies together simply for the exhilarating sensation of skin moving against skin. Crouching over her like a wildcat, I ran my torso over her body, pressing down on her breasts to knead them gently with my own, dragging my body down across her belly, her waist, her legs, then back again. I dropped my head down to let my hair, which I'd been growing out for more than a year now, dangle lightly against her skin.

That night was touch for its own sake. We explored each other's bodies until dawn, kissed once, briefly, and slept. Sometime during the morning, Laura called in sick to work, and we stayed in bed until midafternoon. At last, I got up and showered, where I found the oils in her medicine cabinet. Wrapped in a towel, I went back into the bedroom and asked her about them, thus discovering the erotica she'd written for Paul. She made tea while I read the piece, understandably nervous about being in the same room with me as I was reading, and soon returned to the bedroom with two steaming mugs. "Tea?" she asked, innocently, ignoring the fact that I'd been reading.

"Come here," I said, getting to my feet. I let my towel fall to the floor around my feet. I was very excited from her story; my erection throbbed, flushed with blood. I took the mugs from her hands, and placed them on the nightstand, enfolding her in my arms. We kissed, and I drew her back onto the bed with me, running my hands along her back through the fabric of her robe. The neck of the robe hung wide, and I nuzzled her skin, running my tongue up to her chin, then back down to slide between her breasts. We rolled over, and she opened the belt of her robe, pulling the dark red fabric back slowly as if she were peeling an artichoke. I wanted to devour her. I leaned over her, bracing myself on my hands, when suddenly my right wrist gave out in a searing wrench of pain. I did not have the splint on, and the pressure of supporting myself had been too much. I bit back a cry, and collapsed on the bed next to her, cradling my injured hand under me, against my chest.

"I'm sorry," I said, "but I'm not up to this, it seems."

"Shh," she said, rolling me over and sliding on top of me. "I don't want you to do anything that will cause you pain." She took my injured hand in hers and gently kissed it. She licked the palm, then ran her tongue down to my wrist and slowly along my arm. When she reached my shoulder, she moved across to my nipple, teasing it with circles of her tongue and gentle bites. But she quickly slid backwards, dragging her body along mine as she kissed down my chest and stomach. The loose folds of the robe billowed about her like a butterfly's wings. Her breath was warm, exhilarating, as she explored my pubic area, rubbing her face against my hard cock as she tickled around my balls with her tongue. At last, her tongue met my shaft—a quick lick, a tentative probe. With her hands, she lifted my cock until it was perpendicular to my body, and slowly lowered her mouth over it, surrounding it, but not touching, not yet, only her warm breath. She held her mouth still for a moment, and I burned with anticipation. Then her lips closed, and suddenly her tongue pressed against the length of my shaft, sliding up and down.

My breathing grew heavy as she drew her lips along the length of my shaft, teasing my balls with one hand as the other grasped the base of my cock and squeezed gently. I was so excited that it did not take long before her touch pushed me into orgasm. "I'm close," I warned her, holding back to prolong the blissful sensation and give her a chance to pull back if she did not want me to come in her mouth. She kept her lips firmly clamped, her head bobbing up and down furiously, and I could not hold back any longer. I let out a cry, which slowly faded into a sigh as I recovered from my orgasm. My lips and hands were tingling with bliss, and I held them against her body.

"How do your hands feel?" she asked, concerned.

"In ecstasy," I answered, with a smile.

Laura smiled as well. "I've found a new form of therapy for them, then. Something your doctor would never think to prescribe."

"They should make you a practicing physician," I said, hugging her close to me and kissing her. My fingertips reflexively began to caress her thigh, but she stopped me.

"I don't want you to do anything that will injure your wrists. Just lie there and enjoy yourself."

I was frustrated with my body's betrayal, but succumbed to the bliss. I lay in the afterglow, feeling self-indulgent and enjoying it. The phone rang. I tilted my head to look at her and smiled as she turned to looked back. Neither of us wanted to get up to answer it. After the fourth ring, the answering machine picked up. It was her lawyer, saying that at last he'd submitted the final papers for her divorce, and that soon, hopefully, everything would clear.

I'd known she had been married, but had not realized the divorce was not finalized. Suddenly a gulf loomed large between us as I thought of where she was in her life with regard to where I stood in mine. But curiously, despite the vast differences in our lives, the closeness between us as we lay entwined, her hand gently squeezing my leg, my fingers still caressing despite her protests, did not dissolve.

"Ah, adultery," I said with a grin as I turned onto my side to look at her.

"A new experience?" she asked, also with a smile. I hesitated, and knew she was suddenly wondering, having noticed. But she did not ask. "Don't worry," she continued, "we've been separated for more than a year now."

I deliberated whether to tell her, wondering what would happen to our relationship once she knew. "It's not new," I say. "For the past two years, up until September when he moved back with his wife to Syracuse, I've been seeing Brian Coney."

I waited for a response, hardly daring to breathe, unsure whether to expect outrage, incredulity, or calm acceptance. She smiled, and after a moment, said, "Well, at last I get to sleep with him, if only vicariously through you!"

I smiled, pleased that she was so accepting. I knew that I could share how special that relationship had been to me. "Only you and he have ever made me feel an orgasm like that," I said. "Made me tingle. Too often it's just an ejaculation." I looked at her and said, "Thank you."

She ran her hands across my chest and said, "I'm glad. You deserve it."

I chuckled and asked her, "Remember when Jo Ann said I looked like a young Brian Coney at the reading in Boston? Right before you said he was so sexy that you couldn't talk in his presence? How I was biting my tongue!"

She was curious about everything, asking questions about him, and my relationships with men in general. The questions were never accusatory, but rather seemed prompted by pure curiosity. I believe the notion may have even excited her, especially when I spoke of Brian. She did not ask me which I preferred, making love to a man or a woman, but rather what I thought were the best things one could do with either sex, and what I enjoyed most from each.

I spoke of finally learning to receive pleasure with Brian, of how before I had simply been going through the motions of sex, with either men or women, without enjoying it. How sometimes a need for physical intimacy will well up inside of me until it's unbearable. How I need to touch and be touched, experience the feel of skin on skin. How sometimes I have to go through other things I don't want, or enjoy, to get that. When it builds up inside of me like that, I almost don't have a choice. And there's almost always a man who wants to get me into bed, and I go with him, for the brief moments of foreplay—before he has my pants off, and his own, his large erection pressing against me—and afterward, as we lie together, our bodies touching.

I think what I like most is lying in a lover's arms afterwards. I can never fall asleep like that, I'm too sensitized to the feel of warm skin against my own, but I relish it for as long as I can. But one has to go through sex to get there. Even if I don't enjoy the sex along the way, I'll go through with it, for that luxurious sensation afterward.

If you haven't noticed, I've been avoiding writing about the event that made me need to write this account. It's so much easier to wallow in the background, spewing forth endless, easy details. There's no emotional stake involved. Even talking about sex is easy, although revealing my desires and fantasies starts to get slightly uncomfortable. That's why I just realized as I was writing the above, how much I'd been avoiding the issue.

Enough of cold feet.

Laura is a portrait photographer, by profession, and we began taking photos of me, to try and reveal my inner self. I've never been terribly aware of what I look like, and a comment to this effect made Laura decide on the project. I readily agreed. I was curious what she could show me. I'd produced a body of work as a writer that was much more familiar to me than my own body.

I hadn't been photographed in a long time and was very nervous as we began. For one thing, I had no idea what I looked like now. Until I had begun to grow my hair out a year ago, my image had not changed in the last seven, eight years. I'd shown Laura two photographs of me, one taken when I was thirteen, the other at twenty, and both looked identical. Now, with shoulder-length hair, and the beginnings of a beard, I had no idea who I was. I'd still been using those photographs of my younger self as my mental image of myself. It's how I'd always defined myself, by the pictures I had of myself. That's how I imagined I looked to other people, and since I had no other way of seeing myself, that's how I looked to myself. Laura was going to show me who I was now.

The first session went awfully. I'd taken the train out to her place after work Friday, and after a quick dinner, we went upstairs to her home studio, on the second floor of the house. I was so tense that it made Laura nervous as well, and seeing that she was now nervous only made me more so. It fed on itself in a vicious cycle, until the air was thick with uncomfortable frustration, and we finally called it quits. We went downstairs, leaving the studio set up in hopes that tomorrow we'd manage a better session. We made love that night, tension dissolving as slow caresses gave way to deeper passion.

Waking the next morning, I felt content to be stretched out in her bed as she moved around me. "I wish you'd been this comfortable last night," Laura remarked.

"You should run get your camera," I teased. "Or rather, you can walk. I'm not going anywhere."

"Yes, you are, dear," she said, tugging me upright and kissing me on the lips. She dropped a white terrycloth robe in my lap. I smiled as I noticed the Hilton insignia embroidered onto it, and wondered if it had been stolen after a tempestuous weekend with one of her previous lovers, like something from the story she'd let me read. I put the robe on and followed her upstairs.

She positioned me in front of a large, freestanding oval mirror in her studio, and stood behind me. Reaching around my waist, she undid the sash of my robe, letting it fall open. "I want you to look at yourself, touch yourself, until you know what it feels like from the inside," she said. "Until there are no boundaries between the you in the mirror, and the you inside here." She tapped her knuckles against my chest, and squeezed me gently from behind. Then, taking my hand in her own, she began guiding my fingers across my chest, pushing the robe from my shoulders until it fell to the floor. She released my hand and stepped back as I continued exploring, running my fingers over my arms and torso. I watched myself in the mirror, studying my body as my hands passed over each area.

I touched every inch of myself, running my hands along the muscles of my neck, even exploring my scalp, the fingers smoothing my own hair as they felt their way along the curves of my skull. I moved my hands down my chest and back, onto my legs, crouching down to reach all the way to my feet. I stood again, my hands always in motion, discovering new areas—my thighs, my buttocks. I caught sight of Laura in the mirror, noticing that both she and the camera were watching me. I smiled, and did not stop my exploration. I grew hard, reveling in the multiple voyeurism: looking at myself in the mirror, looking at Laura looking at me. I could tell she was also turned on, and began tantalizing her, staring into her eyes through the lens as I moved my hands over my body, grabbing my erection with one hand as the other circled a nipple or explored elsewhere.

And suddenly, I turned and looked at her over my shoulder, directly, no longer through the mirror. The camera clicked, the shutter winking open and shut like the lips of her labia moving apart and together again in fast motion. She put the camera down and I went to her, almost giddy with desire. We kissed fiercely. I undid the sash of her robe, and she shrugged out of it quickly, as when, in old stories of the sea, seals shed their skins and become women. When I glanced in the mirror, I saw my hands running up and down her back. I snorted with amusement and pointed. Laura turned towards it, and in that moment I leaned down to kiss her neck, her breasts, the entire time watching myself perform these actions in the mirror.

I took the café chair she used for portraits and positioned it in front of the mirror. I sat down on it and held my arms for Laura to come to me. She eased my knees apart with her hips, and kissed her way down my neck, her breasts surrounding my erection. She licked my nipples, sucked on them, then began to drop lower, towards my cock. I stopped her, pulling her to her feet. "I want to be inside you," I said.

She looked at me for a moment, and I could sense her hesitation. I ran my fingers over her nipples, pinching them slightly. I pulled her towards me and she climbed onto the chair with me, slowly lowering herself onto me. I moaned as I slid into her, watching in the mirror as she rocked her hips backward and forward. I threw my head back, reveling in the sensation, and no longer cared about the mirror or watching us. I no longer needed it. I could feel my entire body from the inside, knew it exactly, perfectly. I wrapped my arms around her waist, and stood from the chair, slowly lowering us to the carpet. I kissed her fiercely, and then, supporting myself on my elbows since my wrist would give out, began rocking my hips, pushing deeper into her. She moaned with pleasure, her fingers grasping my shoulders tightly. I began to build speed, exploring deeper inside of her with each thrust, reaching for the places that would thrill her most. I was quickly hurtling toward climax, but held back, an almost painful sensation as each thrust brought me closer and closer. And finally, just when I could not restrain myself any longer, she arched her back and cried out as we pushed over the edge into orgasm at the same time. We laughed, kissed once, and collapsed in each other's arms, spent.

It's ironic that now, after she's pushed me from defining myself by words to showing me what I truly look like, I am writing about it. But perhaps that's exactly what I should do. It shows how much I have grown. My body of work was more familiar to me than my own body was. Now, having explored myself by sight, by touch, so that I truly knew my own interiors, the only thing remaining was to explore it once again, in words. To make the two bodies one.

HOT TODDY

Rachel Sherman

It was called a toddy, hot with whiskey.

I could taste enough to let me wonder. Two will get you somewhere; hot toddies led him from his house to mine. Hot toddies, hot from the stove, then in my living room warm from thermos mugs, made it all the way across town.

If you stir whiskey and cider in a vat, then add cinnamon, you have it. Three hot toddies get me a compliment and four get me in bed.

There, my stomach is warm from the juice. I worry he can smell me, and that the basement boiler is past its point. I feel its heat through my mattress and worry that it doesn't work.

Does a boiler get past the boiling point? Do plugged-in outlets ever blow up and die? Can he smell me? Do I have that hot toddy smell?

Sick toddy does smell in the bathroom toilet. It's ironic, getting this way from something so good. Having made its way down my throat from his polite persistence (please, please), hot toddy splashes its way out from up. How strange that, although so sweet, in the mug it already looked like vomit.

The small particles I had taken for the sweetness of apples and cinnamon were worthy of a grave for a dead fish, or worse, plain shit.

I am thinking all this the next day on the train, sitting close enough to the silver bathroom to bump my way into it, where I sit with my pants down on the dirty toilet. I look through its hole to the ground and watch the earth go by; those dirty pebbles, not to mention the tracks that just keep going. All this keeping the train steady on the rail. Or perhaps just this, just thin steel bars, making for a slight balance when flying by the water on one side, a lake on the other.

I watch the water. All its lapping is not worth my fright. Hot toddies, I realize, are not worth the fight. I want the compliments that seep through his lips after three mugs. And that sucking of the large toe, how that teased me into my head!

After closing my eyes, I put the toddy down. My father's middle name was Todd and that boy who lived across the street when I was little, who sang opera to my patient mother, his name was Todd, too.

I close my eyes.

On the train I can assess, slowly, where I might have put the mug down like a strong drumbeat on my fragile coffee table. It seems things would have been different had I done so; no opening and closing of the damn bedroom window all night.

He sighed in his sleep and I smelled his unbrushed breath. I could smell me over the toddy in his mouth and I kept thinking. While he slept, he inhaled both my insides until I threw up the drink, and then it was just the smell of one part of me I couldn't get rid of.

The train stops short between a big river and a small lake. The conductor says in a voice that is not his that something with two legs has jumped in front.

I worry where this two-legger has come from. There is water on all sides with telephone poles standing out from it. The tracks are in the direction of the land. I wish I could see.

Half-out and half-in my train seat, and half-out and half-in the one next to me, there is nothing to do but wait. The wheels are so delicately balanced that I might as well help with each cheek of my ass. You can get bedsores from sitting and cold sores from kissing, and tumors from thinking if you think enough to burn a hole. I worry about that, and him, too. There is no reason to be running in a hurry, so fast.

SEX IN THE PRE-APOCALYPSE

Anne Tourney

Whores have their heaven, and by whatever Lycra-clad, bleary-eyed grace that leads us to it, I have arrived. For the past thirteen nights I've been summoned by a man with a voice like the syrup my mother poured over Sunday morning pancakes. Sweetly he invites me to his apartment, always hesitant, always saying "please." I sashay to his neighborhood in my leopard-skin pumps, stepping lightly over sidewalks rich with sewage, holding my nose in the flatulence of an ongoing urban disaster. Multi-headed monsters watch me weave past bars and massage parlors and gelato stands and jewelry stores. I show up in the lobby of his building, where he buzzes me in, and I ascend to the twenty-first floor in a box made of glass, steel, and pure light. In a drawl that never comes out fast enough, he asks me if I'd like a drink, and I take his fine bourbon, then follow him to his bedroom, where he's already turned down the sheets.

"Could you take your clothes off, ma'am?" he asks every time, because he knows how it blows me away—not so much the hilarious request, but the velvet dip of the word "ma'am."

I wear a starched white blouse for him—pilgrim collar, tight sleeves—the same blouse I would wear on any date in a building like this, where you could get a nosebleed trying to estimate the average income of its tenants. Under the blouse I wear a black lace bra, the same bra I would wear for any oil-rich, fundamentalist Christian boy from Texas—if I had had one before him. After our third time together I don't have to pinch my nipples secretly to get them hard; they get hard all by themselves as I watch him stretch his pretty self out on the mattress. And after thirteen times with me he's still so shy that he lies down with his pants on and covers his crotch with his hands, as if he were just leaning back to reflect for a minute, instead of waiting to be blown into intergalactic nowhere by the woman with the most skillful throat west of the Rockies.

Before I get to touch him, he talks to me. He makes me lie down—in my Christian Dior panties and garter belt and stockings, with my painted face and hair teased to what he would call "Kingdom Come"—and listen to his stories. He tells me about the school he went to in Texas, a Pentecostal school, where they taught the kids how to tell the false Christ from the true Christ. He tells me that every time a child was out sick, the teachers would say that the Rapture took him or her off to heaven. While he's telling me all this, he starts touching me a little, stroking my shoulder or hip, and eventually he pushes me over on my back and eases his left hand under my lace panties, and with his thumb and forefinger rubs my lips together. He doesn't stop talking. While he's testing how wet I am, he tells me about how they made him memorize the Book of Revelations. He tells me about the Four Horsemen as he makes circles around my clit. He talks about signs and portents and the resurrection of the dead while my back arches and my hips buck up and down. As I'm bursting in a liquid star shower, he whispers about Judgment Day.

Then, while I'm drifting down, he takes the remote control and turns on his television. He changes channels till he gets the Christian Broadcasting Station. By now it's eleven-thirty: time for "Patty-Jane and the Pre-Apocalypse Brigade," and time for me to unzip his trousers.

"These are the days," he sighs, as I free his swollen cock. "These are the days of hope and anticipation."

Patty-Jane appears on the TV screen. Her lavender hair is bigger than mine, and she wears twice as much makeup. Her cheeks can hardly move with the weight of it. Her eyes labor under the burden of three coats of blue Maybelline Great Lash. While I stroke him, I watch her for a few minutes; I listen to her sing about the glory of the coming millennium and the ecstasy of the saved. Sooner or later my God-fearing client grasps the back of my head and moves it in slow circles. Patty-Jane turns him on. She wears bonbon dresses that show off a bosom nourished on God's Midwestern wheat. After she's finished singing, she sits down in her gilded stage set and talks to her guests. They are men full of wisdom, men with multiple chins, men who wear brown suits and chuckle contentedly about who will "get in" and who won't.

"Lately there's been a strange phenomenon in the Middle East," claims one of these lucky fellows, "a proliferation of vultures, which no scientist can explain. Well, the Pre-Apocalypse Brigade knows what it is, don't we, Patty-Jane? God's own clean-up committee. Just waiting to swoop down and devour the corpses of the sinners who have been left behind, once Jesus has carried the saved away." Patty-Jane closes her eyes, murmurs nonsense, clasps her hands tightly in front of her chest till her breasts leap upward.

I suck industriously on my Texas boy while this fat man chatters about vultures and sinners and the thundering of hooves. I work him up and down, head to tail, my lips and tongue a fury of wet motion. I cradle his ass in my left hand and grip the base of his cock with my right while I drag on him as hard as I can. When Patty-Jane sings "Amazing Grace," he lets his sweet salt ebb into my mouth. I savor the last of him on my lips—a lick of hellfire.

"If you were saved," he whispers, "you could be there with me on Judgment Day." I press my face against the damp furnace of his thighs. "You'd never have to worry about the fate of your soul. I can show you the way to salvation, honey."

"I can save myself and you," I reply.

"You can sure try," he sighs, as I climb on top of him. He's hard again.

"I told you," I murmur, sliding down his shaft, digging in for a long ride. "I told you I had the power of resurrection."

† † †

I inform my Pentecostal sweetheart that whoredom is better than boredom. Nothing is worse than waiting for time to pass on some cosmic calendar. My days are full of kisses and used condoms, the smell of deodorant and body fluids. Cuticle softener, fast-food grease, and K-Y jelly. Clouds of hair and skin cells. I'm so busy keeping the stream of consumption and excretion going that I don't have time to think of death, much less what comes after.

In high school I was voted "Most Likely To Be Found Strangled With Her Own Pantyhose." I like that. I cherish it, because it hasn't come true, and it never will, as long as I'm observed by guardian angels. Violence likes me; I know how to caress and manipulate it. I know the savagery of cities and small towns. I lived in Pawsupsnatch, Oklahoma, till I reached fifteen, when my lust ballooned into a demonic appetite. My high-school guidance counselor told me, as I was sitting stark naked on his lap, rocking back and forth and rubbing my nipples against his prickly jaws, that I would never be happy at any profession unless it fulfilled the deepest longings of my soul. Right after I came, I walked out of that school, hitchhiked to the Greyhound station, and rode to a nice, dirty city where I could settle in and fulfill the deepest longings of my soul. If what my Texan says is true, and unrepentant hookers will be dragged off to hell on Judgment Day, then we'll probably ride down to the devil on a Greyhound bus.

"You're the one who's sinning," I tell the Texan. He's standing naked in front of the widest bedroom window I've ever seen, watching the teeming mass of the damned below. "I'm just following the deepest longings of my soul."

"This town is crawling with signs," he says softly. He's not listening to me. He points to a green neon eagle in the sky.

"That's a beer logo," I laugh.

He turns from the window. He's about as hard as he can get—big and pink and gorgeous. He smiles. I open myself up for him.

"Sugar, that is a sign," he insists.

He lies on top of me and plows into me right away. It's going to be rough. I like that.

"Whatever you say," I moan, getting into my act, moving my hips in a dozen directions as he nails me. Then he stops.

"Would you just lie back for a second and quit selling?" he asks.

So I do it. I shut off the scream-siren, the hip-jack, the pussy-pump, and settle back for the first real fuck of my career. He starts slowly and does me at about fifty strokes per minute. Unconvinced, I swallow a yawn. What seems like an hour later, he's still doing me slowly, and I'm feeling like a rubber doll laid out on hot asphalt. I flex my claws, ready to dig them into his shoulders. He catches me by the wrists and holds me down. I moan. Squirm. He won't let go. In small circles he rotates his pelvis against mine. With his groin he locates the nub of my clit, and he refines his thrusts so that he abrades me every time. He starts moving faster—swift, shallow beats. He bites my breasts, giving me some serious pain. Helpless, I stare at him, with his damp mouth and flaming eyes, and I come. A sigh leaks out of my open lips as my soul lifts off like a jet. The spasms of my cunt are as loud as the beating of wings. Time takes a long, long break. Descending, I turn my head to gaze out the window at the yearning thrum of neon, and I think I might have a handle on what these holy people want.

When I walk down to the drugstore to buy lipstick or lubricant, I look up at the sky and wonder if it's getting darker as the days pass. I listen for hoofbeats and the panting of lions. I hand out dollar bills to any sore-stricken bum who asks. I deck myself in dog collars, lacy confirmation dresses, plaid skirts, whatever stirs my clients' souls. In my four-inch heels and microscopic leather minis, I teeter toward the flaming horizon, and whenever I get on a bus, I board the great, smoke-spewing Beast. I watch stiff-necked young professionals, dressed in Eisenhower white, scuttle towards their livelihood, and I dream of rescuing them with my lips and breasts and cunt. Looking up at the skyscrapers, I imagine them toppling slowly, like falling erections. I lick the dripping strawberry ice-cream cone that a runaway holds out to me, and I kiss her feverish mouth. I look for ecstasy wherever I can find it; I offer it to anyone who needs it. At night, in my bedroom, I watch the illuminated windows in the building across from mine. I watch a thousand bodies fucking, coming, and as their backs rise in an alphabet of omens, I come too, as enraptured as the rest of them.

SNAKEFRUIT

Anne Tourney

Octavia sits at the kitchen table, spooning peanut butter from a jar. Her husband's cat tiptoes toward the litterbox. Octavia growls; the tabby retreats. To the cat, Octavia must look like a devourer of felines—her belly huge, her teeth gleaming—but the thought pleases her. Her pregnancy has been full of epiphanies, ranging from the comic to the frightful. Nausea, bizarre forms of water storage, the endless exposure of her vulva to doctors and nurses. She feels as if she's spent a lifetime with her heels in stirrups.

Her husband Reggie lives in awed expectation. Out

of reverence and terror, he has stopped making love to her. Most of the time Octavia doesn't mind. Since her pregnancy, she enjoys solo sex more than ever. Alone in the afternoons, she explores pleasure like an unfamiliar neighborhood—a shabby, wild neighborhood. When she comes, a new pulse thunders in her groin, and her tiny conspirator rollicks inside her. Reggie reads his mother's yellowed copy of Dr. Spock and balances the budget. Octavia masturbates.

Closing the peanut butter jar, she pushes herself away from the table. She hasn't worked on her thesis or written a line of poetry since her first trimester; she's diverted her creativity into a search for food. The quest begins in the morning, after Reggie's chaste farewell kiss, and ends after midnight. Two monstrous, dueling appetites—for food and sex—propel her through the day. No desire to read or write. She never even picks up a pen anymore, except when she writes out a check at the grocery store, which she raids several times a week. The cashiers, all middle-aged women, smile sympathetically. The teenage stock boys blush at her fecundity. Pushing her cart through the parking lot, Octavia chomps pretzels or pickled okra. The madonna's privilege is a serene ignorance of appearances.

Octavia had expected to finish her doctorate,

publish a book of poetry, and coast comfortably from literary to maternal fulfillment. She and Reggie would enjoy a few self-indulgent years before facing the stark engagement of parenthood. And as they came to know each other deeply, their love would sink taproots into the mulch of their prosperity.

Everything changed.

They've been married for eight months when Octavia discovers Reggie's secret. She's furrowing through the storage closet, looking for her wedding album, when she finds a box of magazines. *Playboy*, *Penthouse*. Some slightly spicier publications: lots of tumescent members on the verge of plunging into prim holes. Then, at the very bottom, scenes from a land without limits. Creamy fleurs-de-lis spout triumphantly over breasts and lips and buttocks. Tongues prod labia of all flavors. Lips vacuum yards and yards of purple prick. Stupefied, Octavia falls to her knees. Pages full of flesh slide shimmering out of her hands. It numbs her, this universe of multicolored tissue, with its constellations of nipples and glistening cuntscapes. Forests of fur and fingers. Endless eruptions of ejaculate. Go West, young man, to a frontier where the cock never softens and the cunt never runs dry!

Octavia stares at the pictures. She has never seen

pure pornography. The most obscene publications have no copy at all. Words detract from the brute immanence of flesh. At first she wants to destroy the magazines. She wants to rip the pages apart and pin them on the walls, to relish Reggie's shame when he sees his home adorned with cunts and pricks. Or she could pile them in the litterbox and set them on fire; flame was more appropriate. She would pour cognac over them and make her husband light the match: Reggie's auto-da-fé.

But she's tired, too tired. Why douse obscenity with violence? Eventually they will talk, quietly and maturely, about Reggie's collection. They will "communicate." And Reggie, his head lowered in remorse, will shuffle out to the incinerator to throw the offensive material away.

Wearily Octavia dumps the magazines into the box. Poor Reggie. She's always assumed he had the sexual imagination of an amoeba. His libido is high, and he knows a trick or two, but he's never knocked her world out of orbit. When they have sex (when they used to have sex) his mind probably teems with the purple iconography of porn.

Well, why not? In her hottest moments, Octavia used to imagine the bass guitarist she fucked after her college graduation party.

† † †

Like Bluebeard's bride, Octavia can't stop thinking about her husband's Secret. She has endowed it with a capital "S"; it gives the noun a lewd Victorian majesty. *My Secret*, by Sir R—. She hovers around the coat closet where the box sits, and her hands itch to touch the doorknob. A week passes. Octavia's sleep is feverish—a symptom of her pregnancy, Reggie reassures her. In the bathtub, she studies her swollen breasts. She watches her hands knead the tumulus of her belly. Her fingernails are cut short, like a child's. Only savagely sexual women wear three-inch blades. When they stroke an erect penis, their nails graze the translucent skin. Their breasts and stomachs are as sleek as varnished bread.

One day, her brain burning, Octavia lumbers to the closet and flings open the door. The box is gone. She pushes past stacks of books, Reggie's golf clubs, her neglected Thighmaster, and a surfboard they've been storing for Reggie's younger brother, Lowell.

Reggie's brother. Undoubtedly Lowell has the magazines. Reggie would be too frugal to destroy them, too self-conscious to give them to a friend. Octavia can picture the solemn coming-of-age ceremony: "I, Reginald Baine, hereby pass down to you, my younger sibling, the images that have fed my secret concupiscence." Lowell would be grateful; he gives guitar lessons for a living and can hardly afford to eat, much less whack off to such a costly cornucopia of smut. Meanwhile, Octavia, who is just awakening to the possibilities of pornography, may never understand its visceral allure. She could buy her own supply, of course, but the image of a pregnant doctoral candidate buying fuck rags at a liquor store makes her cringe.

Octavia phones her brother-in-law. "Lowell," she says coldly, "have you seen Reggie recently?"

"Hey, Octopus. I saw him Saturday, as a matter of fact. He came up with a few boxes he wanted to give me. Some clothes and stuff."

And stuff. How chivalrous. Never mention pornography to a woman: she'll pitch a fit. Octavia gets to the point.

"Did he give you any magazines?"

"Yes," Lowell drawls.

"With lots of pictures of genitalia?"

"Are you psychic? Or did you two have a fight over Reggie's hobby?"

"I want them back!" Octavia snaps. "I'm using them for my thesis. I'm doing a feminist analysis of pornography, and I was using those as my research materials."

"I thought you were writing about Emily Dickinson!" Lowell protests.

"Dickinson's poetry has an erotic subtext that the lay reader wouldn't recognize," says Octavia haughtily. "There's more than a hint of submissive sexuality in 'He put the Belt around my life,' for instance."

"So do you want the three issues of *Belts on Butts?*"

"You can keep *Belts on Butts*."

"What about *The Wide World of Water Sports?*"

"We'll pick and choose when I get there. Are you busy this afternoon?"

"Come on by," says Lowell.

Lowell is twenty-six years old and has never had a permanent job. Four years ago he went to L.A. to seek work as a studio musician. Reggie loaned his brother his Volvo and a credit card to be used for emergencies. Lowell promised to return the credit card and the car within two weeks. Three months later, he straggled back to the Bay Area on a Greyhound. He had maxed out the card, sold Reggie's car, and contracted chlamydia. Besides the infection, he brought back nothing but his beloved guitar. Reggie calmly took that, sold it, and pocketed the cash.

Octavia drives to San Francisco after a Pantagruelian lunch of cold fried chicken, liverwurst, and leftover kung pao beef. Her stomach burbles as it digests her meal—how she loves eating and its placid aftermath! Her mouth is the only orifice that gets filled anymore, she thinks sadly. She used to love a hard, slow fuck, the kind that made her pelvis rock like a Ferris wheel car. She has seen men gazing at her hungrily; she is ripe enough to eat. She fantasizes about following one of these fertility worshippers to a sordid motel, letting him roam with tongue and fingers over her extravagant curves and savor the unusually heavy flow between her thighs. Those skyward-pointing nipples, that easy wetness, not to mention her perpetual horniness—shouldn't someone besides herself enjoy them?

Lowell lives in the Haight. After climbing the hill to his apartment, Octavia is exhausted, and she collapses gratefully on his mammalian brown sofa. Lowell grabs her feet and props them on a crate. He brings her a glass of water, then disappears into the bathroom. He comes out carrying the familiar cardboard box.

"Were you pissed off when you found this?" Lowell opens the box and dumps its contents on the carpet. "Incredible! There's a fetish for everything. Feet. Amazons. Women with facial hair. Did you have any idea that Reggie was a secret porn fiend?"

"No," Octavia says frostily. "He kept the box in a closet, under our wedding album. I had no idea he was attracted to women with facial hair."

"Well, these magazines usually come in packs of three. And they're wrapped in plastic, so you can only see the one on top. Poor old Reg probably slithered into an adult bookstore, snatched up a couple of three-packs, and left. It's a crapshoot. You never know exactly what you're getting."

"That's comforting," Octavia sighs. "Do you think Reggie's addicted?"

"This stuff is snakefruit. Once you've sunk your teeth in, it's tough to forget the taste. Reggie knew you'd blow up if you found his collection, but he still has the craving. You can bet on it."

Octavia studies Lowell as he sorts through the magazines, stacking them according to fetish. He is wearing a goatee now, and his hair has grown below his shoulders. Whenever she sees Lowell, with his secondhand clothes and aimless freedom, she feels sorry for Reggie. She can imagine the boys growing up together, Reggie forever forced to be vigilant and prim, Lowell allowed to sink into voluptuous failure.

"I posed for some magazines like this," Lowell says suddenly. "I don't think I'm in any of these, though."

"You posed for them? My God, when?"

"When I was down in L.A. and starving to death. It was an OK job. I had sex with a few women and got paid for it. No big deal." Lowell's face is the color of a boiled lobster. "I think that's when I got chlamydia. It could have been a lot worse."

"I cannot believe you did that. Even without the medical risks, it's so degrading! Screwing total strangers, while someone took pictures of it! I can't believe that, Lowell. And you're so skinny!"

"What difference does it make that I'm skinny?" Lowell asks in a hurt tone. "I'm photogenic, in a retro-hippie kind of way."

Octavia tries to imagine Lowell posing nude with a woman—maybe two or three women. She imagines a mattress covered by a cheap polyester bedspread, pocked with cigarette burns, in a room with aggressively white walls. Before the camera rolls, the actors exchange jokes and sticks of chewing gum. The setting she envisions is about as sexy as a surgical theater.

"Was it hard to get an erection?" Octavia asks.

"Not really. The cameras didn't bother me. I thought the photographer would be some kind of space ape, but he could have worked at Disneyland. It's weird, but the only time I had a problem was when I brought in one of my girlfriends. With strangers it was easy."

"Wasn't it disturbing to make love to strangers?"

"Sometimes. One girl had a bizarre smell. I tried to be polite about it, but sheesh! It was tough. I just closed my eyes and pretended I was drinking miso soup."

Octavia shakes her head. "I can't see it. Didn't you feel cheap, or guilty, or at least sad? Didn't you think about how it could affect the rest of your life? What if you get into a high-profile career, or decide you want to start a family?"

"Right. You're looking at Mr. High-Profile Family Man."

"You could change your lifestyle someday," says Octavia defensively. "You never know."

"Believe it or not, I did think before I tore off my clothes and launched my modeling career. I could have gotten a job flipping burgers—that would have taken care of food and money in one blow. But I wanted to do it. I wanted to be out there, naked. I mean, that was the closest thing I've done to art. The guitar's just a hobby. When I had the chance to be in those magazines, something inside me said, *Give it up, Lowell. All or nothing.*

He is holding a copy of *Big n' Busty*. The magazine quivers in his hands. Around him lie the fruits of commitment, indifference, carelessness, need. So many bodies, so many hungers between those pages.

"I didn't mean to condemn you, Lowell," Octavia says gently.

"I know it looks sleazy. But it's the only thing I've done that was authentic. Everything else has been half-assed, floating. Trailing other people, picking up the stuff they drop. But I can appreciate why you don't understand."

"I do, a little. I have to confess, I didn't want those magazines for my research."

"I thought that sounded kind of weird, even for you," Lowell smiles. "I didn't quite believe the line about Emily Dickinson."

"She wasn't as genteel as you might think," Octavia says. "'Ourself behind ourself, concealed—/Should startle most—' But you can keep the magazines. I don't think I could handle a hoard of snakefruit."

Octavia shifts her weight. The apartment is cool inside, and she doesn't mind the murky light. The magazines lie strewn like shiny coloring books on the floor.

"Could I see your stomach?" Lowell asks. "I've never seen a pregnant woman's belly."

The request startles her at first, but in this atmosphere of revelation, it seems natural, even necessary, that she expose something. "Why not?" she says, lifting her T-shirt.

"Jesus, it's a pod!" Lowell exclaims, staring at the shimmery hummock. "Can I touch it?"

Octavia nods. Lowell kneels in front of her and runs both hands over her skin, stretched nearly to transparency. Blue veins course over the milky slopes.

The tissue gleams. Octavia closes her eyes.

"I should warn you about something," Lowell says, "because you're my sister-in-law and everything."

"What?"

"I'm getting a hard-on. And I don't know why."

Octavia's eyes fly open.

"This has got to be the weirdest thing I've ever seen. It looks like a chrysalis."

He leans forward and applies his tongue to the pale globe. Slowly he encircles Octavia's stomach, then stops.

"I thought it would have an arctic taste," he comments. "But it's warm."

Octavia closes her eyes again. This doesn't feel like any form of betrayal, more like a surreal game of show-and-tell. She knows, when Lowell raises his body and rubs his erection against the southern slope of her belly, that she should protest, but the contact makes her weak. Lightly his lips clasp hers—it's natural to keep your eyes closed while you're kissing, Octavia thinks. It doesn't mean you're trying to deceive yourself about the strong possibility that you're going to make love with your brother-in-law. Now he's lifting her hair, murmuring in her ear.

"Can pregnant women have sex? I've got a condom in my wallet, and I desperately need to use it."

"Don't you care about your brother?" Octavia asks. A liquid reproach.

"It would just be borrowing," he pleads. "Not taking. I'd give you back."

"I'm not a Volvo," Octavia sighs. "Don't let my size fool you."

"Couldn't we do it as a scientific experiment? It wouldn't be fucking, it would be more like intercourse. I promise not to hurt you. And Reggie will never know."

"Can I keep my eyes closed?"

"You can keep your eyes closed if I can lick you."

"Lowell!"

"Please, Octopus. I'm fulfilling several fantasies here."

Lowell helps her scoot out of her pants. For what seems like hours, his tongue weaves through the crevices of her cunt, pulling her into a dream of honey and hot milk. She unhooks her bra so that he can slide his hands underneath and rub her swollen breasts, tweaking the hard nipples. Octavia laughs softly; opening her eyes, she sees Lowell's head below the hill of her belly, and she grasps the back of his neck, coaxing him to go deeper. As his tongue slides to her clitoris, he fucks her slowly with two fingers. Her clit has never been so sensitive; it feels like a small planet, with each side delivering a different sensation in response to Lowell's tongue.

"You are wet, wet, wet," he whispers.

"Don't stop. I'll kill you if you stop."

It starts with a tingling numbness, sharp as needles, and builds to a crest of joy that's almost painful. Lowell buries his face in her as she comes, and when she reaches the very top, the baby seems to hammer the wall of her womb with its tiny heels. Lowell beams at her, his cheeks glistening with her juices.

"It's your turn," Octavia sighs, shutting her eyes once more.

She hears Lowell unbuttoning his jeans and kicking them off. She hears latex squeaking as he slides the condom over his erection. It takes him a few minutes to adjust himself comfortably. First he tries kneeling in front of her, then propping himself up with his hands on the back of the sofa. Finally he slides a pillow under her rear end, then brackets himself between her thighs and slowly enters her. She's tight inside, in spite of her wetness—it's been so long since she's been prodded with anything other than a speculum.

"Could you spread your legs a little wider?"

She obeys. That's better. His penis slides into her with the blunt curiosity of a child's finger. Lowell is tentative and overcautious, but she's glad to be desired. He glides in and out a few times, but it's not going to work; he's too worried about hurting her, he says, and he's getting a fierce cramp in the back of his thigh.

"Doesn't hurt," she murmurs.

"It was only an experiment. Will you keep your eyes closed for a few more seconds?"

She opens them. Lowell is standing over her, his face strained with lust and maybe guilt, holding his stiff penis in his hand. He has taken off the condom; his cock's secretive eye is watching her.

"I told you not to open your eyes!"

"I want to see you," she says.

"I've got a Polaroid camera," he grins. "It's Reggie's. I could give you a souvenir."

"I won't forget." Octavia settles into the sofa's primordial softness. Vast and lush, it welcomes her as a member of its own species. Lowell cries out as his warm come rains over her stomach. Moistening her fingers with his fluid, Octavia draws maps of desire on the globe of her belly.

After an infidelity, a formal feeling comes.

"You don't have to lie about this, if you don't want to," Lowell tells Octavia. "You can tell Reggie. I'll just hang out here and wait to die."

"I'll think about it," Octavia says. "But I doubt I'll tell him anything. I needed that."

"So did I," Lowell grins. "I needed it a lot."

Now she will have a bed of secrets, painful and strange, to tend. Lowell walks her down the hill, and she's grateful; she didn't want to see his pale form withdrawing into the dim room. To her relief, he shambles toward a coffeehouse after helping her into her car. She turns on the radio and plays kinetic jazz as an antidote to the odd afternoon. As she leaves the city, the traffic thickens until her car is barely moving. Usually she panics in rush-hour traffic, but today it reassures her to be part of a slow-moving river of people, many of them tired and hungry or irritable and lonely, longing to be fed or touched. A heavyset bald man rubs his eyes. An elderly woman massages her neck. Octavia's baby turns in its bed of microscopic tendrils, giving her a sound kick as it dreams of its own desires.

DREAM OF SHADOW, SHADOW OF LOVE

Larry Tritten

In a world full of vogue-conscious beauties, Miriam was unique. Her sense of style was the product of a combination of raw instinct and a quirky taste for the offbeat and startling. This applied to her ideas of fashion as well as her behavior, and of course made her controversial, no less than provocative, the sort of woman whose image ranged along a spectrum from brat to enchantress depending on whose point of view.

Miriam had grown up in the mountains of northern Idaho, a dreamer through high school whose dreams soon enough drew her to Hollywood, where she made her living in ways both versatile and capricious, including temp work as a word processor, occasional modeling, a bit of X-rated movie performing (more for the outré experience than for the money), and quite a bit of this and that (which included being a writer for a lurid tabloid newspaper, tending bar, and verbally roasting party guests as a party-perker-upper). Like legions of people in Hollywood, she was writing a screenplay (based on her adventures), but unlike most of them hers was a double threat: literate and fascinating.

At home in the fantasyland of Hollywood, Miriam's favorite day of the year was Halloween. It was the one night in the year, she thought, when extraterrestrials might land and mingle with the people and none would be the wiser. It was also that adventurous night when she made every effort to end up with a lover whose identity and appearance were a mystery obscured by his costume.

There were always several Halloween parties to choose from, but on this Halloween Miriam decided to give priority to one being given by her friend Vale, a designer of sunglasses, at her apartment in Westwood. The invitation bore a lipstick print of Vale's voluptuous mouth, two coral pink parentheses, across the features of a new-wave witch with a Neapolitan mohawk.

By Halloween morning Miriam still hadn't decided on a costume. Some people planned theirs weeks in advance, but she was essentially spontaneous and tended to improvise something at the last moment. Even after spending much of the morning at a café on the Strip sipping coffee and watching the Mercedes and Silver Ghosts glide past in the sunlight, she still had no idea what she would wear. It was only when she found herself late in the afternoon back in her apartment that she started to think concertedly about it. In the kitchen, over a shot of tequila, she tapped her fingers on the table, deliberating.

Going to her closet, she started to rummage through clothing, touching silk and satin and denim and lace, pondering the possibilities. It wasn't until she glanced at her shadow on the closet door that the idea came to her: she would be a shadow. Yes. Perfect! She would wear a black leotard, black nylon stockings, and a black wig to hide her golden hair. She would paint her fingernails black and wear black velvet boots and use stage makeup to darken her face and hands. Only her eyes, as blue as cut sapphires, would contrast with the blackness, but she would wear a black domino mask to subdue their intensity. Excellent.

An hour later, as dark as mystery from head to foot, she stood before the mirror in her bedroom. She lifted her hands caressingly up over the undercurving of her breasts, beneath the jet-back fabric of the leotard, lightly stroking the sketchy presence of her nipples. She slid her hands slowly down to the planes of her thighs, bending slightly so she could glide her fingers lower to the curvaceous backs of her calves and down all the way to touch the sooty velvet tops of her boots with her gleaming black fingernails. Looking at herself in the mirror, she stuck out her tongue; its pinkness was startling by contrast. A thought came to her, and grinning, she went into the kitchen and took a licorice whip from a bowl. She ate it, chewing it leisurely to juicy bits, then returned to the mirror. Her tongue, as she extended it, now gleamed with dark light. She touched two fingers to the juncture between her thighs where the folds of her cunt could be felt against the fabric of the leotard. As she did so the musculature of her cunt pulsed and she savored an incipient sensation of wet heat there, a little shudder tremoring her body.

Patience, Miriam told herself, and then whispered, "Oh, fuck it." Within seconds she was standing ankle deep in a puddle of black leotard and with the fore and middle fingers of both hands was prying open the slit of her cunt. There was a tiny and all-but-subliminal peeling sound as she separated the adhesive labia, and at once the tips of four of her fingers were touched with wetness. With a murmur, Miriam looked down to see a sheen of pearly glitter in the vestibule of her vagina, a fat droplet clinging in tenuous suspension at the very base of her cunt in the manner of one of the last droplets of milk to spill from a carton.

Trick or treat, she thought, biting her lower lip in a straining smile. Miriam moved a forefinger to her clit and began to serenade her nervous system with gentle strokes. The droplet of come fell onto a thigh and she licked her lips in reflex, then slid three fingers up inside herself, very gently, her other forefinger moving to her clit. The viscid musculature enveloped her fingers, her mind filmed over, and her cunt became radiant, as her buttocks began to oscillate, her finger dabbling her clit as a flow of sensation seized her. Her mind became an art gallery of nonobjective painting, sparks skipping across shimmering blue water, fountains of light erupting, colored stars imploding, storms of confetti and twisting collops of iridescent light glowing, pulsing. She brought her fingers out of her cunt, saw them ornamented with turgid swirls of come, and almost swooned. Impulsively she marked her cheeks with the alabastrine stuff, white paths on the black, like war paint. She closed her eyes, and her mind reeled with images of black cats and bats careening, and she was coming, coming, rising into the coming, the other three fingers restored to the interior of her cunt to circle round and round the soggy lining. The orgasm carried her, mounting, cresting, and she felt the heat of her cunt, her nerves sparkling, her mind spinning, until she was forced, finally, to her knees, still coming, moaning, fading, turning slowly, then sprawling on the floor, the redolent fetor of her cunt enlivening her nostrils as the residual thrills in her brain and body faded. Miriam licked her delicious fingers in the aftermath, grinning lewdly.

Time to begin Halloween!

When Miriam left her apartment a full moon as lucid as a chunk of candy shone in the sky. Darkness had blanketed the horizon and was absorbing the last of the sky's twilight lavender. She drove toward Westwood along Santa Monica Boulevard. At Century City, stopping for a light, she watched a boisterous trio—a mummy, pirate, and Bedouin—caper across the street, obviously on their way to revelry, and their merry mood charged her with anticipation. She arrived at Vale's as the last of the light was vanishing. Vale lived in an old-fashioned building of sky-blue stucco. On the second floor her windows were open, an undertone of eerie Halloween music filtering out. Miriam recognized the music from the Warhol party sequence in *Midnight Cowboy*.

Vale met her at the door, a tall slim woman with swarthy Mediterranean beauty, costumed as a toy soldier: she wore blue pants, a red tunic festooned with gold epaulets, her cheeks highlighted with balls of pink greasepaint, a silver shako tilted at an angle in her waves of black hair. They exchanged greetings, a quick mimicry of the obligatory showbiz hug, and Miriam followed Vale inside, where the rooms were lit with candles set in carved grimacing pumpkins. A dozen or so guests circulated.

"See if you can recognize anybody," Vale said, and with a touch launched her toward the party. An haute couture ghost in an opulent violet satin sheet caught her eye, staring at her intensely through the two eyeholes in the sheet. Was it someone she knew? Miriam turned away and found herself confronting someone inside a papier-mâché tree reminiscent of those that threw their apples at Dorothy on the road to Oz. Reaching up with a gnarly hand, the tree plucked a plastic apple from one of its leafy branches, and offered it to Miriam, who took it with a smile.

"Enjoy this, Eve, it's forbidden fruit," the tree said in a male voice.

Carrying the apple held against her thigh, Miriam headed toward a table across the room where someone in a white rabbit suit was pouring a glass of azure punch. She served herself a glass and sampled it, giving her head a little shake as the strong alcoholic impact of it jolted her. The apple and drink in hand, she wandered into another room. Someone in a policewoman's uniform, replete with a real .38 holstered on her hip, passed her. Miriam, who had grown up with guns and done a lot of shooting, including killing dozens of birds and even a bear, wondered if the woman knew how to use the gun. Looking around the room, she noted a fortyish woman incarnated as a forties teenager in baggy, rolled-up jeans, a white blouse, saddle shoes, and white socks; Dick Tracy in a butter-yellow suit; and someone in a penguin costume smoking a Kool. She didn't see anyone she knew. Of course, it was still early.

She decided to find Vale and get the lowdown on some of the guests, and was on her way when suddenly in the hallway a dark figure loomed ahead, drawing her gaze. Abruptly she was staring at a virtual duplicate of herself: a shadow of her shadow. The woman, exactly her size, also wore black stockings, a black leotard and domino mask, and her face and hands were blackened with greasepaint. She was indistinguishable from Miriam except for her fingernails, which were bright red, and the black satin pumps she wore instead of boots. The blue light of her eyes was so intense and familiar that Miriam took a step backward, alarmed.

"God," she whispered.

"Oh," the woman exclaimed, and she took a step forward so precisely that it was like an inverse replication of Miriam's movement. She stared at Miriam as Miriam stared at her. In that moment a unique sense of peculiarity came over Miriam and she suddenly felt the kind of giddy sensation that might accompany a glance over a railing from the top of a tall building. Moreover, the moment seemed to disassociate itself from time so that she had an impression of reflecting the woman's gaze for an interminable period while the sounds of the party receded into a sort of incontiguous subreality. Then a vivid premonition of sensuality came over her, a surge of strange desire as she stared at the woman.

"Beautiful," whispered the woman, and Miriam saw the black semaphore of her tongue as she spoke.

Then the woman abruptly turned and walked away.

As she disappeared into the kitchen, Miriam moved to follow her as if by reflex. As she entered the kitchen, she saw the woman simultaneously exiting through the back door, and she hurried after her.

A flight of steps led down to a small lawn and garden that Miriam knew well from occasional afternoons of nude sunbathing. She paused and put her glass and apple on the porch's handrail, then followed the woman down the steps, her heart beating quickly.

At the bottom the woman waited, smiling up at Miriam as she descended.

Now Miriam felt a sense of excitement beginning to absorb her, starting a tactile simmering along her arms and legs. She felt a stirring of warmth in the depths of her sex. One hand seemed literally drawn to her crotch and her fingers lingered there, finding the fabric of the leotard flushed with dampness.

"Oh," she murmured with burgeoning arousal.

"Oh," echoed her facsimile. The shadow came toward her, her face moving toward Miriam's until their lips met and the woman was taking the pad of Miriam's upper lip softly between her lips and sipping on it. Then she slipped her tongue fully into Miriam's opening mouth, curled it coaxingly around Miriam's tongue to conjure it irresistibly into her own mouth. There was a moment of total blankness in Miriam's mind, followed by a sense of complete commitment as she began to participate in a thirsty exchange of kissing and tonguing in which the two disgorged delicious gobbets of spittle into each other's mouths until it began trickling down their chins.

"Darling," the woman whispered, and with the tip of her tongue painted halos of saliva around Miriam's mouth, licking the greasepaint off her cheeks and turning her head to feed in the aperture of an ear.

Miriam's head swam under the sorcery of her tongue, becoming balmy with desire and yielding fully to the hands now touching her, the fingers fanning out over her breasts, slinking down to seek the throbbing presence of her sex.

On the lawn, on her back, Miriam opened her eyes to see her shadow standing over her, taking off her shoes and leotard. She turned half onto her side and quickly removed her own leotard, slipping off her boots. They were both naked except for stockings held up by black garters. Miriam's legs were drawn up, her feet firmly on the ground, arms spread. The facsimile put her hands on the inside of Miriam's thighs and parted them until her knees were tilted at angles, and her cunt, labia uncloaked, was displayed like a lustrous bloom in the moonlight. Miriam drew her double down into her arms for more kisses, their mouths blending and tongues flowing in concert. She murmured with exhilaration as she felt a finger winnow into the vestibule of her cunt, then forge deeper into the slippery channel, a thumb pressing into the resilient clutch of her asshole.

They began to kiss and embrace each other like possessed houris, writhing about on the lawn. Miriam knew only motion and the exquisite flowing of a powerful sensual continuity that gradually became a mounting flood of orgasmic sensation as both bodies merged and fused, sex to mouth, mouth to sex, both of them finessing little effusions of sweet creamy come from the other's cunt.

Finally, her cunt exhausted and lips and tongue strained, Miriam opened her eyes and saw what she had somehow known all along. Her lover, drawing back to smile at her, removed her mask and wig to reveal that she was indisputably Miriam herself.

Miriam stared at herself in the soft moonlight. They were identical. Every contour of her body was repeated in the woman's figure: the same slender arms and legs, the exact full roundness of her breasts, with thickly peaked nipples in broad tea-colored aureoles, the pubic thicket so lush with densely massed curls that it extended in twin hedges along both sides of her cunt to the brink of the perineal gorge, and the choppy tangles of wavy honey-colored hair that tumbled down to the curves of her chin.

Miriam closed her eyes again and lay back, feeling the beating of her heart, and waited. For something, anything.

"My love," she heard herself whisper into her ear, and she felt her fingers on her body, touching her throat, her breasts, fingers rippling the taut nipples, trailing over her stomach and into the mulled flux of her sex, stroking her arms, legs, the lightly sweated fragrance of her hair as the wig was discarded. As she caressed herself, she heard herself whispering, "Yes, you; I came through the mirror for you." It was the sound of her own voice (which a former lover had once described as volcanic ash and gold dust). She heard the familiar sound of her own laugh, then: "My love, I'm really you. Remember the scientist you dated? The biochemist. Remember?"

Miriam remembered David, a lover of months ago; it had been a brief and failed affair, just a fragment of the past now. "David," Miriam's own voice whispered, "needed only one cell, just one of your cells, love, to recreate you, to clone you, to make me so he could let you go and have you as well."

The words were like veils of moiré through which Miriam glimpsed, waveringly, a spellbinding vista.

"But I love you, Miriam."

Drifting into somnolence with the flow of whispered words, and delicate caresses, Miriam receded into the depths of her mind and body, enclosed by shadows.

Some time later she opened her eyes and sat up to discover herself alone under a full moon, wearing only her stockings and mask. She stood up and remained motionless for a long while as the odd dream replayed itself in her mind like a film running backward: the ineffable pleasure of the lovemaking, the descent to the backyard, the first sight of her other self at the party. A sound of party activity came from the apartment: music and a mingling of voices and laughter.

Miriam dressed. She was eager to be back inside, to disperse the strange memories with conversation and drink.

Then, as she glanced about for her boots, she felt a sudden chill, sensing even before she discovered it that the boots had been replaced with a pair of shiny black satin pumps.

She put the shoes on, knowing they would fit perfectly, as they did. Looking at them, she flexed her toes comfortably, admiring the mirrored gloss of the black satin.

"Miriam, what the hell are you doing down there?" shouted Vale from the porch. "I thought I saw you leave out front."

"I—" Miriam began. "I'm coming." She waved to Vale, then started up the steps, wildly wondering how long it would be before her phone rang at home, how long she would have to wait before she called herself to whisper the words she knew she would hear herself say.

1–900–FANTASY

Alison Tyler

Ian and I found each other at a bar in Hollywood called Ye Olde Rustic Inn. It wasn't like a 1940s movie where our eyes met and held and we fell in love. It was more a floundering lunge together out of sheer necessity. Most of the other patrons were die-hard drinkers, decades older than both of us (some older than the two of us put together).

Ian and I gravitated to each other as if pulled by a magnetic force. In the dimly lit bar, we moved from the counter to a booth in the back, and we got to know each other over a few unhurried shots of hard liquor.

Ian was trying to obliterate a pretty waitress named April from his memory. I was trying to erase the fact that a handsome truck driver named Miles even existed. Together, we sat in the deep, dark vinyl booth and drank Wild Turkey and talked about the very love affairs we were doing our best to forget. We covered reasons for the breakups, and we discussed what it was about our mutual exes that we missed the most.

On that first night together, I took one of his hands in mine and turned it face up.

"Are you a palm reader?" he asked.

"An amateur."

"What do you see in my future?"

"It's cloudy," I said, "But I can see your past. Lonely nights. Lots of them. Trying to forget..."

"Her smile," Ian would say some evenings. "Her smell," he'd say on others. "The way she looked at me when we weren't talking, you know, just sitting at some café. She'd look at me like she loved me."

"She did."

"And then I ruined it by having a fling with her sister, so there truly was no going back."

When it was my turn to share, I'd feel slightly less poetic than Ian. Mainly, I missed Miles's cock. And, though I had been the one officially to end the relationship, it had been his mean streak that had instigated the breakup.

At some point, Ian and I realized we were talking less about our exes and more about each other. We realized we were sitting closer together in the booth, that our legs just happened to bump and our thighs rub as if our bodies had wills of their own. Weeks after our first meeting, I took his hand in mine again.

"What do you see this time?" he asked. "Still only my past?"

I shook my head. "There's a tigerish redhead in your future," I told him, and that led him to ask me back to his apartment at closing time. We walked the few blocks in silence, a strange occurrence for us. We were drinking buddies and talking buddies. Silence was new, startling, and difficult to deal with.

At his place, he ushered me in ahead and turned on the light. It was a small apartment, immaculate, with very few personal objects. Once inside, he took me to the sofa and then got a bottle and two glasses. Just because we'd left the bar didn't mean we were done drinking for the night. I was happy to have a glass in my hand; it made me feel secure.

Ian settled himself on the other end of the couch and looked at me. Suddenly I could relate to the way he'd said April had looked at him. He was staring, as if mesmerized, and I had to ask, "What?" smoothing my hair, wondering if I looked worse to him out of the dim light of the bar.

"You're beautiful," he said, as if awed. "You're spectacular." I relaxed and looked at him. Ian has curly blond hair and green eyes, a strong jaw, a lopsided grin. He nudged me with his foot and I settled back into the sofa, still staring at him. We'd never had a difficult time with words—not until now. I wondered how we were going to get over our shyness.

Ian seemed to be wondering the same thing, or brainstorming on the same problem, because he stood and got his cordless phone, then came back to the sofa.

"I've gotten addicted to 976 numbers since the breakup," he said, something he hadn't told me before. "It's so bad, I've been thinking of blocking them from my phone."

I tilted my head at him, curious. "I've never called one before."

"They're fun." He placed the phone at his side, reached for my hand. I felt a charge when he began playing with my fingertips, tickling them with his. "I don't talk to the same girl, or anything. But I always get off, listening."

I felt myself growing aroused, unsure of the exact reason for the wetness in my panties. I thought for a moment, then said, "I'd like to listen while you talked. That is, if you wouldn't mind?"

His eyes glowed. I thought he'd had the same idea. I asked, "Do you have a separate line I could listen in on?" His studio was so small that I doubted he'd need two phones, but he surprised me by handing me the one at his side and returning with a second.

"I have one in the bedroom and one in the kitchen." He was dialing while he spoke. I lifted my receiver but he said, "I'll tell you when." Then, after a few moments, he nodded and I pressed the red button on my handset.

The woman's voice was low and husky, exactly how I would talk if I were working a sex line. I knew her goal was to keep Ian on as long as possible, and she did a good job, starting slowly, asking him his name, describing herself for him, then asking his fantasy.

"Two women," he said immediately.

"Oh," she purred. "Me and a friend of mine...or do you have someone in mind?"

"I have someone." He moved closer to me on the sofa. He was gripping the phone with one hand, but he stroked his fingers up and down my thighs with the other.

"What's her name?"

"Miranda."

"Pretty name. Is she a pretty girl?"

"Spectacular." His mouth was away from the phone, his lips against my ear as he spoke.

"What do you see us doing?" she asked.

"Why don't you tell me?" Ian suggested, now being more forward, cradling the phone against his shoulder and sliding both hands under my skirt. I trembled as his fingertips met my naked thighs, swallowed hard as he dragged his thumb down the sopping wet seam of my panties.

"I see us in a tub," she said, "a bubble bath. Do you like that?"

"Mmm," Ian murmured, to keep her going.

"The three of us soaping each other all over." She was getting a little louder as she spoke, as if she were really turning herself on.

"I like that," Ian said, then looked at me and mouthed the words, "Do you like it?" I nodded.

His fingers were probing up to the top of my panties; then he slid them down my thighs and off. The woman was still talking, but I could hardly concentrate on what she was saying. Ian was on his knees on the carpet, between my thighs, and he had set the phone down while he moved forward to taste me. I spread my legs wide and tried to stifle my moans.

She continued to describe the scene for us. "Your

girlfriend is sitting on the edge of the tub, Ian. Her pussy needs to be shaved. Do you want to shave it, or should I?"

I tapped Ian's shoulder, wanting him to pick up the phone and talk, but he shook his head, the movement spiraling me into bliss as his whiskers tickled my outer labia. "You do it," he said against my skin. "You talk."

"This is Miranda," I said into the phone, startling the sex lady from her monologue. "Could you shave me? Ian's a bit...busy."

She didn't falter. "Of course, darling. What color fur do you have down there?"

"Red," I said, sighing as Ian stroked it with his fingers, tugged gently on my curls. "Dark red."

"Pretty," she said, "But I'm going to shave it all away and make you nice and clean for your man and me. I'm dying to taste you, and I want you bare before I give you my tongue. Wouldn't you like to be all nice and clean and pretty for me?"

I mumbled something. She kept talking. I was having a hard time concentrating: the combination of Ian and his magic tongue between my legs and the phone-sex lady and her hypnotic voice transported me. As I neared orgasm, I handed the phone to Ian, insisted he take it from me, and he said, "Ginger? It's been a pleasure. We'll call you again."

As he hung up the phone, I said, "Next time you'll listen while I work you." He smiled and let me know that would please him just fine.

I think we're both going to mend our broken hearts without a problem. I foresee a long and powerful love filled with sexual heat and fire. I may be an amateur soothsayer, but I've got a real good feeling on this one.

ANTONIA'S BEAST

Alison Tyler

My best friend, Antonia Miller, is a wisp of a girl, with pale blonde hair as soft as eiderdown and a translucent complexion reminiscent of a Pre-Raphaelite model. Sometimes she wears layered antique slips snagged from secondhand stores on Melrose. Clad in faded rose satin with lace at the collar, she might have just stepped out of a nineteenth-century print, a low flush on her cheeks, a secret half-smile on her lips. Other times, she wears gauzy, ethereal dresses. Always, she looks like a half-frightened wood nymph, her cherry red hair loose and alluring around her cameo face.

I know that her fashion sense makes it sound as if she's not shy, but bold and forthcoming about both her sexuality and sensuality. This is not the case. She has a beautiful body which she dresses seductively. But her composure is one that Miss Manners would approve of entirely. She is discreet and charming. She doesn't have a bad word to say about anybody. She blushes whenever anyone stares at her for one beat too long.

I am often guilty of this mild infraction.

Antonia works at a café across the street from my office. She makes dreamy confections behind the counter, piling on whipped cream, chocolate shavings, dashes of cinnamon, and just a touch of amaretto. On my breaks, I come over and sit at one of the high-backed stools, waiting for her to take a moment and serve me, to come out from behind the wood and chrome counter to sit at my side.

My best friend is a demure spirit, and yet within her heart lingers an impish creature who peeks out from time to time. When this fiend takes over, Antonia changes. She becomes bolder. She speaks louder. She drapes a diaphanous shawl across her bare shoulders and teases me with the fringe.

She tells me stories.

"Did you ever hear about Marc?" she asks, innocent-sounding, but I recognize the undercurrent of her tone.

"The musician?" I think to myself that the fiend is loose, the imp is out, the beast within Antonia's breast is free for the afternoon.

She nods and sips from my café mocha, leaving a sparkly lipstick kiss on the rim of my cup. The whipped cream makes a mustache on her upper lip, and she flicks her tongue out to lick it clean. I find myself teetering on the brink of fainting when she does that, thinking of so many other dirty places she could place that darting kittenish tongue.

Antonia brings me back. "Yes, the musician. Did I ever tell you about the time with the baby oil?"

The businessman seated at Antonia's right perks up. I can tell that he's stopped reading his newspaper and is paying close attention to our conversation. At times like this, when Antonia's beast roams free and she is ready to share, all eavesdroppers are in for a treat. The change may occur in a bookstore, at a theater before the film starts, in line at the grocery store. I watch the man lean slightly closer to Antonia. I wait for her to notice, but she doesn't.

"The baby oil?" I widen my eyes, urging her to continue, to thrill me. "No, I don't believe you ever told me about the baby oil."

She takes another sip of my drink. Then she says, "Marcus used to play his guitar all the time. Whenever he wasn't onstage, he pretended he was. It wasn't about practicing, for him. It was about performing."

I have clients in the music industry. I nod to show that I understand.

Antonia's story goes like this: Marcus was sitting on their water bed strumming his guitar. In his mind, he was performing for an audience of a thousand beautiful women. In reality, his one beautiful woman, Antonia, was taking a shower. The door was open, and she could hear the faint melody of his songs above the spray of the water. When she emerged, wrapped in a towel, she stood in the doorway and watched him play. Marcus was a particularly appealing performer. He had long black hair that hung straight and glossy down his back. He was thin and looked good in tight leather pants. He had colorful tattoos on his biceps and across his chest. He was the perfect Hollywood masturbatory fodder.

When Antonia caught his attention, he looked up at her with a glazed rock god expression. She stood there, with the steam from the shower still dispersing behind her, red hair curling from the moisture, face flushed from the heat. She approached and he put down the guitar. She had a bottle of baby oil in one hand. She gave it to him and he took her over his lap and spread the clear oil all over her legs, from her ankles to her thighs. He worked her thoroughly, as if still onstage in his head, as if still in the part of the performer. He played music on her body, using his fingertips, using the full palms of his hands, rubbing, rubbing. Then he moved higher, massaging the cheeks of her ass, and in between them.

Stop the story: The man at the counter is having heart palpitations imagining lovely Antonia on her stomach, ass up, legs spread, her honeyed nectar mingling with that pure, undiluted scent of baby oil. I swallow hard. The man swallows hard. Antonia continues, oblivious.

She tells it like a bedtime story, in a low lilting voice that has a rhythmic pulse to it. They've never fucked like that.

She hesitates, makes herself continue. They've never had anal sex. He's never tried, and she certainly wouldn't have suggested it. But his fingers begin to probe her back door. His pointer and his middle finger push their way inside this tightest of openings. She sighs. She clings to his leg. She lets him continue. He makes circles with his fingertips as he delves further. Antonia's breathing speeds up. She feels as if she's going to pass out. She begs him to stop, but she doesn't mean it.

Marcus is gentle, but persistent. He lubes her up and massages her until she is relaxed and ready. More than ready, dying for it. She is inexperienced and suddenly she wants to be experienced. She moves off his lap and waits while he undoes his faded jeans and pulls them down. He mounts her on their rolling, bucking water bed, moving with the motions, gliding inside her. She buries her head in her arms, her face crimson with a combination of shame and lust. They don't speak, but as he builds up to climax, he strokes her hair and murmurs something under his breath that sounds like one of the lyrics in his songs.

Freeze-frame. The man at Antonia's side wants to know the lyric. I want to know the lyric. He's leaned over so far that he's practically in her lap. She is still unaware of his intrusion. I don't point it out for fear that she'll stop talking, for fear that Antonia's beast will shape-shift back into the wood nymph I am accustomed to.

She squirms on the chair as if the retelling of this memory has excited her in the same way that it's excited her audience. I can't help myself. I ask, "What did he sing?"

She looks at me, her eyes registering me for the first time during her story. She says, "I don't remember," but I can tell she's lying. She says, "The best part was the way he moved. He always moved as if he were in front of an audience. I don't mean posing, but confident, strong, in control. He made love the same way, he fucked"—unless the beast has come out to play, Antonia never says "fuck"—"the same way."

And when he took her like that, like an animal, like a rock god should, the imaginary audience of thousands broke into thunderous applause.

DIAL "O" FOR OYSTERS

Alison Tyler

"Ohh, baby," he says, sounding like Elvis, a blond Elvis, with his thick, wavy hair slicked back off his forehead, his lip curled into that trademark sneer.

"Baby," he says again, and then smiles, and the Elvis similarity disappears. It's Anthony, my handsome, boyish lover, grinning down at me, pale blue eyes still glazed with an orgasm-high. He doesn't ask if I came, which makes me want to marry him on the spot. I hate that awkward pause after a guy explodes inside you, and then squeaks pitifully, "Did you, uh, you know...?"

Anthony knows because I'm loud when it's good, and the neighbors have been pounding on our floor (their ceiling) with a broom handle for the last ten minutes. I've seen them before in the foyer. They look so straight, so uptight. I wonder what they'd think if they knew about our video camera, on a tripod in the corner of the room, recording our actions for future late-night viewing. Anthony has a thing about watching us making love. He likes to fuck me from behind, but he likes to see the changes creep across my face as I come. To accomplish this feat of spectatorship, we have mirrors in our bedroom, but he likes the video camera best.

"Do you want another cherry, Julia?" He slides down my body and rests his head on my left thigh, watching me from beneath heavy-lidded eyes. "Huh, Jules? Huh, baby? Want another sweet cherry?"

"Cherry" is his pet word for my climaxes. "I want to taste your cherry," he'll whisper against the hollow of my throat, and then he'll move down, lower, grabbing hold of my waist and dipping his tongue between my netherlips, working me until I come and come again.

"Please," I beg now, blushing at how hungry my body is for his magic tongue. Anthony smiles at my need, at the urgency of my desires. But he doesn't tease me, doesn't make me wait. He parts my kittylips with his fingers quickly, spreading me open wide, and begins lapping at the flood of juices awaiting him. Lapping and licking and pursing his lips around my tiny pearl, bringing me as close to heaven as I'll probably ever get in this world.

He's videotaped me up close while he's gone down on me. He wanted me to see what he sees, the delight of my cunt at close range. He says it's the prettiest pussy he's had the pleasure to know. That embarrasses me, but I like hearing him say it anyway.

I didn't want to watch the first tape after we made it. Anthony kept asking if I'd view it with him, but I refused. It wasn't that I didn't want to see him, it was that I didn't want to see myself.

"What if I look bad?"

He reached over and pushed my bangs out of my eyes, then traced his fingertip down the bridge of my nose.

"How could you look bad?" he asked, trying to dissolve my fears. "You're gorgeous. I wouldn't go for a girl that wasn't, would I?"

I said no, but I didn't mean it. He could tell.

"Do I have to tie you down to get you to see it?" He liked the thought. He described it for me. He would use two of my scarves around my wrists, binding me to the four-poster bed. He could position the television to one side of the bed and hold my face down, making me watch it while he fucked me again. He could even set up the camera to film us watching the film. The possibilities were endless.

"I'll watch," I said finally. "But if I look bad, I want you to stop the tape."

He promised, lying, and pushed the cassette into the VCR. And, actually, it wasn't bad at all. It was much more fun to watch than the silly X-rated flicks we've gotten at the video store. I especially liked watching while he went down on me. I had never been able to see myself from that angle before.

Anthony's favorite time to eat me is after we've had sex. He says that the blend of our flavors is intoxicating, like wine and honey, that he can get drunk off our taste. He is slow with me, and when he feels my body start to tense, straining forward, he lifts his mouth and admonishes me.

"Relax, Julia, and let it happen. Baby, relax." His words calm me, and I settle back in bed and let him take care of my needs. He drinks from me as if my come were the nectar of the gods, and my body responds by growing ever wetter, readily supplying more ambrosia as quickly as he laps it away.

"That's right, darling, just let yourself go." That

means he wants me to make noise for the camera, to moan and sigh and call out his name. It's hard for me if I'm thinking about it, but when I get close to coming, it happens naturally.

I feel it beginning, the warmth spreading through me, the tightening inside my body as he takes me there....

Anthony says that he can tell when I'm going to come, that my juices get sweeter at the second of climax. "Sweeter than candy," he says, his blue eyes wide with the wonder of it. "How can you be sweeter than candy, Julia? How is that possible, angel?"

His lips caress my clit, and then he swirls his tongue in rapid circles that take me up, up, and over the edge. As I ride the waves, those rumbling crests, he uses his entire mouth on me, rubbing his golden evening whiskers against my thighs and moving his head back and forth in rhythm with my endless contractions. Then he kisses along the ridges of my hipbones, tickling me, and I squirm away, laughing, happy.

He makes my life with George seem like nothing more than a bad dream.

While I'm still basking in that glorious afterglow, my skin warm and smooth, my thoughts lazy, Anthony turns me on my side and enters me that way, one of my thighs over his knees, my body split in two. He's going for a marathon, and I wonder if the tape will last or if we'll miss the finale when we hold the screening. We'd just have to film it again, though. No worries.

He lightly fingers my clit while his cock fills me, pulsing inside me, withdrawing until just the knobby head of his powerful rod is held within me, then thrusting in deeply again. He adjusts my position slightly, holding onto my waist as he increases the tempo. He's already come twice, so that means I'm in for a long ride. I ache inside from his pounding rhythm, but it's a good ache, both filling and fulfilling.

I roll over onto my stomach and spread my legs even wider apart, hooking my feet on his legs, gaining leverage on his tight calves. He strokes my ass very gently, an amazing contrast to the speed and the friction of his cock throbbing inside me.

"You have the most beautiful bottom, Jules," he tells me, his caresses lingering now between the cheeks of my ass, parting them slightly for a better look at his cock driving that wild staccato beat. He likes to watch, likes to see his shaft move hard and fast in its journey to delirium. I feel his balls slap against me. Suddenly they tighten as he starts to come. The sexy way he moans as he releases makes me shudder, and the tremulous waves wash over me again, echoing through my body.

"Jules!" he yells it as he comes. "Oh, my sweet Julia. . . ."

Afterward, he relaxes on top of me, his cock still inside me. We fall asleep like that, stuck together, one being joined at the pelvis, joined with sex and sweet cherry juice. The red light of the video camera is still on. I don't mention it to Anthony. I'd like to see how we look when we dream.

A second before I slide into sleep, a picture of George floats before my eyes. "I miss you," the apparition says.

"Then miss me," I say back. "You screwed up, George."

"Yeah, I guess." And the vision vanishes.

I never thought I'd get bored with George. I mean, I've seen those couples, the ones who sit in coffee shops and don't say a word to each other for an entire meal, the man's eyes glued to his newspaper while his wife stares unhappily into her coffee. I never, ever thought we'd become one of them.

But we did.

After Letterman, I'd switch off the TV, make sure the dog was inside and the cat was out, set the breakfast table, and then climb into bed next to George. I even caught myself thinking of him as an "it," a living, breathing, snoring IT. My life went: Run, Shower, Work, Groceries, Dinner, George, TV, Cat, Dog, Sleep.

Sex became routine, too—simply another thing to check off my "To Do" list. Our lovemaking escapades were infrequent, often "quickies" that took place between 6:00 and 6:03 A.M., before I was even fully awake. That's pretty sad when you think about it, pretty sad that a twenty-five-year-old woman and a thirty-two-year-old man were in the kind of a rut I had always reserved for couples in their Golden Years.

The most confusing part of the situation was that the less attention George gave me, the more attention I got from other men: guys at work, on the street, even at the market. At first, when I noticed that George's interest in me was slipping, I tried to win it back. I still thought I loved him, or the him he used to be. And I just wasn't ready to give up on a five-year relationship.

At the advice of my coworkers, I went to a fancy Beverly Hills salon and had my hair straightened in the style that he liked. I became a regular at the expensive grocery store around the corner from our West Hollywood bungalow, preparing challenging gourmet dinners nightly. I even tried wrapping myself in plastic wrap after reading about it in an article titled: "How to Light His Fire." Nothing worked. Maybe I needed a blowtorch.

I found myself asking more and more people for advice. My hairdresser said that I should consider going blonde. The lady at the lingerie counter suggested an animal-print teddy. Even the man behind the fish counter at the upscale market got into the act.

"How'd he like the grilled salmon?" he asked.

"So-so. The Dodger game was on, and George had his dinner in front of the TV, washing everything down with beer."

"Have you considered oysters? They're supposed to be an aphrodisiac."

"Do they really work?" I was willing to try almost anything.

"So I've heard," he assured me.

"Well, have you tried it?"

"I haven't ever needed to 'recapture' someone's affection," he answered. "I can't believe that you'd have to, either." He paused, as if he thought he'd overstepped his boundaries. But then, gaining confidence in my blush, he continued, "You're beautiful."

I looked up at him from my spot in front of the lobster tank where I'd been watching the poor, homely creatures climb over each other. I knew just how they felt: trapped. Suddenly, I wanted something more, something else, but I wasn't sure exactly what it was.

Without saying a word, I continued to stare at him, realizing that this was the first time he'd said something beyond the fishmonger-to-shopper casual dialogue. I found myself looking at him from a completely new perspective.

His blond hair has a reddish tint, and it's lighter than the hair that curled in the open V-neck of his pale blue work shirt. He has a very broad chest and hard, muscular arms, and the name tag on his shirt said "Anthony." For the first time, I noticed that the uniform shirt was the same faded denim color of his eyes. He waited modestly while I checked him out, and then he asked my name.

"Julia."

"Well, I'm serious, Julia." He paused. "That's a lovely name. Do people ever call you Jules?" (He said "Jewels," as if he meant something precious.)

I nodded.

"I'm serious, Jules. Maybe instead of trying to win this guy back, you should consider looking for someone else."

"Like you?" I kidded, but he just shrugged innocently and smiled, a grin that seemed to clash with the look in his eyes, and went back to cutting fish.

I brought home a pound of oysters and took my time setting up a feast. I tried to keep the image of Anthony out of my mind while I chilled a bottle of white wine and arranged an artful display of wildflowers in the center of the table. Then I put on the little black dress

George had bought for me in Paris. How long ago that vacation seemed, a trip on my twenty-first birthday. Had we really been in love? I wondered. Can love simply disappear?

I touched a bit of perfume behind my ears and knees, and on my wrists and neck, using the subtle fragrance of rose petals to whisk away my disturbing thoughts. I took time to do my makeup, using a deep red lipstick that would leave smeared kisses on his mouth—kisses like the echoes of our love, kisses that could be rubbed away to nothing.

At 6:30, I lit two ivory candles, turned out the rest of the lights, and sat down on our crimson velvet sofa to relax with a CD of classic Elvis. George was due home in about ten minutes.

When I woke up, it was 11:23. Elvis's baby had left him, and he had found a new place to dwell. My candles had burnt down to sputtering stubs. I stretched, let out the howling cat, and very calmly took the oysters upstairs to the bedroom. I opened George's underwear drawer and put a cold, raw oyster in each one of his neatly folded BVDs. Then I poured wine in his sock drawer, packed my favorite clothes in one suitcase, my mementos and photo albums into another, threw everything into the trunk of my Alfa, and drove to a very classy hotel overlooking the Palisades.

Something had snapped inside me. Some fine elastic wire pulled to its absolute limit had snapped and set me free.

I am now two months into my new life, and I feel alive for the first time in five years. On my first day "out," I called Daniel at the hair salon and had my hair done in glorious auburn curls, the way I like. Then I rented a studio in a very cool area in Hollywood. And then, after I bought a futon, pillows, and some basic kitchen utensils, I called Anthony and invited him over after work to cook some fish with me.

He arrived with a bottle of champagne, a basket filled with fruit and flowers, and a portable CD player.

"I can't deal with fish," he confessed. "Not after smelling it eight hours a day."

"No problem. It was only an excuse."

"What I would like to do, Jules, is dance with you."

I turned off the overhead light and opened the curtains. The mostly empty room was flooded with pale silver shadows from the moon and the purple-red neon glow of Hollywood. Anthony chose a CD—The King, of course—held out his arms to me, and I slid gracefully into his warm embrace.

"Oh, baby," he said, sounding like Elvis, a blond Elvis, with his thick, wavy hair slicked back off his forehead....

CHAIN REACTION

Leslie What

Evangelina had been married almost twenty-five years. She worked as an underwriter at an insurance agency. Her best weekday friend, a woman in claims named Margaret, had scored from their boss two invitations to a posh garden party. He was wealthy enough to be a patron of the arts. So the crowd was peppered with literarti and painters. Now, both women stood in an elegant courtyard surrounded by people they didn't know, all of them gathered around a mildly famous poet who called himself Dante.

He was a large outgoing man who told stories with enough confidence that Evangelina knew he was in on the joke.

"What's the difference," asked the poet, "between a clitoris and a remote control?"

The response all around: "I don't know."

"A man will spend a half an hour searching for the remote," said the poet.

There was a round of laughter and a few groans, all from women.

Evangelina's husband, no doubt, at this very moment held a remote as he watched the big game. Lately it seemed that there was always a big game, always something much more interesting than her.

She could not take her eyes off the poet. He was a bit unkempt, as if too busy confronting the world to look closely at himself, intelligent enough to make her feel insecure. Kind and not at all pretentious. His shirt was snug in the belly. When someone spoke, he was attentive, a good listener. Evangelina said something only slightly amusing; he nodded his head, as if every word were important to him. He asked her thoughtful questions about her life.

She stared at his dusky lips and decided he was one of the sexiest men she had ever met. They exchanged significant glances, or so she thought. He was younger than she was by several years.

A while later, Margaret pulled her away. "Time for a drink," she said.

The bar had been set up on the far side of the cement fountain. The server recommended a Merlot from Chile.

Evangelina and Margaret stood against the wall and sipped from their glasses. The bricks had smuggled a fair amount of heat from the sunny day. The wine was thick; its influence spread across her tongue. "This is good," Evangelina said, words slurred.

Margaret glanced at the poet, leaned close to whisper, "He's cute, isn't he? Bet he'd spend a half-hour with his finger on the right button."

Evangelina said, "It's best not to think about it." This was something of a lie. She thought about it all the time. She had been with the same partner more than half of her life. Sex was good and plentiful, predictable. Some amount of love was involved. Still...

The poet was loud, boisterous. She could easily hear him from across the courtyard. He'd had many lovers and told rousing tales of conquest. Normally, Evangelina would not have wanted to hear this. Not tonight.

There was something about him. Maybe the way he watched her while he spoke, or his worldliness. Maybe that he seemed unashamed of anything. She had always thought that understanding one's feelings would allow one to control them.

The poet told another story. He had gone to dinner with a group of friends. A young lady had practically thrown herself at him. "Buy me some apple pie and I'll give you a blow job," she had teased.

"If it's à la mode, will you swallow?" he had said. The deal was struck, dessert consumed. But after leaving the restaurant, the young lady went back on her agreement. He smiled at the loss, letting slip the young lady's name.

"In any case, she wasn't worth a slice of pie," he said.

"Is he for real?" said Margaret with a laugh. By now it was obvious she had a crush on the poet.

Evangelina nearly sighed. It had been many years since a man had offered to buy her dessert. She excused herself and walked inside to use the bathroom. The hallway was long and dark; on the way back, she passed the poet.

"Hello," he said, extending his hand. "We haven't been officially introduced."

She was still thinking about pie, imagining the fragrance of cinnamon and the tart burst of green apples. She managed to state her name.

He held fast to her hand.

"You certainly lead an exciting life," she said, uncomfortable with the silence.

"What do you mean?" he asked.

"You get around a lot," she said, wishing she knew better words to express to the poet all that she was feeling.

He took a step toward her. "And you don't?"

"No," she said. She had already admitted too much, so went on. "I just think about it."

"Why don't you let me kiss you?" he said. He wrapped his arms around her waist.

She felt his breath hover in the shallow above her lips.

He smelled sweetly of skin, nothing more.

What the hell? she thought. *It's only a kiss.* She opened her mouth.

His tongue was warm, soft, precise.

She felt like someone reading a restaurant menu, trying to decide if she could afford to eat or if she should leave quickly before being noticed.

It was too late: He was already serving her the sampler plate, filled with every possibility imaginable.

He cupped one breast in his large hand. He grabbed her ass, pressed his fingers between her thighs. In less than thirty seconds he had found her remote control.

She did not try to push him away.

It was a sexual encounter with a thesaurus: sucking,

pumping, groping, licking, sniffing, hardening, lubricating, panting.

She was thinking, *ohmygod, I've kissed another man!*

But he was way ahead of her. He pulled two of her fingers into his mouth, suckled and left them covered in kisses. "Think of me when you use these later," he said.

He brought her other hand to his crotch. His body was soft, his penis hard, quite the opposite of her partner.

"You have very nice tense," he whispered in her ear.

"Nice tense?" she said, and laughed, utterly immersed in the present.

"Tits," he said, "I said tits," and gave them a gentle squeeze.

She was excited, maybe scared, and a bit ashamed. She wasn't sure what was supposed to happen next.

The decision was his to make. "I have to leave," he said, and parted her lips one final time.

Regret quickly followed relief. She stood in the hall for several minutes before she was ready to go back into the garden.

"Where were you?" asked Margaret.

"It doesn't matter. I have to go," she told her, and hurriedly left.

Everything had changed in those few moments.

She had eaten from the apple; now she knew she lived in a world where anything could happen.

She knew she was capable of being unfaithful.

She fantasized being a complete slut with the poet, rather than the incomplete slut she had been without him.

She wanted her pie à la mode.

On the slow walk home, she composed the first seven lines of a sonnet.

from **SAFE WORD**

Molly Weatherfield

We must have fallen asleep. Because the next thing I remember was the sun coming through the curtains. It was low, and the light was pink. Sunset.

I was lying on my side. Jonathan was behind me, one arm flung across me, his hand on my breast. Long, tapering fingers, beautifully articulated bones spreading out from his wrists. My skin looked pink in the light, pale pink against the olive of the back of his hand. I could probably bend my head down to kiss his hand if I tried, I thought.

I wanted to, a little. To show him how good I was feeling. Not that I'd exactly been keeping it to myself, but still. It was all so luxurious, so warm and indolent. During the past year, I'd thought occasionally of his hands, the bones in his wrists. Their images would drift, unbidden, into my thoughts, late at night, perhaps when the day's challenges had overwhelmed my defenses. I'd remember their weight on my body, their elegant curve around my breasts. And I'd remembered correctly, too, as it turned out. I'll move, I'll do something soon, I kept promising myself. But right at that moment, I didn't want to do anything but lie there with the slanted light of the sunset lengthening against us on the bed. Well, perhaps I could shift backward a little, a little closer to his hip....

His hand tightened. He was beginning to wake up. I lifted my head and licked his fingers. I inched my ass closer to him. He turned a little, and I could feel his cock—still a little moist, but not yet hard—jumping a little against me.

I turned a little more so that my ass was directly against his cock, and he moved his other hand under me, reaching for my other breast. He kissed the back of my neck. I arched my back, stroking his belly, his stiffening cock, with my ass until I felt him move into its furrow. Slowly now. I moved back and forth—teeny movements really, stomach contractions, rotate an inch forward, an inch back—while he grew against me.

"Okay," he whispered, and we moved onto our knees, him on top of me.

The bed had a headboard. I grasped it. I didn't want him to have to balance on his hands. I didn't want him ever to take his hands off my breasts. He spread his fingers a little, enough to catch my nipples between them, and then tightened. And while I gasped at the pinch, while I lost a beat in thralldom to that sensation and he felt me lose that beat, he moved his cock against my asshole.

I wasn't ready for him, quite. He knew that, he'd been looking for that moment. He wanted to feel me yielding to him. He pushed slowly and I gave way, arching my back, opening to him, forgetting everything except that yielding, that always frightening letting loose.

It hurt a little on every thrust. (It always does. I hope it always will.) I pushed back against him. He moved more deeply into me, and I teased myself a little. It hurts too much, I thought; I have to ask him to stop. Yeah, right. I felt myself opening my mouth and trying to shape some words—please, or slower, or something—but all I could hear was the sound of myself coming.

He moved his hands from my breasts to the wall above the headboard, leaning forward heavily, surrendering to his own orgasm. Somehow we slid down together to the bed, my sweaty back plastered to him while I felt him shrink slowly in me.

I began to believe, for the first time that day, that I was actually here. With Jonathan in a small hotel with faded blue shutters at the windows and geraniums in the courtyard. Lavender and lemon verbena in a vase on the dresser; the sheets of our bed still smelling distantly of sun and fresh air, underneath our darker, saltier smells. Vacation—you know you're on holiday when the smells, the colors, begin to take on this sort of painterly solidity. And when the other stuff—the rules, the plans—become vaguer, hazier. Yes, really a vacation, time out from rules and plans, from fantasies, and from reciting his letter to myself as though it were a mantra. No need for romantic endings, or for any endings at all, just yet. Just this lovely, wonderful, all-enveloping lust, in the sweet, simple, objective, declarative present. It would do for now. It would do quite nicely.

Jonathan:

It was dark outside now. I didn't want to get out of bed, but finally I had to untangle myself from her to pee. Use the bidet. Nice. Always a surprise how nice, how sensible.

"We never did have that picnic," she called from the bedroom. "I'm starving. Where's that food you bought?" I heard paper rustling.

When I came back in, I found her cross-legged on the bed, munching a piece of bread.

"Crumbs in bed," I said. Surprising myself by how compulsive I sounded—like a bad parody of myself in a more commanding persona. Still, there was a perfectly good table in the corner of the room, with two perfectly good chairs standing beside it—was it really so impossibly middle-aged to want to use it? I opened a bag of food, began setting it out. She shrugged, giggled, watching me search my pockets for my Swiss Army knife. I cut pieces of cheese, spread pâté on bread, opened the bottle of wine. I set everything out on paper, found the napkins and plastic wineglasses I'd remembered to get.

"In return," I said, "you're responsible for entertainment. I want a story from your year." And surprised myself again, this time by my eagerness to hear, to know, everything. Insults, punishments, humiliations; all the ways she'd been used, forced, bound, whipped, punished—how, and (trickier business) by whom. So that I could lay claim, begin to possess the experiences she'd had this past year. *Droit du seigneur.* My right to demand that she spin straw of experience into gold of narrative, for my entertainment. For the gentleman in the audience's edification and delectation.

She looked thoughtful for a moment. "Well, okay," she said slowly. "If you want to. But when we're done eating. And back in bed."

Fair enough. We were both so ravenous that the food disappeared pretty quickly, and the night air was chilly enough to drive us under the covers.

"Okay then," she began, snuggling against me. "Well, I think I'd better begin at the beginning. . . ."

Carrie's Story Continues:

So there I was, less than an hour after being auctioned off, kneeling on the floor of a limousine in front of my new master. I could feel the car's suspension under my knees—we were driving over cobblestones. We picked up speed on the paved streets; perhaps the driver had turned onto one of those small highways they sometimes build around the perimeters of ancient cities. I was naked, under a rough black cloak, except for tightly laced high boots. I'd been taught some new rules during my stay in the warehouse: I had to keep my eyes lowered, instead of maintaining eye contact, as you'd insisted. It was difficult for me—fixing my gaze on his very neat suede shoes, the thickly carpeted floor, while his hands methodically probed, opened, examined me. I wanted to know what he looked like. All I'd ever really seen of him were his tinted glasses.

He took his hands away now, reaching for a small package next to him on the seat. I could hear the faint clink of metal. Buckles, I thought. He tore open the wrapping paper and I could smell the leather—I think he was rubbing it between his fingers, to check its thickness. I relaxed my shoulder blades, lengthened my neck for him. The collar was tall and stiff—I would have to get used to holding my head very high. And in front, dangling down over the gap between the bones of my clavicles, I felt a heavy iron ring. Was it three inches in diameter? Four? Big enough for him to grasp in his hand.

Yes. He used it to pull me down to his crotch, unbuttoning his fly quickly with his other hand, filling my mouth with a swollen cock that reached insistently for my throat. It took some effort to move my head back and forth over him with my neck bound so cruelly. I think he sensed that, and I think he enjoyed it, too, pulling me closer with the ring, and holding me down firmly while I swallowed.

And then—well, that's easy. Put him gently, humbly, back in his pants. Straighten out his clothes, with light, deft hands. And then lean back on my knees—

back straight, head high, eyes down, tits out, waiting at attention in case he wanted me again. He reached over me to a magazine rack and selected a newspaper, opening a *Wall Street Journal* and relaxing behind it. I realized that he hadn't said a word to me since... well, he'd never said anything to me at all. I wondered if he ever would.

It was becoming difficult to stay still. Not just the aches at my knees or having to keep my balance as the car sped up and slowed down, but the silence, the poverty of images. I scanned my memory for stray glances I'd caught of him. I didn't think he was tall. His hands were large—I had the impression that he was built squarely, broad for his height. In good shape for his age— late forties, maybe? I'd heard his voice at the auction, when he'd come over to where I'd been displayed on my little carpeted pedestal. He'd parted my ass with blunt, dry fingers, and commented to an assistant about my "pure passion for obedience." His English was precise, accentless; I suspected it wasn't his first language. He'd laughed a little when he'd seen how jolted —how summoned to attention—I'd been by his fingers in me. He was right; I did want to obey him. Although maybe he'd meant that I want to obey everybody.

Only now, maddeningly, I didn't. I felt fidgety. I

needed to hear his voice. I could obey him happily, if he'd tell me to do something, but I was having a difficult time doing the most important thing of all—which was waiting. I realized (tacky, obvious, but there it was), that I'd expected him to give me a little discourse on himself—how tough he'd be—Sir Stephen informing O of his fondness for habits and rituals. He wouldn't have had to say a lot; just something to give it, you know, a story line.

Yeah, I told myself, as the limo's wheels rolled over smooth road and sunlight flickered through the tinted windows, that's you all over, Carrie—life's real only when you've made it into a story. But the more I scolded myself, the more I found that I wanted to lift my eyes and peek at him. One peek, I told myself. Just to see what kind of a mouth he had.

Wide. Determined. The cheeks lined, the jaw squarish. That was all I allowed myself, through my eyelashes. A little something to go on, to settle me down for the rest of the ride. To allow me to imagine what sort of person might have those hands, that taste and smell. He was very rich, the assistant had told me. And he liked a bargain.

Finally the car stopped in front of a hotel, and he stepped out and turned, to allow someone to drape a topcoat around his shoulders. I caught a glimpse of black cowboy boots—Stefan, the assistant from the auction, murmuring assent to Mr. Constant's instructions respectful: get her ready, after she's fed and bathed and rested. "I'll be back for her at eight," Mr. Constant concluded, in his mild, accentless voice. "Oh, and give her two strokes to remind her to keep her eyes where they belong."

The strokes had been swift and furious, the first making me gasp, the second wrenching tears and a few gurgled sobs from me. And neatly placed, I thought now, examining myself in the mirror while I waited for the large bathtub to fill.

It was taking a while, even with water pouring full force out of the taps into the square tub, its deep bottom sunk below the bathroom floor. Black marble. Ugly, expensive. Black tiles on the walls with water lilies etched into them to echo the metallic faux-Monet wallpaper on the ceiling and upper part of the walls. And too much light. Too many mirrors, too, in front of me and behind me: I stared curiously at the infinite parade of pale naked girls in cruel black collars, angry red stripes neatly X'ed across their infinite parade of asses. It was like seeing the year I'd signed on for, spread out before me.

I looked tired, my eyes much more deeply shadowed than usual. I'd been awakened early that morning, to get me ready for the auction. And I'd stood for I don't know how long, chained to my pedestal while the buyers had examined me. I was glad I'd get some time to rest. I just hoped, as I stepped carefully into the tub, that I wouldn't fall asleep in it.

The hot water felt great, the tingly buttermilk bath salts soothing my ass. But—no need to worry about falling asleep—the collar felt even tighter that it had on dry land. I couldn't dangle my head back as I wanted. And the leather would stiffen, too, as it dried. Get used to it, I told myself, as I experimented with how to duck my head under the water to rinse my hair. Get used to it; you'll be wearing it all year.

And when the makeup lady woke me later that afternoon, I wondered if I had fallen asleep in the bathtub after all. But no—I remembered then, through an enormous yawn, that after I'd finished my bath I'd been fed small cubes of cheese, fruit, and raw vegetables on a heavy white china plate on the floor near the bed. And water, in a big bright yellow plastic dog's bowl—I remembered feeling grateful that it was a big bowl, for German shepherds or Akitas, because I'd been so thirsty. And glad that the pallet, that Stefan had prodded me down to, for my nap, was soft, covered with a sheepskin, and placed near the floor vent, in the warm air currents.

I was lying on my side, my hands behind my back. Stefan had buckled a pair of leather cuffs around my wrists, and attached my hands behind my back—I'd had to dip from the waist to get to the food and water —and he'd also tethered me in place at the end of a long chain leash. But I must have slept well, I thought, because I felt a lot better, and amused to hear the makeup lady—a small, cheerful woman with bronzy dyed flyaway hair and rouged pink cheeks—ordering me imperiously in French that I must wake up and sit *au-delà*, at the vanity table across the room, my leash dangling between my legs.

She worked cheerfully and carefully, humming to herself, chattering about what a sweet little boy I looked like in my haircut, entirely unperturbed, it seemed, by my chain and nakedness. Was this something she saw every day in this hotel, I wondered. Or did Mr. Constant's money override people's usual expectations? I gazed at myself in the mirror. I looked better after my nap—my eyes huge and startled above pale pink and ivory cheeks, mouth painted the color of a purplish bruise—while she rubbed a little more of the purplish lip gloss on my nipples.

"Stand up," she told me. "Turn around slowly," while

she considered what else to do with me. She brushed and trimmed my pubic hair a bit, used a little more of the lip gloss at my cunt, but that was about all she could come up with, since I'd been manicured and depilated within an inch of my life that morning, for the auction. She stroked my ass pensively, and then she packed up her makeup kit quickly, tossing away used Q-Tips and cotton balls, prodding me gently back down to the bench, this time facing away from the mirror. "Be good, *petite*," she called to me, clattering out of the room on high, slightly broken-down platform shoes, the room suddenly very quiet, the wrought-iron vanity-table bench cold and hard under me.

Next act, I thought, hearing a sound at the door a few minutes later. Opening acts for my own performance in this commedia, all the characters sketched in broad strokes. The dressmaker was thin, with features as sharp as the pins and needles stuck into the front of her dress, her eyes glittering behind spectacles. Her assistant, a bored, chunky teenager with lots of black eyeliner and a nose ring, grimaced under the burden of the big garment bag and various other packages, and chewed bubble gum to the rhythm of the Walkman plugged into her ears. I could hear the tinny ghost of a backbeat when she bent to smooth long black stockings up my legs.

No garter belt—the stockings went all the way up my thighs and seemed to cling there. The shoes had very high, straight heels, straps at the ankle, and an inch of platform sole. The backbeat from the Walkman changed slightly as I stood up—a new cut, reggae-inspired, perhaps. I swayed a bit to its distracting rhythm, my hands still bound behind me.

They let me sway until I got my balance, then freed my hands, and unhooked the chain from my collar, to put the dress on me. It was really two pieces. The top was dull, matte black, a boned corset with cups for my breasts—a bustier, but with laces in the back so you could tighten it. And the bottom was a skirt made of many layers of white tulle or organdy, one of those tired, old-fashioned-looking sheer fabrics that prom dresses—the good kind, that you get in thrift stores—are made of. The hemline was uneven, sometimes above my knees, sometimes below it. And above the organdy, there was a layer of what felt like thin, transparent vinyl—well, more like cellophane really—stiff, iridescent, unnatural.

I heard the skirt's odd rustle as the assistant slipped it over my head. The dressmaker tugged it here and there, turning it a bit, putting in a few clever stitches near the hem to make it less even, more raffish. Now the bustier—the assistant hooked it up the front, pulling at the laces behind me, and then indicating, with a nod and a little shove, that I should walk around the room, so her boss could see the effect.

"The darts aren't right." Stefan must have come in from the adjoining room. The dressmaker murmured what sounded like grudging agreement, and the assistant rolled her eyes in exasperation as she struggled to undo the hooks and hand the corset to her boss for alteration.

Oh yes, much better, they all agreed, after the adjustments had been made and the garment was hooked up again and relaced. Even Ms. Walkman's eyes widened and her mouth slowed as she watched my second circuit around the room. I was still a little tentative; I'd mastered the shoes but I was dizzy from how tightly I'd been laced—the dressmaker had pulled them a full inch tighter than before. And when I passed the mirror, I saw that her alterations had transformed the dress entirely. Or had I just been too stupid to notice, my first time around? The tight lacing, the billowing skirt, the bare, vulnerable expanse of chest below the cruel collar. This was the Roissy dress, updated as expensive trash, nouveau-punk pastiche. Involuntarily, I felt around the skirt, front and back, for the strings, the hooks, that I knew had to be there.

"Yeah, sure, try that part," Stefan said in a bored

tone. And it wasn't very difficult to hook the little tabs of cloth in place, so that the skirt was lifted, front and back, to expose my ass and cunt.

"Keep it rolled up while you wait for him," Stefan added. He'd been thanking the dressmaker, tipping her, perhaps. I heard the door shut behind her, while he turned off some lamps. "You can sit on that bench until fifteen minutes before he comes for you—I'll let you know when that is."

I thanked him. No need for him to expand on those instructions. I knew he meant that fifteen minutes before Mr. Constant was due, I'd move down to the floor, in the center of the room, to wait for him on my knees. And that there was no need for me to know what time it was now, and how long it would be before that happened.

They're not exactly boring, those long stretches spent waiting for a master. You're hyperconscious of your body—you hope it will be pleasing, after all the preparation and grooming it's had. You breathe with your whole body, that's so open and displayed and ready. You're a little afraid of the moment when you'll be judged, examined. You're afraid, but you also can't wait—to be seen, to be touched, to be commanded, forced, used.

I don't know how much time passed while I sat on

the iron bench in the darkening room. There was a clock ticking on the mantel, but Stefan must have turned it around while I was asleep, so that I couldn't see the time. I watched stars appear in the evening sky, and I looked down at my body, and at my dress. The bustier felt even tighter than when I'd been standing, and my breasts swelled, plump and white, over the bra that barely covered the rouged areolas of my nipples. The odd, synthetic fabric of the skirt billowed to either side of my waist, iridescent as insect wings, crinkly as gift wrap, surrounding my pale thighs and dark naked cunt. Even with the skirt unhooked, so that my cunt and ass would no longer be visible, so we could go out—and I knew we'd be going out, this was a dress for going out—this was a dress for announcing precisely what I was. In some ways, it was simply a setting for the collar and cuffs—the way some black velvet evening gowns are settings for fabulous diamond jewelry. I swallowed, resolving to wear my restraints proudly. And then I snorted, wondering where I'd copped that pretentious notion.

But I stifled the snort quickly, at the sound of Stefan's footsteps. Down to the floor now—he pointed out the spot with his toe, training a reading lamp at it, and dimming a few more of the other lamps. And perhaps because he'd told me I'd wait fifteen minutes, it felt like an eternity until he nervously led Mr. Constant into the room. I was surprised by the edginess in the air—it was the first time, all afternoon, that I'd wondered what Stefan might be feeling about any of this—and at his palpable relief when Mr. Constant commended him on the dress and chuckled appreciatively at how my ass had been marked. "Stand up, turn slowly," Stefan commanded me.

"And let down her skirt and get her cloak," Mr. Constant commanded him, before leading me quickly and silently to the elevator and outside the hotel, down a few crowded, brightly-lit downtown streets to a restaurant. Showtime.

I followed the maître d' across the floor, the big ring in my collar catching the light of candles on tables, Mr. Constant walking close behind me like an impresario, my cloak over his arm. I could hear murmurs. I blushed, but kept my chin lifted, even higher than the collar forced me to. I could feel my nipples stiffen, my cunt get wet, my whole body open and swell under the stares directed at me.

An image floated into my mind. I guess I thought of it because we were going to Greece the next day, but it was from an old fantasy, one I'd played over and over again, late in bed at night, during high school. I was naked, chained from a collar much like the one I was wearing now, the chain tugging me along behind a chariot. Booty of war, a slave captured at Troy, following barefoot behind the warrior who'd loaded me on his ship. He'd also gotten a wagon full of pottery and weavings, and some sheep and goats. The minor Greek island kings had squabbled, had even come to blows once, over how to divide the spoils, especially the pottery. It had been raucous, cruel, violent, petty—like the rest of the war. They'd enjoyed it. And now, ship safely in harbor, we were marching through the gates of his city in a victory parade. The crowd lining the road seemed huge to me—I tried not to look at them, but I could hear, I could feel them—drunk, laughing, jeering. I thought I could hear them that night in the restaurant, though it was really just the tinkle of silver and china and crystal, and perhaps a few polite gasps.

Chill, people, I thought. If I can deal with it, so can you. But it's probably easier for me. Because I have to concentrate on walking in these shoes, and breathing in this dress, while you can hang out at your tables feeling...well, what *are* you feeling? Shamed curiosity, self-shielding contempt, outraged desire? Or envy, which is what Mr. Constant is really hoping for. He wants you to desire me, and to envy him terribly. And I know this because it's what I want, too.

It couldn't have taken more than two minutes for the maître d' to guide us across the restaurant. But it felt like an hour, with that Technicolor epic running in my head. And its coda, when everything caught up with me.

As we entered the private dining room at the back of the restaurant, Mr. Constant whispered, "Brava." I smiled. It was the first thing he'd said to me.

A waiter held a chair for me. I spread the stiff, oddly smooth and crinkly skirt when I sat down—it wasn't exactly stuff you'd sit on. The seat cushion tickled my bare ass. My cunt was moist; I was going to leave a sticky little wet spot on the dusty-rose velvet. I sat as straight as I could while the waiter fussed with the flowers and glassware.

"And pull her dress down so that I can see her breasts." Mr. Constant added.

The waiter's hands were deft, circumspect. He used a finger to lift each of my breasts out of the bra cup that held it, and to fold the stiff cloth below it. My breasts rose under Mr. Constant's gaze, their painted nipples standing at obedient attention. I kept my eyes down while the waiter answered all Mr. Constant's questions about the menu, and disappeared silently.

Mr. Constant and I looked at each other across the

table. That is, I looked at the flowers, the silverware, his hands, everywhere but his face. And I felt him looking at me all over, sternly, while I struggled to manage my body, my eyes. I realized that he was speaking to me.

"...Much better," he seemed to be saying. "I'm glad you take instruction so well. You'll have to learn a great deal of patience and control. But you seem to be making a good start."

"You can look at me tonight," he continued. "I know you've been waiting for me to tell you a little about what you can expect. And you can ask me some questions."

I raised my eyes slowly, past his wide chest and shoulders, the aggressive set of his short neck. He had salt-and-pepper hair, in a brush cut. Large, blunt, decisive features, ruddy skin, large pores. And the glinting glasses. I was glad to be able to look at his face, but I was disappointed by how little it revealed, with the glasses hiding his eyes.

"You like being publicly displayed, don't you?" he asked. "You like it much more than you thought you would."

"Yes, Mr. Constant."

He nodded. "I thought you'd respond that way, but it was just a guess. It's a relief to know that my buyer's instincts were correct. Because I intend to show you, on the dressage circuit."

I'd seen dressage shows, of course. You'd taken me to some, Jonathan, to show me how much I had to learn about submissiveness. I thought of the participants, offering their open, vulnerable bodies to an enthusiastic crowd, to judges who would decide which of them had presented the most appealing and comprehensive tableau of availability and obedience. I knew how much control it took, and I didn't think any owner in his right mind would enter me in a difficult competitive event like that.

"I employ an excellent trainer," Mr. Constant was saying. "You'll receive a lot of instruction. Of course, it will take a lot of work, but I think you'll try hard for me. I think you'll want to present your body in all the difficult, painful modes we'll teach you."

I found that I didn't quite have the breath to give sound to my assent, but I mouthed the words, whispering that yes, Mr. Constant, I would try very, very hard.

"But ultimately," he said, "I see you as a racing pony. I find pony races very entertaining. Have you ever seen one?"

"Uh, no, Mr. Constant."

"We'll take you to one, so you can see. They're

loud, fast, a little dangerous. And people bet large amounts of money."

"But Mr. Constant," I said, "I've only had a week of beginning pony training, and I've never raced or competed at all...."

"Yes," he nodded, his glasses opaque in the candlelight, "the odds will be stupendous."

I thought of protesting, but of course I couldn't do that. Instead I giggled nervously.

He didn't seem to mind. His body spread out a little in his chair, his neck relaxed a bit. "I'm rather an arriviste," he confided. "I wasn't born so wealthy—I've just perfected a few tricks that seem to work very well in the current financial environment. We work from my place in Greece, mostly, except when I have to go to New York from time to time. The way we approach the market takes very good satellite technology and lots of time and concentration; so my only amusements, really, on the island, are the occasional party and checking in on your training—yours and Tony's. And then attending the races and competitions where you're shown.

"I suppose," he said slowly, "that outside of my work—outside of the risks and quick decisions and high stakes—what I most enjoy is a disciplined body, painfully bound and displayed for my entertainment, either at a public competition, or at night, in my room."

"Will it be very painful, Mr. Constant?" I felt my voice wobble.

"Painful enough to entertain me," he said somberly. "You can buy slaves, you know, whose specialty is pain. But I know you're not one of those. And neither is Tony. I prefer material like you, it turns out—fast, eager learners who can be taught to bear what they have to, but who never quite get used to it."

He seemed to have scoped it out pretty well.

And then he added, laughing a little, "Oh, and don't waste your time wondering whether I'm really one of those tycoons whose dearest wish is to be tied down and beaten. I've met a few of those gentlemen, but we don't seem to have much in common."

"Well, uh, it all seems very, uh, *simple*, Mr. Constant." It scared me a little. I didn't know if I'd be good at simple.

"You'd like a bit more mystery," he nodded. "Hidden motivations, complex revelations. Ah, yes, like your Jonathan."

How did he know this about me? I didn't know how much information the auction people collect, in the folder that's available to interested buyers. But I guessed there would be some pretty elaborate psychological profiles in there. And, oh shit, of course—he'd read your note, Jonathan. Well, after all, I thought,

Stefan wouldn't have given it to me without routing it by his boss first. He'd read it and he seemed to find it amusing. Or perhaps not so amusing. A hint of rancor crept into his voice.

"Oh, yes," he said, "I've met him.... He puts in an occasional appearance at a party or exhibition. I think Ms. Kate Clarke must have introduced him to me a year or two ago.

He grimaced slightly.

"Quite the master," he said, "for a girl who's read so many books. Fancy bastard. Handsome, too. And he seems to have had all the time in the world to amuse himself by playing at being in love with you. Kept you guessing, I expect. Was he really in control of things, you wondered—or was he secretly pining—no, what's the word? Oh, *languishing*. Yes, that's it—was he languishing for your little soul?

"He wants you to guess about it all this year," he added. "On my time. Well, you have my permission. As long as your body is obedient. I'm less concerned about your soul, I guess, than he supposes he is.

"He spoiled you terribly," he concluded, "but he didn't ruin your good instincts. I think a little *simplicity*, as you put it, will improve you tremendously."

"Avignon," he chuckled, as the waiter came back into the room with the first course. "Avignon, March 15 next year—well, the place d'Horloge is a nice venue for a reunion. And we'll keep you too busy to fret much about it in the meantime. But"—he trained his glasses at me—"it's rather an old story, don't you think, Carrie?"

"Yes," I said softly. "Yes, thank you, Mr. Constant."

And then we both turned our attention to the food that the polite waiter was setting out. Oysters. Very cold, with a peppery sauce. Lots of them, too, piles of them. I'd never had oysters where you didn't have to count how many you could have. The waiter opened a bottle of wine. He didn't make a big deal of staring at my breasts, but he didn't look away, either. I dipped an oyster into the sauce and swallowed it slowly.

"It's very good, Mr. Constant," I said.

"Yes," he answered placidly, the rancor drained from his voice. "And it's nice to watch you, Carrie."

"Thank you, Mr. Constant," I breathed, trembling.

"What else did you talk about?" Jonathan asked sourly. Well, it's no fun being dissected so neatly by someone you have absolutely no memory of meeting. Still, he enjoyed thinking of her, eating oysters in her pretentious collar, bare, painted breasts above the punk Roissy dress.

Carrie scanned his face.

"He didn't say anything else about you," she assured him, a small, opaque smile on her lips.